THE CALLING OF EMILY EVANS

JULIA'S LAST HOPE

ROSES FOR MAMA

JANETTE OKE

The answer
had come.
She would go
alone.

THE CALLING
OF
EMILY
EVANS

JANETTE OKE'S

Women of the West

THE CALLING OF EMILY EVANS

JULIA'S LAST HOPE

ROSES FOR MAMA

Published by Bethany House Publishers
A Ministry of Bethany Fellowship International
11400 Hampshire Avenue South
Minneapolis, Minnesota 55438

ISBN 0-7394-4380-1

Printed in the United States of America by
Bethany Press International, Minneapolis, Minnesota 55438

To those women
whose dedication and courage
opened many of the
community churches
for the Missionary Church
(formerly the Mennonite Brethren in Christ)
in the Canada West District.

Children's Books by Janette Oke

The above titles are also available as
CLASSIC CHILDREN'S STORIES for older readers.

Books by Janette Oke

Another Homecoming* / Tomorrow's Dream*
Celebrating the Inner Beauty of Woman
Dana's Valley†
Janette Oke's Reflections on the Christmas Story
The Matchmakers • Nana's Gift
The Red Geranium • Return to Harmony*

CANADIAN WEST

When Calls the Heart   When Breaks the Dawn
When Comes the Spring   When Hope Springs New
Beyond the Gathering Storm
When Tomorrow Comes

LOVE COMES SOFTLY

Love Comes Softly   Love's Unending Legacy
Love's Enduring Promise   Love's Unfolding Dream
Love's Long Journey   Love Takes Wing
Love's Abiding Joy   Love Finds a Home

A PRAIRIE LEGACY

The Tender Years   A Quiet Strength
A Searching Heart   Like Gold Refined

SEASONS OF THE HEART

Once Upon a Summer   Winter Is Not Forever
The Winds of Autumn   Spring's Gentle Promise

SONG OF ACADIA*

The Meeting Place   The Birthright
The Sacred Shore   The Distant Beacon

WOMEN OF THE WEST

The Calling of Emily Evans   A Bride for Donnigan
Julia's Last Hope   Heart of the Wilderness
Roses for Mama   Too Long a Stranger
A Woman Named Damaris   The Bluebird and the Sparrow
They Called Her Mrs. Doc   A Gown of Spanish Lace
The Measure of a Heart   Drums of Change

———

Janette Oke: A Heart for the Prairie
Biography of Janette Oke by Laurel Oke Logan

*with T. Davis Bunn   †with Laurel Oke Logan

JANETTE OKE was born in Champion, Alberta, during the Depression years, to a Canadian prairie farmer and his wife. She is a graduate of Mountain View Bible College in Didsbury, Alberta, where she met her husband, Edward. They were married in May of 1957, and went on to pastor churches in Indiana as well as Calgary and Edmonton, Canada.

The Okes have three sons and one daughter and are enjoying the addition of grandchildren to the family. Edward and Janette have both been active in their local church, serving in various capacities as Sunday school teachers and board members. They make their home near Calgary, Alberta.

Table of Contents

Prologue

Although Emily Evans is totally fictional, the story she tells may well have happened. The Missionary Church was not the only denomination that sent young women out to pioneer new works in the Canadian West. It was not an easy task. There were times when they did not even have horses to help with their traveling. Many lonely and difficult hours were spent walking the dirt roads and paths in order to make calls on all the homes in an area.

But even when a mission worker was blessed with a team and buggy, her lot was not always that much easier, for often the roads were little more than winding trails through the countryside. And sometimes heavy rains or drifting snow made them nearly impassable.

Her accommodations were not that fancy either. Wooden crates stacked one on top of the other could comprise a good share of a room's furniture. Sometimes the girls boarded with an area family, but most often they were on their own.

The Sunday offerings were the workers' source of income. Many area farmers were good to share their farm produce, but in those early days on the prairies there was little extra to pass on to another household. The young women suffered the pioneering hardships right along with the families in the community.

In researching material for Emily's story, I scanned Conference Journals dating back to 1917, which for the Missionary Church was the twelfth annual conference. That would date the first conference as 1905, the year Alberta became a Canadian province. The efforts of the "Sister Workers" were reported along with those of the male ministers'. These reports included evangelistic meetings, tabernacle work, conducting the church services in local mission churches, working in a home established for unwed mothers, and "taking meetings over the needy prairies"—all done by "Approved Ministering Sisters," as they later were called.

In reports by women in the Journal of 1919, I saw references to the flu epidemic and concern for the returning soldiers of World War I.

The 1920 Journal tells of the committee appointed to decide the "uniform" of the Sister Workers: ". . . and that they dress in plain attire becoming to their work and the dignity of their calling, the wearing of low-necked waists [known to us as blouses or shirts] not being allowed, and the skirt must be ample in length and width." A simple dark bonnet was also a part of their dress.

Incidentally, the committee consisted of three women.

In the 1928 Conference of the Mennonite Brethren in Christ, held in Allentown, Pennsylvania, the presiding elder (later known as district superintendent) from the Canadian West field, Alvin Traub, reported to the conference: "Our preachers and workers are wholehearted and self-sacrificing and are devoted to their work."

I found twenty-eight names of Sister Workers listed in the early Conference Journals. Perhaps that does not seem like many, but, remember, in the beginning years of their ministry the Missionary Church had only three or four established parishes on these "needy prairies."

I recognized many of the names as those I had known as a child—missionaries, lady evangelists, college teachers, and wives of pastors.

I personally owe much to those dedicated young women, for one of them, Miss Pearl Reist, began the work in the community where I grew up. My home church, Lemont Memorial, is named in her honor. She married an area farmer, Nels Lemont, and continued as a supporter and ardent worker in the little church long after a minister was found for the congregation.

Another woman, Mrs. Beatrice Hedegaard, was the children's camp evangelist when I at age ten made my personal decision to commit my life to the Lord Jesus Christ.

Mrs. Alma Hallman, though in her mid-nineties, is still able to care for her own apartment, attend our local church, and chat with good humor and a great deal of insight about the happenings of the church over the many years of her involvement. She showed me her "papers" and her "button" and shared tales about the hardships and dedication of the women who served the Lord and the church in the early years of this century.

Only God knows the full extent of the cost to those who gave totally of themselves. And He alone knows the number of lives their ministry affected through the chain reaction resulting from that service. We do know that from many of these small mission works have come pastors, missionaries, and lay workers.

Most of the Approved Ministering Sisters have now passed on to their heavenly reward, but the product of their selfless ministry remains.

Chapter One

Training

Emily Evans lifted a slender hand and pushed back a wisp of wayward brown hair. She arched her back slightly to try to remove a kink in her tired muscles, then reached up to gently rub the back of her neck. Her whole body was protesting the position she had held for what seemed to be hours. She slid the opened book back and pushed away from the small wooden table, which was her desk. She was tired. Tired of studying. Tired of bending over the printed pages. Tired of trying to fit all the historical facts into her weary brain.

She lifted herself from the straight-backed wooden chair and walked to the window. Her left hand reached out to the lace curtain and lifted it back, allowing her to see the silent scene before her. Had it not been for the moon smiling down from overhead, she would have seen nothing but blackness. As it was, all she could make out was the outline of another building, looming dark and plain in the silvery light.

Emily knew the scene by heart. She had looked out upon it many times since her arrival at Gethsemene Bible School nestled in the western Canadian town of Regis. Not a large school, it was not known for its greatness. Only those interested in its teachings seemed to be aware that it even existed. Except for the town folk, of course. To them it was another way of adding to their coffers in the sale of produce, toiletries and winter boots.

There were only four buildings on the small campus. The main structure housed the two classrooms, the library, and the offices. The ladies' residence was to the right and the men's to the left. Behind the main building and centrally located between the dormitories was the small chapel. Emily wished she could see it from her window. It was the chapel that was dearest to her heart.

She turned silently from the dark window so she would not disturb the sleeping form in the bed across the small room.

"I've studied quite enough," she murmured quietly. "What I don't know will just have to be left unknown. I can't think one moment longer."

She looked at the sleeping form. *How can she breeze through the exams so easily?* was Emily's exasperated thought. *She never needs to study.*

Emily's dour assessment was not quite accurate. Ruth Raemore did study. But of course it was unnecessary for her to spend the time over her textbooks that Emily did. Though Emily was not brilliant, neither was she a poor student. Her high grades throughout her school days had resulted from disciplined hours of study. In Bible school, anxious to make the most of her years in training, she quickly found that diligent studying was the only way to make good grades.

The silence was broken by the unmistakable squeak of the second step of the stairs. Emily's head lifted, her breath catching in a little gasp. She did not hesitate to wonder who was making the silent ascent up those stairs and, then, down the hall. Each night the rooms were checked after "light's out," and Emily was tardy again.

As quietly as she could, she hurried across the distance between the window and the desk and quickly turned out her light. She could hear the quiet opening and closing of doors as the woman made her way down the line of bedrooms. With one swift movement Emily was out of her shoes and under the covers beside the sleeping Ruth.

Ruth stirred, turned over on her other side, and resumed deep breathing. Emily held her breath and made sure the covers were tucked snugly under her chin. Then turning her back to the door, praying inwardly that all of her long skirt had followed her under the quilt, she closed her eyes and waited.

Her door soon opened softly and with the light that filtered in from the hall, Emily could imagine herself being counted. Two forms in the bed. Two young ladies properly retired for the night. The door closed just as softly and Emily could sense, more than hear, the silent figure move on down the hall to the last room on the left.

Emily breathed again. She was saved from a scolding or more kitchen duty—at least for this time.

She dared not stir until she heard the footsteps descend the stairs. At last all was silent, and Emily folded back the covers and rose from the bed.

Now in the dark, Emily felt her way across the floor and removed the combs from her hair. She shook out the long strands, her fingers running idly through its silkiness. Tonight she didn't even stop to mourn the fact that her hair was plain— plain brown. Quite dark brown. How often she had looked at Ruth's raven black tresses, or Olive Tyndale's glowing blond crown, and longed for her hair to be such a color. But tonight she was too tired to care.

She stumbled over her kicked-off shoes as she felt her way to the clothes cupboard where her nightgown hung. She could not even see to properly hang up the clothes she had lifted over her head. She reached out and released them, hoping they were placed on the chair where she had been sitting. She wasn't sure if she heard them slide to the floor or not, but she did not feel for them in the darkness. She slipped into the printed flannel gown and carefully made her way back across the floor. The cold boards gave way to the braided rug, and she knew she had headed in the right direction.

Carefully she eased herself again into bed beside Ruth and snuggled into the warm blankets. She hadn't realized how chilly the room had become until she felt the warmth of the bed. Her sore muscles seemed to soak up the heat, and her head, now nestled on the pillow, began to ache in protest.

She chided herself. *I must start getting to bed earlier or I'll be sick again—just like Father warned.*

But even before Emily closed her tired eyes, she argued back.

But how can I? If I don't study, I'll never make it. They might not even let me stay. But if I don't go to bed on time . . .

Emily let that thought go unfinished. She knew there were good reasons for getting sleep. Her health depended upon it. She had never been physically strong. She was also breaking school rules, and at this small Bible school, rules were made to be kept. Emily chafed under the guilt that hung over her. What would they do with her if they ever found out that she was pushing "lights out" all too often? That she had bounded into bed on more than one occasion as she heard the preceptress's footfall on the stairway?

Emily shivered even in the warmth of the blankets. She did not welcome the thought of being sent home in humiliation. She wanted to be here. She had so much to learn. In a way that she couldn't explain, she felt compelled to study God's Word.

So why did she continue in her disobedience? Emily could only shake her head. "It's their rules," she mumbled, half asleep. "Nobody could live with such silly rules."

Ruth stirred again and Emily realized she had been pressing a bit closer than she intended in order to draw from the warmth. She shifted her body away and allowed herself to drift off to sleep. The rising bell would sound all too early, and everyone was expected to be at the breakfast table, properly combed, washed and dressed for another day in the classroom.

———

When the bell rang the next morning, Emily stirred restlessly and would have rolled over and gone back to sleep had not Ruth called, "Emily. Emily! It's time to get up. You'll be late for breakfast again."

Emily moaned and pulled the blankets a little higher.

"Emily! You told me not to let you sleep—remember?" Ruth scolded softly from in front of the room's only mirror. "Come on. You've got to get up."

When Emily still failed to respond, Ruth leaned over the bed and tugged the blankets from Emily's possessive hands.

"Emily!" Ruth said sharply.

Emily's eyes immediately flew wide open. Panic filled them as she looked up into the dark-brown eyes of her roommate.

"What is it?" she asked, raising from her bed.

The sternness left Ruth's face and a smile turned up the corners of her lips.

"Nothing," she answered with a chuckle.

Emily flopped back to her pillow.

"Then what are you—?"

But Ruth did not allow her to finish. "It's past time to get up. You'll be late again. You asked me to be sure to get you up. Remember?"

Emily sighed. "Oh, yes," she admitted in a half whisper.

"Then get," urged Ruth, sternness back in her voice.

Reluctantly Emily sat up on the edge of the bed, and slowly

rose to her feet to begin her morning preparations. The bathroom down the hall was shared by all the young ladies in the dorm, and Emily slipped into her robe and began to gather her toilet articles. Her eyes swung to the clock on the desk and she gasped.

"It's already ten to," she moaned. "Why didn't you get me up sooner?"

"I tried," said an exasperated Ruth. "How I tried! You are impossible to awaken in the morning. *You* ought to try it!"

Emily said nothing, grabbed everything she thought she would need and left on the run for the bathroom.

She was soon back, scrambling into her long gray skirt and fresh white blouse with the lace collar. Then she set to work on her unruly hair, running the brush through it as quickly as she could and fastening it up at the back of her neck. She hoped it would hold. Emily was often embarrassed by the hairpins coming out halfway through class. She poked in another pin as an extra measure of insurance, but even that did not make the roll feel any too secure.

Ruth was already moving out into the hall when Emily turned to follow.

The last breakfast bell sounded. At least she would not enter the dining room alone, in breathless fashion, while the rest of her classmates were ready to seat themselves. She cast one last look around her room.

She had tidied nothing after her return from her morning toilet. Her brush and comb lay on the desk where they had fallen. Her nightgown dangled haphazardly from the bed. Her dress from the day before reclined half on, half off the desk chair. Emily sighed deeply and resolutely hastened her step. She would have to do all her tidying after her morning kitchen detail and sometime before having her devotions. She would be expected to be on time for her first class—the one with the Bible History exam, and she had hoped to be able to spend a few moments in review.

Well, there most certainly won't be time for review this morning, she concluded reluctantly. She might even have to skimp on her devotions in order to get everything done. Emily hurried into the dining hall and was able to reach her assigned table in time for Carl Tyndale, Olive's blond brother, to hold her chair while she was seated.

"Good morning, Miss Evans," he whispered in a teasing voice. "I see we made it this morning."

Emily gave him a withering look. She wasn't quite ready for jokes.

"Shall we stand for the blessing?" came the voice of the preceptress. "Mr. Russell, would you lead us in the Grace?"

Emily stood and bowed her head. Subconsciously her spirit began to quiet, her soul to respond. Fred Russell always seemed so close to God when he prayed. Emily wanted that more than anything in the world. She wished with all her heart that she knew his secret. She strained to hear every word of the prayer above the quiet rustle of the dining room. A new calmness descended upon her as she began to sense the presence of God.

When she sat down again at the table, a new attitude possessed her. Her tiredness and anxiety seemed to disappear. She knew—she knew without a doubt what she was doing here in school. She knew what she wanted with her own life. She knew that no matter how difficult it might be for her to keep up with the studies and the multitude of scheduling bells, she was where she belonged. Where she needed to be. She longed with every fibre of her being to know God better, to understand His way, to find His will for her scattery life.

She sighed again—this time not in impatience and frustration but in longing. She lifted her eyes to face her fellow classmates around the table and gave them one of her lovely smiles. She was ready for the day now. She'd get her chore of dreaded pots and pans over in quick order so that she might properly tidy her room for morning check. Then she'd take the time to have a meaningful morning devotional time. What she didn't know for the exam would just have to be endured. She knew she needed God's presence more than high test scores, as important as she knew her studies to be.

And just as it seemed Emily's thoughts and day were well under control, she felt the hairpins give way at the base of her neck and knew that one side of her loosely held roll was spilling down her back. With a red face she excused herself from the table and went to re-pin her hair, firmly and properly.

Chapter Two

School Days

When Emily's Bible History test was returned, she was relieved to see that she had received a good grade. Excitedly she hurried off to her dorm room to share her wonderful news with Ruth. But Ruth was not alone when Emily bounced into the room. Olive Tyndale's blond hair was flowing freely down her back while Ruth snipped at the ends of the golden tresses with her blunt fabric scissors.

Emily slid to a stop. She could hardly just burst in, waving her test paper and boasting about the grade she'd received.

"—and do you know what he said to me?" Olive was saying. "He said, 'Your hair looks like spun gold.' That's what he said. I couldn't believe it." She gave a little giggle.

Ruth's scissors continued to snip. Her expression did not change. Olive was always spilling some secret comment of one young man or another. Ruth listened but paid little notice. She simply was not given to swooning over beaus, but if Olive wished to do so, that was her privilege. Besides, the compliment was certainly not very original.

"And then he said—"

"Emily," Ruth cut in, "Mary Friesen was looking for you. She said she had to go to the store for some shampoo and wondered if you would like to walk along."

"I would," Emily admitted, "but I just don't have the time. I have my report for tomorrow's Pentateuch class to prepare—and I have resolved to get to bed on time tonight."

"Then maybe you should let Mary know. She's been waiting for you."

Emily went down the hall and rapped lightly on Mary's door, but it was Mary's roommate who called, "Come in."

"Ruth said Mary was waiting for me," Emily explained.

"She was," answered Pearl, "but she finally left. She has to be back for detail so she asked Liz to go with her."

Emily nodded.

"Is that your Bible History test?" asked Pearl, noticing the paper in Emily's hand.

Emily glanced at the paper she was still absent-mindedly holding and excitement filled her again. She nodded, trying to keep the pleased gleam from her eyes.

"What'd you get?" inquired Pearl candidly.

"Eighty-seven," answered Emily.

"Eighty-seven percent?"

Emily nodded.

"That's good," Pearl replied admiringly. "I got sixty-eight and I thought I did well. Even Fred got only eighty-two. That was a hard test."

For a moment Emily was swept with a feeling of pride. *I even beat Fred Russell!* she exulted. Then her instant glory faded away. Fred had not been able to study for the test. He had been called home because his mother was ill, and he had only arrived back on campus the night before the exam. Her pride quickly changed to sympathy for Fred.

"He didn't get to study—remember?" Emily reminded Pearl.

"I know," agreed Pearl. "Still, you did beat him—and rather handily, too."

"Well, it hardly—"

But already Pearl was changing the subject. "What are you wearing to the Missions dinner on Friday?"

"I don't know. I haven't even given it a thought."

"Are you being escorted?"

Emily shook her head. She still wasn't sure if she wanted to be escorted. The only fellow on campus that she really liked had invited Olive. Olive with her blond spun-gold hair. Emily had long since given up her secret dream that Ross Norris would ever notice her.

"No-o," she answered hesitantly.

Pearl sighed. "Max asked me, but I said no. So I guess I'm stuck with going alone." She sighed again. "I was really hoping Carl would ask me first. Now I won't be able to accept when he does ask."

Emily wondered why Pearl thought Carl would be asking her, but she didn't voice the question. Instead, she responded good-naturedly, "You can sit with me if you want some company."

Pearl nodded. "Thanks," she said. "I might."

Emily left to return to her own room. She had to get busy with her assignment. It would soon be time for the dinner bell.

Olive was still there. Ruth had completed the task of trimming her hair, but Olive had not bothered to re-pin it. Instead, she sat on the edge of the bed, running long slender fingers through the silken strands.

"—and Rob said that I shouldn't worry my pretty head about it," she commented coyly.

"Rob?" questioned Ruth without too much interest.

"Rob. Robert Lee. I call him Rob," answered Olive with a toss of the golden hair.

"You are supposed to call him 'Mr. Lee,' I believe," commented Ruth dryly.

Olive chuckled. It was school rules that the young men and women address one another with proper respect—not on a first-name basis.

"Oh, I do—whenever we're within earshot of one of the faculty," she assured Ruth, then cast a look toward Emily. "Are you going to study?" she asked incredulously as Emily cleared a spot on the crowded desk and arranged her books.

"I must," Emily answered. "I have an assignment to get done for tomorrow."

Olive sighed. Due assignments were such a bore.

"I need to get busy, too," Ruth informed Olive in a courteous but firm dismissal. Reluctantly the girl eased herself from the bed, still running her fingers through her hair, then tossed it back over her shoulders and picked up her hairpins and combs.

"Okay, Bookworms," she chided pertly. "Stick your noses back in your books." She left the room humming a popular song often played on the radio.

Emily settled herself at the small desk. "Do you need some room?" she asked Ruth, trying to figure out what she could move to give Ruth space on the one small surface.

"No, I think I'll go to the library. I need some reference books for my report."

Then Ruth noticed Emily's Bible History paper.

"How did you do?" she asked with interest.

Emily could not keep her eyes from lighting up. "Better than I thought I would," she enthused. "I got eighty-seven."

"Good," Ruth rejoiced with Emily. "From what I've heard, that's one of the higher marks of the class."

"Is it?" Emily could hardly believe that she was topping her classmates. She who always had to work so hard for her grades.

"Even Fred—" began Ruth.

"I know. Pearl told me. But Fred wasn't here to study," Emily said once more.

Ruth just nodded her head and gathered up her books with a "See you later."

From down the hall came Olive's giggle followed by a little shriek from Pearl. Olive had not returned to her room to prepare for the next day's classes. She and Pearl were likely exchanging stories about the cute things that the young men on campus had said to them recently.

Emily bent over her book and set her mind to studying—but the words seemed to blur before her eyes. Through her mind ran the catchy little tune Olive had been humming. No matter how hard she tried, the tune insisted on going round and round in her head.

Oh, bother! fumed Emily. *I might as well have gone up town with Mary. I can never study with all the commotion.* She concluded that she would never get in step with dorm living. Waiting for late-night quiet seemed to be her only recourse.

But Emily did eventually get into her report. She even became so engrossed that she missed the warning dinner bell and might have missed dinner had not Ruth arrived back from the library to inform her that they must rush or they would be late. Emily pushed back her books and rose to follow Ruth. In her hurry she bumped some papers from the desk and stopped to retrieve them. Ruth's Bible History test had big red markings giving her score. She had made ninety-two percent! Emily's eyes widened.

"And without any effort," she muttered to herself. Suddenly she felt that life was not fair.

Then she hastened from the room and ran the few steps down the hall to catch up with the other girls. Nobody had ever said that life was fair, she told herself, and besides, if anyone deserved it, Ruth did. Emily pushed her agitated feelings from her with determination. She refused to be jealous over her roommate's ability. God expected Emily Evans to do only what she was capable of doing. No more—and no less.

Chapter Three

Classmates

Emily found that it was all she could do to accomplish her assignments in time for the next day's classes. On more than one occasion she broke the lights-out rule, though she didn't intend to do so. And she was occasionally still late for breakfast—in spite of Ruth's insistence that she must get up. But Emily tried. She honestly tried to keep up with the demands of the school. It seemed to her that she was always rushing, always pressing, always scurrying to keep up with the rest. Yet in all of the hurry, she was conscious of a strange serenity that she was in the right place, doing the right thing. Her knowledge of the Bible continued to grow daily.

To Emily the most special time of the day was the chapel hour. She loved to hear the hymns as the students joined in singing, the men on one side and the women on the other. She thrilled with the testimonies of fellow students. She drank in the preaching hungrily. There was *so much* she longed to know. She felt unworthy to be at such a place of learning—yet deeply thankful that God had allowed her to come.

Not all of Emily's activities were serious and studious. She enjoyed the parties held in the dining hall. Skating was allowed at the local pond. Interaction was encouraged, though formal dating was limited. But during the school year the young men and women became acquainted in a proper and chaperoned environment. Emily soon learned to identify each of her classmates, not by name or appearance, but by personality traits.

As far as Emily was concerned, Ruth was the perfect example of what a young Christian woman should be. Though rather plain in appearance, perhaps, she was alert, capable, intelligent and devout. Her no-nonsense approach to life fit well with her deep desire to serve the Lord. Emily thanked God many times for giving her a roommate like Ruth.

Olive, the one with the pretty hair, was flighty, flirty, and seemingly out-of-place at a Bible school. *But perhaps God has His own reasons for bringing her here,* Emily concluded.

Mary, quiet and studious, asked little of others and gave much in return. Emily found Mary easy to love. She was of the stuff that close friends were made from.

Though not as enamored with the opposite sex as Olive was, Pearl was certainly more attractive, and she didn't pretend not to know that young men occupied the same campus. She was quick to laugh and witty in her responses. In a way, Emily could have easily envied Pearl.

One by one Emily mentally reviewed her dorm sisters. They came from many backgrounds, looked quite different, had varying personalities, but they shared many things—besides the large common bathroom with its curtained showers and stalls. They shared dreams and hopes and aspirations. They shared a desire to study the Word and to share that Word in some way with others. At least, *most* of them were on campus to study and grow.

Emily was also aware of the young men on campus, though not nearly as much so as Olive and Pearl. Carl Tyndale, blond like his sister, was the campus tease, the one who was usually thinking of some silly prank to pull on an unsuspecting fellow student. Occasionally there were whispers of Carl being sent home if he didn't conform to the school standards of conduct, but the days passed by and Carl remained. Emily thought the dean was patience personified when it came to his dealings with Carl.

To Emily, Fred Russell was as much the example for the men as Ruth was for the young women. A spiritual leader, he was studious, sensitive, committed and deeply respected. The faculty counted on Fred to set the tone of the school. One could not dislike Fred. It would have seemed near to blasphemy.

Robert Lee, known to Olive as "Rob," was the campus flirt, or so Emily thought. He may have told Olive not to worry her pretty little head, but he told every girl on campus some such silly rubbish. Emily paid little attention to the cute sayings of Mr. Lee.

Morris Soderquist, his heavy glasses framing deep blue eyes, was a slight, wiry young man with a deep sense of commitment to his goal. He intended to go overseas to the mission field, and he pored over his Bible with intensity as he prepared himself for service. Conversations with Morris were few and far between, for he was always in the library or in his own room studying.

Lacey Beckett, a big farm boy, was tall and heavyset. His voice matched his appearance and his laugh rumbled through a room. Emily felt that fate—or whatever or whoever was responsible for naming Lacey—had somehow played a cruel trick. The name simply did not fit the man. Lacey was anything but fragile or feminine. Emily had to keep herself from giggling every time she heard or read his name. She was glad she had to call him "Mr. Beckett"—she was sure she could not hide her amusement if she were to call him "Lacey."

Thirteen young men in all filled the men's residence. Each one added a personal dimension to the student body and, together with the fifteen young ladies, formed a unit of learning and growing, each contributing in some sense to the other.

———

Emily went home for Christmas to share some special times with her father and two sisters. Emily had been twelve when her mother was taken from them. Being the middle girl in the family, Emily had nearly been overlooked in the changing household. She had not had to take on the home duties that fell on Ina, nor was she petted and pitied like younger Annabelle. Only her father, who had always seen Emily as the most like her mother, had carried a special spot for her in his heart. Her rather frail body was his constant concern. Slight of stature and subject to flus and colds, Emily often carried out her responsibilities by sheer determination.

But Christmas had been a good time for all. They went to Grandma Evan's on Christmas Eve and to Grandma Clark's for Christmas Day. Ina was spared the burden of preparing a Christmas dinner, and Annabelle, now thirteen, was fussed over sufficiently to carry her through the months ahead.

Though Emily enjoyed Christmas, she secretly longed to get back to school. But she tried not to let her restlessness show, for she could feel her father's thoughtful gaze upon her. There was little chance for the two of them to talk privately, so Emily answered all the general questions about the school, her work, and her health. She thought she had given a satisfactory report until one night when she sat reading her Bible after Ina and Annabelle had retired.

A rustling of paper preceded her father's question. "How's school?"

"Fine," Emily answered simply, her eyes not leaving the page.

There was a moment of silence.

"How's school?" her father asked again.

This time Emily lifted her eyes and looked directly into his warm brown ones, now crinkled with interest and concern.

"Fine," she answered evenly. "I like it."

He nodded and his work-worn hands laid the newspaper in his lap. "You've been keeping well?"

Emily was about to nod in agreement when she remembered a bout with the flu that had kept her in bed for three days, and the last cold that bothered her for a week.

"Mostly," she said honestly.

"Are you takin' your cod-liver oil?"

The very mention of it caused Emily's pert little nose to wrinkle up, but she nodded vigorously.

"Good! You look a little peaked."

"Peaked" was one of her father's favorite words. He referred to any one of his children as being "a little peaked" whenever illness struck.

"I'm fine," Emily insisted.

"Got a good roommate?" was the next question.

"Ruth. She's great. I really like her. I just wish I could be more like her," Emily said sincerely.

"Nothin' wrong with you," her father was quick to assure her, and Emily flushed with the simplicity of his appraisal.

"Any special fellas?" asked Mr. Evans, and Emily's head lifted in time to catch the twinkle in his eyes.

She smiled slowly, then shook her head. She knew that Ross really didn't count. He still seemed to be carrying a torch for Olive, even though Olive responded positively and then ignored him, by turn.

She shook her head. "No one special to me—in that way," she admitted.

"Will Pearson still asks about you," Mr. Evans said, causing Emily to blush. Will Pearson had been asking about Emily for too many years. He was much older than she—nine years, in fact, and he had been living with false hope for a long time. Emily had no interest in Will Pearson, even if he did own his own farm.

"He thinks it a bit foolish that I favored you gettin' Bible learning. Seeing as how girls aren't preachers and all."

Emily lifted a stubborn chin. "Some girls are," she argued, as though Will Pearson were right in the room. "We've had women in chapel who are. They came with their preacher husbands. Both of them. Mrs. Witt, the district superintendent's wife, she can preach, too."

Mr. Evans looked surprised. "Women preachers? Never heard of it."

"Well, you can just tell Will Pearson the next time he asks that there *are* women preachers—aplenty."

Emily's chin lifted higher. What right had Will Pearson to dictate the role of women anyway?

Mr. Evans was quite intrigued by the news. "Ordained?" he asked, and Emily had to quickly think about what he was asking.

"No," she answered slowly. "Not ordained. But they preach— and they help in the church. And they lead people to the Lord, too."

"If they aren't ordained, how can they run a church?"

"They have a special—a special position. The denomination even gives them papers. It says right there that they are approved to minister."

"Do they do everything? Everything that a man preacher does?" queried her father.

"No-o," Emily had to admit. "They can't do things like marry or bury. Or baptize. Things like that."

"But they preach?" queried her father, scarcely believing that a woman could be placed in such a role.

"They preach," Emily assured him. "Mostly when their husbands have to be away. But Rev. and Mrs. Jackson—they take turns, Sunday by Sunday."

It seemed preposterous to Emily's father. "Well, I don't guess I'd care much to have a daughter of mine bein' a preacher— even if her husband was," went on Mr. Evans. "Seems to me that one preacher in a household is quite enough." He thought for a moment and then spoke again, quietly. "Not sure I'd want to be listenin' to a woman either, come to think of it." Emily wasn't sure if the words were meant for her or were just a quiet expression of the way her father felt.

"I think—I think—" and then Emily hesitated. Was she breaking a confidence? Her father looked at her, waiting for her to go on.

"I think Ruth might like to be one," she said at last, speaking barely above a whisper. "She hasn't said so yet, but she loves to study and says that she would love to preach. She just wants to teach and preach. She can hardly wait for her turn to share in chapel or at prayer meetings."

But Emily's father was shaking his head.

"Must be a strange one," he observed and then rose from his chair, signaling that it was time for them to put out the light and retire for the night.

Chapter Four

A Call

Emily arrived back at school with new resolve. She had no intention of going home to Jamestown and marrying Will Pearson—whether he was still waiting for her or not!

Several times she recalled the conversation with her father and realized that she did not share some of her parent's views. She believed a woman could join with her husband to serve in the role of church leadership. Emily began to secretly think that she would be honored if the Lord would favor her with a preacher-husband so that they could serve Him together. She began to look at her male classmates in a different way. Which ones would make good preachers? Which ones might answer a call from God to serve? Emily had never evaluated fellows in such a fashion before. But as she observed, she soon became convinced that Ross, for all his good looks and magic charm, would *not* be the man for her, even if he hadn't been smitten by the elusive Olive. Ross just was not preacher material, in Emily's estimation.

Carl was a bit too unsettled, a bit too frivolous to make a preacher. Fred, of course, would make a first-rate preacher—but Fred already had a lady friend by the name of Agatha. And comparing Fred with herself, Emily felt inadequate and lacking in spiritual depth. She would never be able to measure up as Fred's wife. She wondered silently if Agatha could.

Robert was not even considered a possibility. He was just too silly—too insincere. Emily was sure that even God would be hard put to make much out of Robert.

Morris was headed for the mission field—and by all appearances he planned to go alone. Morris did not even seem to realize that girls were a part of the world.

Lacey, with his huge frame and boisterousness, was easily scratched from Emily's list as well. God would have to do a lot of polishing before Lacey could be ready to serve Him.

One by one each of Emily's fellow students was assessed and found wanting in one area or another. There just didn't seem to be anyone in her class who was right for Emily. Oh, she certainly knew young men with sterling qualities, but those whom Emily might have selected were already attached to someone else, or had stated their intentions of going back to the family farm or on for secular training. Emily couldn't see much future for her in the current prospects.

Yet the insistent desire to serve the Lord continued to fill her thoughts. "What can I do, Lord?" she kept asking in her daily prayers. "I have no place of service, no particular skills, and no one with whom to share a call."

In her devotional reading, scripture passages such as "Calling the twelve to him, he sent them out two by two" seemed to leap off the page and burn themselves into her heart. *What did it all mean?*

Emily did not wait patiently for the answer. She chafed inwardly, posed hard questions in class, sought counsel from fellow students, and listened intently in the worship services.

It wasn't until her first Bible school year had almost ended that Emily received her answer. Rev. and Mrs. Paul Witt, the district superintendent and his wife, were visiting chapel. Emily sat on the edge of her seat, her hands clasped into nervous knots in her lap, her hazel eyes opened wide with intensity.

"We have countless areas open to us," Rev. Witt was saying. "Places where they are begging us to come and start a church, and we have no one to send. God does not call us to sit idly by while the people perish. He has called us to go—to give—to preach the Gospel."

Emily could not help stealing a glance at the men's side of the chapel. Surely many of them would be profoundly moved and anxious to answer the call to serve.

"We need to be willing to obey His voice as He speaks to us. Where are the men who are willing to bridge the gap—to answer, 'Here am I. Send me'? For how can they hear without a preacher? How can they preach except they be sent? We, as a denomination, are here to send you forth. We are here to back and support you. We are here to help you to obey God's call—to take up your cross and follow Him."

Is he speaking only to the men here? The question suddenly flashed through Emily's mind. She looked around her and caught Ruth's eye, then turned her attention back to the speaker.

"I urge you, if He is speaking to your heart, obey His voice—follow His leading today. Come. Come acknowledge His call on your life. Come forward and kneel here at the altar of prayer. Offer up your life as a sacrifice of love and obedience to the Lord who loves you. Who died for your salvation. Come. That others too might know the joy of knowing God."

Fred Russell was the first to move forward. Morris Soderquist was close behind him. And then, to Emily's surprise, Lacey Beckett was moving quickly toward the altar, tears on his round cheeks.

And then Emily could bear the intensity of the feeling in her heart no longer. With a sob in her throat, she hastily rose and practically ran to the altar railing where she knelt down and unashamedly buried a tear-streaked face in her clasped hands.

The answer had come. If God had no helpmate with whom she could share His call, she would go alone. It was as simple as that. Will Pearson might think it impossible for a woman to preach, but Emily knew otherwise. Hadn't she heard God's call? Hadn't He promised all of His children that He would be with them? Of course! Of course God could call a woman to serve. Emily had no idea just where and how—but she did know that her heart yearned to be of service to God.

"Yes, Lord. Yes," she prayed silently. "I'll go. Wherever you want me—I'll go."

A strange peace settled over her heart. She had been obedient. She was committed to Christ and to the goal of serving Him. She was only a girl, but God would be with her. He would lead her. Emily was sure of that.

———

Emily later learned that she had not been the only young woman at the altar. Ruth had, as Emily would have expected, joined those at the altar as well. Ruth, too, had answered God's call to serve Him—maybe even to preach.

After the altar service was over, the good Rev. Witt spoke softly to those who had stepped forward. As Emily lifted her swollen, red eyes and looked shyly about her, she was surprised to see seven of her classmates on the front benches.

Rev. Witt went slowly down the row, speaking to each person by name.

"Why are you here, Mr. Russell?"

Fred answered without hesitation. "I feel called to serve."

"And where would God have you serve?"

Fred shook his head. "It matters not," he answered just as firmly. "I will serve wherever my church places me."

The district superintendent smiled and nodded in agreement.

"And you, Mr. Soderquist?" he went on.

"God called me to the mission field when I was a boy," answered Morris with a trembling voice. "I came forward today to publicly testify to that calling."

Again the superintendent nodded.

"And you, Mr. Beckett?"

But Lacey Beckett could not readily answer. He was still weeping with the enormity of his conviction that he was called to serve.

Rev. Witt passed on. Emily felt a quiver go all through her body. She was next.

"What about you, Miss Evans?"

"God has called me to—to serve Him—somewhere—in some—some new church. I—I don't know where," Emily responded.

"God will show us where," the good man said with confidence, and the tears streamed down Emily's face again. She had been accepted. As simply as that, she had been accepted to minister for the Lord, to preach.

The superintendent heard testimony from each of the other students. Occasionally he stopped to praise God or to wipe his eyes with his handkerchief before continuing on.

Emily was filled with emotion at the intensity of this time. Surely great things would happen as a result of the day's chapel service. Eight more servants! Eight more to serve her God!

And then the service was dismissed and Emily was free to embrace her roommate and share in the excitement of being *called*.

All that week Emily walked on air. She was actually going to serve God in a new work—somewhere. Even now she was preparing herself for that service. She would prepare herself well. She needed to thoroughly know the Word. She would be sharing that Word with hungry people Sunday after Sunday.

And then, unbidden, a new thought came to Emily. She remembered the late nights—the stolen minutes after lights out and the jumping into bed under false pretenses to fool the preceptress. Surely God could not honor such actions. She was smitten with conviction, and tears stung her eyes. She had to make things right before she could go one step further. She had to confess her sin and ask for forgiveness. *Maybe they will refuse me an assignment someplace when they know how deceitful I've been*, she thought, her heart constricting with fear.

Reluctantly Emily placed one heavy foot before the other as she made her way to the office of Miss Herrington. She dreaded the stern look she no doubt would encounter in those sharp gray eyes. She could picture the pointed nose lifting slightly, and the lips pursed in a thin, tight line, expressing displeasure. Miss Herrington was a kind, godly woman, but Emily knew the preceptress did not have much patience with disobedience. Timidly Emily knocked at the door and was told to enter.

"Miss Herrington?" she addressed her dean hesitantly.

"Miss Evans," the woman responded, smiling pleasantly. "Come in. Do come in."

Emily closed the door behind her.

"You can't imagine how pleased we all are that you have presented yourself for service," the woman went on, beaming at Emily.

Emily's smile was shaky in return.

"Well, yes, I—"

"Have you had the opportunity to share your good news with your family?"

"No-o," Emily admitted and again remembered the discussion with her father. She wondered if her father would deem the "call" good news.

"You haven't written?"

"Well, no-o. I'm to go home this weekend. I thought that I'd rather—rather tell them firsthand."

The preceptress smiled. "Of course," she said. "It is always nicer to share those things in person."

The woman looked searchingly at Emily and seemed to sense that something was troubling her.

"Can I be of help in some way?" she asked solicitously.

Tears gathered in Emily's eyes.

"I—I have a confession," she admitted.

The smile left but the eyes still held softness.

"Go on," the woman urged.

"I—I haven't always been to bed on time. I—I mean I have studied after—after lights out. I—I'm rather slow—I mean in my studies. I need to spend much longer studying than Ruth, and so I—I—"

Then Emily finished lamely, "I broke the rules."

"But your light was always out when I came around for bed check," the woman puzzled.

Emily's face felt hot. "I—I would put the light out when I heard the stair step squeak," she admitted.

There was a moment of silence.

"I see," said the preceptress slowly.

"And—and on occasion, I—I got back up and put the light on again—after all was quiet, so I could study some more," Emily admitted. "I—I even laid my rolled-up towel at the door to cover the crack."

More silence. Then Miss Herrington commented, "I have watched your grades. You have been doing well."

"But I wouldn't have—without studying," Emily assured her, her words tumbling over each other. "I have always found learning more—more difficult than some. Even in grade school I had to work harder than Ina or even Annabelle—my sisters. I—"

"Miss Evans," the preceptress interrupted softly, "do you understand why we have the 'lights out' rule?"

"Yes." Emily's voice trembled.

"Why?"

"So that we get the proper rest."

"Correct. Lights out is not some casually contrived policy. Lights out is for your benefit. But that is not all. It is for the benefit of the total student body—so that you do not pass on an illness to the rest. You are cheating yourself when you break the rules. And perhaps endangering your fellow students."

Emily had not considered that before.

"You have been remarkably free of sickness this winter—but your faculty has been praying for you week by week."

Emily's eyes widened. She had no idea that her health was the subject of faculty prayers.

"Perhaps God has seen fit to answer those prayers in spite of your disobedience." Miss Herrington's gentle tone took some of the sting out of the words. "Because—because," she went on, "He saw a girl who wanted to get all she could from her studies."

Emily blinked.

"But," continued the preceptress, "one should not press, or be presumptuous, with God."

Emily wondered if the preceptress had been on the verge of saying "press one's luck." In spite of her mortification over the interview, she found it hard to suppress a smile.

"From now on, I shall expect you to be in bed at the proper hour."

"Yes, Miss Herrington," agreed Emily in a subdued tone.

"If you need to have more study time, we will try to find some other way for you to manage it."

The kindness and consideration of the older woman surprised Emily. She had not expected such understanding.

Emily's eyes brimmed again. She felt more chastised than if she had been assigned further kitchen duty or soundly scolded for her crime.

"I am sorry—truly, I am," she sobbed. The woman offered her a clean handkerchief and Emily murmured her thanks.

"Miss Evans," the preceptress said, "you realize that if you had not come to me about your disobedience and I had discovered it another way, I could not have avoided disciplinary action."

Emily nodded and wiped her eyes, greatly relieved that she had been moved to seek forgiveness.

Miss Herrington reached out and patted her hand.

"Let's hear nothing more about it," she stated matter-of-factly, and Emily knew she had been dismissed. Dismissed and forgiven. Feeling a load had been lifted from her heart, she slipped from the room. She had not been condemned. She had not been removed from the list for future service. With great relief, Emily went back to her room to wash her face.

"Now if only Father will understand about my call . . ." she said under her breath and reached for her towel and washcloth.

Chapter Five

Sharing the News

Spring was knocking at the back door of winter when Emily stepped off the train at Jamestown station for her weekend at home. Here and there a bird twittered in expectation of warmer days. Bits of hardy green showed in small patches against the southern side of buildings where the snow had been forced to give way by warm sunshine. Emily took a deep breath and smiled her anticipation of milder weather, which she yearned for. Her health was always much better in the summertime.

If I go home with a bounce to my step and a healthy glow on my cheeks, Father won't be quite so hard to convince, she had reasoned to herself on the train ride home.

But even with those positive thoughts, Emily wondered.

Just how would her father accept the news of her "calling"? Besides his feeling regarding women preachers, he had inferred that Emily needed a hardy, solid man to care for her, to protect her from the strains that life often imposed. That probably was why he considered Will Pearson a good candidate. It was true that Emily's shoulders were not broad, nor her frame strong. *But God has other strengths He gives His servants,* Emily reasoned.

Emily's father greeted her at the station. She could feel his eyes scan her quickly. *I'm glad I had my coat properly buttoned,* she thought to herself. Then her glance followed his to her feet. She had neglected to wear her overshoes again.

"The streets were quite clear in Regis," she said defensively. "I didn't even think to wear my—"

He just nodded, his face solemn, as he reached for the small valise she carried. Emily knew he was not pleased with her carelessness.

She circled a spring puddle and had to run a few steps to catch up to her father, who had splashed directly through with his farm boots. She sought for something to say, but she couldn't think of anything except, "How are Ina and Annabelle?"

"They're doing good. Ina's fixin' supper and Annabelle wasn't home from school yet, so I came by myself." They lapsed again into silence.

When they reached the team and wagon, her father nodded for her to get in while he placed the valise on the floor boards. Emily climbed stiffly over the wheel and settled herself for the ride.

They were almost home before her father said, "How's school?"

"Fine," responded Emily, continuing to watch a distant V of returning Canada geese.

There was a moment of silence, and then her father spoke again.

"How's school?"

Emily jerked to attention. Her father had always used this device with his children. If they answered absent-mindedly, he simply repeated the question until they gave it proper consideration.

Emily's heart began to pound. *Is now the time to tell Father about my call?* She took a deep breath and decided to get it over with. Perhaps then they would have the rest of the weekend to sort it through—work it out.

"We had a wonderful chapel service recently," Emily began with a deep breath. "The Witts were there, and Rev. Witt spoke about the need for church workers. Then he gave an altar call. He asked those who felt God was calling them to serve Him to step out and come forward."

Emily stopped for breath—and courage. "Eight students went forward."

She hesitated again.

Her father had been watching her face as she spoke, and Emily turned to him now. She saw his eyes were alight and he answered almost under his breath, "Praise God."

Emily was pleased with his response. She knew her father was deeply interested in enlarging their mission of reaching local communities, particularly ones that had no church.

Emily took another deep breath and then blurted out hurriedly before the gleam left her father's eyes, "I was one of them."

A startled look passed over his face. Emily waited for the lecture to begin. There was nothing. Only silence. His eyes shifted back to the team he was driving. One foot stirred restlessly on the wooden boards of the wagon. Emily could see his hands tighten on the reins.

Still he did not speak. He had just thanked God that young people had been called to preach. And now he had to face the giving of his own flesh and blood—and one not too strong at that.

At length he nodded—just nodded his head in acknowledgment. He could hardly take back his expression of praise to God. But Emily could see the uncertainty in his eyes.

"Where?" was his simple response.

Emily shrugged her slim shoulders. "I—I don't know where—yet. Rev. Witt said that—that God would show us where."

He seemed to relax then. "You know you're not very strong," he began gently.

Emily's chin came up. "Scripture says that God often chooses the weak things to confound the strong," she reminded him.

He nodded, his expression saying there was no use arguing against Scripture.

They rode in silence again. Emily could tell that her father was mulling over the news. Finally he spoke again. "So who's the young man?"

Emily did not understand. "The what?" she asked.

"The man. When you were home at Christmas, you told about a preacher and his wife both servin' together. I don't recall your writing about someone special. I would like to know the man my daughter will be sharing her life with. Who will you be goin'—"

"Oh," cut in Emily quickly, "I—I'm not interested in anyone. I'm quite prepared to go alone."

This did bring a sharp reaction from her father. "Alone?" he thundered. "That's absurd. You can't just go off and run a church alone. A young girl like you—sickly and—"

"I'm not sickly," Emily protested. "I've much more strength than you credit me with, Father. And I will have God to—"

"It's unheard of," her father continued, paying little attention to Emily's arguments. "It wouldn't even be decent for a young woman to be on her own. To try to manage a church. How can the district superintendent even consider such a thing? I won't hear of it! Not for one of my girls."

Emily bit her tongue. Now was not the time for the discussion to continue. Tears stung her eyes, but she wisely made no further comment. Inwardly she prayed. Prayed that He would speak to her father. If she was to answer God's call, He would need to convince her father that it was proper and right for a young woman.

"We'll talk later," he said at last, patting her arm a bit stiffly and flicking the reins to hasten the team.

He needs time to think—to pray, Emily concluded.

It was not until Mr. Evans was driving Emily back to catch her train that the subject was broached again.

"You know you are often ill," he began softly.

Emily nodded in silent agreement. It would have been foolish to try to deny it.

"You know that directing a church is hard, hard work."

Emily nodded at that as well.

"Why don't they send out two women together?" he demanded.

"There aren't enough of us to double up like that," Emily tried to explain.

"You'll likely spend many hours alone."

"I know," whispered Emily, the tears threatening to come.

"You'll have no one there to lean on."

"God will be there," Emily insisted in a trembling voice.

The plodding of the team, the creaking of the wagon wheels, and the occasional twitter of a bird were the only intrusions on the silence.

"And you still wish to do it?" Emily's father finally asked.

Emily turned pleading eyes to him. The tears clung to her lashes and she swallowed the lump in her throat.

"It is not what I want that is important," she murmured in a whispery voice. "I have been called, Papa. To disobey would only bring heartache. I must—I *must* answer my call."

She called him Papa only at very intimate times. It was what her mother had often called him. "Go ask your papa," the girls would be told. Or, "Call your papa for dinner." He turned his face slightly to hide his deep emotion. After a time, he cleared his throat and turned back to Emily.

"Then by all means, be obedient," he said huskily. "I—I will do—whatever I can to help."

With a glad little cry Emily leaned against her father and took his large hand in both her small ones.

"Thank you, Papa," she said through her tears. She knew her prayer had been answered.

Chapter Six

Preparations

Emily went home to help Ina at the farm over the summer months. She had wished she could go out on some summer mission, some endeavor that would fit in with preparing herself for her future work. But her father had requested that she spend the time with them, and she was anxious to honor his wishes where possible.

The summer eventually was over, though it seemed to Emily twice as long as normal. She was glad to pack her trunk and her suitcase and board the train for school.

But just maybe, she reasoned with herself as her train chugged south, *just maybe these weeks of canning beans and tomatoes with Ina were the very best way I could have spent the summer. Maybe even the best preparation. . . .*

Back into the rhythm of school life, she conscientiously obeyed the dorm rules, which meant that she was in bed on time. *I might as well be up studying,* she sometimes grumbled as she lay in bed with her eyes wide open, the threat of an impending exam hanging over her troubled head. Her grades slipped a little, but she struggled on, willing herself to make use of each precious moment of her day. *Lord, I trust you with my time, my health, and my grades,* she prayed.

Her social life dwindled down to almost none, and she soon became known as "Nose-In-A-Book Emily." She seldom had time to indulge in a leisurely stroll uptown or a game of table tennis in the recreation room. But Emily didn't mind. She knew she needed to cram as much Bible learning into the short year as she possibly could.

She'd already had two interviews with the district superintendent, and on both occasions he had assured her that he would see she got a position as soon as she qualified.

A reading course had to be fulfilled, and Emily laboriously tried to fit it in along with her studies. It was difficult for her to read and report on all the required books, but if she didn't she would be delayed in getting a church posting. Her effort to keep pace left Emily hurried and exhausted.

Emily daily thanked God for strength, feeling that He truly was watching over her, certain He was as anxious for her to make it through the grueling school year as she was. Then two and a half weeks before the end of the term, she felt the familiar ache in her bones, the pinching tightness to her throat.

For a few hours she tried to deny that she had the flu, but her throbbing head and the flush of her face drew others' attention to her dilemma.

"Are you sick, dear?" Miss Herrington asked, touching a cold hand to Emily's forehead, and she had to nod in truthfulness.

"I think you should be in bed," responded the practical preceptress.

"I can't," moaned Emily. "I have a paper due tomorrow."

"I'm afraid the paper will have to wait," the preceptress continued. "Who is the teacher? I'll speak to him."

Emily told her and reluctantly headed for her room. By now the stairs were moving strangely. Emily clung to the bannister, scarcely knowing where to place her foot for the next step.

Miss Herrington came with some medication just as Emily pulled the covers up over her flannel nightgown and settled her head on the softly floating pillow.

Emily found it difficult to swallow as she tried to wash the pills down with a glass of orange juice.

"I will have Ruth double up with Judith tonight," the lady said. "That way you will not be disturbed and Ruth will have less chance of catching the bug."

Emily nodded.

"Do you feel sick to your stomach?" the preceptress asked.

Emily shook her head.

"Well, I'll leave this basin handy just in case," Miss Herrington went on. "And I will look in on you often."

Emily mumbled her thanks and willed the pills to work soon.

It was well that Miss Herrington had the foresight to leave the basin. Emily was soon in need of it—over and over again. *The medication won't have any chance to work,* Emily moaned.

Miss Herrington was kept busy rinsing the basin and bathing Emily's flushed face.

For four days the chills and fever raged. Emily could feel the strength being sucked from her slight body. When she could think nearly coherently, she felt angry and disappointed that the day of graduation was drawing so near and she would not be ready. Her assignments were not completed. *If only—if only*—she argued; *if only the flu could have waited for a few more weeks!*

And then Emily had no more strength to fight. She gave in to the ravaging illness and was content to lay her weary, aching head upon the pillow and try to rest.

When she finally felt a little better, it was only a few days until the term would end. *I'm so far behind, I'll never catch up,* Emily concluded despondently. With reluctant and unsteady steps she made her way to the dean's office.

Professor Henry was more than considerate. He looked at all Emily's courses, promised to talk to the teachers, and assured her that they would do everything possible to help her to get the necessary work done the week she had left.

Concessions and shortcuts approved by the faculty along with Emily's hard work meant that she was somehow able to meet the requirements. But she had to lay aside her required reading. So when she finished the school term, graduating with her class, she was unable to present herself for service as a mission worker along with the others.

It pained Emily deeply when Ruth showed her certificate of approval and told excitedly where she would be serving.

"There is no church there—not yet. I am to start one," Ruth enthused. "I will have two Sunday services, actually. One in the Midland schoolhouse on Sunday mornings and the other at the Dunnagan school in the afternoon."

It sounded like a big undertaking to Emily. It also sounded wonderful. She gave Ruth a firm hug and wished her well, but tears flowed freely down both faces.

"Where will you live?" Emily asked when she had her emotions under control.

"I'll be boarding with a neighborhood family. I'm sure it will be crowded. They have a family of six, I've been told."

"Well, there's a good start to your church right there," Emily said with a wobbly smile, and Ruth answered with another hug.

But both girls knew that the situation would not be easy. Ruth had been raised as an only child and was not used to the noise and activity of a crowded house. And Ruth liked a lot of quiet time in which to think and pray and plan her sermons.

"I'll make it—somehow," Ruth said in response to Emily's look of concern.

Emily nodded, trying to coax up a confident smile.

"And what will you do?" asked Ruth seriously. "I know how much you wanted to be ready—now."

Emily nodded slowly, trying to mask the disappointment she was feeling.

"I'm going home," she said with just a small tremor in her voice. "I've been told I must regain my strength—and I still have to complete the reading course . . . so-o . . ."

She shrugged and forced a smile.

"When do you think—?" began Ruth.

"Two or three weeks," Emily cut in. "I hope. Of course Rev. Witt has urged me to take a bit longer. Well, we'll see."

———

A few days later the two girls stood on the Regis station platform waiting for the train that would take Ruth to her first posting.

"Isn't it exciting about Verna?" Ruth asked enthusiastically.

Emily's eyes lit up. Verna Woods, another classmate, had also responded to God's call to serve, even if it meant going alone.

"That will make three of us who are deaconesses," Emily said. "And we even get to go to conference—and vote."

Both girls laughed and gave each other an unrestrained hug. To sit on the conference bar was quite an honor.

The distant train wailed against the silence of the spring morning, and Ruth placed her luggage closer to the boarding dock.

"You'll write?" urged Emily.

"Of course. And you?" responded Ruth.

"Oh, I will. Promise. I'll have more time than you," Emily answered.

"Not if you are going to hurry through that book list," Ruth quipped, but Emily merely shrugged and nodded in reply. The reading course was demanding, and she knew her father would be carefully watching her to see that she didn't overdo.

There was just enough time before the train wheezed in for Emily to take Ruth's hand and bow for a quick prayer. Then the two friends parted—Ruth excitedly boarding the train to her first mission work, and Emily reluctantly returning to the dorm to wait for her train home.

More preparation, Lord? Emily prayed wistfully. But then she resolutely set her mind to the task at hand.

But rather than the two or three weeks Emily had anticipated, it was a full seven weeks before she had her books read, papers of approval, and was ready for her first assignment. By then her health was improved, her walk more steady, her face less strained.

Emily would not be boarding. A small living accommodation was available, she was informed by the superintendent in his letter assigning her to the small community of Wesson Creek. It was a two-day drive away from home by horse and buggy. Her father himself was providing her with a steady team of grays and a secondhand buggy.

Emily was relieved yet anxious about her assignment, for she had never lived alone before. She would be glad for the solitude, which would help her in studying and prayer time. But at times it would be lonely, too, she reminded herself.

She felt thoroughly confused and strangely agitated as she saw her father reluctantly load the buggy for the trip, occasionally giving her long, questioning glances. She was both excited and fearful, exuberant and solemn, eager to be off and doubtful about leaving the home she had known and loved.

But she would not let the doubts and fears show. She kept the smile on her face, the spring in her step, and indicated that she was perfectly at ease with the path her life was taking.

Emily didn't know what all her father was piling into the already heavily loaded buggy. Gunny sack after gunny sack and box after box were stacked beneath the seat, spilling into the back of the democrat. She remembered that Ruth had set off to her assignment with just her two worn suitcases. *But Ruth is boarding,* she reminded herself. *I'll need to set up housekeeping on my own.*

At last the final trunk and small valise were settled into the packed buggy. "I do hope the weather holds," her father remarked with an eye on the cloudless sky. "Will Darin borrowed my only canvas tarp, and when I went over there this morning to collect it, his missus said he won't be home until next week."

Emily was totally unconcerned. With a sky as clear as the one that stretched above them, she was sure she could make a two-day trip without mishap.

Hugs and goodbyes were exchanged with her sisters and father, and Emily was off down the dusty road. A hand-drawn map from her father was tucked securely in her coat pocket.

The tears did not spill over until Emily was well hidden by the stands of poplar lining the country road. Then she allowed all the deep emotion to run down her cheeks and drip from her quivering chin.

This totally new venture—one she had been called to—was something she had to do, but it was not without some trepidation, some tearing away of old and dear bonds.

Emily made no effort to control her tears until she spotted a team approaching. She sniffed, took a handkerchief from her pocket, and hoped that she was successful in repairing the damage. A neighbor merely nodded and tipped his hat as they passed.

The sun was hot overhead, and Emily was glad her father had insisted she bring her everyday bonnet. She wore it now in place of the brand-new dark bonnet that was required to identify her as a church-approved deaconess. That treasured piece of headgear was protected from dust and sun in the small box at her feet.

Her father had picked a gentle team. Though Emily was by no means a horse-woman, she had often driven her father's well-disciplined team of bays. Shadow and Star, her new horses, needed little attention except to steer them in the right direction and urge them forward when they tried to loiter along the track.

Around noon Emily pulled the team into the shade of some larger poplar trees and climbed stiffly down from the buggy. Not used to driving a team for such a long period of time, she looked at her hands with dismay. Her fingers cramped and her hands felt as though blisters were forming. *So much for being a sturdy farm girl,* she thought wryly. She pulled off her bonnet and let the wind blow through her hair.

Emily unhooked the team and led them to water in the ditch. Shadow, eager for a drink, almost upended her in the dirty puddle. She spoke sharply to the horse and jerked on his bridle. Emily finally let go of the rein and stepped back to let him find his own way. She wasn't going to argue with the big gray.

After the team had satisfied their thirst, Emily tied them to posts where there was ample grazing, then lifted the bag with her lunch from the wagon. Ina had prepared it for her, and Emily's eyes misted as she looked at all the things Ina knew to be her favorites.

She was so filled with emotion that she could hardly swallow, so most of the lunch was rebundled and placed back in the buggy. Perhaps she would feel more like eating later.

The team was reluctant to give up the tall grasses. Emily had to drag on their reins and shout at the horses to get them back to the buggy. By the time she finally had them re-hitched, Emily was hot, sweaty, and angry.

At long last she was on her way again, the afternoon sun beating down upon her head.

"At least it's not raining," she muttered to herself as she flapped the reins over the two broad backs in front of her. The country road could be almost impassable when the heavy rains rutted the thick clay soil.

She was going to stay overnight with Fred and Agatha Russell, newly married and now in charge of the church at Conner. She was a little shy about seeing her former classmates for the first time as husband and wife. But as the afternoon wore on and the long shadows lengthened to darken the road she traveled, Emily no longer was concerned about fitting in at the home of newlyweds. She would be so thankful to see her friends and the parsonage that marked her abode for the night. She strained forward, eagerly scanning the road ahead for signs of civilization.

But it was almost dark before she finally spotted the small frame house. With a silent prayer of thanks, she turned the horses in at the gate. Her friends must have been watching for her and came out on the porch to greet her warmly. Fred took the team, and Agatha ushered Emily in to refresh herself at the kitchen basin before the evening meal was served.

Chapter Seven

Starting Out

Emily made her way down the path to the team that Fred had hooked to her loaded buggy. The sun was just making its way up into the summer sky. Emily knew it was going to be another hot day, and she firmly placed her bonnet on her head.

With warm thanks to Fred and Agatha, she settled herself on the buggy seat, picked up the reins and clucked to the team of grays. They responded with eagerness and Emily felt a twinge of guilt, sure that the horses expected to be on their way home. At the end of the lane, Emily had to force the team to make a right-hand rather than a left-hand turn. They reluctantly responded to her tug on the reins. She waved one last time at Agatha, and then Emily was alone once more.

Emily felt refreshed and eager after her night's rest. Her hands had been carefully washed and salved, and Agatha had even cut the feet from a pair of Fred's heavy discarded socks and snipped holes in the remaining portion for Emily's thumbs—a mitt of sorts to protect her from the wear of the reins. Emily wished she had thought of something like that before she left home.

The day grew hotter and hotter. Emily feared that even with the protection of her hat, she wouldn't be able to endure the heat much longer. A breeze stirred just in time.

As she had the day before, she stopped to eat, this time much past the noon hour. She had been watching for a place to water her horses, but the ditches along the dusty road had been dry.

At last she spied a small pond. There were no sheltering trees nearby, but there was grass in the ditches. She guided her buggy off the road the best she could and climbed down. She was even more stiff than she had been the day before.

The horses, anxious to get to the water, were not too patient with Emily as she struggled with tugs and yokes. At last she separated the team from the buggy and led them carefully down the sharp incline to the edge of the water. The big mare was fairly cooperative, but Shadow, the gelding, lumbered forward and stepped on Emily's heel enough to cause her pain. When she squealed and jerked the rein, he threw his head angrily into the air, almost knocking the unsuspecting girl into the pond.

The two horses drank deeply, at length both turning their interest to the grasses at the water's edge. Emily tied each to a post and hobbled back up to the buggy to get the lunch Agatha had sent along. She was hungry. She was also thirsty. Even though the bottle of water Agatha had prepared was warm and uninviting, Emily drank nearly as long as the horses.

She removed her hat and pushed her hair back from her damp face to catch the full benefit of the afternoon breeze. Pulling her father's map from her coat, she saw she still had a long way to go.

She packed up the remains of her lunch and placed it where she could easily reach it if she grew hungry again before arriving at her own small parsonage. She eyed the horses as they greedily pulled mouthfuls of the coarse grasses. They hadn't been feeding very long, but, oh, she was anxious to be on her way. Her eyes went to the sky and to her dismay she saw large storm clouds boiling up in the west.

"Oh my!" she said aloud in alarm. "It looks like rain and here I sit right in the open! I don't even have a rain cape with me."

Rain was another thing Emily had not thought to prepare for.

She retrieved the team and hitched them hurriedly to the buggy while they switched angry tails and tossed defiant heads. But Emily paid no attention.

"We've got to hurry," she said firmly to the balky team. "It's going to rain and we are miles away from home." She smacked the reins on their round rumps, and they moodily started down the road at a brisk trot.

The trot did not last long. Emily knew the team was as tired as she, and she didn't have the heart to run them. They returned to a walk and Emily drove with one anxious eye on the sky.

The wind increased and Emily took another look at her map to be sure she was still on the right road. The impending storm didn't seem to threaten the horses in any way. They trudged along just as carelessly as they had done in the heavy heat.

But Emily was fearful enough for all of them. The dark, scudding clouds looked as if they would soak everything that was in the buggy. Emily cast furtive glances backward, trying to determine what was in each of the sacks and crates her father had packed.

She spotted bundles of sugar and flour. What use would they be to her if they got wet? She tried to think of some way to cover the supplies, but she could think of nothing. She began to pray, earnestly, fervently, for some divine intervention.

Just as the storm began to spatter angrily about Emily, she came around a bend and spotted a farmyard. Then for the first time she used the buggy whip, and the team started off at a brisk trot that Emily found difficult to control.

She did manage to direct the team into the yard, thankful that here was some help, but her relief was short-lived. The place was deserted. Tall grasses grew up around the buildings. Glass was missing from some of the windows of the aging house. Shingles flapped noisily in the tearing wind, and a large padlock held the door securely in place or it would have been flapping too. She knew immediately that no help would be found here.

She looked around and saw a sagging barn with a one-hinged double door and wondered if there was some way she could get the buggy in there and out of the storm.

It was hard work, but Emily at last managed to pull the huge door sufficiently open to fasten it back against the barn face. Then she tugged and pulled at its companion until she forced it open also.

She crawled back onto the now wet buggy seat and urged the team forward. There was just enough room to make it through the doorway. The horses were reluctant to enter the strange barn and snorted and sidestepped, but Emily would have none of their foolishness. She gave the gelding a sharp slap with the buggy whip, and his forward thrust encouraged the mare to follow.

Outside, the thunder rolled and crashed, and Emily prayed

that the sagging barn would stay in one piece for the duration of the storm.

The horses restlessly complained about their unfamiliar surroundings. Emily decided she would unhitch the team and put them out to graze. The rain on their backs would bother the horses very little and they did need more grazing.

She struggled with Shadow and eventually unhooked him from the buggy. Star objected to her teammate leaving and tried to follow. Emily knew that she was going to have problems but spoke to the horse and hoped fervently that the mare would wait patiently until she returned for her.

The wind was whipping the heavy rain into lashing torrents now. Emily struggled against it to reach a fence where she could tie her horse securely. It would not do for Shadow to decide that now was a good time to head for home.

Against the wind and cold rain, Emily forced her way back into the gloom of the barn. Star had not been patient and, to Emily's dismay, had tramped around until she'd managed to break the buggy tongue. Emily nearly wept when she saw the damage. What would she ever do now?

She untangled the horse and led her, too, out into the beating rain. She found another post near to Shadow and tied the mare securely.

Back in the barn, soaked to the skin and ready to cry, Emily realized the first thing that she needed to do was to get out of her sopping clothes and into something warm and dry. The storm had dropped the temperature significantly, and her fingers felt like icicles. She rummaged in the semidarkness and found her valise and a fresh change of clothing. She drew back into the shadows, stripped the clinging wet garments from her shivering body and hurried into the dry clothing. Then she pulled the blanket from under the buggy seat and folded it about her. She needed all the warmth she could get.

Her eyes had adjusted to the darkness of the barn, and she spotted a welcome pile of dry straw in the corner. She made her way to it and tried to make herself comfortable.

Just when she thought she might have found some measure of comfort, rain began to drip from the roof above her head. Emily changed her position and went through the settling process again.

Then she noticed a small stream of water falling directly into her buggy, and Emily jumped up to make sure the sugar bag or flour sack was not immediately under it. The sugar was threatened, so she shifted the sack to a drier spot.

Back she went to her post on the straw pile again. A few new drips had begun since she vacated the spot, and Emily wondered if there was any place in the building where she was safe from the rain.

She hugged the blanket about her. There were more blankets in her trunk, but she hated to haul them out in the dirty old barn. She shivered and bundled herself more closely. She would just wait out the storm and then be on her way.

But the storm did not pass quickly, and Emily became more and more concerned. Occasionally she went to the door and listened for the horses. She could hear them stomping and chomping, quite content to feed while the storm raged about them.

Emily, too, was feeling the need for nourishment. She went to the buggy and found the rest of her lunch. She was glad she had left some of it for later. She wouldn't have known quite where to begin looking for a snack among the supplies in the wagon. Raw potatoes, ground flour, or bagged sugar did not have much appeal.

Emily ate the bit of lunch and still did not feel satisfied. If there were something to drink, she would feel much better. But the bottle of water had long since been exhausted.

Overhead the steady stream of pounding rain beat on the weathered roof.

"This is silly!" Emily said aloud. "All that water—and nothing to drink." She took Agatha's bottle and set it outside the door, hoping to collect enough rain to at least moisten her mouth and throat. Then she huddled down into the straw and tried to find some comfort from the cold.

She finally had to admit that the lack of daylight was no longer a result of the passing storm but because night was falling. Emily had never been brave in the dark. To be at home alone would have been one thing. To be in some old deserted barn was quite another. Emily was shivering now from far more than the chilly night air.

Again she went to the door and strained to look through the darkness to find the team. They were still there, feeding hungrily on the heavy grasses. Emily knew that she should remove the harnesses, but she could not bring herself to step out into the unknown blackness into the puddles and wet foliage.

With a shiver she realized that she was stranded for the night. Stranded with only moldy straw for a bed and no way to even lock the door against night prowlers. Emily had never spent a night in any kind of similar conditions before, and a knot of fear tightened her stomach. *My reading list surely didn't prepare me for this,* she thought wryly.

In the distance an owl hooted and Emily shivered again. In the corner something rustled in the straw and Emily had to stifle a scream as she scrambled to her feet. It was just a mouse, she was sure, but Emily was no more willing to share her habitation with a mouse than with a bear.

With what little twilight remained, Emily began to rummage in her trunk until she felt the warm, coarse fiber of a woolen blanket. *Dirt or no dirt, I've got to get warmer,* she told herself. She managed to tug it from the rest of her belongings and climbed up into the buggy. While pushing and shoving bags and boxes to make herself some kind of resting place, Emily came across a piece of heavy fabric folded neatly in a square. Opening it up, she discovered a rain cape her father had thoughtfully provided. *I should have paid more attention—I'm sure he told me about this,* Emily thought as she held the cape close to her heart and tried to swallow the lump in her throat. She wrapped up in the blankets as snugly as she could and spread the cape over herself as she settled in for the night. It was not comfortable, but at least it was dry—for the moment—and she hoped it would be reasonably free from other occupants.

Some time during the night the rain stopped. Then the wind died down, and from her cramped position in the buggy, Emily was able to hear the creaking of the harnesses and the tramping of the horses. The sound brought some small measure of comfort. At least she was not totally alone.

"Of course I'm not alone, Lord," she prayed. "Those were not just words I said to Papa—you really are here."

When Emily at last dropped off to sleep, her body ached, her throat felt dry from breathing straw mold, and her feet were cold in spite of her blanket, but the fear had left her. She knew in spite of her difficult situation that God was with her—just as He had promised to be.

Chapter Eight

Dubious Aid

A loud crack awakened Emily from her fitful sleep. She lurched up, surprising herself at her cramped position in the front of the buggy. For a moment she couldn't get her bearings, and then in a flash it all came back to her.

There was more commotion outside and Emily realized it was coming from where the horses were tethered.

She scrambled out of the buggy and ran to the door of the old barn. Shadow was causing the stir. He had exhausted the supply of grasses that he could reach on his short tether. In his greediness to feed on the rain-drenched grasses, he had managed to break the post and was now doing battle with a rickety fence. His halter rope still held him prisoner, for which Emily was thankful, but he had entangled himself in broken rails and rusty wire.

Emily ran forward, wondering how she was going to get the frantic horse and the broken fence free from each other.

"You think *you're* hungry," she scolded in frustration. "You've been feeding most of the night, but I've had nothing and—" But Shadow, still stomping and blowing, was in no mood to sympathize.

The horse needed to be quieted and the harness removed. Emily found this task most difficult, for the horse would not cooperate. At last she was able to pull the harness free and hang it on a portion of still-standing fence. Then she set to work trying to get the gelding to step through the broken rails and boards while she coaxed and urged him with tugs on the halter rope. He balked and snorted and dug in his hooves with each tug, finally backing up to the place where he had started.

Through the whole process Emily couldn't help but notice Star. She stood apart, head up, eyes alert and ears forward. Now and then she gave a quick snort as if to tell Shadow that life had played some cruel trick on him and she was in total sympathy.

Emily wished she could voice her own opinion about the circumstance. At last she did, speaking directly to the mare. "It's his own stupidity that got him where he is. I don't feel one bit sorry for him—and you needn't, either!"

"Oh, I don't. I don't," a male voice responded, and Emily whirled around, her face red with exertion. She had been so engrossed that she hadn't heard anyone approach.

The man who stood there was big and burly and roughly dressed. His beard—not trim and well kept but bushy—seemed to be there simply because the wearer felt it too bothersome to be rid of it. His clothing hung haphazardly on his oversized frame, and his trouser legs were tucked carelessly into the tops of his boots as protection against the wetness of the morning.

As Emily's eyes took in the appearance of her unexpected visitor, he leaned slightly to the side and spat on the ground. "Whatcha doin' here?" he asked gruffly. Emily realized he had not moved an inch toward helping her.

"I'm—I'm trying to get my horse," she answered defensively, her eyes flashing as she spoke.

"Thet I can see," the man threw back, "but what's yer horse doin' on my property?"

His comment sobered Emily as she quickly surveyed the damage that Shadow had done and was still doing to the fence. At once she became contrite.

"I—I'm sorry," she began lamely. "I—certainly didn't mean to damage your—"

But he cut in sharply. "I never suspected ya set out to tear down my fence. But ya still ain't answered my question."

Emily's attention went back to Shadow, whose head was jerking up and down against the rein. Emily didn't really blame him. He was standing in an awkward position, his legs sprawled over broken rail poles while two people who could help him continued to chatter. Emily tried once more to lead him to better ground.

Again he balked and snorted; then Emily felt herself being jostled to one side as the halter rope was grabbed out of her hand and the big man took charge.

Emily was glad to move out of the reach of both of them. She scrambled across the broken boards just as Shadow made a giant lunge and sent pieces of wood scattering as he headed for clear ground.

"Whoa-a," called the big man. Shadow obediently whoaed.

Without a word to Emily he tossed the halter rope her way and began to throw the broken bits of board and poles back to where the fence had stood.

A flush washed over Emily's face.

"I am terribly sorry," she apologized. "I'll see to it that your fence is fixed."

Even as she said the words, she wondered just how she might do that. She had no money with which to purchase fencing materials, and no idea about how to make the repairs even if she had.

The big man straightened and looked sharply at Emily. Neither his voice nor his eyes softened. "An' how ya plannin' on doin' thet?"

Emily backed off another step and fidgeted with the rope in her hands.

"I—I don't know," she admitted. She'd made a mess of everything. "Perhaps—perhaps I can send for my father—"

"Jest like younguns," grumped the man, and he spat again. "Git theirselves in a fix an' yell fer their pa." He leaned over to grab another armload of broken fencing.

With nothing more to say, Emily led Shadow toward the barn. All she wanted to do was get away from those angry eyes as quickly as possible.

The man suddenly quit tossing broken rails. Emily, without turning to look, could feel his eyes on her retreating back.

"Jest a minute," he thundered; "we ain't done talkin' yet!"

Emily turned to face him, pulse racing, her face red.

"You still ain't explained what yer doin' here. You runnin' from home or somethin'?"

His words brought the fire back into Emily. Her head came up, her chin thrust out. "I am *not* a runaway child," she said with all the dignity she could muster. "I am the new deaconess for the area."

He stared at her in silence for a long minute, then blurted out, "The what?"

"The deaconess. I've been sent here by my church to start a mission work."

"Well, I never—" sputtered the man and he spat again.

Emily eyed him as calmly as she could, willing herself to get better control. After all, she was sent to the area to minister, not to enrage.

"An' who told yer church, whatever it is, thet we in this here area need to be 'missioned'?" asked the man, straightening to his full height until Emily felt as if she were looking at a giant.

Emily wasn't sure how her denomination had arrived at their decision to establish a mission in this community, so she held her tongue.

"Well—?" he thundered.

"Well, I'm not sure exactly," she began. "Perhaps—perhaps they were invited." She knew that was the case in many communities.

"*I* shore didn't invite 'em," the man declared, his eyes boring through Emily.

"No," she responded evenly, her eyes unwavering. "No, I'm sure you didn't."

They stood there, their gazes locked, some kind of challenge passing from one to the other. It was the big man who moved first.

"So how'd ya get here? I didn't see no wagon."

"No," replied Emily, shifting uneasily. "I have a buggy."

"Where?" The question was curt, short.

"In the—in the barn there." She motioned with her hand.

"So ya used my barn too?"

"I'm—I'm sorry. I thought the place was vacant. I didn't know anyone lived here. I—"

"The place *is* vacant. I don't need ta live here to own it, do I? It's bein' vacant gave ya license to walk right in and make yerself to home, did it?"

"No. Of course not. But when the storm struck—"

"Ya had to take shelter from thet storm? What's the matter? Ya made of sugar? Ya'd melt in a storm?"

"Of course not," answered Emily, trying hard to keep from responding angrily. "But I had supplies in the buggy that would have spoiled if they had gotten wet. I—"

"Supplies. An' ya didn't have 'em covered?"

Emily shook her head, feeling young and foolish all over again. She wouldn't bother explaining that her father had loaned his only canvas to a neighbor. The man would think her too young and irresponsible to care for herself, regardless.

He strode forward as if in a hurry to get the strange and troublesome interview over and the girl out of his yard and life.

"Well, let's git ya hitched up and outta here," he barked as he walked toward the barn.

"It's—it's not that simple," began Emily.

He stopped and looked at her.

"The wagon tongue—the horses—Star spooked in the storm and stepped on the tongue, and it's—it's broken," she finished lamely.

He just stared at her, open-mouthed and unbelieving. "You jest keep yerself an' those horses outta my way and outta trouble," he said tersely, and stalked off toward the sagging barn.

Emily's hand tightened on the lead rope and she jerked up the head of the feeding Shadow, tugging him toward the fence where Star still remained tied to a post.

"C'mon," she said to them in almost a whisper. "Let's not get into any more trouble," and she untied Star and led the team away from the fence, away from the barn, toward the lane.

Then she spotted the dilapidated Ford truck that stood at the entrance to the lane. For a moment her heart jumped, thinking another human was close by who might be able to rescue her from her present circumstance. And then she realized dismally that the truck likely belonged to the man who was fussing and swearing in the barn as he surveyed the broken tongue.

He was soon back outside, storming angrily as he headed for the truck at the road and rummaged in the back for some tools. When he walked back down the lane, he reminded Emily of last night's thunder storm.

Emily stayed out of his way all the while she heard the pounding and grumbling. When at last the commotion subsided, Emily debated whether she should approach the barn.

Fighting to keep the horses' heads up so they would not be grazing on any more grass that did not belong to them, Emily was hard put to hold them steady.

A gruff voice behind her said, "You can hook 'em up now."

Emily just stared at him.

"You can hitch a team, can't ya?"

Emily's face began to flush and she fought for control of her emotions. She sighed, looked at the big man, and replied, "Yes. Yes, I can."

She gave a sharp tug on the ropes to get Shadow and Star

going in the right direction. *But the buggy is still in the barn,* she thought.

Then even as the thought flitted through her mind, Emily saw that the buggy had been backed out of the barn and was standing on the grass, waiting for the approaching team.

She led the two horses into position before she realized that Shadow's harness was still hanging on the fence. With a red face she looked around, expecting to see the big man leering at her. But he was nowhere around, and then Emily heard the chug of the engine as he started his truck.

Emily led both horses around the barn so she could keep an eye on Star while she harnessed Shadow. Emily struggled as she made one attempt after another of getting the harness over the big horse's back. At last she got it on, and she sighed with relief. She was flushed and dirty and shaking from her exertion.

Maybe the girls who have to walk aren't so bad off, after all, she reasoned.

Emily led the team to the waiting buggy and hitched them for the remaining trip. She did hope that it wasn't far.

Noticing her dirty hands, a new thought came to Emily. She really was in quite a mess. Her hair was disheveled, her dress wrinkled and covered with dirty spots. She had planned to put on her deaconess bonnet just before she entered the town. Now, she reasoned shamefully, she would not wish to disgrace the hat.

"Oh, God," she prayed, "I've really made a mess of things. Could you show me a back way into town, Lord? I don't want to shame the church or you by coming in looking like this."

Emily clucked to the team and took her leave of the farmyard. It looked even more desolate and run-down in the light of day than it had in the darkness of the storm.

How could he make such a fuss about the broken fence? she asked herself. *Most of the fence is falling down.*

But even as Emily spoke the words to herself, she knew she had no right to wreck another's property—no matter what its seeming worth—without taking responsibility.

"I'll have to find some way to make things right," she said slowly. "But I've no idea how to go about it."

Emily remembered that she did not know who the man was that owned the property. Nor did she know how to get in contact with him.

"Oh, dear," she sighed, "that means he will have to contact me—and that makes it look like I'm trying to avoid my responsibilities. Oh, dear. I should have asked him—"

Emily turned the team onto the road and took another quick look at her map. But she wouldn't have needed to, for as she lifted her head she could see in the distance the small town where she was to serve. Her heart began to thud; then her mind quickly cautioned her emotions—both anxiety and excitement—to slow down.

"Surely the people won't all be like him," she voiced out loud. She reminded herself that though he was gruff and uncouth, he had rescued her horse from the fence, fixed the tongue of her buggy, and single-handedly pushed her buggy out of the barn. Even though he had been in a hurry to get her off his property, perhaps he really wasn't all bad and rude and uncouth.

Then another thought came to Emily, and it brought another flush to her cheek.

"I didn't even thank him," she said in a whisper. "What kind of deaconess am I?"

Chapter Nine

Beginnings

Emily could see no unobtrusive entry into the small town. As far as she could tell, there was only one road leading into it—right down the main street, between the houses and shops and the eyes of the townspeople.

Emily, her cheeks coloring, really did not wish to place the distinguishing bonnet upon her head. Nor did she wish to greet any of those who might be her new parishioners. But she did both. At the very edge of town, she reached for the carefully wrapped bonnet and lifted it out. With trembling hands she brushed her hair back from her warm face and attempted to push stray brown curls into proper place before settling the bonnet on her head. She brushed the dust from her skirts and tried vainly to brush away the wrinkles as well, and then clucked again to her team.

If she was going to minister to these people, she had to be friendly, she decided. So with that determination, Emily headed into the heart of town, ready to greet anyone she met with a warm smile and a nod of her head.

Though it damaged her pride, she kept her resolve, smiling and nodding to all she passed as though she were properly groomed and attired. She could feel their curiosity as she continued on down the street.

When she reached a large building called Wesson Creek Mercantile, Emily pulled the horses up before the building next to it. According to her map, this was to be her home and the church for her parish.

It was not an impressive looking place. The paint had long since washed from the plain board sides. The door was sagging slightly, the two front windows dirty and broken, the walk in front of it covered with clutter. Emily looked at it in dismay. It couldn't be expected to draw people to worship.

For a moment she felt like crying, and then her sagging shoulders lifted and she forced a smile. It wasn't the building that mattered. She was here to share the Gospel. She would do that.

She tied the horses to the front rail, hoping that it was secure enough to hold them, and set off to survey her domain.

Through the gate that swung open on squeaking hinges, along the grass-hidden, broken walkway, toward the back where she understood her living quarters to be, Emily made her way.

The door would be secured with a padlock, Emily had been told, and so it was. But ironically, right beside the padlock, the key hung on a piece of rusty wire. Emily could not help but smile.

She opened the protesting door and entered the small closed-in porch. It was dusty, reeked with mustiness, and was full of spider webs. Emily ducked the webs and proceeded to the next room.

It too was small, with stained walls and a dirty floor. It held an old-fashioned wood stove and a small painted cupboard, with a wooden table and two chairs standing beneath the room's single window. In a corner a rough shelf supported a few discarded items. Two overstuffed chairs, ugly and defiant, sat right where they had been left.

"It sure isn't anything fancy," Emily breathed to herself, and then felt guilty about her evaluation.

"It's not that I expected it to be a palace, Lord," she apologized. "I just want neighborhood folks to feel welcome here."

Emily spotted a small door leading off the main room. The room behind it was not much bigger than a large-sized closet. A cot almost filled it. There were several nails sticking out of the wall boards, and Emily assumed they were meant for hanging garments on. No cupboard. No dresser of any kind. The bare window looked out into a weed-covered lot, and beyond was a weathered board fence.

Emily looked around her for a door to the part of the building that would function as the meeting room for church. There seemed to be none. She concluded that the only entry was from the outside and went around to take a look.

She knew the building had been used for a billiard room and assumed that it would be spacious.

The door was a little reluctant to open, but at length Emily was able to push it far enough to crowd her slight body inside. It took a moment for her eyes to adjust—and then she shuddered.

The room was truly a mess. The walls were dark and stained, the windowpanes shattered across the floor, broken chairs strewn here and there, and it looked as if the sparrows were in residence.

The floor was the worst. It was almost completely covered with litter, and where the wood did show through, it was stained and blotchy. Emily imagined that it had been used freely as a spittoon for as long as the building existed. With another shudder she fled outside. It was too much to deal with at the moment.

She closed the door tightly and hurried back to her little lodging. The two small rooms and the shed looked good in comparison to what was to be her church.

"Well," decided Emily, lifting her shoulders, "if I am to be settled by tonight, I'd best get busy." She went back to the street and began to laboriously unload her buggy.

Emily thought about conscripting some of the older children who gathered to watch her to help. After all, their backs were stronger than hers, she was sure. But she held herself in check and kept right on working in the afternoon sun while her little audience continued to grow.

Across the street, five or six youths lounged against the door of the blacksmith shop watching the goings-on with good humor. "Yeah, I heard rumors 'bout someone comin' to start a mission church," Emily overheard one of them say, "but I'd no idea that it'd be a *woman*—and she'd be nothin' more'n a young girl!" They jostled and teased and winked at one another, while Emily sweated under the weight of her loads.

Emily carried in all the boxes and bags of supplies and belongings, then the suitcase, and turned in dismay to the remaining trunk. How in the world would she get it off the buggy alone? Her father had had help from a neighbor to load it. She would just have to unload it item by item and leave the trunk itself on the buggy, or else she would have to drive the buggy away with the trunk and its contents still on board, with hopes of getting it unloaded later.

Deciding on the latter, Emily was turning from the buggy when a voice spoke from behind her.

"Need some help?" There was a hint of amusement in the tone.

Emily turned to see two young fellows standing near, their faces slightly red, their eyes twinkling.

The question caught Emily quite off guard, but a youngster who had been watching the proceedings with interest responded quickly, "She's got thet there big trunk. She cain't lift it."

"Want it in the house?" one fellow asked.

"Oh, if you could, please," Emily replied. "I would be so grateful."

One of the young men sprang easily up into the buggy and slid the trunk to the end where the other could reach one of the handles. With a bit of showing off, they hoisted the trunk and carried it down the broken walk to Emily's door.

"Where ya want it?" the talkative one asked, and Emily motioned to a corner of the room. The trunk was duly placed where she had indicated and the two were off, nudging and poking each other as they left with big, self-conscious grins on their boyish faces.

"Thank you! Thank you so much," Emily called after them and heard another nervous guffaw.

With the buggy finally empty, Emily took a deep breath and went back outside. She managed a smile in spite of her aching back and arms, her flushed face and disarrayed hair, and spoke as kindly as she knew how to the little group that still stood watching, "I'm Miss Emily Evans. I have been sent here to start a church. I do hope all of you will be able to be here on Sunday morning for Sunday school."

Some of the older boys, whom Emily judged to be ten to twelve, turned away quickly in seeming embarrassment. She had invited them to Sunday school—right along with the little kids.

Others looked at her blankly or nodded with shy smiles. Emily wondered how many of them had no idea what Sunday school was.

"We'll have singing and stories, and we'll learn about Jesus," Emily explained.

As the small group began to disperse, Emily untied the horses, picked up the reins and crawled wearily back into the buggy. Through the district superintendent, her father had arranged for the horses to be boarded at a small farm on the edge of town. Referring to her map again, Emily drove there now. It was not far to the farmstead, but Emily would have to walk back and she was anxious to begin her cleaning, so she urged the horses to a trot.

When she reached the farm, she noted that it really wasn't in much better condition than the one at which she had spent the night. A young lad met her when she turned her horses in at the gate. Emily was surprised to see that it was one of the fellows who had stood by and watched her unload.

"Hello," she greeted him. "I understand that my father has made arrangements for me to keep my horses here."

He nodded but made no comment.

"Would you like to show me where?" she asked him.

"Jest put the buggy over there," he said, with a motion of his head. "The horses can go to pasture."

Emily drove the buggy to the indicated place by the fence and climbed stiffly down. The kinks of the night before had still not left her body.

The boy stood and watched as she unhitched the team.

"What about the harness?" she asked him.

"Guess you can hang it in the barn," he answered casually.

Emily was about to move the team closer to the barn when a shrill voice came from the small house to her left. "Claude! Shame on you for making the lady do the work. You take those horses to the barn and unharness them. Then turn them to pasture. We're not paid for doing nothing, you know."

Emily turned to see a little bit of a woman standing on the porch. Over her small frame she wore an apron, startlingly white against the bleakness of the house. Her hair was pulled back into a severe knot at the back of her head, and from where Emily stood, the lady's face looked so tired that it seemed drained of emotions.

"Come on in," she nodded to Emily, "I'm Annie Travis. I'll fix some tea."

At the mention of tea, Emily's stomach reminded her painfully, sharply that she'd had nothing to eat since last night and it was well into the afternoon.

She wanted to decline the invitation and get back to cleaning, but her insides protested and so did her back. A cup of tea would be a good pickup. She managed a smile and moved forward.

"Tea would be nice," she admitted.

The contrast from outside to inside the little house surprised Emily. In spite of its simplicity, everything was spotless. Emily couldn't help but notice the small bouquet of summer flowers that graced the table and the clean shine of the cracked windows.

"Have a chair," Mrs. Travis invited and Emily accepted, worrying about her dusty dress on the clean wooden seat.

The woman bustled about her kitchen, pouring boiling water into a flowered teapot. Emily noticed a crack where the spout joined the pot.

"Sorry I don't have a cake or something," the woman apologized, then went on. "I do have some fresh bread—just out of the oven. You care for a piece or two of that with some strawberry jam?"

"It sounds wonderful," Emily responded and then checked her enthusiasm. She didn't want to sound as if she were starving. She blushed. "I—I always enjoy fresh bread," she added.

Mrs. Travis turned to cut the bread and get the jam from her cupboard. As she opened the door, Emily could see that the cupboard shelves were not crowded with provisions.

"So you're the new preacher?" Mrs. Travis said as she brought china cups from the cupboard and poured the tea. The cup that she handed Emily was without blemish, but the one she kept for herself had a large chip. She seated herself at the table and poured the tea.

"Well, I—I guess I don't really think of myself as a—a preacher," Emily fumbled. "More of a—a—teacher."

Mrs. Travis nodded. "Well, whatever you call it," she said, "we've sure been needing someone."

Emily's heart responded with a joyous flutter. *Here is someone with a welcome.*

"I was raised in church myself," explained the woman, "but my babies—haven't had a bit of church—any one of them." Her eyes darkened. "Sometimes I fear that it's too late for some of them. They've already been shaped to be what they're gonna be."

Emily was surprised to see tears form in Mrs. Travis's eyes, and she wondered if the mother was thinking of young Claude when she spoke.

"It's never too late for God," Emily said softly, and the woman's head came up, tears spilling slightly before she turned away.

A little girl entered the room and Mrs. Travis scooped her up onto her lap and broke a piece of bread for her. Then she brushed back the child's damp, curly hair and spoke softly, in a voice meant just for Emily.

"We don't have much. Used to be much better off, but my husband—he's—he's not been well—for some time now. Doesn't get things done like he used to. Things are getting—" But she did not go on. A haunted look flitted across her face as if she might already have said too much, and she abruptly broke off and lifted the cracked teapot.

"Care for another cup?" she asked and did not wait for Emily's answer before she began to pour.

Emily enjoyed a second helping of bread and would have eaten a third and perhaps a fourth had not her good manners kept her in check. It would not do for her to be eating food that should be for the occupants of this needy home. So after her second slice of bread and her second cup of tea, she thanked her hostess, explained that she was most anxious to get her home scrubbed, invited the family to church, and excused herself.

At the gate she met another young boy—he, too, was a member of the little band that had watched her unpack. She smiled at him as she said "Hello," and he smiled shyly back. She noticed the thin, patched clothing, but she also saw a clean face and carefully combed hair. She decided that this boy also belonged in the simple farmhouse.

As Emily hurried back down the dusty road toward her own little dwelling, the picture of the small woman stayed in her mind. Here was someone in deep need. With very little means, she was endeavoring to care for a family—keeping the house clean, the clothing patched, the place a home, and doing it in spite of the fact that she had an ill husband. By the time Emily trudged down the crude main street, the warm summer sun beating down on her new black bonnet, her mind was already thinking of ways in which she could mobilize the community to aid the Travis family.

It's a shame, she thought, *just a shame that something hasn't been done.*

And then Emily felt a deep sense of joy. Annie Travis had wanted a church. A church for her growing family. Well, God had sent Emily in answer to that need. Emily vowed to do her best in ministering to this woman and her children.

Chapter Ten

Cleaning House

Pail in hand, Emily made her way to the backyard pump. It took a good deal of working the handle before a small stream of discolored water dribbled out of the pipe. She feared that her water supply might be unusable, but gradually the flow began to clear and soon clean-looking water filled Emily's bucket.

After returning to the house with the water, she carried in some wood for a fire. The thought of a stove burning in the little kitchen on such a warm day was not a welcome one, but Emily knew of no other way to get hot water for scrubbing. She was thankful for the good supply of wood that was stacked against the backyard fence.

After the fire was heating the tub of water Emily had placed on the stove, she turned to her suitcase for an older garment in which to do her cleaning.

"This dress is wrinkled and dirty," she said to herself, "but I don't want to ruin it entirely. I do need to change into something else. But where?"

Emily looked about her. The small windows of the kitchen-living room had no coverings. She looked into the bedroom. There was no curtain or shade on that window either.

"One of the first things I need are some kind of shades or curtains," Emily murmured, and then picked up her clothes and left the house for the small building out back.

The outhouse too was full of dust and spider webs. Emily cringed as she entered. Dried leaves and grasses rustled beneath her feet.

"I do hope there are no living creatures in here," Emily muttered as she closed the door, then slipped her dress over her head and stripped off her good stockings.

Emily pulled on her old housekeeping dress as quickly as she could. She breathed a sigh of relief as she stepped back out into the sunlight.

By the time she had swept the two small rooms, she judged the water hot enough to begin her cleaning.

"Thank you, Lord, for soap and water," she breathed quietly as she picked up a cleaning brush and some soap, pushed up her sleeves and set to work on the bedroom. There wasn't much she could do about the skimpy, soiled mattress that flopped across the cot, but she could wash the walls, the windows and the floor. She would feel better about that.

When she turned to the kitchen-living quarters, she had to add more wood to the fire and more water to the tub.

By the time she had completed her scrubbing, dusk was falling. Then Emily remembered that she hadn't eaten supper yet.

She threw out the last of the dirty water, filled the basin afresh with warm water, and thoroughly washed her hands, arms and face. When she had finished, she turned with an aching back to her kitchen supplies. She was much too weary to spend a lot of time cooking, so she reached for a frying pan, scrambled a couple of eggs, and sliced some of Ina's bread.

She was about to sit down to eat her light meal when she noticed the kettle on the stove. In spite of the intense heat of the little room, she decided that another cup of tea would taste good. Then she settled at the table and bowed her head in prayer.

She was thankful—truly thankful. But as she raised her head the room before her made her tired shoulders sag. *Will this ever look like a home?* Even with her scrubbing, she had succeeded only in uncovering more blemishes on the walls, more cracks in the windows, more worn spots on the painted floor boards.

The dirt was gone, but her unpacked boxes and bags were stacked all about. Would her things fit in this tiny place? What could she do for cupboard space? The one tiny cupboard would hold very little besides her few dishes. Emily sighed. It was going to be very difficult.

But even as she looked with dismay at her surroundings,

Emily thought, *At least I'm here—not off in a tumbled-down barn. It's clean, and there's no storm dripping water on me.*

Emily remembered the big, gruff man who had come to her rescue. She wondered again how she would contact him. She either had to fix his fence herself or pay for the damage that Shadow had done. She wasn't sure how she would accomplish either, yet it was very important that she not start off in this new community with a debt to one of the residents.

Emily sighed again. Perhaps someone who lingered around the blacksmith shop would know who he was. How could she describe him? There might be many big men in the area, and for her to ask if anyone knew a big, sour grouch with sloppy clothes and an unkept beard seemed hardly appropriate.

Emily sighed again. She would have to tread carefully. In the meantime she was weary and needed some sleep. She lifted her lamp from the small kitchen table and went to find blankets to make her bed.

The morning sun was already streaming in the open window when Emily awakened the next morning. For a moment she wished she had left it unwashed so the sunlight would not shine so brightly in her eyes. She wearily pulled herself from the cot, her sore muscles screaming their silent protest.

The thin, lumpy mattress had not allowed for a good night's sleep. The springs underneath sagged until her body nearly draped to the floor. She had not been able to properly turn over during the night. Emily stretched to loosen her cramped limbs.

She was running a brush through her long hair when she distinctly heard a woman's voice call loudly, "You boys get down off'n thet fence." The shout was followed by a thumping and scrambling, and Emily looked up just in time to see youngsters scrambling down off the fence that separated her yard from the mercantile next door.

"They were spying!" she whispered in horror. "The young rascals were spying on me." With a flaming face Emily whipped a blanket from her bed and hung it from nails on each side of the window. She looked down at herself, thankful that she still remained modestly attired in her "proper" cotton nightdress.

"I must get some blinds or curtains first thing," she announced to herself, hoping that something would be available at the mercantile next door.

And Emily hoped the prices would be reasonable. "I'm really going to have to watch my pennies," she went on. "It could be several weeks before the offerings are enough to support me."

After breakfast and devotions, Emily set to work trying to find a place for all her belongings. As simple as her requirements were, she still was hard-pressed to find room to store her things. It was afternoon before she had everything put away. Then she took a basin of water, her washcloth, and towel to her bedroom where, though she had little room, she was assured of privacy with the blanket over the window. After a quick sponge bath and a change into a clean dress, she tidied her hair, set her black bonnet in place, and took up her small handbag. It was time to do some shopping.

The few steps to the mercantile took only moments, and Emily pushed open the heavy door and stood quietly while her eyes adjusted to the darkness inside.

"Can I help ya?" a female voice asked, and Emily noticed someone behind the counter.

"Oh yes, please," she began, moving into the store. "I'm Miss Evans, the new mission worker. I—"

"I know who ya are," the woman interrupted, but there was no animosity in her voice even though it was curt and gruff.

Emily looked across the counter to the face of a tall plain woman. Her graying hair was pulled back tightly to form an odd kind of roll at the top of her head, her ample frame was shrouded in a cotton dress covered by a stiff dark apron, and her lined face looked as if it had long since forgotten how to smile.

But it was her eyes that drew Emily's attention. They were intense and piercing. Perhaps at one time they had danced with merriment or glowed with understanding.

"Oh . . . oh," Emily's voice faltered. Then she continued nervously. "I need some—some coverings for my windows. I have—"

"Yer right," said the woman briskly. "I chased them kids off the fence three times this mornin'."

Emily flushed.

"Oh, it—it was you. I—heard a voice—I . . . Thank you," she finished lamely.

The woman just waved an arm and advanced toward a shelf at the rear of the store. "Jest curious—like kids always are." Then she went on. "Whatcha wantin'?" she asked.

"Well, I—I don't wish to spend too much. I would like curtains for the—the hominess, but I might have to settle for shades—if you have them."

"We do," the woman responded curtly. "Both. An' not too expensive either."

Emily was relieved. She followed the woman to the corner counter and waited for her to produce her merchandise.

Emily still felt as if she could not see clearly enough. She wasn't sure if the bolt of material the woman pushed toward her was blue or green.

"Could I—do you mind if I take it nearer the window?" asked Emily hesitantly. "I'm having trouble telling just what color—"

"Thet's John. He won't let us have the light on here in the daytime. Can scarcely see to get around. Says it's bright 'nough without it. Might be—if the place had some decent windows. Jest a waste of good money, he says. And besides, he says thet the light would jest heat the buildin' up more, and it's hot enough in here as it is in the summertime. Won't let no doors be open. Says the flies will come in—an' nobody wants flies in their molasses or pickles." She finished with a "humpf" and passed the bolt to Emily.

The material was green. Emily hated to say so, but she didn't like the color.

"Then we have these here blinds," the woman continued when Emily laid the bolt back on the counter top. "Not expensive. You could maybe make some light curtains to go with 'em for the same price as thet there heavier material."

Emily brightened. She looked at the light material. It had a soft ivory background and a small flower print, and Emily much preferred it to the rather sickly green.

Emily pulled out her measurement calculations. "How much would it be," she asked, "for the blinds and the curtain material?"

The woman did some quick figuring on a piece of paper and quoted Emily a price. It would cost more than she had hoped, but she did need to have some protection from curious eyes.

She nodded. "And I will need a spool of thread," she added. "I wasn't planning on sewing the curtains."

The woman added the spool to the list, and Emily drew out the required cash. It cut deeply into her meager finances, and she fidgeted as the woman cut the cloth and bundled her purchases. Emily was glad to escape the dark shop and head for home.

The remainder of her day was spent in putting up her blinds and hand sewing her curtains. In spite of the cost, when she was finally finished, she was pleased with the results.

But in some ways the clean, bright little curtains made the rest of the room look shabbier than ever. Emily sighed. She did wish that there was some way to cheer things up a bit.

———

The next morning Emily was back in the dark mercantile again.

"Do you have calcimine?" she asked the woman behind the counter, and the woman nodded her head and moved to a shelf behind her.

"Ya want tinted or white?"

Emily hadn't thought of getting tinted.

"White, I guess."

"How much ya need?" the clerk asked.

"Well, I—I don't really know," responded Emily, embarrassed. "I've never used it before—but the walls are in desperate need of some cleaning up, and I figured it would be the cheapest—"

"Yer right," the woman answered curtly. "Much cheaper'n paint."

Emily was relieved to hear that information.

"Ya doin' all the walls?"

"I would like to—in the living area. I haven't checked the—the church yet."

The woman nodded but said nothing. Emily wondered if she found it difficult to think of the former billiard room as a church.

"This ought to do if'n ya jest put on one coat," the woman said, lifting a can from the shelf. Then added, "Ya have a brush?"

Emily fumbled. She hadn't thought of a brush. "No-o," she stammered.

"Ya need a brush. No use buyin' one. You can use the one I used on the back shed."

"Thank you so much," Emily told the woman with a smile when a nice, clean brush was produced. "I do appreciate your lending it to me. And I'll make sure it comes back clean."

She paid the bill, mentally cringing as each coin left her hand, and then went home to tackle the job of whitewashing her little parsonage.

When the task was finally accomplished and the blinds and curtains were back in place, Emily looked around with contentment.

"Well, the calcimine didn't cover up all the problems, so it's not perfect, but it's much better—and it's clean," she declared. "Now I won't be embarrassed to have ladies in to tea."

Humming to herself, Emily set about washing up the borrowed brush. *Maybe she was going to feel at home here, after all.*

Chapter Eleven

The Church

Benches and a small pulpit would be arriving on the following Wednesday, thanks to arrangements by the district superintendent, so Emily wanted to have the meeting room cleaned up before then. The idea of a Sunday passing without a service distressed her, but there was really nothing she could do.

With a good deal of self-determination she gritted her teeth and picked up her broom and dustpan. The first task would be to remove the piles of debris from inside the church building. Then the scrubbing would begin.

Emily found an old apple crate, lined the bottom with a piece of cardboard so it would hold the clutter, and loaded it again and again as she swept the floor. Each time she filled it she had to carry it out and empty it at the back corner of the fence. She had quite a pile when the task was done—and the day was already spent. There would be no time for scrubbing this Friday.

Emily emptied her box one last time and dragged her tired body back to her living quarters. Her back and shoulders ached. Her face and hands were smudged with dirt. All she wanted was a chance to wash up, have some tea and a sandwich and fall into her bed—lumpy though it was.

It was early when Emily crawled from her bed the next morning and lit the fire so she could heat water for the scrubbing. During her work of the day before, Emily realized that some of the scattered chairs appeared to be fixable. There were also five or six crates scattered about the floor of the building. She was sure she would find a use for them. She had even found a back closet with shelves, which probably had been used as some type of billiard equipment room. It too was dirty, but Emily was thrilled at the discovery. It would be perfect for Sunday school supplies and hymnbooks.

As Emily entered the meeting room with her first pail of hot, soapy water, three sparrows made their exit through a broken window.

Emily set her pail on the stained floor and looked about her.

"I'd better fix the windows—somehow," she spoke quietly. "There's no use scrubbing if the birds are still living here."

Emily searched around until she found some scraps of board that she thought would do. She had discovered a few rusty nails on the shelf in the closet the previous day, and she went for them now. She was too short to reach the windows that needed repair, so she chose what she considered to be the safest chair to stand on. But she had no hammer.

Emily thought of crossing the street and asking the blacksmith to loan her one; instead, she went outside and searched her backyard until she found a rock large enough to use as a hammer. With that firmly in her hand, she began her repairs. It wasn't a good job, but as Emily studied the boarded-up window, she decided it should keep the birds out until a proper job could be done. Then she set to work with her water and scrub brush.

It was another long day for Emily. Twice she had to take rest breaks for her aching back and arms. At those times she found something lighter to do in the parsonage. She organized her books on the newly scrubbed small shelf and swept the rickety steps that led down into the cellar hole beneath the kitchen.

"I'm going to have to start cooking properly," she told herself as she sat down to another meal of tea and sliced bread. "If Father were here, he would say that I'll be making myself sick."

Emily quickly put the few dirty dishes in the pan on the cupboard and hurried back to her scrubbing.

She didn't finish the task that day either. She groaned as she surveyed the small area she had managed to clean, wondering if she could possibly be ready by next Wednesday. Tomorrow was Sunday. There would be no scrubbing then. Emily felt a bit impatient that she could do nothing further till Monday, yet she was appreciative of a day of rest. She allowed herself the luxury of sleeping later and then arose to a leisurely breakfast and a long time of Bible study. She let the words from the Psalms and the Gospels rejuvenate her soul.

Then Emily prepared a nutritious dinner with vegetables from her father's garden and some of Ina's canned chicken, washed up the dishes that had been stacking higher and higher in the dishpan, and lay back down on her bed to read one of her favorite books. But the warm day outside beckoned to her. "I need to get out," she told herself. "A walk might help me settle down."

She debated about wearing her black bonnet and decided against it. *I'm not on church business,* she reasoned. *I'll just slip out down the alley and into the country.*

Walking felt good and Emily followed the road until she came to a little creek, crawled the fence, and followed the creek bank.

She loved the little stream, even though it seemed lazy and joyless, sometimes seeming to sit in disjointed, stagnant little pools.

She continued walking along the creek until she came to a spot where it truly did gurgle along. She sat down, her back against a tall poplar, and let the song of the stream ease some of the weariness from her mind and body.

"I must remember this spot," she murmured to herself. "It is restful here." She closed her eyes and listened to the song of the birds and the faraway bawl of a milk cow in the pasture beyond.

Just as she was close to dropping off to sleep there was a crashing through the undergrowth and Emily's eyes flew open. *Surely there aren't bears here!* was her first frantic thought. But it was a man with a fishing pole who broke through the bushes.

Emily wasn't sure which one of them was the most surprised at seeing the other. He stared while she scrambled quickly to her feet, her eyes mirroring his surprise.

"I—I—was just resting," she stammered, and he seemed to gain some composure.

His smile was slow in coming, but when it did, Emily noticed that it was delightful. He nodded his head, let the smile come in full and then spoke slowly. "I'm not too used to finding a girl in my woods," he said with a chuckle. "Hello."

"But I'm not—not a girl," Emily quickly pointed out, making his eyes crinkle even more deeply at the corners.

"I—I mean, I'm Miss Emily Evans," Emily finished, as though that should be explanation enough.

"Miss Evans," returned the man with a nod.

Emily's face began to redden. She knew he still assumed her to be a young girl.

"I—I mean I'm the new deaconess. The mission worker sent here to start a new church."

For a moment the man's face showed surprise; then he smiled again. "Well, I should expect you won't have much trouble finding a willing congregation," he teased. "A pretty young girl—I mean, woman—" Then surprisingly his voice turned serious. "I guess your church knew well what it was doing."

Emily was at a loss to understand his words.

"What do you mean?" she asked softly, reading the irony in his voice.

He cast a quizzical glance her way. Emily's puzzled frown assured him that she truly didn't understand.

"People are always a bit more tolerant of girls," he replied. Then he cast a meaningful look her way and added, "Children—or defenseless young women."

By then Emily's face was flushed and her eyes flashing as she straightened to her fullest height and lifted her chin.

"I am not a girl," she repeated stubbornly. "Nor—nor am I a—a 'defenseless young woman.' I have been sent here to start a mission, not to—not to lure people to the church through pity. I—"

At the sound of his chuckle, she stopped and lifted her chin even higher. *He is insufferable!* she fumed. She would not stay and have him mock her further. With a defiant toss of her head she started back down the trail, but was quickly jerked up short. Her pinned hair had somehow become entangled in a branch.

Emily refused to cry out in spite of the sharp wrench. She lifted a trembling hand to disentangle herself. She could hear further laughter, and her anger increased.

In spite of her efforts, all she managed to do was dislodge the pins until her hair was tumbling about her shoulders. Still the small branch held her prisoner. She tugged and fumbled but could not free herself.

"If you don't spook, I'll help you," said a quiet voice from behind her.

Emily wanted to cry, but she choked back her anger, took a

deep breath and willed herself to respond in a reasonable fashion. "If you would, please."

Never had she felt so humiliated. Never so at the mercy of another, particularly one so arrogant and irritating.

She heard him put down the rod he carried and step closer. Then she felt his hands on her hair. She sensed now that he was much taller than she and thus had an advantage—he could see what he was doing.

"Here's a—a peg," he said, thrusting a pin into her hand.

Emily almost corrected him, but she bit her tongue.

"Here's another," he said, and again passed her a hairpin.

"You *are* stuck!" he said as he began to untwine the locks of Emily's hair. In trying to free herself, she had managed to make things much worse.

At last he had untangled her hair and stepped back while she ran shaky hands over her hair to get it under some measure of control. She could hardly walk back to town with her hair flowing wildly about her shoulders.

"It's a shame you can't always leave it down," he surprised her by saying, and Emily looked at him evenly, making no comment in return.

His broad shoulders shrugged indifferently. "But I guess a mission worker couldn't do that."

Still Emily didn't answer. She feared he was taunting her again.

"Is this . . . your land?" Emily asked hesitantly, hoping to change the subject.

He shook his head. Emily was relieved that she hadn't trespassed a second time since coming to this community.

"It belongs to my uncle," he went on, and Emily's eyes expressed dismay.

He noticed, and another smile played at the corner of his mouth.

"It's okay," he assured her. "My uncle is a generous man. He'll share his creek with you. He even lets me call it mine."

It was Emily's turn to smile. He had understood her concerns so accurately.

"I don't even live here," the young man went on. "I've come to my uncle's farm every summer since I was a kid. I grew up in Edmonton. Live in Calgary now."

Emily hoped her face gave no hint of her confusion—he seemed so rude one minute and rather gentlemanly the next.

Her hair was secured as well as she could manage without brush or comb. Emily took a deep breath and made sure that no low overhanging branches obscured her path.

"Well, I must be going," she explained. "It'll be dark before I get back to town if I don't hurry."

"I have a car. I could drive you," he offered simply.

Emily blushed. What on earth would the town's folk say if she came driving into town with a complete stranger? She shook her head quickly. "No—no, thanks," she hastened to say. "But—I . . . thank you." She began to stumble down the path, anxious to get going.

"Good fishing," she called back over her shoulder in an effort to be neighborly. He waved a hand, and she heard another chuckle.

She dared not look back. He might still be standing there, watching her go. She really did need to hurry. It would be dark before she could cover the distance back to town. Then a new thought came, *I don't even know his name!*

Chapter Twelve

A Busy Week

On Monday morning Emily was anxious to get back to her scrubbing in the church, but she did take the time to wash three of the orange crates thoroughly and give them a coat of calcimine. They could be stacked as shelves in the corner of the bedroom, giving her some storage place. Emily could hardly wait for them to dry so she might place her clothing on the little shelves and hang one of her towels over the front.

Back in the church, Emily scrubbed all day Monday, all day Tuesday and Wednesday morning before she completed her task. Even so, she had been able to wash the walls only as high as her rickety chair would allow her to reach. The higher portion of the walls was not as dirty as the lower, except where the sparrows had been, but still the dust hung heavily on them. She had tried tying her cloth to the broom and scrubbing above her head with that. But it did a poor job at best, and finally Emily decided to leave them just as they were.

She was just throwing out her last pail of dirty water when the truck with the furnishings pulled in. Excitement filled her whole being, but as she watched the two gentlemen unload the benches, Emily's heart sank. The pews were very old and very used. Some church had replaced them and they obviously had been stored where the weather was able to get at them.

"They'll need a good scrubbing, too," Emily said to herself and looked down at her already rough, red hands.

The men were no more impressed with the little building than Emily had been.

"The windows need to be fixed," said the man named Herb Collins.

"The whole thing needs some paint," added Dick Lowe.

"I—I didn't have a ladder," Emily explained, pointing at the line on the walls.

Mr. Lowe nodded. "Must have been a dirty job," he said sympathetically.

"Is there a phone around?" asked Herb, and when Emily informed him there was one at the mercantile, he left the two of them and was gone for several minutes. When he came back he was carrying a ladder, which he put in the meeting room. Then he left again. Emily knew the men were no doubt hungry, so she excused herself to prepare a meal and went back to her little kitchen.

She was surprised when she returned to the church to call the men to dinner. Not only had the ladder been set up, but window glass, paint cans, brushes and various tools were all laid out. And the men had already set to work. Their first task was repairing the broken windows. Now Emily really felt excited. She would have some help in getting her church building in order.

The men decided to stay overnight to finish the repairs. Emily had no parishioners yet with whom to board them. She knew it would be senseless to offer her one small cot. The two ended up sleeping in the truck cab, assuming that the padded seat was somewhat softer than the church benches. Emily could only imagine how uncomfortable it must have been for them. She gave them her one spare blanket, then pulled the other one from her bed for them, too. She could do without the blanket far better than they.

The next day the men went from replacing the window glass to cleaning away the sign of birds, and then to the painting. Emily knew there was nothing much they could do about the splotches on the floor.

While the men painted the walls, Emily scrubbed down the wooden pews. But they were deeply stained and weathered, and washing wouldn't help that. She did wish she had some way to cover the discolored wood, but she was getting more help now than she had expected. She would not ask for more.

The men finished the painting just before the supper hour, moved in the pews that Emily had left drying in the sun and sat down for one last time to Emily's table. Then the truck disappeared down the dust-covered street and Emily was left waving at her gate that now swung on steady hinges. Mr. Lowe had somehow found the time to fix that as well.

Though dreadfully tired, Emily felt euphoric. It was only Thursday night. She had all day Friday and Saturday to make calls and invite the community people to the Sunday services. She could hardly wait to get started.

She lingered at the simple wooden pulpit after the two men had driven away, trying to envision what it would be like to face her congregation on Sunday morning. Her finger idly traced a large gouge that traveled over the pulpit's entire surface. It looked as if it had served for years in many missions as small as Wesson Creek.

But even the battered pulpit could not daunt Emily's buoyant spirits. It was not the building or the furnishings that mattered. It was the Word. The Bible was pure and righteous and unscathed by time or wear or even indifference. She could hardly wait for the opportunity to share it with this little community.

The next morning Emily bounded out of bed with the sunrise, eager to get started. *I'm doing much better at getting up in the morning than I did during Bible school days,* she thought wryly to herself. She spent extra time in her morning devotions—she needed God's help and wisdom as she went from door to door inviting people to the Sunday services. Then she groomed carefully and pinned her bonnet securely to her hair in case a breeze might come up. It would not do for the new mission worker to appear in public looking wind-blown and frazzled.

Emily set out, Bible in hand, with a brisk step. In her other hand was the borrowed paint brush to return to its owner. Besides, she knew no better place than the mercantile to begin her invitations.

Emily entered the store and paused to adjust her eyes as quickly as possible to the dim light. A figure stirred behind the far counter, and Emily hastened toward the spot, her voice preceding her with a merry, "Good morning. I am returning your brush. I can't thank you enough—"

But a gruff voice stopped her in her tracks. "My what?"

Emily instantly recognized the voice. It belonged to the man with the vacant farmhouse and the sagging barn. The man whose fence she had unwittingly dismantled.

"I'm—I'm sorry," she stammered, frozen where she stood. "I—I thought the store owner was here."

"He is!" the man snorted.

Emily's eyes had adjusted now. There he was, his huge frame towering over the counter, his face just as dark, just as challenging as she remembered it.

"I—I thought—" Emily stumbled.

Just then the woman who had helped Emily previously entered the shop. Relieved, Emily motioned in her direction, "I thought she—"

"Well, she don't," the man countered gruffly.

But the woman did not appear to be one bit intimidated by the size or the roar of the man. She approached Emily with an outstretched hand and accepted the brush from her.

"Did it work all right?" she asked amicably, to which Emily nodded dumbly.

"Did ya have enough calcimine?" the woman went on, and Emily nodded to that as well.

"My brother John owns the store," the clerk explained simply. "I keep his house and help out in the store a bit when he's not around."

Emily's eyes turned from the man to the woman. "I . . . I see," she managed.

"Ya had some help with the—the church," the woman went on, and the shine came back to Emily's eyes.

"Yes," she responded enthusiastically. "It's ready now—ready for Sunday. I—I dropped by to extend an invitation for service. Ten o'clock."

But the glow in Emily's eyes was not reflected in the eyes of the woman. "Reckon John and me don't feel much need for church," she answered firmly.

Emily had known she could expect refusals to her invitation, but now that she had one, she hardly knew what to do.

She quickly regained control, managed a wobbly smile, and said, "Well, should you ever change your mind, you'll be more than welcome."

Emily heard another snort from the tall man, but she did not turn to look at him. Instead, she addressed the woman, "And you are most welcome to come for tea—anytime."

She wasn't sure how to read the quick change in the woman's eyes, but the man scoffed, "Tea partyin' now!"

Emily turned to him then. She did hope her face showed a calmness she did not feel.

"I—I am glad to meet you again, Mr.—Mr. John. I didn't know where to find you, and I do still owe you for the damage done to your fence," she said.

"And thet ya do," the man asserted.

"I'm a little short of cash right now," Emily continued with flushed cheeks, "but if we could arrange for monthly payments—" She fumbled in her purse as she spoke and took out some coins as a token of good faith. She held them out to him, but the woman brushed her hand aside.

"Thet fence weren't worth a plugged nickel," she said firmly. "The rest of it is gonna fall down any day now."

The man cleared his throat awkwardly. "Vera's right," he admitted. "No need to make payment fer the fence." He turned abruptly and left the room through a door directly behind him.

Emily turned to the woman. "Thank you," she said sincerely, "but my horse really did damage his fence."

"I know. I know," replied the woman with a wave of her hand. "He told me 'bout it. But thet fence wouldn't have held nothin'—let alone a work horse. I have no qualms 'bout takin' money where money is due—but thet broken fence weren't worth nothin'."

Emily let the coins drop into her purse.

"And besides," the woman continued, "thet farmstead, old and out of shape as it is, it belongs to me jest as much as to him."

Emily murmured another thank you and left the store to continue her visiting.

Chapter Thirteen

Sunday

By the time night had fallen, Emily had visited nearly all of the homes in the little town. Though no one had been outright rude, Emily was wise enough to know that the various evasive answers she received to her invitation would likely not result in a high attendance come Sunday.

Still, there were a few homes where she had felt accepted and even warmly welcomed. At least some of the children appeared excited about the prospect of a Sunday school. Emily went to bed feeling that she had done her best, and promised herself that she would spend the next day traveling some of the outlying country roads.

But when Emily arose the next morning, it was to another thunderstorm and drenching rain. She knew it would be foolhardy to attempt taking the horses and buggy out in such weather. She settled in to prepare a Sunday school lesson and her sermon for the next day.

All day long the rain poured down. It was midafternoon before Emily thought of making some kind of signs to announce the meetings. At her kitchen table she wrote out the pertinent information on cardboard. Bundled up in a rain cape and galoshes, she started out, not quite sure where she could post her signs. One was tacked to the church door. She wished she could put one on the door of the mercantile. But with the poor impression she had already made on the owner, she dared not even suggest such a thing.

The blacksmith shop didn't seem appropriate for such notices, so she passed it by and went on to the drugstore next door. The man behind the counter seemed eager enough to welcome her until she explained her mission. Then his eyes grew distant and he fumbled for an explanation.

"Don't allow advertisin' here," he mumbled, but Emily knew differently. She had seen other local notices posted on his door and in his windows. He saw her eyes drift over the premises and hastened to add, "About religious things. Some folks are touchy about such things. I don't want to offend anyone, you understand?"

Emily understood all too well. She smiled brightly and left the store.

At her next stop, Sophie's Coffee Shop, Emily met with a warmer reception.

"Sure," said the plump, youngish matron called Sophie in a rather boisterous voice. "Stick it wherever ya want. This town needs all the excitement it can get."

Emily wasn't sure that her church service would be considered exciting, but she thankfully posted her little notice.

"Haven't had many folks in today," the woman commented. "Rainin' too hard. Why don't ya sit down and have a coffee," she continued. "Ya gonna make yerself sick, runnin' around in this weather."

How many times had Emily heard her father say those words? "I didn't bring my purse," she stammered, but the woman waved aside her comment.

"No matter. This one's on the house. Made this whole pot here, an' hardly anyone's been in. Hate to jest throw it out." Then Sophie paused and said apologetically, "Unless ya have beliefs against coffee drinkin'."

Emily smiled. She didn't care much for coffee, but she had no feelings about it being forbidden. "I would appreciate a cup. Thank you."

The woman took two cups from the shelf and filled them from the steaming pot, placed one in front of Emily and pulled up a chair to the table. "I'm Sophie," she said, pointing toward the sign on her door. "And you are . . . ?"

After Emily told her, she commented, "So yer startin' a church."

Emily nodded.

"I used to go to church when I was a kid," the woman continued. "My ma saw to thet."

"She sounds like a good mother," Emily replied with a smile.

But the woman quickly changed the topic of church. Emily wondered if she was a bit fearful of where it might lead.

"Whatcha think of our town?" Sophie asked.

Emily took a sip of the hot coffee. It did taste good and felt even better. In her short time in the pouring rain, she was already damp and chilled.

"I've been so busy trying to get things ready for Sunday that I've scarcely had time to form an opinion—but I'm sure I'm going to love it."

"You grow up in a small town or a city?" Sophie asked next.

"Neither," smiled Emily. "I was a farm kid."

"Me, too," the woman responded. "Hated it. Went off to the city when I was fourteen."

"Alone?" asked Emily before she could check herself.

The woman nodded her head and fidgeted with her cup, lifted it up and set it back down, then abruptly spoke to Emily again.

"Ya mind if I smoke?"

Emily was caught off guard. She did mind. The thought of a woman smoking—and in public—was, to her, shocking. She wondered if as the new mission worker she should express how she felt, but she looked at the nervous woman and said instead, "Go ahead, if you wish." Emily hated the smell of the smoke drifting around their heads, but she tried not to show it. After all, it was Sophie's cafe.

Sophie inhaled deeply, blew more smoke into the air above Emily's head and spoke again. "Didn't like the city, either. Tough place. Bunch of pushy people. I wasn't trained for any kind of good work. Cleaned rooms—tended bars. I hated it. Then I met Nick and we came here and got us this little cafe. Well, things was goin' great 'til Nick decided this town was too dead for 'im. He went back to the city an' I stayed on here."

She blew another cloud of smoke into the air. Emily felt that she should respond, but she didn't know what to say.

The woman went on. "Heard later thet he got married again. Well, I have the cafe. Not much, but it's a livin'. Me an' the kids are makin' out fine."

Here was something Emily could respond to. "How many ch—kids do you have?" she asked.

"Four. We had 'em one after the other. They was four, three, two and one when Nick left me."

"I'm sorry," Emily whispered, picturing in her mind how difficult it must have been.

Sophie grinned bravely. "So was I—at the time," she responded. "But now I figure as how Nick didn't do me so bad after all. He really weren't all thet great a guy. Though he was the best thet I seemed to be able to get. Now—life's really not so bad. I enjoy the kids. Turned out pretty good, if I do say so."

"How old are they now?" asked Emily.

"Eight, seven, six and five," the woman answered, pride in her eyes.

"I do hope they can come to Sunday school," Emily suggested shyly.

Sophie puffed silently on her cigarette. After blowing a blue cloud into the air, she smiled at Emily. "Sure. Why not?" she agreed. "Didn't hurt me none."

On Sunday Emily awoke to the sound of more rain beating methodically on her roof. Her first thought was of the Sunday service. "No one will come in this weather," she moaned and climbed reluctantly from her bed.

It was even worse than she feared when she looked outside the window. The street was one large muddy pool. There was not a soul in sight. Emily sighed deeply. She couldn't expect anyone to brave such weather.

A morose Emily sat down to her breakfast. All her preparation had been in vain—at least for this Sunday. She wouldn't be using the lessons today after all.

An hour before the appointed time for the service, Emily shrugged into her coat, wrapped her bonnet, Bible and lessons carefully in a towel and tucked them into a large pail, put the lid on and started the short walk around to the front of the building. She would be there, with a warming fire in the pot-belly stove, just in case someone did come.

Emily opened the front door to the church, pleased at least about the clean meeting room, but her happy expression turned to dismay. The roof leaked. Badly. Emily's scrubbed floor was now covered with dark puddles. A steady stream of rain water fell in a dozen places, the newly painted walls were streaked with trails of dirty water.

Emily was heartbroken. There were only a few benches in the room that were not rain-soaked. What would she do now?

With a heavy heart she put down her pail and moved toward the stove.

The fire started slowly, and Emily wondered if the chimney was plugged, but suddenly the flames began to lick at the wood, and warmth spilled into the dismal room. Emily warmed her back at the fire and looked forlornly out the new windows while the minutes ticked by.

No one is coming, she finally conceded. *It is well past time. I might as well go back to the house.* She picked up her pail and started out the door, securing it carefully behind her.

The long day was not helped when the rain slackened in midafternoon—it was too late to aid her planned service anyway.

She went to bed early, hoping to sleep away the storm and her discouragement.

When she arose the next morning the rain had ceased, but the sky was still dark and glowering. Without hesitation she drew out her writing materials and began a letter to the district superintendent.

After a formal salutation and greeting, she got to the crux of the matter.

The church looked so nice, she wrote, *after Mr. Lowe and Mr. Collins kindly gave me so much aid in fixing the windows and painting the walls. But the recent rainstorm has brought to light the fact that the roof leaks badly.*

Is there any way that we could have some aid in fixing it?

I would normally expect the parishioners to care for such, but as yet we have no established church here. The nasty weather over the past weekend made it impossible to hold a service, so I do not even know who my parishioners are to be—or how long it might take to find them.

I would be most pleased if something could be done before the next heavy rainstorm. Of course, I know that funds are not in abundant supply, so I will await your good judgment.

May God grant you His peace and blessing.

Yours sincerely,

Miss Emily Evans.

After posting her letter, she took one more peek into the church building. Water still stood here and there, and Emily knew it would need to be sopped up before it could do further damage. She went again for her scrub pail and a heavy mop.

———

Emily's letter had more effect than she had dared to hope. Word came back by return mail that a crew would be there to repair the roof the following week—Lord willing—and might even have time to give the walls another coat of paint. Emily could scarcely believe it. *Thank you, Lord. You truly are here with me,* she prayed. With quickened resolve she decided to do more calling. As yet she had visited none of the outlying farms. She must remedy that before the next scheduled service. So bright and early the next morning, Emily determined, she would walk out to the Travis farm where her horses were kept, and begin her rural calling duties.

Chapter Fourteen

Visiting

Emily turned her team first toward the west. Consulting her map, she decided she would try to cover a seven-mile radius before the coming winter set in. She knew that it would keep her busy, but once she discovered where the prospective parishioners lived, she would concentrate her calls on those places.

There was no one home at the first farm. Disappointed, Emily drove the team on for another mile down the road to the next place. There she found a bachelor, and he made no bones about the fact that he wasn't interested in her little church service.

It was almost two miles to the next farm. Emily was pleased to see a woman at the clothesline, hanging out a washing that included a number of children's articles. Emily thought that home looked like a good prospect and turned the team in at the gate.

The woman stopped and lifted a hand to shield her eyes from the sun. Emily could imagine that the lady was studying the horses and buggy to determine which neighbor was calling.

By the time Emily pulled up to the hitching rail, two children had appeared from somewhere. A little girl clung to the mother's skirt, peeking shyly at Emily. The other, a boy of about eight, flopped a thatch of dark hair out of his eyes and studied her boldly.

"Hello," greeted Emily in her friendliest voice as she stepped down from the buggy so that she might be on even ground with the woman.

"Lovely day, isn't it?" she continued.

The woman was hot and damp from bending over the sudsy

water of the washtub. She blew a straying wisp of hair out of her face and looked up at the sizzling sun. Emily wondered if she had made a poor choice of words.

"You sellin' somethin'?" the woman asked candidly.

"Oh no. No," Emily quickly assured her.

"Come on in then," the woman invited, nodding toward the door with her head. Emily tied her horses and followed.

"Ed always says that the only people who call on us are peddlers—either of no-good products or unwanted religion."

Emily's breath caught in her throat.

"Sit down." The woman nodded toward a kitchen chair. The cat already had it occupied. Emily didn't know whether to shoo the cat off and take possession or remain standing. The little girl solved the problem. She stepped forward and smacked the cat off with a pudgy hand. Emily took the seat.

"You new here?" the woman asked while she pushed the teakettle forward and poked another stick into the fireplace.

"Yes—yes, I am," Emily answered rather breathlessly. She wasn't quite sure how to handle the situation. "I've been here only a couple of weeks, in fact." There was heavy silence. "I—I decided that I should get out and meet my neighbors," Emily continued. Well, it was the truth as far as it went, she told herself. "My name is Emily," she added.

"I'm Clara. Who's farm you on?" asked the woman.

"Oh, I'm not on a farm," Emily admitted reluctantly.

Clara frowned as she lifted down the teapot. "In town?" she asked doubtfully.

"Yes. In town," responded Emily with her best smile.

"Well—I never," the woman said.

"Pardon me?"

The woman turned to look at Emily. She was shaking her head. "Never a town woman called to make acquaintance before," she observed dryly.

Emily felt as if she were living a lie. She knew she must clear up the matter quickly or she would not be able to live with herself. Her face reddened as she stood to her feet.

"Actually," she said slowly, "I am the new—new mission worker in town. My church hopes to start a congregation here. I—I am just trying to get acquainted so that I may find out who—who would be interested in joining us."

Clara had set down the teapot. She stood with mouth open, staring at Emily.

"Just like Ed says." The farmwife spoke quietly, a look of disappointment in her eyes.

"You aren't interested in church?" Emily asked shyly.

The woman turned her back and put the pot back up on the shelf.

Emily did not wait for her answer. "Then, perhaps—perhaps I could call—just as a friend. We wouldn't talk church at all—just visit."

The woman said nothing, but Emily noticed that she was taking the teapot down again.

Emily held her tongue for the moment, thinking quickly. She must try hard not to say anything that might jeopardize the delicate opportunity.

"I noticed that you have some lovely flowers, Clara," she ventured and the woman's eyes lit up for the first time.

"I'm not familiar with that blue one at the corner of the house," Emily went on.

"Got those seeds from my mother," said Clara. "She always had a patch of 'em. Called Blue Cups."

"They are beautiful," continued Emily sincerely.

"You can have a few seeds come fall—if you'd like," offered Clara, then added slowly, "That is, if you're plannin' to stay over the winter."

"Oh, I am," Emily spoke hurriedly. "I hope I can stay for a long time."

Clara smiled slightly.

They had their tea together and chatted about flowers, family and housekeeping. Emily did not bring up the subject of church again. Nor did her companion. Emily sensed that Clara was starved for the fellowship of another woman. Although Emily hated to leave, the sun was climbing directly up overhead and she knew she should be on her way. Besides, she was afraid that Ed might suddenly make an appearance, and she was not sure she was prepared as yet to meet the man, who would immediately assume she was a peddler.

When at last she bid farewell, Clara was reluctant to let her go. Then Emily turned her team and called back as she drove off, "You must have tea with me when you're in town. I live at the back of the old pool hall," deciding it was wiser in this case to identify her residence by what the building had been.

"Well, I certainly haven't added many members to my congregation this morning," Emily mused as she turned her horses onto the road and set off for the next farm.

This one belonged to the Browns, Emily learned when she was cordially greeted, though not asked to come in. Mrs. Brown listened to her invitation, thanked her for her kindness and said she would consider letting her children attend. Emily was afraid she would not see them in her little church. She lifted her heart in prayer for the Brown family.

By the time Emily had taken to the road once again, she discovered she was hungry and decided to break for the light lunch she had tucked beneath the buggy seat.

"Most people will invite the visiting preacher in for a meal if it is anywhere near mealtime," Rev. Witt had told the students during a school chapel service. "But one is wise not to count on it. Take a bit of a lunch with you if you are expecting your calls to take most of your day" he advised.

As soon as she felt the team had fed long enough, she arose from the grassy shade, stretched, and climbed back up in her buggy.

There were still some bad potholes in the low spots from the last heavy rain, and Emily drove carefully. She had no desire to get mired down while dressed in her best Sunday frock and shoes.

She seemed to drive endlessly before the next farmyard came into view. Emily turned in at the gate and was met by a fiercely barking farm dog. The horses were reluctant to enter the yard and began backing their way toward the gate again. Emily had a hard time keeping the team under control. She knew there was no way she was going to climb down from the buggy until the dog's owner made an appearance.

But though Emily saw the curtain at the window moving as if some hand were sweeping it aside, no one appeared at the door. Emily finally managed to get her team turned around and back to the road.

It was late by then and Emily wearily decided to head for home. It was a long drive back to town and she wanted to make it over the potholes while there was still plenty of light.

It was close to the supper hour when Emily again passed the farm she had visited that morning but found no one home. Now a small truck stood in the yard and a man carrying a pail crossed toward the barn. Emily could see a woman in a printed housedress coming from the chicken pens, a basket in her hand.

Impulsively, Emily turned her horses in at the gate. She would make a quick call while she was passing. She couldn't do any worse than she had already done.

At the sound of the approaching buggy, the woman stopped and turned to watch it draw near. A light breeze toyed with the strings of the woman's apron and lifted wisps of graying hair. There was a slight smile of greeting on her pleasant, motherly face. Emily felt it was the most welcome sight she had seen all day, and responded with a bright smile.

"Hello," called the woman before Emily had even stopped the team. Emily returned the greeting.

The woman did not wait for Emily to alight, but as soon as the horses arrived at the hitching rail, she set down her basket of fresh eggs and moved forward to tie the team herself.

"You out calling?" the woman asked.

"That's right," Emily answered, surprised that she would know. Emily brushed the wrinkles from her skirt, trying at the same time to shake some of the kinks from her back and legs as she stepped down from the buggy.

"I'll just stop a minute," Emily said. "I know it is an awkward hour, but you weren't home when I passed by this morning."

"You've been calling all day?" the woman asked, then quickly continued, "My, you must be exhausted."

Emily just smiled.

"Come in," invited the woman, picking up her basket again and shooing away a kitten that rubbed against her leg.

"Oh, but I mustn't stop now," Emily answered. "It is almost the supper hour."

"So join us," she replied pleasantly. "It won't be fancy, but we fare quite well—and we love company. There's just George and me. Come on."

Emily gratefully followed her into the restful coolness of the farmhouse.

"I take it you are the new church worker." The woman again surprised Emily. She added, "But I don't know your name."

"It's Emily. Emily Evans."

"I'm Molly Reilly. I heard you were in town. My, what a job you have—making that old hall into a church," she chuckled lightly.

Emily nodded. "I thought I had it pretty well in hand," she admitted, "until that heavy rain over the weekend."

"It leaks?" the woman asked sympathetically.

"It leaks," agreed Emily. "Badly."

"Oh, dear!" exclaimed Mrs. Reilly kindly. "What a shame."

Emily liked her immediately; perhaps drawn toward the woman because of the mother she had lost. Emily was glad she had decided to stop.

"Take off your hat and lay it on the shelf there," her hostess invited. "The washbasin is right over there and there's no shortage of water."

Emily moved to comply.

"I believe you met our nephew," the woman said off-handedly as Emily freshened up at the basin. Emily wondered if their nephew was one of the young lads who had carried in her trunk.

"Shad Austin," the lady explained further.

Emily still drew a blank. She shook her head slowly.

"He came back from fishing and said you had met along the creek."

Emily could feel her face burning. What else might the young man have told about her?

"He thought you looked awfully young to be taking on so much responsibility," the woman added comfortably as she bustled about her big farm kitchen.

I'll bet he did, Emily wanted to retort, but she bit her tongue.

"Shad's father was a preacher," the woman explained, surprising Emily beyond measure. From the young man's response to her "calling," she hadn't expected him to have had Christian rearing.

"At one time Shad planned on being a preacher, too, but that was before—" Mrs. Reilly sighed and her shoulders sagged, and she said no more.

Emily pondered what it all meant. At one time? Before what? What had happened? She wanted to know but of course didn't feel free to ask.

"He's a banker now," his aunt continued. "In Calgary. He still comes to the farm whenever he can. His folks are both gone now, and he's always been like a son to George and me."

Then she chuckled. "He came home last Sunday and said, 'Aunt Moll'—he always calls me Aunt Moll—'guess what I just found along the creek. A new preacher. A little bit of a girl. Going to start services in town. Maybe you'd better check her out, Aunt Moll. See if she's teaching the truth.' "

Emily's face flushed deeply. She winced at the thought of being "checked out." Certainly she planned to teach the truth. It was unkind of the young man to suggest she might do otherwise.

"Well, George gave me a wink, but Shad seemed quiet—almost moody—for the rest of the day. And he's never like that. After we'd gone to bed, George and I had a long talk. Wouldn't it be something if our Shad made his way back to God? It would sure be an answer to his mother's prayers—and ours." She sniffed and turned back to Emily, wiping her eyes.

"Forgive me," she implored. "It's just that we've been praying for him for so long. We grasp at any signs of softening toward the Lord, I guess."

Emily managed a smile and whispered a quiet, though sincere, "I'm so sorry." Mrs. Reilly returned the smile and went back to her stove.

"George will be looking for his supper," she said as she worked. "He's only milking two cows now and it doesn't take him long."

"Is there anything I can do?" offered Emily, certain now that she was staying for supper.

"You can set the table," Mrs. Reilly invited. "You'll find the dishes in that cupboard right there."

Chapter Fifteen

Another Week

Emily's calling continued to be met with varied responses. Very few folks gave her a definite answer, but there were some who said they would consider coming to her little church, or would think about sending their children. Emily found their indecision frustrating, but she had to accept it and keep praying for these families. Those long buggy rides between farms were good times for that, she discovered.

"The weather can't be an excuse *this* time," Emily mused as she looked out on a perfect Sunday morning.

Singing to herself, she prepared for the service. Surely today would be very different from last week.

At two minutes to ten, Mrs. Travis and two of her children found their way into one of the pews. Emily smiled her good morning, hopeful that they were only the first of many.

They waited for another fifteen minutes, but no one else came. So Emily, with a heavy heart, started the Sunday school lesson. Maybe others would join them later for the morning service, but she was disappointed in that as well.

Don't despair, she kept telling herself. *This is only the beginning. And perhaps God wants me to spend special, personal time with this woman and her children.* Emily endeavored to make Mrs. Travis and her two little ones feel as much in the presence of the Father as she knew how.

When the short Bible lesson and the worship service had ended, the woman took Emily's hand and smiled her appreciation.

"It is good to be in church again," she said in a soft voice. "I have missed it so much. Especially since Mr. Travis is—is ill."

"I'm so glad you could come," Emily responded, and then impulsively gave the older woman a warm hug.

The woman left with tears in her eyes, and Emily lingered about the room, straightening the few worn hymnals and studying the stains on the walls.

Her first Sunday had not been as she would have chosen. But certainly God cared even more about this community and these people than she did. He would help her get their attention.

On Tuesday a work crew of six men in two trucks pulled up in front of Emily's little church. She was both excited and concerned when she saw the number of men. She would be expected to feed them. Emily knew her cupboards didn't hold much in food staples.

She smiled her welcome, reminding herself that she had written the letter asking for help. God had answered her need. And, surely, if He had supplied the men and the materials, He would supply their food as well.

And He did—through Shad's Aunt Moll. Mrs. Reilly was shopping at the mercantile when the trucks pulled in and the men busied themselves setting up their ladders. Quick to assess the situation, she hastened to Emily's door and rapped hurriedly.

Emily answered, still a bit flustered by the situation.

"I see you have a whole crew out here," said Mrs. Reilly.

"Yes," responded Emily.

"And I suppose you're expected to feed them?" asked the woman.

Emily nodded, her face showing her concern.

"I guessed as much," the woman went on. With a hint of apology she lowered her voice, "Can you cook?"

Emily nodded and smiled.

"Good!" said the older woman. "So many of the younger generation . . ." But she stopped and changed direction, "Well, you fix something for their noon meal, soup and bread—or whatever you have—and I'll fry a couple chickens and make some pies for their supper."

Emily couldn't believe her ears. "Oh-h, but—" she began, but the woman stopped her with a wave of her hand.

"You have vegetables?"

Emily thought of the garden produce her father had sent along. She nodded.

"Then you take care of that. I'll see to the other."

And she was off before Emily could even find the words to express her relief and gratitude.

As Emily watched Molly Reilly hasten down the broken walk, a thought flashed through her mind. *I wonder where you were on Sunday?* but she quickly checked herself. That was none of her business. She was not sent to judge the people—only to present truth and lead them to the Lord.

Emily was just about to reenter her little home when she saw Sophie waving a tea towel from down the street. "Yoo-hoo" came the call. Emily hastened across the dusty road, hoping nothing was wrong at Sophie's place.

"Is—is anything the matter?" she exclaimed when she was within earshot.

Sophie laughed with unchecked hilarity. "No. No. Nothin' like thet. Jest saw yer big crew and figured ya might not have a coffeepot big enough to serve 'em all. Why don't ya send 'em all over here at coffee time? I'll supply the coffee—you send the men."

Emily stared open-mouthed. She hadn't even thought about coffee time.

She nodded her agreement, thanked Sophie and asked what time she would like the crew to come.

"Tenish," the woman responded. Emily scurried back to the house to get some cookies in the oven. At least she could supply that much to go with the coffee.

———

At ten the crew was called from their labors and sent over to Sophie's cafe for morning coffee and cookies. At noon, Emily served thick vegetable soup and sliced bread. In the afternoon, Sophie again served coffee, and Emily had time to bake a chocolate cake. And, right on time for the supper hour, Reiilys' truck pulled up in front of the building and Mrs. Reilly came in bearing her dishes of fried chicken and apple pies.

When the long day had come to a close, the roof was repaired and the walls repainted. One older man had even found time to replace the broken boards in Emily's walk, while a younger member of the crew worked a scythe in her backyard, taking down all the tall grass and garden weed patch. Emily couldn't believe how much had been accomplished in such a short time.

Deeply thankful, Emily lay on her bed that night. The little church and her small abode were now in good order. She could concentrate her efforts on reaching out with love and truth to the people of the community.

———

Emily's days were mostly taken up with her calling. At times she came home weary and disappointed. There just didn't seem to be much interest in her little mission church. With difficulty she left her burden with the Lord and tried to sleep in spite of her anxiety.

A letter from Ruth was filled with excitement and good news. She loved her community, she loved her boarding place, and she had crowded twenty-five people into one little country schoolhouse on her first Sunday of preaching—twenty-nine in the other and the numbers had continued to grow. Now the attendance had settled in at thirty to forty at each service.

Ruth is such a good preacher that they are sure to come to hear her, thought Emily, holding the pages loosely and staring out at the vacant lot. She was happy for Ruth—but in comparison, Emily did seem to be a total failure.

She went to bed feeling discouraged and lay tossing restlessly. Finally she crawled out and knelt down on the braided rug by her bedside.

"Lord," she prayed, "I was sure I heard your call to serve. I don't seem to be very good at it. I can't preach like Ruth. I know that. Maybe I misunderstood the feeling I had in chapel. I don't know, God. I'm so mixed up." Emily paused a moment to think. "But that strong desire to serve you in some way was there even before I went to Bible school. Surely that was from you, Lord." She paused again. "If you really want me to start this little church, then I need your help. I can't do it without you. Please, dear God—give me wisdom and direction.

"I'm willing to work here—for as long as it takes—if that is your will. Show me, Lord. Show me what to do.

"And help me to be patient. I know I'm always in a hurry. I know I push. I've always pushed myself, Lord. I'm not good at learning things and I've had to work harder at it than others.

"But help me to not push other people and to understand that this is your work, not mine. I don't need to push here. I need to obey. And I need to wait for you."

Emily continued praying, the tears wetting her cheeks. At

length she felt a peace steal over her heart and she rose from her knees, brushed her tear-stained face with a sleeve of her nightgown and climbed back into bed.

She slept then. A restful, much-needed sleep.

Whatever happened at Wesson Creek Mission was up to the Lord. Emily was only an instrument for Him to use.

The next morning Emily arose with better spirits. It was Sunday and she expected to again welcome Mrs. Travis and her children to the service, intending to use the time together as well as she was able. But when the Travis children arrived at the door of the little church, they were alone.

"Mama's not well," they informed Emily in quiet voices and selected the same seat they had occupied the previous Sunday.

Emily was about to begin the lesson when the door opened again and Mrs. Reilly scurried in, her face red, her hat slightly akimbo. But she flashed a smile at Emily.

"The cows got out. Just when we were ready to leave. George is still rounding up the last of them. Neither of us would have made it to church if we'd had to drive all the way to Tomis like we've been doing. It's nice to have our own church here in town."

She slid into the seat beside the Travis children, still panting slightly. "Don't know why such things always happen on Sunday," she puffed, drawing a white handkerchief over her perspiring face.

Emily smiled, welcomed her little audience and began her lesson.

She had just announced the story of Noah and the ark when the door opened again and Sophie stuck her head in. "Sorry," she said in a hoarse whisper. "They was scared to come alone the first time." She pushed four children with shiny-clean faces and slicked-down hair into the room, withdrew and closed the door again.

Emily, happy indeed for a congregation of seven, greeted the four newcomers.

When it was time for the morning worship service, three more people joined them—two country women, one leading her child by the hand.

That's ten! thrilled Emily, but she did not pause long to rejoice. It was not her doing. God had sent them to her. Now it was her responsibility to teach from His Word.

As soon as Emily had eaten her simple dinner, she placed some cookies and a loaf of bread in a pail and set out for the Travises. She knew there wasn't much she could do about the illness itself, but at least she would express her concern and see if there was any way that she could help.

She expected to find the woman in bed, or at least in the house wrapped in blankets and drinking broth. But when Emily arrived Mrs. Travis was in her garden, pulling carrots. She straightened and her hand fluttered to her face. She looked surprised at Emily's visit, and Emily knew she had caught her off guard.

Emily almost blurted out, "The children said you were not feeling well," but said instead, "I brought some cookies. Thought we could have tea. How are you? I—I missed you at the service."

Emily noticed that the woman turned sideways when she answered.

"That's—that's kind. Come in. I—I wasn't feeling so well this morning. Better now." And she led the way to the house.

It wasn't until they were seated at the kitchen table having tea and cookies that Emily noticed a large discolored area on the left side of the woman's face. Mrs. Travis seemed to sense immediately that Emily had seen the bruise.

"I fell," she offered quickly. "It's nothing."

"But it looks . . . shouldn't you see a doctor?"

Mrs. Travis shook her head stubbornly. "No need," she insisted.

"Did you faint?" asked Emily. Perhaps the woman was sicker than she realized. But Mrs. Travis brushed aside the question.

"No. No. Don't think so. Just—just clumsy, I guess."

Emily let the matter drop. She could sense that the woman was agitated.

While Emily was on her way home, she tried to puzzle through the situation. *Perhaps she has seizures and doesn't want to admit it,* she reasoned. *But there must be some kind of medication that could help her. But, then, maybe not . . .*

Maybe Mrs. Travis would not visit the doctor because of lack of funds. Or she might just refuse to admit the seriousness of her illness because of the children. Mr. Travis was hardly able to care for them with his own ill health.

Whatever the situation, the Travises needed her support and her prayers. She hoped that other members of the community were aware of their circumstances and ready to help as well.

————

After another busy week of calling in all kinds of weather—hot one day and a cold rain the next—Emily awakened early on Friday. She lay in her bed staring up at the ceiling while it seemed to sway and tilt every which way. She felt flushed, her throat hurt and her body ached.

"Oh no!" she groaned. "I can't be sick. Lord, please don't let me be sick."

She pulled herself into a sitting position and willed herself to get up. But as the day dragged on she felt worse and worse. At last she had to concede defeat and take to her bed.

Maybe if I rest today, I'll be fine by tomorrow, Emily hoped.

But she wasn't fine the next day. Her fever increased and her pulse raced. It was all she could do to make it from her bed to the kitchen.

I must drink fluids, she reminded herself, but it was difficult even to swallow.

She placed a pitcher of water and a glass beside her bed and again lay down.

"Please, God," she prayed feverishly, "make me well for Sunday." But when the first of the children arrived on Sunday morning, Emily was not there to open the door. They stood on the walk, wondering what to do.

Mrs. Reilly was the next to arrive. She greeted Sophie's four youngsters and chatted while they waited for Emily.

"It's strange," she murmured as the minutes ticked by. "I wouldn't expect her to be late."

"Maybe *her* cows got out," quipped young Nicky, and all the little cluster shared in the laughter.

Mrs. Travis arrived, her two children close behind her.

Mrs. Reilly greeted her warmly and then said, "It's strange, I wouldn't expect Emily to oversleep. It's past Sunday school hour." She fidgeted a few moments more and then moved resolutely toward Emily's gate.

"I'll just go see," she told the waiting group, and off she went to Emily's door.

There was no answer to her knock, and since there was no lock on the door Mrs. Reilly opened it and let herself in.

She found a very ill Emily. She could scarcely lift her head from her pillow, but she still fussed over the fact that she was not there to open the church building.

Mrs. Reilly sent Nicky for Dr. Andrew and tried to make Emily more comfortable in the meantime by putting a wet cloth on her forehead. There was nothing for Emily to do but to accept the ministrations. There would be no service that Sunday.

———

It took me nearly a week to get back on my feet, Emily wrote to Ruth. *I don't know what I would have done without Mrs. Reilly. She came every day to see how I was and to make sure I ate her nice, hot soup. Even Sophie from the cafe sent her Nicky over with a sandwich, and Mrs. Travis baked a loaf of bread for me.*

I don't dare write to my father about how sick I was, she continued, *or he would really be worried.* Emily finished her letter with words of enthusiasm for Ruth's fine progress and continued hope for her own situation.

Chapter Sixteen

Autumn

Other than the handful of women who had become her friends, Emily's adoption into the Wesson Creek community came slowly. She wished that Big John, as he was known in the area, didn't treat her quite so gruffly and that the young fellows did not loiter about the doors of the blacksmith shop staring at her as she walked to the post office or did her shopping. She wished the neighborhood women were more free to drop in for a cup of tea and that the young children didn't still dip their heads in shyness when she spoke to them.

"Be patient," she kept insisting to herself, but sometimes it was very hard to do so.

Gradually the attendance in the little church picked up. But just when Emily began to exult over the possibility of higher numbers, others would drop out.

"How do I keep them faithful? Consistent?" she lamented to the Lord. "I know I'm not a good preacher—but I try to make it interesting."

Letters from Ruth still included glowing reports of the growth in her church, though she too acknowledged a setback or two.

Things were even more difficult for Verna Woods, Emily concluded after reading her letter. The community where Verna served seemed to have less interest in church and spiritual matters than Wesson Creek. In fact, Verna was already admitting that she often thought of giving up and going home. Emily sent her an encouraging note and prayed daily for Verna.

Emily knew several households quite well by now and that encouraged her.

Whenever she was passing, she dropped in on the lady who had no interest in "religious peddlers." She seemed so lonely that Emily ached for her. Emily didn't mention anything about church when she called there, though she longed to do so. She was sure she knew the cure for Clara's lonely heart. It was found in the pages of the Book Emily carried, tucked protectively in a corner of her buggy.

Soon the community was astir with harvesting activity. In the fields along the road, Emily observed teams of draft horses or chugging tractors from morn to dusk as she made her calls. Womenfolk took over the choring and cooked hardy meals, drawing on their abundant gardens. The children scurried to the fields with pails of fresh water or beef sandwiches and lemon tarts. Everyone was busy and Emily observed all the productive commotion as well as tension in the air as she visited the farm families. Every cloud was viewed with alarm. Would rain bring the harvesting to a standstill? Could there be a chance of snow?

Emily continued calling on folks, but she respected the harvesting situation. She certainly did not expect a farmwife to turn away from the pie crusts to prepare her visitor a cup of tea. She did not pause for polite conversation when a farmer was on his way to the granary with a wagonload of grain. Emily had grown up on a farm. She knew the pressure of the harvest.

Thus Emily decided to concentrate her efforts in town for the present. Sophie always seemed glad to see her, and cheerfully served her coffee and sat down to chat when she wasn't busy. Big John's sister at the mercantile, too, didn't seem to mind an occasional chat.

Also there was much to do around her own small place. While the harvesting was being completed, she busied herself cleaning up the weedy garden, patching her broken fences, repairing seams in aging dresses, and securing buttons on her winter coat.

She had more time for Bible study in preparation for future Sundays and caught up on her letter writing, baked cookies for an elderly lady down the street, and sewed a new, much-needed winter skirt.

She even took time for the luxury of a few walks in the woods. Beneath her feet the fallen leaves rustled with each footfall. Above, those that remained danced joyfully in the autumn breeze. Still higher in the sky, the Canada geese honked their goodbyes in V-formation as they flew their way to warmer climates. Other birds that would stay for the winter fluttered anxiously about to locate each berry tree, each rose bush, for future use. Squirrels scolded and bush rabbits ducked for cover when they saw her coming. Emily found great pleasure in the life of the woods.

Her feet always found their way back to the same spot—the cluster of trees along the creek where she had been resting the day she met Shad Austin. The creek had slowed further with the passing of summer. In some places it barely moved at all, but here, at the place Emily was sure was a favorite fishing hole, it still gurgled and played over stones as it left the small pond. Dragonflies zoomed in and out, and hornets settled on fallen leaves to ride a moment on the water.

Emily loved this restful little hideaway. Its peace refreshed her with each visit. On some days she brought her Bible and read as she basked in the serenity. Occasionally she wondered about the man whom she'd accidentally met in that place.

Mrs. Reilly had not mentioned the young man again. Emily did not wish to pry, but she often found herself trying to imagine what had brought about the change in his life. Why had he given up his calling and seemingly deserted his faith? What had happened to both of his parents that he was alone? *When* had it happened? Emily mulled over the questions as she watched the pond's activity.

Her thoughts always led her to prayer. Whatever the situation, she knew there was a need. She pictured the tears in Molly Reilly's eyes and heard again the words, "It would be an answer to his mother's prayers," and Emily added her voice to those prayers on Shad's behalf.

———

Emily met Mr. Travis for the first time when she went to get her team from the farm one day.

Claude was usually there to bring her horses. Though he was scarcely taller than Emily herself, he insisted on harnessing them. Emily allowed him to do so, assuming that he was likely being schooled by his mother to act the part of a gentleman. She had all she could do to keep from trying to help him as the lad struggled to lift the heavy harness over the backs of Star and Shadow.

On that particular day, instead of Claude, a man walked out to meet her.

"Mawnin'," he greeted, and touched his cap.

"Good morning," Emily responded, quickly making some deductions and extending her hand. "You're Mr. Travis?"

The man chuckled as he shook Emily's hand. "Been a long time since I been called mister."

Emily didn't quite understand his little joke, but she told him her name.

He nodded and said, "Ya wantin' yer team?" Emily assured him that she was.

"You go on in to see the missus an' I'll fetch 'em for ya," he said good-naturedly and Emily agreed.

He certainly was gaunt, she noted as she moved toward the house. His whiskered face seemed to sag in where his cheeks should be, and his clothing hung on his slight frame. He walked with a slow, lumbering step, and Emily wondered if he would have the strength to make it to the barn, let alone the pasture where the horses fed.

Oh, dear, she scolded herself, *should I be letting him exert himself this way?* Uncertain about what to do, she went on to the house.

Mrs. Travis welcomed her and put the teakettle on to boil.

"Hope you're not in too big a rush," she said slowly. "Claude is off to the neighbors and Wilbur might take a while getting your team."

"Should—should I have allowed him—?" began Emily and then changed it to, "Is he well enough to deal with the horses?"

Mrs. Travis cast a glance at Emily. "He's fine," she said crisply. "Best he's been in some time."

Oh, my, thought Emily. *The poor man! If that is his best, he must have really been ill.*

The team eventually arrived at the door, and Emily bid Mrs. Travis goodbye and left. She felt even more concerned for the family. Over the months she had noted bruises on Mrs. Travis on more than one occasion and wondered if the woman needed to see Dr. Andrew about her continual falls.

"I do wish there were a way I could help. The poor man. Poor Mrs. Travis!" Emily said under her breath as she drove from the yard.

———

After that Emily often spotted Mr. Travis on the town streets. She realized she had seen him before without knowing who he was. On some days he could scarcely walk, and Emily wondered why he came into town when he was obviously so weak. Surely the man's precarious health should be guarded carefully. If his condition continued to deteriorate, the Travis family would soon be without a father.

Emily wondered if she should speak to anyone about the situation. Surely the townspeople were aware of what was going on. Didn't anyone care? Had anyone attempted to get help for the family? Had the man ever had medical attention?

Emily fretted but didn't know what she could do.

———

Carefully Emily counted her money. She was getting awfully low on funds. The Sunday offerings she had depended on amounted to only a few coins. *What can one expect when the congregation is mostly children?* she thought. She was very glad for the eggs and milk regularly supplied by Mrs. Reilly, but items such as salt, soap and flour had to be purchased at the mercantile. It was the lack of soap that had Emily concerned now.

Well, I must have it, she concluded. *I can't run around in dirty clothes.* Emily picked up her near-empty purse and headed for the store.

"Good morning," she greeted Big John cautiously. She had been hoping his sister would be minding the store. From the back rooms came the sound of activity, and Emily knew that Miss McMann was busy with housekeeping duties.

"Humph!" Big John snorted.

"I—I need some soap," stated Emily, giving up on conversation.

"What kind?" he snapped.

"For my laundry," responded Emily.

"Duz? Maple Leaf? Oxydol? Sunlight? Iv—?"

"What—which one is the cheapest?" Emily asked, embarrassed.

Big John swung around. "So ya bargain shop? Well, at least thet shows *some* sense." If he had not emphasized "some," Emily might have felt strangely complimented.

"How big a box?" he asked her as he reached for the soap. "Large or Family?"

"No—the—the small box—please," said Emily, her cheeks growing hotter.

"Thought ya was bargain smart," huffed Big John. "Now thet ain't wise buyin'."

"Mr.—Mr. John," Emily said, her voice more stern than she intended, "I would love to be a wise shopper. I know that one does save more by buying the larger box, but—I—I only buy what I can afford to pay for."

She dropped the money on his counter, spun on her heel and left the store with the soap, her head high.

How that man manages to rile me, she fumed and then felt guilty. She was there to show love—whether people were loving in return or not. She was the one who was to be gracious and forgiving. *I've failed again,* she mourned. She could never hope to win this neighbor if she responded that way. She turned around and went back into the store.

"Ferget somethin'?" Big John gruffly greeted her.

"Yes. Yes, I did," faltered Emily, her cheeks crimson, her eyes bright with tears. "I—I forgot my manners. I forgot my Christian upbringing. My father would be embarrassed by my behavior, and I'm sure my—my heavenly Father is disappointed. I am sorry."

By the time Emily had finished her little speech, her voice was little more than a whisper. "Please—please forgive me," she asked, blinked back the tears, and left the man staring after her, his mouth open in astonishment.

Chapter Seventeen

Celebrations

I visited Bible school last week, Ruth wrote again, *and thought you would be interested in all the news. I hardly know where to start. Each time I heard another report about one of our classmates, I jotted it down so I wouldn't forget to tell you.*

Morris expects to leave for the mission field next May. He is so excited. He is going to Nigeria.

Word has it that the Russells are doing well in their pastorate at Conner. They are expecting their first child next April. Guess Agatha has not been at all well, so I do hope things soon improve for her. Poor Fred has had to be preacher and nurse and housekeeper all at the same time.

Olive broke off her engagement to Ross. I heard he was devastated. Seems that she and Robert Lee, her dear little Rob, are planning a December wedding. Hope they make it. Maybe they deserve each other.

Another engagement has also been announced. Lacey Beckett and Mary Frieson. I think they make a nice couple. Perhaps Mary will help to polish him up a bit.

But the biggest surprise for me was how much he has already changed—Lacey Beckett, our big, boyish Lacey. He seems so much more mature. And has such concern for others. I couldn't believe my eyes and ears. He is still planning on the ministry, and Pearl told me that Rev. Witt views him as the prize candidate for a new church work in the city. In the city, mind you! Was a day when I thought the poor boy wouldn't even make it on the farm. God sure is full of surprises!

Emily had to agree. "Isn't it amazing what God can do with a life given completely over to Him?" she murmured. Then she smiled, "Especially Lacey's—and mine!"

Ruth had other bits of information about faculty members and people they both had known. It was a long, newsy letter and it left Emily feeling very homesick for the school and those like Miss Herrington who had nurtured and loved her.

She wiped away unbidden tears as she folded up the letter and returned it to the envelope. Then she hastened to get out her pen and writing paper. She would write to Ruth while all the news was still fresh in her mind.

Mrs. Reilly was the first to mention the Harvest Picnic to Emily. "Of course you'll go," she declared. "Everyone does. It will be a wonderful opportunity for you to meet the neighborhood in a less formal way."

"I haven't even heard about it," said Emily. "Tell me more."

"We have it every year as soon as the harvesting is over. Everybody comes. It's at the fairgrounds. The meat is supplied by various farmers. We all take turns. Then everybody brings favorite dishes and potluck for the rest of the meal. It's great fun."

"It sounds fun," agreed Emily. She hadn't done anything just for fun in a long time.

"There are races and tugs-of-war and a ball game. Sometimes we even have booths for the kids. You know—balls to throw, a fish pond, apple dunking . . . things like that. They love it. It's the big event of the year."

"I'd love to go!" exclaimed Emily enthusiastically.

From then on the fall picnic came often to Emily's attention. Everywhere she went people were talking about it. Posters, made by the school children, began to turn up all over town. Word had it that Big John was going to provide some firecrackers for the event, and the farm kids were already coaxing their folks to stay late enough to be able to watch them.

Emily wondered what she should bring as her share of the meal. Her grocery supplies were depleting rapidly, and she still faced the long winter months.

Maybe I should take a trip home and get some more, she wondered, but it was such a long way to go and it was late enough in the fall that a winter storm could sweep in at any time. No, if she had been going to travel home for supplies, she should have done it weeks earlier.

She refused to write home to her father for money. She was sure he would send what he could if he knew of her plight, but she was on her own now—and serving the Lord. Didn't she believe that the Lord would provide? Where was her faith if she had to rush to her earthly father when the cupboard got a bit bare?

"Hold steady!" Emily often said to herself. "Be still, and know that He is God," she quoted from her beloved Bible.

But Emily had to admit that the coming event was a worry on her mind.

I have milk and eggs, she thought suddenly. "I'll make a custard," she announced, brightening.

That made Emily feel better, but she was sure she was expected to bring more than one dish. *I do have potatoes—and onions,* she mused. *I guess I'll just have to experiment.*

But Emily didn't feel too confident about experimentation when the community at large would be sampling her work.

On the day of the picnic Emily made her custard as planned and was pleased that it turned out just right. She sprinkled nutmeg over the top and turned to her experimental dish. She cooked a pot of potatoes and mashed them until they were light and fluffy, generously adding some of Mrs. Reilly's farm cream. Then she stirred in a few chopped onions. Last of all she whipped up some eggs, which she seasoned, then poured the mixture into the little pockets she had scooped in the potatoes in her pan.

"If I just had some cheese to sprinkle over the top," she murmured thoughtfully as she slid the pan into the oven.

A knock at her door turned out to be Mrs. Reilly.

"How are you coming?" she asked. "Ummm, that custard looks good."

"I've just popped my second dish into the oven," Emily responded cheerfully. Then she stopped short. "Oh no!" she wailed.

"What's wrong?" asked Mrs. Reilly anxiously.

"The supper—it won't be eaten till evening! Who will want to eat cold potatoes and eggs? I didn't think—"

Mrs. Reilly looked relieved. "Is that all," she said, waving aside Emily's consternation. "Don't worry about it. Keep it for your Sunday dinner. You can rewarm it later. Anyway, the custard is more than your fair share. There's always much more food than can ever be eaten. I've got to run. I'm helping with the ice cream. Here's your milk and eggs. And there's a bit of cheese there, too. George's sister brought me a great wedge of it. We'll never manage to eat it all on our own."

Cheese! Emily's eyes opened wide.

"Now don't be late," the older woman admonished as she hurried off.

Emily prepared herself carefully for the outing. She chose her prettiest housedress, pinned up her hair extra carefully, and for a long moment debated about her deaconess bonnet. Should or shouldn't she wear it? Would the parishioners expect to see her appear properly attired as the town mission worker, or would she look foolish attending a picnic in her ministry garb?

At last Emily laid her bonnet back on the shelf. She would go without the hat.

She could smell her cookery as she entered her kitchen to lift the hot pan from the oven. Emily was tempted to try a small forkful of the food.

It *was* tasty. She scraped a few shreds of cheese onto another mouthful and took another bite. That made it even better. *Just one more bite,* she decided. It was good. Really good.

"Oh, dear," she giggled. "I won't be able to enjoy any of that beef if I don't quit!" Emily paused long enough to pick up her custard and grab her coat in case the evening was chilly, then left excitedly for the town fairgrounds.

Emily couldn't remember when she had last had so much fun. She shared in the laughter as the sack racers toppled and scrambled for the finish line. She licked ice cream that ran down her cone before it could spill on her hands, she shouted encouragement to her Sunday school students as they took part in the wheelbarrow race, and cheered on the softball players. She even tried her hand at dunking for apples, soaking her face and the curls that framed it. The children laughed and squealed their delight when she tossed the ball that sent the mayor of the town into the dunk tank and urged her to try her hand at it again with the schoolteacher.

Before she knew it, it was time for the picnic supper.

Emily stood in line with Sophie's Olivia on one side and little Rena Travis on the other. The food smelled delicious in spite of her sampling from the potato dish.

The line was long, and the two children got fidgety.

"Go ahead," urged Emily when they saw an opportunity to dart ahead and join their own family members. "Your mothers are waiting for you."

Emily stood near the end of the line, humming softly to herself. This was the first time she had really felt a part of the small community.

"How's the preacher?" a voice asked at her elbow.

Which one of those young fellows is teasing me now? Emily's thought as her head came around. *They still laugh and jostle and throw out silly dares to one another whenever I come in sight.*

But it was Shad Austin who stood next to her, a teasing smile on his lips.

"If you are referring to me—I'm just fine," she answered evenly.

His eyes conveyed an apology, though he did not express it aloud. "Actually, Aunt Moll sent me to get you. There's an extra spot at the table over there. She said to tell you to join us."

"Thank you," Emily replied and moved up a step in the line.

He followed her. Emily noticed that he carried an empty plate.

"I didn't realize you were here," Emily commented for something to say.

"I never miss the Harvest Picnic," he said. "I've been here most of the afternoon."

Emily wondered fleetingly where he had been and why she hadn't seen him.

"I was manning the dunk tank," he continued, laughing. "I helped you dunk the mayor," he remarked.

"But I—I thought the ball did that when—" began Emily.

"It should—if it's working. Ours doesn't work quite right. So someone has to be underneath to pull the rope and tip the seat."

"Oh-h," laughed Emily. "I didn't think I was that good a shot. Well, thanks for the help."

He smiled. "I just hope the mayor doesn't find out who was responsible," he quipped.

The line moved by tables weighted with the community's bounty. Emily was faced with some difficult choices.

"That's Mrs. Long's potato salad," Shad offered. "She makes the best salad I've ever tasted." Or, "Mrs. Tennet's pumpkin pie. I'm surprised there's any left," and again, "I knew it. Not a scrap of Mr. Willmore's fudge cookies."

"Mr. Willmore's?"

"He brings them every year."

Emily chuckled. She couldn't imagine the no-nonsense schoolteacher standing over a hot oven baking fudge cookies.

"Which dish did you bring?" Shad wanted to know. Emily pointed out the custard, and he helped himself to the last serving.

When they had their plates filled to capacity, Shad directed her to the table where George and Molly Reilly ate with several neighbors.

Emily was content to sit and listen to the chatter and laughter. Occasionally a question was directed her way and she answered pleasantly.

"So what do you think of our Harvest Picnic?" a big farmer in bib overalls and a white shirt asked her.

"I love it," she answered honestly. "I haven't had so much fun since I was a school kid."

"I agree," enthused Molly Reilly. "I think we should have community picnics more often."

"Guess the next big social event is the school Christmas program," said a woman at the end of the table.

And so the talk and laughter continued. Emily snuggled into the warmth of belonging and wished that the evening could go on and on.

But eventually the women began to gather pots and dishes and the menfolk moved to take down the tables and load them on Eric Thorn's farm truck. One by one families with young children began to leave, the little ones whining at missing the fireworks.

Emily gathered her own things under a nearby poplar. A soft darkness was beginning to steal across the open fairgrounds. With the night came a coolness and Emily buttoned her coat.

"Did you bring a blanket?" Mrs. Reilly called as she walked by, looking for a suitable place on the ground.

"I thought you'd gone," answered Emily. "No. I didn't even think of a blanket."

"Well, come share mine," the woman offered, "and no, I didn't go. Shad drove George home to do the chores."

So Shad is gone. For a brief moment Emily felt a twinge of disappointment. Then she quickly put the thought out of her mind and went to catch up to Molly.

As soon as Big John was satisfied that it was dark enough to properly show off his fireworks, he sent the first one whistling into the sky. Emily had never watched such a display before, and she thrilled at the burst of sparkling color.

She was clapping enthusiastically with the crowd when she heard, "Are you warm enough?"

Emily looked up to discover that Shad had returned. He sat down beside her, situating himself to shield her from the cool night wind.

"I'm fine," whispered Emily, not sure why she whispered. Others were shouting or cheering with every new explosion of color and light.

All too soon the display ended and Emily found herself shivering. She wasn't sure if it was from excitement or cold. She stood to her feet and pulled her coat more tightly about her small frame.

You'll be sick, her father's voice played in her memory, and Emily prayed fervently that it might not be so.

"Can you come for dinner tomorrow?" Mrs. Reilly was asking as she folded up her blanket.

"I'd like that," Emily admitted. She had eaten with the Reilly's a number of times and always enjoyed it.

"Good. We'll see you after church."

And then Mrs. Reilly was gone, leaving Emily standing with Shad.

"Come on," he said, taking her arm. "I'll drive you home."

Emily eased her elbow from his hand. *Aren't you being a bit presumptuous?* she could have asked. *Not "may I," or "do you mind?" but "I'll drive you home."*

But Emily walked with Shad to his car and accepted the lift. The night was cool, her coat inadequate—and his company pleasing.

Chapter Eighteen

Troubles and Woes

The attendance at the worship service the next morning was down. Emily was sure that many of the children, and perhaps some of the adults, had found it a little more difficult to get up after yesterday's celebrations.

But George and Molly Reilly were there for Sunday school. Emily had let herself wonder if Shad would accompany them and worried about how it might affect her presentation of the lesson if he did.

"Shad volunteered to do the chores to give George the morning off," Molly volunteered, and Emily felt both disappointed and relieved.

After the service Molly approached Emily as she re-stacked hymnbooks. "I'm going to scoot on home and see to dinner," she said. "I'll send Shad in for you in half an hour or so."

Emily could only nod in agreement.

She finished tidying the small church and dumped the coins from the offering plate into the palm of her hand. She had been hoping for a bill or two—she was low on so many things she needed. And then she chided herself. She was not serving for the money. Times had been tough for everyone. The whole community was still feeling the effects of the recent drought. This was the first decent crop year for many of the area farmers, and Emily could well imagine that they had a lot of debts of their own. *I can't look to them for what I need any more than I can to my father,* she decided firmly.

"My God shall supply all your needs," she quoted aloud as she returned to her quarters to freshen up before her dinner engagement.

Shad arrived in the half hour stated and Emily was ready and waiting.

"How about bringing along walking shoes?" he suggested. "We might feel like a visit to the creek this afternoon."

Emily tried to keep the flush from her cheeks and went to get her other shoes.

"It's a beautiful fall day," Shad remarked as he reached for the shoes Emily carried. "It might be the last opportunity to take a walk before the winter snows come."

Emily agreed with a nod, waiting while Shad held the door of his car for her.

Shad broke the silence.

"Have you been out to Wesson Creek lately?"

Emily was puzzled. "I *live* in Wesson Creek," she reminded him, feeling a little silly but not knowing what else to say.

Shad smiled. "I mean the real Wesson Creek," he responded, and Emily suddenly knew what he meant.

"Oh-h—the creek. Is that what it's called?"

Shad nodded and Emily chuckled. "It makes perfect sense, doesn't it? I just hadn't heard it called by name before."

"So?" he asked. "Have you been back?"

"Many times," Emily admitted. "I go there as often as I can." She blushed, hoping Shad didn't think her trips to the creek had anything to do with him.

"So do I," Shad stated simply. "Ever since I was a kid."

"It's so—so peaceful there. Sort of—sort of like being in church," Emily dared to say.

She saw a slight shadow pass over Shad's face, but all he said was, "The most peaceful spot I know."

Dinner with the Reillys was enjoyable for Emily, who often ate alone. Shad seemed to fit well in the family of George and Molly. Emily thought it was a shame Molly had not had children herself, but certainly Shad acted as if he belonged.

After Emily had helped Molly with the dishes, Shad suggested they take their walk and Emily nodded in agreement and changed her shoes.

From the Reilly farm it was not as far to the creek as it was from where Emily lived in town, and soon the two were approaching the special pond.

Shad tossed his jacket over a fallen log and motioned for Emily to sit there. He flopped down on the grass beside the small stream.

"It's almost dry in some spots," he said as if to himself. "When I was a boy, it often overflowed its banks. The drought has changed that, but it's coming back now," he added on a more hopeful note.

"Those years were hard on everyone—everything," murmured Emily, watching the leaves floating on the surface. "I'm glad they're over."

"I'm not really sure they are," Shad surprised her by saying.

But he quickly changed the subject. "So where did you grow up?" he questioned, and the rest of the afternoon was spent exchanging bits of information. Emily found herself telling him about her father, Ina and Annabelle. She talked of her school years and her home church and even shared some about her two years at the Bible school.

They walked slowly back to the Reilly farm, feet shuffling through the autumn leaves, laughter coming easily as they shared a joke. Emily had never experienced an afternoon quite like it before.

As they came to the rails that divided the farmyard from the pasture land, Shad spoke softly to Emily. "I owe you an apology for the smart-alecky way I acted on the day we met by the creek."

Emily turned to look at him. "Oh, but—" she began, but he lifted a hand.

"But I do," he continued. "I had no reason to tease you as I did. I've felt sorry about it ever since."

"Really, I—I've thought nothing more of it," Emily fumbled.

"Well, I have—with embarrassment. Do you suppose we could sort of—start over?"

Emily laughed then, a merry, good-humored sound. "Well, I guess we have," she stated.

Shad smiled. "You'll forgive me?"

Emily's eyes sparkled as she turned to the young man and reached out a small hand to his. "Forgiven," she said simply, and Shad accepted the proffered hand and held it after the shake until he had helped her through the rail fence.

Back at the farmhouse, Molly had coffee ready. Emily didn't think she was hungry, but when she tasted the sandwiches, they were so good that she ate two of them.

The talk around the table was cheerful and lively and Emily wished it could go on forever.

"As much as I hate to," Shad finally said, "I've got to head back to Calgary. It'll be late by the time I get there."

Emily had not thought of him driving back that night.

George nodded his agreement. "Don't want you fallin' asleep on the way," he said, and Molly looked toward him with concern.

"I won't," Shad quickly assured her. "But I do need to get going." Then he turned to Emily. "If you're ready," he offered, "I'll drive you home."

Emily hurried to get her purse and her extra pair of shoes.

"I could walk," she told him as they started for his car. "It's not far and it would do me good."

"And deny me the privilege?" he teased.

"Well, it would save you some time," she continued.

"I'm not *that* pressed for time. It'll only take a few minutes to drive into town," he said as he helped her into the car.

After a moment or two of peaceful quiet, Shad said, "I'm not sure when I will get out again. Maybe not until Christmas."

"I'm hoping to go home at Christmastime," Emily said, thinking wistfully of her family.

Shad was silent, and Emily could sense that something was wrong.

"Yes!" Shad finally said softly. "I hope you can. Your family must really miss you."

Emily realized then that he had been wondering about seeing her again, and she had unthinkingly slammed the door on the possibility. She did not know what to say next.

"Of course, I will need to be here for Christmas Sunday," she said slowly.

He was quick to pick up the slightest invitation. "Maybe I could drive you home," he suggested almost shyly.

Emily felt her pulse quicken. It sounded almost like a date. What would her father think about her bringing a man home who did not share their faith? No, she could not do that. To take Shad home with her would be like acknowledging that he was her beau. And even beyond her father's concerns were her own. *I cannot think of him in that way—ever,* she told herself. There was no way she could accept the company of a non-Christian man except as a friend.

"I—I will need to do a great deal of praying about that," responded Emily.

Silence hung heavy about them.

"I take that as a no," Shad said softly.

"I guess it is," spoke Emily, nervously clasping her hands on her lap. "It isn't that I wouldn't like to say yes."

"I understand."

Emily wondered if he really did. She was near to tears and hoped fervently that he wouldn't notice.

When they arrived at the little church, Shad held Emily's car door for her. She gathered her purse and her shoes and climbed out slowly. She hated for things to end this way, but there seemed nothing else she could do.

"I enjoyed the day," Shad was saying close to her ear.

"I did, too," Emily echoed. She felt near to tears again.

"Goodbye, Emily."

But Emily choked on her answer. She hated to say goodbye, for she knew how final this goodbye would be. She didn't say, "Can't we just be friends?" for she knew instinctively that they both wished for more than friendship.

She blinked back the tears that threatened to fall, managed a wobbly smile and said a soft "Thank you" before leaving.

———

Emily was nearly blinded by tears as she stumbled down the walk leading to her door. She had heard the car reverse and then leave the front of the church. Shad was on his way back to the city. That was as it should be. That was as it *had* to be, but Emily couldn't deny the ache in her heart. She had never felt this way about a man before.

She was about to reach for her doorknob when she stumbled over something. Her eyes looked through the darkness for the cause and a gasp escaped her lips. It was Mr. Travis, collapsed on her doorstep! *Maybe he had been coming to me for help while I was out spending a frivolous day mooning over a man I can not have.* Frantic thoughts raced through her mind.

Emily dropped her shoes and purse and leaned over the man. He smelled of vomit. Emily felt both revolted and frightened. *He must be very ill. I have to get help right away.*

It was too far to Dr. Andrew's. She ran to the closest person.

"Mr. John! Mr. John!" she cried, beating loudly with her fist on the mercantile door. "Please. Please! Let me in."

When the door opened, Big John stood there, a slice of unfinished bread and butter in his hand, his jaws still working on the last bite he had taken.

"What is it?" he asked, concern in his voice. But Emily was shaking so hard she could not speak.

He tossed the unfinished bread onto a nearby counter and grasped Emily by the shoulders.

"What is it?" he asked again.

Emily found her voice then. "It's—it's Mr. Travis."

Big John's eyes flew wide. He steadied Emily with one huge hand and studied her trembling lips. "What did he do to ya?" he asked sternly.

"No—no, not to me. He—he's sick. He collapsed—on my doorstep. Quickly—he needs help."

Big John strode toward the door. He still had not released Emily's arm, and she scrambled to keep up.

Mr. Travis was lying right where she had left him.

Emily pointed one shaky finger. "He's—he's fainted or collapsed or something."

Big John pushed her back and stepped deliberately in front of her as he moved forward, stopping by the fallen man.

"He's stinkin' drunk," he hissed as he bent over him. "He's stinkin' drunk like he always is."

Emily gasped. She had never encountered a man in Mr. Travis's condition.

"The scum," hissed Big John again, raising to his feet and pushing the inert man's arm to his side with a booted foot. "If he weren't on yer doorstep, I'd leave him right where he is." And Big John spat in the grass.

"Is—is he often like—like this?" faltered Emily.

"Only on the weekdays an' every weekend," responded the big man with a sarcastic growl.

"What about—what about Mrs. Travis? Does she know?" whispered Emily as though she were afraid her remark might betray the secret.

Big John looked at her steadily. "I guess she knows," he said deliberately; "seein' how he knocks her around whenever he can stand up straight."

Emily's breath caught in her throat.

"Where ya been all yer life, kid?" John asked gruffly. "Where'd ya think she got all those bruises? Runnin' into doors?"

Emily just shook her head. *So—so the whole town knows the truth, and I never guessed. Poor, poor Mrs. Travis,* she thought to herself.

Big John hoisted the fallen man to his back and carried him off down the walk.

Emily picked up her purse and shoes, stepped across the vomit on her walk and let herself in her door. She felt sick herself as she carried a pail of water out to slosh her step clean once again.

Later, Big John was back. Without a word he went to work, placing a sturdy lock on Emily's door. Emily watched in silence.

When he finished, he lifted his eyes to hers. "An' see thet ya use it," he said, and then was gone.

Chapter Nineteen

Winter

Emily felt awkward and ill-at-ease the next time she had to go to the Travis farm to pick up her team. Mrs. Travis waved her usual greeting and called to see if Emily had time to stop for tea. She wished she could decline but really had no excuse. She found it difficult to converse naturally with the older woman now that she knew the dreadful secret.

Emily even found herself inspecting the woman's face to determine if she had any new bruises. She caught herself, lowered her eyes in shame and prayed silently that God would help her to show the same love and concern for Mrs. Travis and her children as she had previously done. Yes, and for Mr. Travis, too.

The children greeted Emily just as warmly as ever, and that helped her to feel a bit more relaxed.

Rena crowded up against Emily's skirts and showed her the new kitten she had discovered in the barn.

"Would you like a kitten?" Rena asked generously as Emily's hand stroked the soft fur.

"I love kittens," Emily confided, "but I'm not sure it would be a good idea for me to have one at the parsonage."

"Why? She could eat your mice."

Emily cringed. She did hate the mice that plagued her small home. "Does she already hunt mice?"

"Well—no, not yet. But she will when she gets bigger. Her mommy catches lots of mice. I always see her taking one to her babies," Rena went on, her pale blue eyes full of the immensity of her knowledge.

Emily's hand moved from the kitten to the head of the child.

What a beautiful little thing she would be if she had dainty hair ribbons and prettier clothes, thought Emily, and immediately checked herself. Mrs. Travis was doing all she could for her little family. It was impossible for her to do more under her trying circumstances.

Timmie came over and lifted the kitten from Rena's arms. "I should take her back," he explained softly to his sister. "She might be hungry again." Then he turned to Emily. "There are three others at the barn if you'd like to choose one." Then he added hurriedly, "They have to grow for a couple more weeks, and then they'll be ready to eat from a dish."

"I'll think about it," Emily promised with a warm smile. She did have plenty of milk from Mrs. Reilly—and if the kitten would be a good mouser, she might be worth her keep at the parsonage. Emily would enjoy the company, without doubt.

———

Winter came softly to the land. Emily had retired one night with feathery flakes drifting slowly down from the heavens and awoke the next morning to a world of white. It was a beautiful sight, the morning sun making the whole drab world outside Emily's kitchen window one glorious wonderland.

Midafternoon it began to snow again and continued on throughout the evening and into the night. By the next morning Emily had eight inches of fluffy snow on her walks. It was Sunday, and Emily did not want her little congregation struggling through the new snowfall to reach her church door.

As she swept vigorously with her kitchen broom, a voice from behind her said, "Hi! Need some help?" It was Nicky, Sophie's oldest.

"Mom spotted ya," he said with a grin. "She said ya won't get nowhere with that." He pointed at the broom in her hands.

Emily smiled. "It's all I have. Hadn't even thought to prepare myself with a shovel."

"I've got one," said Nicky, holding a battered but serviceable shovel out for Emily to see. "I'll shovel and you sweep behind me."

Emily thought it was a good plan. They worked as a team, their breath puffing out before them in little silvery clouds.

"Look," called Nicky, "I'm a dragon."

Emily shared in his laughter.

In the weeks ahead, winter was no longer kind to the folks of the town and community of Wesson Creek. Emily watched the snow become deeper and deeper in the piles beside her walk. Each time she shovelled more onto the pile, she thanked the Lord for His answer to her prayer for a shovel of her own. One day, quite unexpectedly, she had spotted a handle protruding from the snow by the backyard fence. Emily tugged and pulled until a shovel made an appearance. She hadn't noticed it earlier in the year because she didn't need it. She couldn't help but say "Thank you, Lord!" right then and there. But then she took a closer look. The handle was broken. It had been put back together, but the patching too had cracked.

At first Emily had felt keen disappointment, but then she brightened at a sudden idea. Maybe for a few of her precious coins, she could buy a new handle. She would pay a visit to the store next door.

Big John McMann stood behind the counter. Emily didn't dread seeing him as much as she had in the past. He was still gruff and curt and still plagued her with jests and testing each time that they did business, but Emily sensed a softening in his demeanor.

"Good morning," she said brightly as she approached his counter.

"Whatcha got?" he growled in return.

"I've been in need of a shovel," said Emily, her eyes reflecting her excitement. "I found this one by the back fence. Can the handle be fixed—or replaced?"

"Fixed, no. But replaced, no problem."

"How much would a handle be?" asked Emily timidly.

"Let's see it," said Big John, and Emily struggled to lift the shovel across the counter.

"Reckon I could put on a new one fer fifty cents," he growled.

"*You* will fix it?" Emily could scarcely believe her ears. She'd been sure she would need to do the replacing herself, though she had no idea how to go about it, and certainly had no tools if it required that.

"Comes with the price of the handle," said Big John, not even lifting his eyes.

"I'll—I'll take it," responded Emily and opened her purse to carefully count out the coins.

But Big John did not hold out his hand for the change.

"Why don't ya jest throw those coins in the offerin' on Sunday?"

Emily could not believe her ears. She looked at the big man uncertainly. He stared back at her.

"Don't believe none in this here gospel-stuff," he hastened to inform Emily, "but always did like to carry a bit of insurance."

Emily's mouth dropped open, her eyes grew big, and then she slowly laid the change on the counter.

"I'm afraid this Policy is all or nothing, Mr. John. It's not insurance—it's assurance." She held his eyes steadily.

Big John reached down, picked up the coins and tossed them into his till. He still said nothing, nor did Emily.

"I'll have it ready fer ya to pick up in the mornin'," he finally said with a nod toward the shovel in his hands.

"Thank you," replied Emily softly. "I appreciate that," and she quietly left the store.

––––––––

The winter temperatures dropped until Emily spent most of some days hauling in wood so she could keep her little house warm and have the small church somewhat comfortable for Sundays. She was alarmed that the woodpile she had considered so huge was rapidly decreasing in size. But Mr. Reilly noticed too and told her not to be concerned. He was arranging with neighborhood men to add to the pile in plenty of time to meet Emily's need.

What did worry Emily was the depletion of her food supplies. Her vegetables, carefully stored in the cellar beneath her kitchen, were nearly gone. But it was her nearly empty cupboard that gave her the most concern. By now it was not at all uncommon for women of the community to drop in for a warming cup of tea or coffee after a cold drive to town. Emily welcomed the opportunity to show hospitality. Some of the women who came did not attend church, and Emily felt the visits were a wonderful time for them to get to know one another better and perhaps give her occasion to share her faith in a nonthreatening setting.

But these visits were hard on her resources. Still she was determined that the women would always be welcome, that she would always try to supply them with tea—or coffee—to warm them and, as long as possible, a cookie or piece of cake to enjoy with the hot drink.

The flour was the first to give out. Then the sugar crock emptied—except for one cupful that Emily set aside for her visitors who took sugar with their cup of tea. Emily was glad she always had cream. Mrs. Reilly kept her in constant supply of milk and eggs.

Emily was also thankful for the eggs. She never needed to go hungry as long as she had eggs in the house—she cooked eggs as many ways as she knew how.

"If I can just manage at least tea and coffee until I go home for Christmas," Emily said to herself over and over. "Then Father will see to it that I get some supplies again."

Emily was looking forward to Christmas and seeing her family again. It would be wonderful to just relax away from all her responsibilities. She loved the work, but it was a constant drain on all her reserves.

She had planned a children's Christmas program. All her Sunday school children were involved and met at the church for practice after school on Tuesdays and again on Saturdays. Along with all the rest of Emily's duties, rehearsals certainly made her days busy. She prayed for continued health so she could keep up to the strenuous schedule. Just carrying in the wood to heat the church on so many occasions was a constant chore.

Emily felt a cold coming on, but she fought against it with all her strength and managed to keep going.

The night of the program arrived, and Emily was very pleased to see her small congregation of between ten and fifteen grow to thirty-nine.

Oh, if only we could have the church this full all the time! she enthused, carefully studying the audience to see where she needed to concentrate her calling on people after the Christmas season.

―――――

As Emily swept and tidied the little church the next day, she felt happier than she had for weeks. The program had been a great success. The children who took part had been so happy with the enthusiasm of the crowd. Those who had attended the little church for the first time seemed quite delighted with the evening. Emily could see great possibilities for growth now that more of the community had been introduced to the small congregation. Perhaps after Christmas there would be a real upswing in progress.

Christmas! Such a beautiful, powerful word to Emily. She stopped her sweeping, thrilled at the thought that God had actually given His Son. What a wonderful love gift to the world—to her.

Christmas! A time to see family again. Emily suddenly realized just how homesick she was. She had not really allowed herself to think of it before, but she missed her father. She missed Ina and Annabelle. She missed her familiar room, the warm coziness of the farmhouse kitchen, the security of warm fires and full cupboards and no responsibilities to make the provision. Emily could scarcely wait to reach home again. Her family was coming for her by car on the morrow, and she would have a full week at home before returning to the duties of the Wesson Creek parish.

After finishing her work in the little church, Emily returned to her rooms in a dreamy mood. With a thoughtful smile she took up her purse with its few cents and slipped into her coat and boots.

Miss McMann was busy adding stock to the shelves. Emily called a greeting, and the woman turned. "Feelin' cheery, ain't ya," she commented, but she didn't appear to share Emily's holiday spirit.

"I get to go home for Christmas tomorrow," Emily offered in explanation, and the woman nodded. But no smile filled her eyes.

Emily presented a short list of items and held her breath while the woman totalled the amount. Emily sighed with relief when she found she would be able to cover the cost of the purchases. She counted out the coins. She had two thin dimes left—but it was enough. Emily picked up her small bag of items and left happily for the parsonage.

In her warm little kitchen, Emily set to work at once, snatches of "O Little Town of Bethlehem" coming from her lips as she worked. Sophie and Mrs. Travis had always been so kind to her. She would say her thank you at this Christmas season by doing some baking for their children.

When the cookies had cooled, Emily decorated them with the resourcefulness of the creative in strained circumstances. When she was done she smiled at the snowmen, angels and holly wreaths. They looked rather cute in spite of the little with which she had to work. She hoped the children would enjoy them, and Emily carefully bundled up her little offerings of love and set out.

At Sophie's cafe she found the place bristling with activity. Sophie was so busy serving coffee and pie that Emily herself picked up the pot and for a half hour scrambled back and forth to keep up with the customers.

When at last the Christmas shoppers had drifted back out to the street, Sophie brushed back her hair with a weary hand and invited Emily to share a cup of coffee.

"I'd love to," said Emily, "but I need to get out to the Travises. I have some cookies for the children, and if I don't make it there soon, I'll be walking in the dark."

"Would ya like Nicky to go with ya?" offered Sophie.

"Oh no. No, I'll be just fine. I've walked that road so often I'm sure I could walk it in the dark if I had to," Emily assured her and shrugged into her coat.

Sophie surprised her by giving her a quick hug. "Thanks for the cookies," she whispered. "The kids'll love 'em. I never seem to get time to do anything special for 'em."

Emily smiled and returned the hug warmly.

Walking briskly to the Travis farm, Emily noticed the air was colder and a wind was stirring the bare branches of the trees along the road. The sun had disappeared behind a heavy cloud cover. Emily increased her speed.

But as Emily hastened up the drive toward the Travis home, she heard a commotion coming from the farmhouse. Angry shouts were followed by shrieks of an even more intense nature. Emily stopped mid-stride, not knowing what she should do.

"Don't go in there," a muffled voice warned from the shadows, and Emily turned to see Rena cowering in a corner of the shrubbery, a skimpy blanket pressed tightly around her slight body.

Emily hurried to the child and drew the little body close to her. Rena shivered as Emily held her, and Emily wasn't sure if it was from fright or the cold.

"You can't stay out here," Emily whispered. "You'll freeze."

"I—I can't go in," chattered the child.

"But—" began Emily and then asked instead. "Where are Claude and Timmie?"

"Claude ran away from home—last week," said the child simply. "I—I think Timmie might be in the barn—or the chicken coop."

Emily pulled her closer. The noise from the house intensified. *Something must be done. But what?* Emily prayed as she stood helplessly, sheltering the child.

Sudden silence. Then the door opened and a tight, sobbing voice called out into the gathering darkness, "Rena. Timmie. You can come in. Rena."

"Guess Pa's sleepin' now," shivered Rena through tightly clenched teeth, and she stirred in Emily's arms.

Emily felt tears streaming down her own cheeks. She brushed at them with the back of her mittened hand. *How can they live like this?* she wondered and let the little girl go.

"Timmie," came the call again.

Emily could see Mrs. Travis standing in the open doorway. Her dress was torn at the waistline and the skirt sagged sloppily into the snow on the doorstep. Her hair was dishevelled and, even from where Emily stood, she could see a small stream of blood as it coursed its way down and over the cheekbone. Mrs. Travis raised a shaky hand to wipe at it with the kitchen towel she held.

"Mrs. Travis," Emily called in a whispery voice as she led small Rena toward the woman. "May I help you? You could spend the night—" But the woman silenced her with a quick wave of her hand.

"We'll be all right now. He's sleepin'. He'll be okay in the mornin'," and she reached out to pull her shaking daughter into her own arms.

Emily hesitated, then knew that the woman needed to get back to her kitchen to tend to her own wounds. And Rena needed to be tucked close to the fire to chase the chill from her little bones.

Emily stepped back and turned to go. "I'll—I'll be praying for you," she whispered, but it seemed such a weak, empty promise to make under such circumstances. Emily drew a deep, shaky breath and turned away.

Timmie was coming toward her from the barn. He too was not dressed to be outdoors on a wintry night. Hay clung to his clothing and hair, and Emily guessed that he had burrowed his way into the hay in an effort to keep warm—or hidden.

Emily suddenly remembered her errand. She still had the package of cookies in her hand.

"I forgot," she said to the small boy. "I came to give you these—to wish you a—a Merry Christmas." Emily could scarcely choke the last words from her throat. A Merry Christmas? Hardly. Not with what Emily had just witnessed.

Timmie took the offered gift and in spite of his circumstance, he smiled and thanked her politely.

Emily turned from the small boy and directed her steps toward the road and home. The tears running freely down her face were soon frozen upon her cheeks.

How frightful! Emily mourned to herself. *What fear and pain they live with! Oh, God, there must be some way to help them. There must. Show us. Show me what we can do.*

Christmas! The most beautiful, special time of year—and they lived with abuse and suffering. Sobs choked Emily's throat.

It seemed that Mr. Travis had his own unique way of celebrating.

Chapter Twenty

Mixed Blessings

The next day a message came to Emily by way of Miss Mc-Mann. Emily was at her kitchen table, her small valise packed, her coat and hat nearby. She was dressed and ready to leave for home when the car arrived to pick her up.

At the sound of the knock on her door she rose to her feet, smiling softly to herself, and grabbed her coat as she went to bid a welcome to whichever member of her family had come to fetch her.

She was startled to see Miss McMann, but she quickly regained her composure and smiled.

"Come in," she offered. "Please come in. I'm expecting my ride anytime. They are sending over a car to take me home for Christmas. I thought that—"

But Miss McMann interrupted. "Thet's why I came. A call jest came. Yer father telephoned and asked if we'd tell ya thet they're delayed. Something's the matter with the car. They have to fix it before they can come. It won't be till tomorrow."

Emily was deeply disappointed. She had so counted on today. She had everything ready. She had nothing more that needed to be done. She—why, whatever would she do with another day on her hands? Besides, tomorrow was the twenty-fourth. Christmas Eve. She had wanted to be there to help Ina and Annabelle with the last-minute preparations for Christmas.

Emily turned back to Miss McMann, her shawl wrapped carelessly about her shoulders, her hair still sprinkled with quickly disappearing snowflakes.

"Thank you. Thank you for trudging through the snow to bring me word," she said and even managed a smile. "Would you have a cup of tea?" she offered rather awkwardly. Emily immediately remembered that she had just disposed of the last few drops of cream.

"I have to get back to the store," Miss McMann answered. "John is away."

Emily thanked her again and the woman left, promising Emily that she would one day come again. The promise brought a stir of excitement to Emily's disappointed heart. Miss McMann had not as yet been to Emily's house for tea.

But after the woman left, Emily felt the tears fill her eyes. She brushed impatiently at them with the back of her hand.

Don't be a child, she scolded herself. *You can wait until tomorrow. Get busy and find something to do.*

Emily looked around her small home. Everything was in place. Her simple furnishings were easy to keep in order. A good supply of wood lined the wall of her small entry. She had also carried an ample supply for the little church. There was no need to carry more.

She could not bake. Her cupboard was once again empty of flour, and only the one little bit of tea-sugar remained. The two dimes in her purse were not sufficient to buy more.

I'll go over to Sophie's and see what I can do, she determined. She pulled her coat over her traveling dress and left a note on her door concerning her whereabouts if her ride should come early.

She was about to leave when she thought, *What if I get to cleaning or baking at Sophie's?* She decided she'd better change into something more practical.

She was glad she had, for after explaining her predicament to Sophie and sharing a quick cup of hot apple cider, Emily entered the upstairs living quarters and set to work with the children, cleaning house and making simple decorations for the Christmas tree. Then they worked together to bake sugar cookies. By then the cafe had closed and Sophie joined them. They shared a supper of pancakes, shaped like little animals and snowmen, and by the time Emily had helped Sophie with the dishes and read a story to the children, it was late.

The day turned out well, after all, she smiled to herself as she let herself in the door. *And tomorrow I get to go home.*

The wind, which had blown all day, rattled the loose pipe that fed Emily's rain barrel, and made the gate creak on its hinges. She snuggled more closely under her blankets and prayed that the Travis children might be safely tucked into their beds, not cowering in some corner where the wind tore at their clothing . . . and then she fell asleep.

———

The wind was still blowing the next morning. Emily hastily prepared and ate a simple breakfast. She had no milk or cream, having disposed of her supply in preparation for being gone, so she again ate eggs—and eggs without anything else. *Oh, well,* she thought, *I'll soon be home for a turkey dinner.*

But as Emily washed her few dishes and tidied her small kitchen, Miss McMann knocked at her door. Another message had come. The roads had drifted closed. The car was unable to make it through. They felt so bad. They would miss her.

She would not make it home for Christmas.

For one moment Emily thought of her strong team of horses. They could drag her buggy through the drifts. If she left immediately she could make it home Christmas night. She might even make it for—but Emily checked herself. It was a foolish idea. She could well freeze in the process or lose her way in the storm.

She nodded her head and mumbled her thanks to Miss Mc-Mann. She did not even extend an invitation to tea as she knew she should. The woman seemed to understand and hurried from her door.

Emily did not fight the tears this time. She sank into the chair by the table, laid her head on her folded arms and cried until her whole body shook.

It was dreadful to be alone in a storm. But it was even more dreadful when it happened at Christmastime. Emily wept until she could weep no more.

———

Emily was grateful that Sophie had heard of her Christmas plight and invited her to share simple celebrations with her and her little family.

It helped to ease her pain at not being with her own family.

She even received a Christmas gift later in the day—one that brought tears to her eyes.

She had left Sophie's early so that she might add wood to her fire, and had just removed her coat when there was a knock on her door. To Emily's surprise, Timmie and Rena stood there when she answered the rap.

"Come in," Emily invited, fear gripping her heart. *Is there trouble at home again?* she wondered, but the children did not appear frightened.

"We came to say Merry Christmas," said Rena as she moved into the warmth of the kitchen, a gleam in her eye.

"Why, thank you," began Emily, but Timmie could not hold back his excitement.

"We brought you something," he declared, his eyes mirroring the glow in Rena's.

Emily looked at their empty hands, puzzled.

Timmie was fiddling with coat buttons, and Emily noticed that he wore no mittens. Then he reached inside his jacket and withdrew a black and white kitten with green-flecked eyes and a pert pink nose. Around its neck a worn hair bow had been carefully tied.

"They are big enough now," explained Timmie with a grin.

"This is the prettiest one," added Rena, one hand gently stroking the soft fur of the tiny animal.

"It's beautiful," agreed Emily, the tears forming in her eyes, and she reached out for the kitten that Timmie held toward her.

For a moment she could not speak. Her eyes brimmed and her throat constricted. *They have come through the drifts of snow to bring me a Christmas kitten. A real gift of love—from my own needy, caring Magi.* Emily fought hard for control.

"Is it a boy or a girl?" she asked when she could trust herself to speak.

"A boy," answered Timmie. "Mama said a girl might be a bother. You'd not know what to do with all the babies."

Emily smiled at the candid appraisal.

"Does he have a name?" she asked, stroking the kitten's back and being thanked with a soft purr.

Rena bobbed her head vigorously. "I named him," she informed Emily, "but you can call him whatever you want. He won't mind."

"What did you call him?" Emily asked.

"Walter," said Rena.

Emily wondered if she managed to hide her surprise. Walter seemed a strange name for a kitten.

"Well, if his name is Walter, we'll call him Walter," she said with finality.

Rena beamed.

"Now," suggested Emily, "let's allow Walter to explore his new home while I get you some hot chocolate."

Then Emily grabbed her coat. "You wait here," she told the youngsters. "I'll be right back."

Never had Emily borrowed from neighbors before, but now she hastened to Sophie's. She could not let the children start out for home in the cold without warming up their small bodies.

The winter was a difficult one for Emily. Often she went to bed with little in her stomach. Her cupboard was seldom supplied with the items she really needed to give her proper nourishment. And now she had to share her milk with Walter as well. She wondered that she was not sick more. All around her, colds and flu kept her parishioners in bed. And whenever possible, Emily called on those who were ill, offering what little help and encouragement she was able. She did suffer from a cold on two occasions and a flu sent her to bed for two days, but for the most part, she managed to keep going.

Severe illnesses kept Dr. Andrew busy day and night for a number of weeks in February. He looked haggard and weary when Emily met him on the street.

Then word came that old Mr. Woodrow had passed away. He was from a family Emily did not know well. She had called there on two occasions but had received a very cool reception. She immediately recognized an opportunity to reach out to the elderly widow.

It was a miserable drive out to the Woodrow farm. The long winter that had piled high drifts of snow was gradually giving way to the mud of early spring. Emily urged her team through the ruts and mud holes, coaxing them to quicken their pace even though the buggy wheels clogged with the heavy gumbo.

At the farm home she found the new widow alone. Mrs. Woodrow had no family to share her mourning, and it seemed that the neighbors either had not yet heard the news or else did not know quite how to respond.

The woman's eyes did not soften as she saw Emily, but she did nod her head for Emily to enter as she held the door.

"I'm so sorry about the—the . . ." Emily did not know how to choose her words. She had heard that the couple had done nothing but quarrel for the past twenty years. "The death of your husband," Emily finished lamely.

Mrs. Woodrow just nodded again.

"I came to see if there is anything I can do."

The woman pushed some papers off a chair, letting them fall to the floor in disarray, and indicated that Emily could sit down.

Emily removed her mud-spattered coat and, without invitation, hung it on a crowded hook on the wall and took the offered chair.

After waiting for what she considered a suitable time, Emily cleared her throat. "Do you need any help with—the—the arrangements?" she asked softly.

"You bury?" asked the woman bluntly.

The words surprised Emily. "Well, no—I have never—never conducted a funeral service," she stammered, but quickly added as she saw the woman's expression, "but I'm sure that Rev. Witt—our district superintendent—would come or send another minister."

The woman looked relieved.

"We need a coffin," the woman said.

"Would you like me to have one sent out from town?" Emily asked.

Mrs. Woodrow nodded.

"When would you like the funeral?" Emily continued.

"The quicker, the better," the woman responded without hesitation.

"I'll see how quickly I can get someone," Emily promised, and Mrs. Woodrow seemed satisfied with that.

"Where is the—the deceased?" Emily asked in a hesitant voice.

"In the back room," the woman said with a nod of her head. "I been sleepin' here on the floor."

Emily looked around her. *The body is right here in this house!* She shivered, then turned her attention to the blankets lying in a heap by the kitchen stove.

Emily rose. "Is there anything else I can do before I go?" she asked. The woman stood and moved toward the aforementioned back room. Without a word to Emily, Mrs. Woodrow opened the door, entered the room, and Emily could hear her moving about.

Soon she was back, a worn, threadbare black suit and a white shirt in her arms.

"Here's his buryin' things," she said to Emily. "Guess he should be washed and shaved."

Emily stared blankly at the woman. The woman was placing the items in Emily's hands and Emily took them dumbly, the truth slowly sinking in. *She expects me to prepare the body for burial.* Emily swallowed and tried to speak but the words would not come.

"There's water in the teakettle, and the basin is there on the corner stand. His razor is on that shelf."

Woodenly, Emily moved forward. She poured water into the basin, gathered together the shaving tools and lifted the much-used towel from the peg. Then, her arms laden, she moved toward the back room.

It was cold in the room. A strange odor seemed to fill the place. Enough light came from the small window to outline the still form on the bed. His eyes were fixed in a blank stare at the ceiling above his head and his mouth, empty of most of his teeth, hung open. Emily shuddered and wanted to run. She had never touched a dead body before, let alone prepared one for burial. She had no idea what was to be done.

She closed her eyes and another shudder ran through her. "I can't do this," she whispered. "I can't."

But a new thought flashed into her mind. *This might be the only bridge to reaching the woman out there.*

Emily steeled herself and set down her basin. She laid the clothes carefully on the bed and prepared herself for the ordeal ahead.

"Dear God, help me," she prayed. "I need your help in a way I've never needed it before," and Emily reached out a shaking hand to touch the arm of the man who lay on the bed.

It was stiff and cold to her tentative touch. A shiver went all through her, but she straightened her shoulders, pressed her lips tightly together and began the unwanted task.

———

Rev. Witt was not available, so Fred Russell was sent in answer to Emily's plea. Emily was disappointed that Agatha did not accompany him, but their baby was due any day.

Emily was relieved to see Fred and to turn the situation over to someone who had some experience in handling it.

Mrs. Woodrow wanted no church service.

"I just want him buried," she insisted in a hard voice, and Emily was glad that it was Fred who would be supervising the arrangements.

The neighborhood men prepared the grave. A number stood silently while the coffin was lowered and a few words from Scripture were spoken. Emily felt rather empty inside, as if something important wasn't quite finished.

As the small crowd drifted away, Emily thought she should invite Fred for supper but didn't know what she could serve him. He solved her dilemma by excusing himself. He was anxious to get back home to Agatha, and Emily nodded understandingly.

As she watched him go, she was glad the day was over. Mr. Woodrow's widow had already gotten a ride home from a neighbor. Emily walked from the cemetery, down the road toward the little town.

She felt discouraged as she trudged along. Mrs. Woodrow had not so much as muttered a "thank you" to anyone who had been involved in helping her.

Emily passed the post office and decided to check for mail. She didn't get much, but occasionally a letter came from home or from one of her Bible school friends. Emily would welcome such a letter now.

There were two pieces of mail that awaited her. One was a letter from the district superintendent with news of the coming conference. Emily was excited to learn that she would be expected to be there. She would see many of her old friends again. *That's almost as good as going home!* she exulted.

The second letter puzzled her as she looked at the bold script and reread the return address. *It's a letter from Ross Norris. Imagine that! Ross, of all people! Why would he be writing me?* Emily had been interested in him when they were in Bible school, but she was sure they hadn't said more than a dozen words to each other during the whole time. Ruth wrote that Olive had broken her engagement to Ross, Emily remembered. Excitedly she held the envelope, but she resisted the urge to open it immediately and made herself wait until she was in the privacy of the parsonage. But that resolve did not stop the questions from chasing through her mind.

Chapter Twenty-one

Conference

Ross's letter was full of newsy bits concerning their Bible school classmates. It was open and friendly, but Emily found herself still puzzling as she read. *Why has he written—to me? He's never done so in the past. Perhaps I'm trying to read more into it than I should. Why should it be so strange for a man to think of a former classmate and drop her a friendly note?* Emily assured herself that the letter was nothing more than that.

But an odd little feeling still tugged at the corners of her mind—especially when she read the last paragraph.

I have been doing some serious thinking recently. I saw Lacey at a youth meeting. He's really changed a lot since our Bible school days. He is so excited and happy about the chance to be in the ministry that I began to wonder if I had missed something important. I am even giving some consideration to entering the ministry myself.

Emily felt excitement course through her. *A minister? Ross? How wonderful if—* But Emily quickly checked herself and carefully folded the letter. She turned her attention instead to the other letter and the information on the coming conference, welcoming a change and a time for some spiritual refreshment.

Emily would take the train to Regis for the conference. On the day of the departure she was up early, took Walter to Sophie's to be cared for by the children, checked and rechecked her packed valise and tried desperately to get her unruly hair neatly tucked beneath her deaconess bonnet.

"Be sure to wear your deaconess badge," Mrs. Witt had instructed all the girls at their orientation meeting. "It lets the public know you are a member of the ministry."

Emily took her button from her handkerchief box and pinned it securely to the lapel of her coat. It wouldn't do to lose it.

She was at the train station much earlier than necessary, but she was too excited and nervous to stay at home. Nicky and Johnnie came by on some errand for Sophie and couldn't resist stopping to chat.

"We're gonna have fun with Walter."

"Are ya takin' the train?"

"How far are ya goin'?"

"When will ya come back?"

"Have ya ever been on a train before?"

"How do ya know when to get off?"

Their questions flowed thick and fast and Emily could not get one answered before the next one came at her. But their chatter did help the wait to pass more quickly.

Emily had another visitor at the train station. Mr. Travis came by, walking a fairly straight line. He had even made an attempt to comb his hair. He gave her a gap-toothed grin. His clothes were still hanging on a frail body and his chin was raggedly shaven, but he did tip his hat and bid her a good morning.

Emily knew he wanted to chat, but she felt herself becoming at once angry and frightened. A man who would beat his wife and children might do anything. Emily did not encourage a conversation.

At length he turned and made his uneven way toward the downtown. Emily was relieved to see him go.

Then a thought flashed through her mind. *Christ died for him, too, you know.* Emily's cheeks grew hot as she thought about her distant treatment of him.

I'm sorry, Lord, she prayed. *You love Mr. Travis—help me to love him with your love.* Emily spent the rest of the time on the station platform praying for the whole Travis family. *And poor little Claude. Such a child to be off on his own. I wonder . . . I wonder where he is and if he is okay,* she thought as she prayed for him too.

Emily jerked to attention as she heard the whistle of the train. The out-dated passenger car was not a fancy one, but Emily sighed with relief as she settled her valise under the worn seat. With a bit of a jerk they were on their way. Emily looked out to see the familiar sights of her little town slip by. *I'm a real deaconess, and I'm on my way to the conference,* she let herself exult.

As they passed through the countryside, Emily recognized many of the farms she had visited. One was the farm of Mrs. Woodrow, and a chill went through Emily again as she thought of her experience preparing a body for burial.

"Well, it didn't kill me," she mused. "I'm still here—and well. But I certainly wouldn't want to repeat the ordeal. I'm sure Ruth will laugh when she hears about the squeamish Emily," and Emily smiled in spite of herself. It would be so much fun to have a good talk with Ruth again.

The blue-uniformed conductor came through the passenger car calling out "Tickets! Tickets!"

Emily fidgeted with her empty purse. She did hope she wouldn't have any explaining to do.

But when the conductor reached her, he looked squarely at her deaconess button, tipped his cap, smiled and said, "Good morning, ma'am. Have a good trip," then passed on to the next passenger. Emily breathed a sigh of relief and settled back into the worn plush of the seat.

Emily decided to pay particular attention to each town they came to so she wouldn't lose track of where they were. When Emily had traveled the train to and from Bible school, she had not had to pass through other towns but had always climbed down from the passenger car at the first stop. It would not do for her to miss her departure at Regis. But before they reached the first town, the conductor came through again.

"Swifton! Swifton!" he called loudly. "All out for Swifton."

Emily audibly sighed her relief. If he did that with each stop she would not need to worry about missing her own station. She leaned back against the seat and tried to enjoy the ride.

What if, for some reason, he does not call Regis? Emily thought. *I'd better be keeping track, just in case.*

But the conductor did not forget Emily's station. In fact, when he came through he looked directly at Emily as he called out Regis. Then he stopped at her seat and smiled again.

"Getting off here, ma'am?" he asked her, and Emily nodded, wondering how he knew.

"We bring a number of folks to conference every year," he explained. He reached for her valise and cautioned her gently,

"Just stay in your seat until the train fully stops. Sometimes the train jerks a bit."

Emily nodded her thank you and waited for the jerk. The conductor then led the way down the narrow aisle, took Emily's arm for the dismount down the iron steps, and handed her the valise.

"Have a good conference," he bade her with another smile and a doff of his cap and then he was gone again.

"Emily!"

Emily wheeled to meet Ruth in a warm embrace.

———

The next two days were spent in meetings. Emily loved singing hymns of praise with the fellow worshipers. She thirstily drank in the messages that were given. She felt excitement to think she actually had a vote in the decisions of the church; and at mealtime or after the sessions were over for the day, she eagerly visited with old school friends and new acquaintances. Mostly the talk was about the ministries in which they were involved. Some brought glowing reports, others, like Emily, faced difficulty and challenge in trying to get a little work started.

But the time after the evening services belonged to Emily and Ruth, and instead of getting much-needed sleep, they often talked well into the night hours in the darkness of their shared room.

Ruth was still excited about being able to preach. "If only I didn't have to go calling," she told Emily candidly, "I would just love the work."

"Calling? That's the part I like most," Emily said in amazement.

"Oh-h, I dread it. I put it off—and put it off for as long as I can. I would much sooner be pouring myself into my next sermon."

Emily began to laugh softly. "We should be a team," she decided. "I would do the calling and you could do the preaching."

Ruth joined in her laughter.

"I do have some problems, though," confided Emily. "One in particular that really troubles me. One of my parishioners has a drunkard for a husband. When he drinks, which is often from what I can gather, he beats her. He would likely beat the children, too, if he could catch them, but they usually run and hide and the mother takes the brunt of his fury. It just sickens me. I don't know what to do."

Ruth sympathized but had little advice to offer. "Why don't you ask Rev. Witt?" she said at last. "He might know of some way to deal with it."

Emily decided to talk with him at the first opportunity. Then the conversation changed direction.

"Do you have a . . . a friend?" asked Ruth hesitantly.

"Well, I guess Sophie is my best friend, even though—"

But Ruth's chuckle stopped Emily.

"I meant a male friend," she informed Emily.

Emily blushed and was glad for the darkness that hid her embarrassment. Immediately her thoughts flew to Shad. But she had not heard from him for months.

"No," she answered in the darkness.

There was silence for several minutes. Then Ruth spoke softly into the night and even though her voice was low, Emily could sense the excitement in it.

"I do."

"You do? Oh, Ruth!" squealed Emily and had to be shushed by her old roommate.

"You'll awaken everyone in the dorm," cautioned Ruth.

"Tell me about him," pleaded Emily. It was almost unbelievable that Ruth—Ruth who never seemed to care about fellows, who seemed oblivious to their existence—was actually confessing to being interested in one.

"Well," said Ruth and the tone of her voice betrayed her, "he is a farmer. He comes to all the services—been a wonderful help to me. He's taller than I am by about three inches, has dark hair and really pretty eyes. At least I think so."

Emily squealed again but quickly pulled a blanket up around her face to muffle the sound. "Are you getting married?" she asked her old roommate.

Ruth hesitated. "I still want to preach," she replied at last.

"Doesn't—doesn't he want you to?"

"He—he says it's fine with him, but . . . Well, it's hard work directing a church. I don't know if I could be both a wife and a—a pastor. And if I wasn't a good wife, I'd feel guilty. And if I didn't preach, I would feel cheated. And if we had children— then I'd really have a hard time trying to do it all."

Emily understood Ruth's dilemma.

Again there was silence. Emily spoke softly. "You are really going to have to pray this one through."

"I've prayed and prayed," admitted Ruth, "and I still don't know what to do."

"I'll pray with you," promised Emily and inwardly added Ruth's situation to her prayer list.

―――――――

Emily did talk with Rev. Witt about the Travis family.

"This is a really tough situation," he said sadly. "One must move cautiously. Has she ever indicated that she needs or wants help?"

"No," admitted Emily, shaking her head.

"Are the children frequently abused as well?"

"They usually run away and hide," Emily answered, "but emotionally, I know they are damaged. I felt little Rena shiver with fear when I held her."

"One could report him to the authorities—but then, Mrs. Travis could do that herself."

"I—I honestly think she still loves him in some strange way. She doesn't want interference, but I just can't stand by and see—" Emily stopped for a moment and then continued. "She speaks of him as 'being sick.' "

The minister nodded again. "And so he is," he agreed, "very sick—in body and soul." He was quiet for a while, then looking up, he said, "It puts the church in a most difficult situation. We do not wish to break up families, but to allow a woman and her children to continue to suffer at the hands of such a man—that is unthinkable."

Emily nodded, sorrow shadowing her eyes.

"Offer the woman and her children all the love and support you can," the kind man went on. "And watch for an opportunity to talk with her frankly about her situation. Maybe from that discussion, something will become clear to you and to her. And keep praying for a change of heart in this man. The next time I visit you, I will look further into the matter."

He placed a fatherly hand on Emily's shoulder. "I know this is difficult," he said sympathetically. "We'll all be praying that God will give you wisdom beyond your years or experience."

Emily thanked him and, with tears threatening to spill over, excused herself.

"Emily! How are you?"

At the sound of the voice and the light touch on her arm, Emily whirled to meet Ross. She hadn't expected him to show up at the conference.

"Ross! What a surprise," she managed as she extended her hand.

Ross grinned. "I had to see all my old school friends," he said easily.

"Well, the last session dismissed about a half hour ago. Some of the people already left," Emily told him. But there was no disappointment on Ross's face.

"Well, you're still here," he countered and laughed at Emily's surprise.

"My train doesn't leave until morning," she explained. "I'll stay in the dorm another night."

"Good," he responded. "Then how about a meal with me at the Royale tonight?"

Emily was surprised. How many were the times she had longed for such an invitation? She stammered now, "That— that sounds like—a wonderful idea."

"Good! I'll pick you up around six then. We'll do all our catching up over a Chinese dinner."

Emily nodded dumbly. She couldn't believe this was actually happening.

Emily wanted her hair and her dress to be just right, and prepared carefully for her evening out. She actually had a date with Ross, something she used to dream about. She smiled as she worked at her hair nervously.

Just before leaving, she automatically reached for her black bonnet and then laughed at herself. *I certainly don't need that tonight!* she decided. And Emily carefully laid the bonnet back on the dresser.

Ross was prompt. He offered his arm and Emily took it shyly.

"You have a car?" she asked as he led her to the waiting automobile.

"Of course. I'm a man of great wealth now," he teased and they chuckled together.

"Well, I'm not," admitted Emily. "I still use a poky old team and buggy. But then, an automobile would never make it through Wesson Creek's mud holes anyway."

They laughed again.

"You really drive horses—through mud?" asked Ross seriously.

"I do. Some of the women still have to walk when they make their calls. I am blessed with transportation—thanks to my father," admitted Emily.

"You shouldn't have to do that," Ross argued firmly. "The men should be out there preaching."

"But there aren't enough men called," Emily countered. "Or, if they are—they aren't answering," she added slowly.

"Well, let's not talk about work tonight." Ross changed the subject smoothly. "Let's have a night of fun—and fellowship—as we used to say at school."

Emily laughed. She was ready for a night of fun and fellowship. It had been a long time since she had enjoyed the company of someone her own age.

Chapter Twenty-two

Back to Work

Emily had been back at her small parsonage for only six days when another letter came from Ross.

I had a delightful time the evening we went out for Chinese food, he wrote. *It made me realize that we have so much in common. I do wish I would have discovered it earlier. It was a shame to have wasted those two years at school.*

Emily frowned. Her two years at school had certainly not been wasted.

I was wondering when you might be this way again, Ross continued. *I really would like to see you. Until then, I guess I will just have to be content with writing—but a letter leaves so much to be desired.*

"Oh, my!" breathed Emily. "Exactly what is Ross trying to say?" she wondered.

Then Ross's letter told about his work managing a hardware store and his family and the town where he lived.

The man who owns the store lives in the next town and he says he may even sell it to me someday, Ross enthused on paper.

Emily frowned slightly. It seemed that Ross had forgotten about his possible call to the ministry. He appeared to be making future plans with no thought of that call.

Emily decided she needed a diversion—a busy diversion—and deemed it a good day to get to work on her small garden plot. She hoped she would not need to go through another winter on such scanty fare. Mrs. Witt had thoughtfully provided each of the young deaconesses with seeds from her own garden. Emily reached for them now and sorted the seeds out on her kitchen table. Then she slipped into her rubber overshoes and went out to check her backyard. It was much too wet for digging. Keenly disappointed, Emily decided to go visit Sophie instead.

Sophie was pleased to see her.

"Sit down," she said. "I'll get us some coffee."

Sophie brought two cups to the table and lit a cigarette. "So how was yer trip?" she asked with interest.

"Great," answered Emily and felt her face flush. Why was Ross the first thought she had in connection with her trip?

"Good," responded Sophie. Then added rather listlessly, "Things ain't been all thet great here."

"Why, what's wrong?" asked Emily with concern.

"It's Nicky. He's been sick. At first I thought it was jest some little bug—but he didn't get no better, so I called Doc yesterday. He don't know what's the matter either."

An unnamed fear twisted a knot in Emily's stomach. "It isn't serious, is it?"

"Don't know. I hope not. But Doc says he don't even know what medicine to give."

Sophie's expression gave away her worry.

"Oh, Sophie," said Emily softly, "we need to pray."

Tears ran down Sophie's cheeks. Emily reached for her hand and bowed her head, "Dear God," she began, "you know all about Nicky and his need. We don't know what is wrong. Even the doctor doesn't know yet what is wrong. Give the doctor wisdom as he seeks for the right medicine, and help Nicky to be better soon. And be with Sophie. It hurts to see a child ill, Lord. Help her to trust you and to be able to rest at night. Thank you, Lord, for all you do on our behalf. Amen."

Emily lifted her eyes. Sophie was still crying softly, but there was a crooked smile playing about her lips. The ash of the cigarette grew longer and longer, some of it spilling onto the table top.

"Thanks," muttered Sophie. "I was about beside myself. Thanks. It's such a relief. It's been worryin' me sick."

Emily was a bit surprised. She gathered from Sophie's simple words that she considered her son as good as well. Perhaps Sophie's faith was stronger than hers. Emily felt a bit of shame. She also felt some fear. She had known the Lord long enough to realize that God's answers sometimes did not come quite as one had asked.

"May I see Nicky?" Emily asked hesitantly.

Sophie smiled. "Sure," she said. "You can take him some of this chicken soup. I made it especially for him, but he ain't been able to eat a bit. He's likely half starved now." And Sophie busied herself with preparing food for her son.

But Emily found a very ill Nicky. His face was flushed a deep pink, his eyes were bright with fever. He moaned as he tossed restlessly on his pillow. Emily sat beside him and bathed his face from the basin on the stand beside him. She tried to coax some of the broth into him, but he could not swallow. Emily now became fervent in her praying.

"Oh, God," she pleaded, "I didn't know how sick he is. Please, dear Lord, we need your help. Nicky needs your help. He's lost weight. He's so sick. Help the doctor. Show him what to do. Touch Nicky's little body, Lord. We need you. Please, God."

Emily stayed all day with Nicky. Sophie, looking puzzled, came and went as her customers allowed. Emily had prayed. Why was it taking so long?

Emily did not go home even that night, except to care for Walter and then slip back. "You try to get some sleep," she urged Sophie, but Sophie paced the room restlessly until Dr. Andrew made a late call and left two tablets that would allow Sophie to rest.

The next day Sophie attached a sign on the cafe informing customers that she would not be opening, left her door locked and her blinds down, and stayed the day with Nicky.

Emily was concerned about the other three children. They too lived with fear. Emily did not know whether to offer to take them to her house and thus leave Sophie alone, or to stay with Sophie and leave the frightened children exposed to the anguish of the illness.

Again that night, Emily stayed with the family. Around one o'clock she slipped into her coat and let herself out the door. Nicky was worse. They needed Dr. Andrew.

Nicky died at quarter to three. There was nothing any of them could do to save him. Emily reached for Sophie to give all the support she could, but Sophie stepped back and pushed Emily's hands away.

"No!" she hissed. "No! No, ya prayed. Ya asked God. Why? Why did He let it happen? How could He? How could He? I was the one who was bad—not my Nicky." Sophie threw herself on the bed and gathered her son into her arms.

"Leave her," Dr. Andrew said softly to Emily. "She must express her grief in her own way. You go home now."

Emily went, dragging her tired body and her confused mind. Over and over her own thoughts echoed those of Sophie. *Why? Why did it happen this way? Why didn't you heal him, Lord? You could have. You could have.*

Emily's faith had never been so shaken. She sobbed long after she should have been asleep, and when she finally did drift off she was totally spent emotionally. *Will I ever be able to reach out to Sophie again? Will she ever let me?*

———

The funeral was held on a sunny spring afternoon. Rev. Witt came for the service. Sophie sat stoically in the small church, holding her three children close to her. Her eyes were sunken and red-rimmed, but she did not weep at the funeral.

Emily wept, sobs shaking her slight frame.

"Oh, Nicky," she cried, "you were such a sweet child. We are going to miss you terribly. And Sophie. The pain of Sophie. I can't imagine the pain!"

After the graveside ceremony was over, Sophie placed a small pink rose on the coffin of her son and turned to go back to the cafe.

Emily wanted to speak to her, but the retreating back was straight, stiff, and the head held defiantly high.

I'll slip over later, Emily promised herself and turned to invite the Witts to the parsonage for tea.

———

Emily visited Sophie three days later. The woman welcomed her cordially enough, but the coldness did not leave her eyes.

They sat at the corner table, their coffee cups before them, each with her own thoughts.

Emily wished to offer some words of hope, but she didn't know how to express them. Silently she prayed for wisdom—for guidance.

"I . . . I would love to have the children stay for dinner after church on Sunday," Emily began slowly.

Sophie's eyes lifted then. Emily could see the hardness there.

"They won't be in church on Sunday," she replied sharply.

Emily's eyes showed no surprise, but she asked softly, "Will you be—be away?"

"No. No, we'll be right here. They'll jest not be goin' anymore, thet's all."

"Oh, Sophie," breathed Emily before she could stop herself.

"Look, Emily," Sophie said frankly. "I don't mind callin' you a friend. Ya stayed with me and Nicky night an' day when he was sick, but don't—don't ever try to shove yer religion on me again—understand?"

Emily looked into the cold, dark, angry eyes.

"As I see it, either He couldn't do anythin' to save my son—or He wouldn't. Either way, He's not the kind a God I want or need."

"Oh, He could have—" began Emily.

"Then why *didn't* He?" spat Sophie, and she rose quickly from the table, her eyes flashing.

"I—I don't know," replied Emily helplessly. "I just don't know."

"Then don't do yer preachin' in here—to me or to my children—ever again!" snapped Sophie, and she turned her back and walked briskly to her counter.

Emily arose and slowly left the small cafe, her shoulders drooped and her eyes brimmed with tears. "I don't know," she wept softly. "I really don't know."

————

Emily, numb with sorrow, hardly was aware of what she was doing the rest of the morning. But that afternoon Mrs. Woodrow surprised her at her door. Emily welcomed her warmly and hurriedly set teacups and a small plate of cookies on the table.

"I didn't come to sip and chat," the woman said gruffly. "I came to find out how to get ready to die."

Emily did not know exactly what the woman meant. "You mean you—you want to arrange for your funeral service?" she inquired.

"Lands no!" exclaimed the woman. "I don't care none if they throw my body in the lake. I need to be ready to die."

Emily understood then, but she could not have been more surprised. "I see," she said slowly, feeling the enormous weight of the responsibility that was hers. She lifted her Bible from the shelf and began to turn the pages. She knew all the appropriate scriptures. She had carefully trained for this moment during her Bible school preparation. *Please make the truth come alive to Mrs. Woodrow,* she prayed as she came to the book of Romans.

"The Bible says that *all* have sinned," began Emily, pointing to the scripture passage.

"I know that," responded the woman. "I've lived long enough to see it for myself."

"And the wages of sin—is death," Emily went on.

Mrs. Woodrow nodded. Emily could see that she accepted that as fair.

"But God loved us and sent His Son to take the death penalty in our place. We are talking now about spiritual death—separation from God and punishment for our sins. We all still die physically."

The woman nodded again, and Emily sensed her impatience.

"What I need to know is how to get that forgiveness," she prompted Emily.

"Well, God's forgiveness is a gift. We need to accept the gift by accepting God's Son. We repent of our sins and we receive His forgiveness in Jesus' name. He will help us turn from what we have been to what He wants us to be. God gives us a cleansed heart. We accept, with gratitude, His salvation. And then we are baptized to show others that we are now members of the believing church."

Emily swallowed quickly. She wasn't sure if she had explained it clearly or if the woman could understand the concept of salvation through faith.

But Mrs. Woodrow nodded again. "And how do you do that?" she asked.

"Is that what you wish?" asked Emily.

"That's what I came for," responded the woman.

Emily flushed. "Well then, you pray. You pray and ask God— and He will do the rest."

"I don't know how to pray," stated the woman. "That's why I came to you."

"Let's pray," invited Emily. "You may repeat after me—if you mean the things I'm saying." And Emily led the woman in a brief prayer of request for God's forgiveness and salvation.

At the end of the prayer Mrs. Woodrow's face had relaxed. Her eyes, formerly so troubled, were shining now.

"When do I get baptized?" she asked simply.

"Well I—I need to make arrangements with Rev. Witt. I don't do the baptizing myself. He will come—"

"Well, just don't wait too long," cautioned the woman. "I could die most any time."

Emily denied the smile that tugged at her lips. Instead she spoke evenly, slowly. "You will want to have fellowship with God, now that you are in His family," she said simply. "We do that through reading His Word, the Bible, and through prayer."

"I can read," she answered, "but I can't pray."

"All you do is talk to your Father—much as you are talking to me now. But it doesn't even need to be out loud. Just open up your heart to Him. Any time. Any place. Whenever you feel you wish to talk to Him. And share your—your troubles. Your hurts. Your joys. Anything. And ask Him to help you to understand more about Him each day."

"Do I have to come to church?" asked the woman, and Emily did smile then.

"You don't *have* to come to church," she said, "but I would encourage you to come. There you can grow as you hear God's Word and fellowship with other Christians. It's very helpful to come to God's house as often as you can."

Mrs. Woodrow nodded.

"Do you have a Bible?" asked Emily.

"My husband's ma gave him one when he was a boy. It's still there."

"Good," said Emily.

The woman's eyes suddenly filled with tears. "I wish he would have read it—believed it," she said softly. "Might have made a heap a difference." Then she quickly added, "But I can't blame him none for the way I been. I had enough smarts to know I wasn't doin' right."

Emily nodded.

"I'd like that tea now," said the woman, sniffing, and she took off her hat that had seen many seasons and settled herself at Emily's table.

Chapter Twenty-three

Autumn Blues

Emily looked dismally at the patchy row of carrots, the few potato plants, the yellowish leaves of the one tomato plant, the skinny beets and the stunted corn in her garden. She would not have much to go on through the coming winter with such a skimpy crop. She heaved a sigh and thanked God for Mrs. Reilly's hens. At least she would have eggs to eat.

"I had so hoped . . ." she mused wishfully, then turned her back on the garden patch.

"Well, at least there are a few meals there," she said to herself as she went back inside to prepare for another day of visiting the families in her community.

During four days of rain, Emily had paced her small kitchen floor waiting for the sky to clear. Walter had chased along after her, playfully grabbing at her shoelaces. It was important to her to make another call on Mrs. Woodrow, who, as she wished, had been baptized by Rev. Witt and was coming to church faithfully. Emily marveled at the woman's hunger for the Word and the change in her over the past few months. In fact, everyone in the town had noticed the change in Mrs. Woodrow.

But word had come that the woman was ill. Emily took one more look at the gray skies and decided to hitch her team to the buggy, rain or not.

It was a mistake. The side road that led to the Woodrow farm was rutted and full of holes at the best of times, but with the heavy rains that had fallen, it was next to impassable. Big John had tried to warn Emily, but she quietly pushed aside his gruff prediction and went ahead.

The first trouble came in the form of another heavy shower.

Emily gritted her teeth against the cold rain and kept her horses headed in the direction of Mrs. Woodrow's farm.

When she turned off the main road onto the side road that led to the farm, she discovered firsthand how accurate Big John had been. The road to the Woodrow house was even worse than she had feared. Deep, gummy mud holes bogged down her buggy, and it was all her strong team could do to keep the small wagon moving.

Emily lurched from one hole to another, trying to pick her way through. To make matters worse, the rain running down her face prevented her from seeing clearly. Much of the ground was under a layer of water, and Emily hardly knew where to aim the team next.

And then the inevitable happened. The buggy wheels careened into a particularly deep hole, and Emily heard the sickening splinter of wood. She had broken a wheel. The horses strained, trying to get the obstinate vehicle free from the cumbersome burden of mud, but Emily knew that to attempt to pull the buggy out would only mean more damage to the wheel.

"Whoa-a," she called, pulling hard on the reins.

Emily looked dismally at the muddy road. Then she slipped off her shoes and stockings, hoisted her skirts as far as her dignity would allow, and climbed down over the muddy buggy wheel.

She gasped at the depth of the hole and the cold ground as she sank down in mud past her ankles. She could hardly move one foot in front of the other. For several minutes she struggled with the tugs, but they were wet and sloppy, and her hands could not get a proper grip. In the meantime the horses shifted impatiently, lifting one foot after the other with a strange sucking sound. Working as quickly as she could, Emily finally freed the team and managed to get them off to the side of the road where she tied the horses to a tree.

"If I had a husband," Emily mumbled, "I would not need to do this."

She padded back to the buggy, retrieved her shoes and stockings, and went on to the Woodrow farm on foot.

Mrs. Woodrow was not as sick as Emily had feared, and Emily was relieved to find her sitting before a warm fire, a cup of hot lemon juice before her and her Bible on her knees.

"My lands, girl, you'll catch your death!" the woman exclaimed when she saw Emily.

Emily only smiled. She had stopped long enough to wash her dirty feet in a cold puddle and slip back into her stockings and shoes. Still, she shivered as she entered the room.

"Sit down, sit down," the woman prompted. "Pull your chair right up there to the fire. Here, drink this. It'll warm you," she encouraged as she shoved a cup of hot lemon drink toward Emily.

After the visit, Emily again removed her shoes and stockings and went back to retrieve her team. She rode Shadow into town, and on to the Travis farm, leading Star behind her, her muddy, dripping skirts spread out over Shadow's broad back.

When the world finally stopped dripping, she had to send the blacksmith out for her buggy. She worried about the expense of the broken wheel, but he waved her money aside. "Seems I should be able to do some small thing for the church," he said, and Emily thanked him sincerely.

After a few days the sun came out in full strength, and the roads began to dry again. Emily had her buggy, solid and sound again, and her horses waiting for her at the Travis farm. Emily was ready to make up for lost time.

She began the rounds of familiar places, greeting people she had come to know. Most of them were glad to welcome her to their kitchen, but not many promised to visit her church in return, though a few did say they'd stop by for a cup of tea.

Emily was about to pass a vacant farmyard when she noticed a wagon in the yard. She took a closer look. Yes, two horses stood in the corral, and the fenced pasture beside the road held a few head of cattle.

With a quickened pulse, Emily turned her horses down the lane. *Here's a new family,* she thought joyfully. *One on which I've never called before. Perhaps they'll be new members for our little congregation.*

A man in the yard was working on a stretch of broken fence. He lifted his head and looked her way. He seemed young—perhaps newly married and starting out on his own for the first time.

"Hello," greeted Emily. "I was just passing and noticed that this farm is now occupied. Welcome to the community."

"Thank you," he responded, and laid aside the hammer,

touched his cap, and stepped closer to Emily's buggy. He had the brownest eyes she had ever seen.

Emily did not know what to say next. He solved the problem for her. "Are you the community welcoming committee?" he asked, teasing in his voice.

"Well, no," laughed Emily. "Actually, I am the—the worker at the little mission in town. I just stopped to give an invitation to our services. I'd love to meet your wife."

"I'd love to introduce you—only I don't have a wife . . . yet."

"I'm—I'm sorry," muttered Emily, embarrassed.

The man smiled. "No problem," he assured her. He went on. "Then there is a church here. Ma was afraid there might not be. She'll be pleased when she hears there is."

"Your mother attends church?" Emily inquired, thinking, *He must still live with his folks.*

"Regularly! And she tries to make sure that all her offspring do too."

Emily felt her heart quicken. *New members for our little church!* She handed the reins to the young man and moved to descend from the buggy. "I'd love to meet your mother," she said emphatically.

He put out a hand to help her down and led her horses to the hitching rail.

"That would be nice," he responded, his eyes sparkling just a bit. "I expect her next Sunday afternoon."

Emily could feel the color rising in her cheeks. "She isn't here?"

"No, ma'am," the young man answered with a shake of his head.

"She isn't moving in until Sunday?"

"I expect her on Sunday—but only to call. She lives in Meldon. I'm on my own now." He stopped long enough to lift the hat from his head, wipe a sleeve across his sweaty brow. "I'm just starting to farm my own place," he said, gazing out across the acres.

Emily looked at the tall, broad-shouldered young man with love-of-the-land clearly showing in his dark brown eyes. She hadn't a doubt that he'd make out just fine.

"Then I guess I should be on my way," she stated.

"I would be happy to bring some lemonade to the porch," he offered.

"That's very kind," replied Emily, "but I really think—"

"It's a warm day," insisted the young man. "I'm about ready for a break. And Mother always taught us to take care of God's servants." He smiled.

Emily returned the smile. "A glass of lemonade on the porch would be nice," she conceded, and fell into step with the young man.

Carl Morgan was in church every Sunday. He brought produce to her door. He volunteered to haul her wood, work on her skimpy garden, and build the fire in the church stove when needed.

Emily enjoyed the attention. She enjoyed his taking some of the burdens that she had carried for so long. But she did not enjoy the strange little warning that kept flashing through her mind.

Ruth's dilemma was a constant reminder. Ruth had written that she had let the young man go his own way. "I could not see how I could be wife, mother and minister," Ruth had written. "God has not yet released me from my call, and I know I could not turn my back on it."

But Emily argued that her situation might be different from Ruth's. Surely she could live right here in the community and still serve the church and be the wife of an area farmer.

Carl had not as yet asked her to be his wife. "He is considerate and manly and a sincere believer," Emily told herself. She was sure all she had to do was to encourage him and he would ask for her hand.

"This is ridiculous," she finally said aloud one evening. "You don't marry simply to have someone to harness the horses or haul the wood!"

From that time on, Emily carefully guarded her words and actions when she was around Carl. She, like Ruth, could not give up her calling until God released her, and He had not done so as yet.

When I marry—if I marry, Emily reminded herself, *it must be to someone who shares my commitment, not robs me of it.* From then on Emily busied herself even more with the task of outreach and nurture of the community.

But regardless of her new resolve, memories of another man, Shad Austin, began to return to her daytime thoughts and her nighttime dreams. *He seemed so comfortable to be with—so right,* thought Emily. *If only . . . if only . . .*

Then Emily's thoughts turned to Ross—Ross whose warm letters arrived each week. Now Emily felt more confused than ever.

———

A knock at her door brought Emily's attention from the Sunday sermon over which she was laboring. She was not expecting company. The women who shared neighborhood news with her over a cup of tea never came on Saturday, knowing it was the time she devoted to her Sunday preparations.

But when Emily opened the door, there stood Ross!

"Ross! What a surprise," Emily managed, and he moved to enter without invitation.

"I thought it was a nice day for a picnic," he answered cheerfully.

It was a glorious fall day. The leaves were delightful shades of reds and yellows. The sun hung lazily in the sky, and birds flitted here and there, calling their last farewells before departing for the south.

"A picnic? It *does* sound like fun."

"Then grab your coat—or whatever you need, and let's be off. I already have lunch in the car."

It was so tempting. "But I'm not ready for Sunday," Emily moaned.

"Sunday?"

"My sermon," Emily reminded him.

"Your sermon? Can't it wait?"

"I'm afraid not. It takes me most of Saturday to properly prepare it."

"But just this once, couldn't you cut short the time? Use an old one or something. No one would remember. Just change a few words."

Emily shook her head.

"You shouldn't be—" started Ross, but he stopped and changed his tone.

"Oh, Emily," he said, and moved closer to her, "I've traveled miles to see you. It is my only free day. I had a picnic lunch specially prepared. I was so looking forward to seeing you again." His hands on her waist, he pulled her closer to him and pressed his lips against her hair. "Please," he pleaded. "Please."

Emily pushed away slowly, not comfortable being held by a man to whom she had made no commitment. She lifted Ross's hands from her waist and stepped back to look at him.

"Ross," she began slowly, "I'm sorry. Truly I am. I enjoy your friendship, but I—my first commitment is to the Lord. And that includes preparation of a Sunday sermon, and I'm afraid—I'm *sure* that is what I must do."

She thought she saw anger in his eyes.

"You—you can't understand that, can you?" she dared to ask.

He shook his head stubbornly. "I thought a woman's place was in the home—as a wife, a mother," he retorted.

"I agree," she admitted, then added quickly, "unless God calls her into something else. Then she must be obedient to His call."

"Let the *men* preach," he countered. "You can't do the full work anyway. You can't marry or bury or baptize. You call that ministry?"

Emily forced herself to ignore his sarcasm. "If I had a husband who would preach, I would be glad to allow him that privilege," she returned firmly. "This community needs the Word of God. Until such time as a man comes to deliver it, the responsibility will be mine."

"Very well," he said in clipped tones. "I guess I will find someone else to share my picnic—and my future."

Emily sighed. "Yes," she replied evenly, "I guess you should."

Then he was gone, and Emily shed a few tears before she returned to her sermon.

"It's all right, Lord," she prayed. "I am quite prepared to serve alone—for as long as you need me."

Emily participated in the annual Autumn Picnic again. But without the presence of Shad, the day was not the same. She joined the Reillys at their table, but they made no comment about Shad missing the festivities for the first time—and Emily dared not ask. *In fact,* Emily thought, *Mrs. Reilly has not mentioned Shad for many months. Has there been some rift between them? He didn't even come visit this summer, as far as I know.*

Emily was puzzled, but her question went unanswered.

Chapter Twenty-four

Winter Wars

"I notice Sophie's kids don't go to yer Sunday school no more," Big John commented as Emily opened her purse to pay for her purchases.

"No, they don't," agreed Emily, sadness in her eyes. She had prayed so often that Sophie would relent after a time, but she was still adamant in her refusal to allow the children to return to church.

"Took it pretty hard, did she?" Big John continued.

How would you expect a mother to take it? Emily wanted to retort. Instead she made no reply.

"Thet's what I don't understand 'bout religion," John mused, almost to himself. "Ya say God loves. Ya say He is powerful. Ya say He can answer prayer. So how come ya didn't pray thet the boy would git better?"

"We did," said Emily honestly.

Big John looked at her triumphantly. "But He didn't answer, did He?"

"He answered," responded Emily evenly.

Big John looked surprised at her reply.

"The kid died!" he shot back at her.

"That doesn't mean God didn't answer our prayer," Emily answered softly, tears glistening in the corners of her eyes. "Oh, I know. He didn't answer in the way we wanted—the way we prayed. But we can't see the future. He can. He answered in the way He knew best."

"Humph!" Big John snorted. "Thet's the baloney ya religious people always spout. Don't make a lick of sense, an' ya know it.

Either He ain't got the power to do what He promises, or else He don't care one little bit, thet's the truth o' the matter."

Emily straightened to her full height. "If I thought that for one minute," she said honestly, "I wouldn't be here."

"So why are ya here?" he challenged. "No man ask ya to wed?"

Emily gulped down her frustration. If he only knew the agony she had been through trying to weigh her desires to be a wife and mother against her call to the ministry. She blinked back tears and answered softly, firmly.

"Being here, as a single woman, is not easy. I do not relish the care of horses. I do not enjoy trying to produce a garden in a patch of weeds. I do not like hauling wood and water. I do not even enjoy the preparations of sermons—all 'manly' jobs, if you will. But God has called me here. I do not know why—nor do I ask. I only try to obey."

She picked up her small parcel. "And you can be assured," she went on, "I will be here—just as long as I feel this is where He wants me." She turned and quietly left the store.

She was annoyed with herself that she let Big John's barbs get to her. She would never, never be any witness to the man as long as she allowed him to trouble her so.

"Lord," she prayed, sitting at her little table stroking Walter's fur, "please help me to respond calmly to his honest questions and overlook the ones he asks simply to bother me. Help me to know what to say and how to say it. And help Big John to learn to love you."

Emily hurried the team home from her calling, feeling the sharp chill in the air. She let her horses through the pasture gate and moved quickly toward the Travis house. She was anxious to see how things had been going with the family. They had missed church on Sunday.

Mrs. Travis welcomed her warmly and insisted that she stop for a cup of hot chocolate. Two new bruises had appeared on the woman's forehead but she made no comment. They chatted lightheartedly over their cups.

"Mrs. Travis," Emily finally began carefully as she toyed with the teacup, "is there any way that I can help you?"

The woman looked surprised.

"I would be glad to make the call if you'd like your husband to get some—some medical help with his problem," Emily dared to continue.

Mrs. Travis looked alarmed and shook her head vigorously. "I don't want anyone butting into our family affairs," she said firmly. "We've made out fine till now. We'll make out fine in the future, too."

"But what about Claude?" Emily challenged.

"Had a letter from Claude," Mrs. Travis said proudly. "He's got him a job with a farmer over east of here. Plans on coming home for Christmas."

Emily was pleased to hear the news and said so to Mrs. Travis.

"But the other children?" pressed Emily. "What if Timmie and Rena decide to leave home at Claude's age? Will that be all right, too?"

Tears formed in the woman's eyes. She dropped her head and shook it sadly. "He's my husband," she whispered. "He's their father. It's just the drink that gets him—upset." Then she lowered her voice even further. "They might come and take him away if they know. I couldn't live with that. Do you understand? . . . No, I don't suppose you can."

"But they could help him," insisted Emily. "Bring him back again after he had conquered the problem."

"No. No—it doesn't work that way. He tried. He tried once before. He just came back worse."

Then she looked at Emily, the tears flowing down her cheeks. "Please, please," she pleaded, "leave things as they be. Please?"

Emily could only nod her head while despair filled her heart. What choice did she have? What else could she do?

———

Winter's snow fell in stinging crystals, biting at faces and uncovered hands. Strong winds swirled it round and round the little town, sculpting drifts in out-of-the-way places and sweeping white, glass-like particles against windowpanes and rooftops.

Emily was glad for a warm fire and plenty of wood, but she couldn't help worrying as she studied her little storage cupboard. Most of the few vegetables she had managed to draw from her little garden had now been eaten. And though the Sunday offerings had increased somewhat with the attendance of a few new members, it was still not enough to adequately cover her living expenses.

God will provide, she reminded herself.

By now she was out of flour and sugar—even the precious bit she kept for the guest's tea had been used. And she needed tea again as well. With the colder weather, more women were sure to be stopping for that cup of warmth and a chat when they came to town.

Emily folded her coat closely about her and hurried out into the driving snow. At the mercantile she carefully counted her coins as Big John waited on another customer. She simply did not have enough money for flour, butter, vanilla and sugar to make cookies.

She wondered what she should do. It wouldn't be very hospitable to serve just tea.

Emily's eyes scanned the shelves and bins and fell upon ginger snaps. Carefully she fingered her money again. She could do it.

When it was her turn, she ordered two dozen ginger snaps, one-half pound of sugar and a pound of tea. Then she counted out her money and left the store.

While Emily served her guests "store-bought" cookies, no one suspected she herself was living mostly on eggs scrambled, eggs fried, eggs boiled and eggs poached. Cream and butter came to the parsonage, along with an occasional frying chicken or small piece of beef, but Emily's diet varied little from day to day.

She tried hard to have at least one serving of vegetables daily, knowing that her body needed the nutrients, but at times it was as little as minced onion in her scrambled eggs.

Periodically, she counted out her coins and purchased another pound of cookies and another bit of sugar. If Big John wondered as he filled her orders, he didn't say anything.

———

Emily had not seen Sophie for several weeks. Even after Sophie's conclusion that Nicky's death was God's fault, Emily had continued to visit the cafe for a cup of coffee and a little chat. But their times together became more strained, and Emily crossed the street less and less. She still prayed for Sophie and the children. She still worried and wondered about them, but she found the situation very awkward.

"If only she would let the children come," Emily often sighed. "They seem to miss it so much."

But Emily did not dare to approach Sophie again with her request.

One morning Emily went to the church earlier than usual. It was a cold, crisp Sunday, and she knew the stove would need extra time to heat the small building. Carl had stopped by the day before to tell her that he would not be able to be there. It was the first time Emily had to build her own fire for a number of Sundays.

She got the fire going, placed the few hymnals on the seats, arranged her teaching notes on the small podium, and then waited for the room to lose its chill and her congregation to arrive.

"There won't be many out this morning," she mused as she rubbed her hands together near the stove, trying to keep warm.

The door opened and Sophie pushed her head in. "May we come in?" she asked self-consciously.

Emily could not believe her eyes and ears. "Oh, Sophie!" she cried, hurrying to meet the woman.

Three beaming children bounded in ahead of their mother.

"We're comin' to church again!" exclaimed Olivia, clapping her small hands as she hopped her way across the floor.

"I'm so glad!" exclaimed Emily, and she knelt before the child and pulled her into her arms. "Oh, I have missed you," she said, a lump in her throat.

"We missed ya, too," said Olivia, wrapping her arms around Emily's neck.

Sophie was silent as she watched the exchange, but tears filled her eyes.

"It was the kids who made me see the truth," she explained to Emily, wiping her eyes.

Emily stood to her feet and took Sophie's hand.

"Last night when I was puttin' them to bed, Tommie said to me, 'Mom, do ya think Nicky's in heaven?' And I said of course I did. Then he said, 'But if we don't live the way Jesus wants us to, we won't be able to go there to see him.' An' he started to cry. 'I want to see Nick again, Mom,' he said. And I knew I wanted to see Nick again, too.

"But I didn't say so to Tommie. I jest couldn't let myself forgive God. An' then Johnnie spoke up. He said, 'Mom, do ya think that's why God let Nick die—so the rest of us would want to go to heaven?' " Sophie paused a moment to get control of her emotions.

"I couldn't answer thet question, but I thought about it long after the kids was asleep. Maybe that *is* why. I mean, if Nick had not died, I would've jest gone right on sendin' my kids to Sunday service, livin' my own life the way I want, never realizing thet I need God more'n any of 'em.

"God could've taken all my kids to heaven someday, an' I would've been left behind. I don't want thet, Emily. I want to go with 'em."

Sophie was crying hard now. Emily led her to a church pew and they knelt down together, and Emily carefully, tenderly led Sophie to understand and seek God's great forgiveness.

Emily was still feeling the thrill of Sophie's conversion the next morning when she went to get her two dozen cookies with the offering money. She even had a few extra cents with which to buy a handful of potatoes. God was so good. He had cared for Sophie. He was daily meeting Emily's needs. At least she had not gone hungry—and she again had enough change to buy cookies for her guests. Emily felt like singing as she entered the store.

"I see yer strays've returned," Big John said in a mocking voice, and Emily wondered if he had nothing better to do on Sundays than to sit and spy on her little flock.

Emily had a notion to ask him, but he continued, "Even Sophie herself."

"Yes," replied Emily, eyes shining. "Isn't God good?"

Big John just "humphed."

"I'm sorry—truly sorry that you are unable to accept the fact that there is a God—and that He loves us, and cares for us," Emily said boldly. She had never dared to talk to the man in such a straightforward fashion before. "Because He *is*. He exists—and He does care."

Big John cleared his throat.

"I've never said thet I don't believe there is a God—somewhere," he argued. "I jest don't think He's much in'erested in me," he countered.

"But He is," Emily responded. "Enough so that He sent His Son, Jesus Christ, to die for you. How much more could He care?"

"An' thet's another thing," Big John hurried to interrupt. "This Jesus bit. What makes ya think thet Jesus is God?"

"What do you mean?" Emily asked, stunned.

"Well, this here Jesus. He was a man—jest like me—or Walt or Jake. No different."

"No," countered Emily, shocked at his statement. "He was born to a woman—but He was God himself in a human body."

"And where do ya git thet stuff?" the man continued. "He died, didn't He? Can a God die?"

"*He* did," affirmed Emily. "He died—for us—because He *chose* to die. But He rose from the dead—by His own power. Can a mere man do that?"

"Nonsense!" snapped Big John. "Thet was a hoax. Men was bribed to say—"

"Then what about all of the people who saw Him after His death and resurrection?" asked Emily. "Is it logical that over five hundred witnesses could be wrong?"

But Big John did not answer her question. Instead he asked, "What makes ya think He's God?"

"The Bible confirms it," Emily replied firmly.

"Ya mean 'cause o' the Trinity?" snorted Big John.

"Yes. The Trinity."

"The word *Trinity* ain't even in the Bible," scoffed Big John.

"I know that," agreed Emily, looking directly into his eyes, "but the teaching is. Over and over it speaks of God the Father, of Christ His Son, of the Spirit that moves in the hearts of people. The concept of the Trinity is there, even though the word is not used."

"How can three people be one, answer me thet?" sneered Big John. "How can a person be spoken of as a son of God an' yet be God. How can ya be yer own son?"

"I don't know," Emily answered frankly. "I really don't know. I—I don't think that a human being can fully understand it. I don't think we have proper words to describe it. I think that God called Christ His Son because that relationship was something we *could* understand. There are no words in our human languages to describe the very special relationship of God the Father and God the Son."

"Pshaw!" exclaimed Big John. "Jest words to prove a belief ya can't support. When ya find reasons to believe all thet stuff ya teach—then maybe I'll listen to what ya got to say."

Emily was shaking.

"He was the son of God—not God," the man still insisted. "A 'little lower than the angels,' the Bible says. Don't tell me thet another man could do fer me what I ain't able to do fer myself. Trinity! Humbug!"

"I might not be able to explain it," Emily acknowledged humbly, "but I know that I believe it. With my whole heart I believe it."

"Yeah, an' men used to believe the earth was flat," Big John ridiculed.

Emily made herself smile and thanked him for her purchases as she left the store. There didn't seem to be any good reason to continue the argument.

"I do believe it," she said aloud as she trudged home through the snow. "I do—with all my heart."

But why? asked an inner voice. *Just because that's what you've been taught all your life?*

Though Emily would not have cared to admit it, her faith had been shaken by the exchange.

Chapter Twenty-five

The Answer

During the weeks that followed, Emily spent hours studying her Bible. *I must know for myself that Christ Jesus is God,* she decided. *It is essential to my teaching—to my whole life. If it is not so—then my faith—my devotion—is all in vain.*

As Emily studied, she took notes, slowly filling many pages. It was true, she discovered, that Scripture referred to Him over and over again as the Son. He himself made numerous references to the Father. *So,* thought Emily as she reviewed those scripture passages, *they are two distinct beings.*

She really never doubted that. Now Big John's next question haunted her. *How could He be the Son of God, and yet God himself?* Was He a created being, as some groups taught? Was He a lesser God, as others taught? How could one explain Christ as God without the concept of the Trinity?

Emily struggled on.

"What evidence do I have," she murmured, "that Christ is God?" and she dug more deeply into the pages of her Bible.

He does have power, she thought as she read the story of the healing of the lepers. But she quickly reminded herself that His followers were given power to heal as well. Hadn't Peter healed the lame man at the temple gate?

But Christ's power was different, she mused. With His own power He had raised himself from the dead. *A live man doesn't have such power,* Emily reasoned, *much less a dead one.*

It sounded like a solid argument.

But Emily needed more.

Again and again she found words like these: "I came from the Father and to Him I shall return." They were spoken from the lips of the Christ. He also stated, "If you have seen me, you have seen the Father." And He told His followers that He had existed from the beginning.

Then Emily began to discover some special evidence. Jesus Christ forgave sins. It was only God who could wipe man's sin from the record books.

Emily found too that the creation references interchanged God and Christ as the Creator.

But it was as Emily gathered the scriptures pertaining to the worship of God that her heart began to sing with joy.

Scripture was very specific. God would allow the worship of no other being than himself. He was a "jealous God." Man was to bow down to one God and one God only.

God's chosen people had learned that lesson through great tribulation and loss of land and even death. They had finally been broken from their idolatry under the rule of the Babylonians. God would not tolerate the worship of false gods.

Yet God allowed, yes, *demanded,* the worship of His Son, Jesus Christ. The religious leaders could not accept the position of Christ as God, and had rejected Him as an imposter.

"If they would have just understood the reality of the Trinity," Emily said to herself, "they could have accepted Christ and stayed true to the Father as well."

In the book written to the Philippians, Emily found the apostle Paul's statement: "At the name of Jesus every knee should bow, of things in heaven, and things in earth, and things under the earth; and that every tongue should confess that Jesus Christ is Lord, to the glory of God the Father."

Emily added page after page, as her notes grew, of accounts where Christ was worshiped, accepted worship, and was approved for worship by the Father.

"They have to be One!" cried Emily. "There is no other explanation. God would not share this honor with another, lesser, being."

It was enough for Emily. She still could not explain the Trinity. Three persons—yet One. But she was at peace in her own heart. Christ Jesus was not an imposter. He was not just a son of God. He was God himself. One in essence, one in Spirit—one with the Father in purpose and being.

Emily let the tears fall unchecked.

"My faith has been restored," she whispered to herself as she lovingly laid aside her Bible. Then she quickly added, "No, not restored. Strengthened."

———

After a great deal of thought and prayer, Emily approached Big John with her findings and some simplified notes. She handed them to him with an earnestness new to her.

"This is what I have discovered to support my beliefs," she said simply. "I do hope that you will study them. They are grounds for a living faith. Jesus Christ *is* God. The Trinity is a reality. I still can't explain it in human terms, but I know that God the Father, God the Son, and God the Holy Spirit do exist—as one."

The big man took her notes with no comment, then muttered something about the weather, his arthritis and his difficult sister. Emily felt it was all bluff. She smiled warmly at him, purchased her small bag of cookies and left the store.

———

Emily's cupboards now were truly bare. She had used the last of her eggs the night before. All she had left were a few cookies that she doled out carefully whenever she had guests, a few teaspoonfuls of sugar and enough tea for a skimpy pot.

"Lord, I don't know what to do," she confided. "I can't beg. But I don't think you want me to starve. I hate to do it, Lord, but I guess I'll have to visit somebody. I—I determined that I would never do my calling just to get a meal—but this time . . ."

Emily decided that though the day was cold, she would get her team and drive to the Reillys'. Not only would Mrs. Reilly welcome her and feed her well, but she would send her home with more eggs and milk as well. That would keep Emily going for several more days.

"Maybe I should even explain why I'm there," Emily told her conscience. She pulled on her heavy coat and tied a warm scarf snugly about her neck. After running a caressing hand over Walter's sleek fur, she checked her fire to make sure it was banked properly and walked to her door.

The thought of stepping out into the day made her shiver. She took a deep breath and pushed against the door. The frost had sealed the edges. Emily pushed harder and felt it give.

Her breath preceded her in silvery puffs of steam.

"It's too cold for man or beast," she said aloud, closing the door tightly behind her.

But as Emily turned to go, her foot kicked against something. Her first awful thought was of Mr. Travis. She had found him on her doorstep once before. If he were there now, he would be frozen stiff.

But it was not Mr. Travis. A small basket, bulging with contents and lightly dusted with snow over its brown paper wrapping, lay at her feet.

Emily picked up the basket, wondering what it held. She'd heard no knock at her door. She returned to the kitchen and tore the brown paper from the bundle.

"It's food!" she exclaimed, unable to believe her eyes. "It's food."

She found a small bag of sugar, another of flour, and went on to pull out vegetables, cheese and bread.

"Where did this come from?" she asked herself. "Whose is it?"

Then softly in Emily's inner thoughts came a beautiful scripture verse: "My God shall supply all your need according to his riches in glory by Christ Jesus."

"Thank you, Lord," breathed Emily. "Thank you." And she set her basket on her kitchen table and sank to her knees at the nearby chair.

"Forgive me for doubting, Lord," she wept. "I should have known you had it all under control—all the time."

And Emily carefully portioned out the food that had been provided. It would do her for many days to come if she used it sparingly.

But the following week, another food basket appeared on Emily's doorstep.

I wonder who is bringing them? she pondered. *Someone is certainly an Angel of Mercy.*

All through the remainder of the long winter, Emily continued to get weekly supplies. None of her congregation knew anything about the baskets when she shared with them her wonderful provision. Emily had thought that it might be Sophie, though she knew Sophie was hard pressed to care for her own family's needs. Then she wondered if it was Carl. He was always watching out for her. But Carl was just as surprised and excited as anyone when he heard the news. The Reillys were not bringing it. They would have brought it openly had they known Emily was in such need, Mrs. Reilly told her.

Others too were surprised that Emily had been so low on provisions.

"But the cookies?" asked Mrs. Cummings. "You always had store-bought cookies."

"That was all I could afford," admitted Emily. "I just didn't have enough money to purchase all the ingredients for baking at any one time."

"Oh, my," said Mrs. Reilly sorrowfully, "if only we'd known. I can't forgive myself for allowing you to go hungry."

But Emily only smiled. "Don't feel guilty," she assured them all. "God meant it for good. I learned more about leaning on the Lord this winter than I have in my whole life. I learned the wonderful truth about faith and trusting God."

Along with the continuing food baskets, her congregation sometimes blessed Emily with a bundle of carrots, a small bag of potatoes, some canned goods or baking, an occasional roasting chicken or piece of beef, and often—very often—with eggs and milk. And, as an added blessing, the Sunday offerings increased.

A letter from Ruth included the news that the two new mission workers who had been approved by the district at the last conference were doing well at their postings. Verna, who had quit the year before, was now married to the grocer in the small town where she had gone to serve. He was an older man, widowed with two small children.

Emily smiled. "Imagine me married to *my* grocer," she chuckled. "Wouldn't we have one jolly time growling at each other!"

The more serious side of Emily kept her praying for Big John McMann. But she wondered if she was making any headway at all.

Emily had begun to feel a thawing on the part of his sister. Vera McMann greeted her warmly when she went to the store. And she came for tea about once a week.

Still, the woman forbade the discussion of "religion," and Emily chafed that she couldn't share the reason for her faith with Vera.

"Lord," she prayed, "I'll love her and you talk to her."

So Emily poured tea and chatted about the weather, the present wave of the flu, and commented on the news Miss Mc-Mann heard over her wireless.

At one point Emily wondered if it was she who was leaving the groceries at her door, but after some candid statements, Emily realized that the woman knew nothing about the food.

Emily's visits with Sophie and her children were bright spots in her week. They never missed a service at church. On Sundays, Sophie's sign hung boldly in her window: "Closed for Worship." At first she had worried that her business would suffer, but she happily told the little congregation that her receipts had actually increased.

One early spring day when the eaves were dripping and water was running in muddy streams down the sides of the town's narrow streets, Emily decided to don her rubber overshoes and take a walk in the woods.

It was a long time since she had visited the creek she loved, and she was sure it was pulsating with new life now that the sun had filled it with melted snow.

Dressed warmly in an old coat, Emily found the creek to be just as she had expected. Here and there, through the winter ice and snow, the stream had managed to flow southward, clearing its path as it wound among the slope of the hills.

Emily sought out her familiar log and settled herself to gaze at the blue stretch of sky above her head.

"I've made it through another winter, Lord," she breathed quietly. "Thanks to you and your care. Now we face another spring. As wonderful as it is, it is a hardship too. The mud will be deep for a while. I won't get much calling done. I do hope my garden is more workable this year—though you did get me through last winter without it. Still, I can't expect those food baskets to keep dropping from heaven forever. But thank you for them, Lord. I much prefer those to food gifts from ravens." She paused a moment and pictured her heavenly Father on His glorious throne smiling with her at her little joke.

"It's been a good year. A hard one in many ways—but I've learned much from you. It was hard to lose Nicky—but wonderful to welcome Sophie as a sister in the faith. And thank you for Mrs. Woodrow and the way she has grown spiritually since giving her life over to you. I'm sorry that I was not able to talk to Mr. Woodrow before he died. Of course, only you know what might have happened in his heart before he passed on into eternity.

"Thank you for bringing Carl here. He has been a real blessing to me. I'm glad he caught on so quickly that we can only be friends. He's such a good friend to have, Lord.

"I guess the thing that has bothered me the most—the oftenest—is the Travis family. Lord, it seems that there should be some kind of a solution to that problem. Surely someone could do something before one of the family members is hurt very badly. If I should interfere, in spite of what Mrs. Travis says, Lord, please make that clear to me.

"And then there is the matter of Big John and Miss Mc-Mann. Lord, I have failed in trying to share the Good News with them. I don't see where I have made any progress at all—though she is friendly now. Almost seems to want my company. If you simply want to show your love to her through me, I'm willing, Lord.

"And Big John? He still growls and grouches when I come in—though he doesn't taunt me anymore about being called to preach. I'm thankful for that—I wonder if he ever checked the scriptures I gave him. Only you know that, Lord.

"And thank you for caring for Ruth—and each of the others who have gone to serve you. Be with Morris as he leaves for Africa. Ruth says that he is to be married before he goes. I never really felt he would take time to find a wife—but you work out some marvelous things.

"Be with each member of my little congregation. I thank you for the Reillys. She's been like a mother to me—and it sometimes makes me miss my own mother even more. But it's been good to have her, Lord. I love to have someone to talk with who is motherly and wise—and who has loved you for a long time. When I visit with Sophie, she's more like a sister.

"And, Lord," Emily hesitated. "Be with Shad, wherever he is. Help him to put aside his bitterness—whatever caused it—and to open his heart to you. He needs you, Lord—and I know you still love him." Emily paused again. "And sometimes I'm—I'm afraid I love him, too," she added.

Emily finished her prayer with tears in her eyes. She wondered why she was unable to forget the man who seemed to have so completely stolen her heart—but who was so wrong for her to love.

Chapter Twenty-six

The Letter

When summer arrived, Emily planted her garden after Carl spaded it for her. She hoped the absence of the weeds might encourage her seeds to grow more prosperously.

"If it does well, I'll share it with you," she had promised Carl.

"No need for that," he assured her. "Ma always plants a big garden and she sends her stuff to me already canned."

Emily laughed. "Well, I won't make any such promises," she said lightly, and thanked Carl warmly for his help.

The garden was doing much better than it had the year before. Emily counted on it supplying vegetables for the entire coming winter.

"My pa is sick." A voice suddenly interrupted Emily's concentration as she weeded her carrots.

Emily lifted her head and saw Rena standing nearby. "Sick? How?" she asked, wondering if Mr. Travis was beating his wife again.

"He keeps throwin' up and he's too weak to get out of bed," said Rena.

"Does your mother need help?" asked Emily.

"She said to fetch you," answered the girl.

"What about Dr. Andrew? Does she want him to come?"

Rena shook her head.

"But I can't do anything for a sick man," Emily told her.

"She doesn't want you to. She just wants your—your company," said the child, and Emily went to her kitchen to wash the soil from her hands and get a light wrap.

"Let's go," she said to Rena and the two set off for the Travis farm.

She found the man in even worse condition than she had feared. Rena was right—he was very sick. His face was sunken, his skin had a yellowish cast, his eyes were bleary and unseeing. From time to time he thrashed about the bed, and then fell back exhausted, the sweat standing out in beads on his forehead.

Mrs. Travis had said nothing as Emily slipped in by her side. Emily sat silently for many minutes and then reached for the woman's thin hand. "I will fix you some tea," she whispered, and went to the kitchen.

She took the tea to Mrs. Travis and kept vigil with her, occasionally quoting a psalm from memory in a soft voice until the evening shadows began to lengthen.

"The children should be fed," Mrs. Travis murmured wearily.

Emily left for the kitchen to see what she could find to make a meal. The cupboards were almost as bare as Emily's had been the winter before. She did find enough to make a batch of pancakes, and soon the griddle was sizzling, the smell of pancakes filling the air.

Timmie and Rena ate hungrily, and Emily continued to flip pancakes until they declared themselves "stuffed"; then she fixed a plate for the mother. But Mrs. Travis only picked at the food. Emily encouraged her to eat even though she did not feel hungry.

At last Emily removed the plate and washed up the supper dishes along with the stack that lined the tiny cupboards. After she finished, Emily prepared the children for bed and read them a story about Jesus blessing the children.

When she was sure the children were sleeping, Emily fixed another cup of tea for Mrs. Travis and offered it to her as she moved her chair beside the woman. Mr. Travis was quiet now. He had ceased to vomit and twist about. It seemed to take all his effort just to suck in another breath. Emily felt anxious and uncomfortable. Would they just sit and watch him die?

"Shouldn't I get Dr. Andrew?" she asked the woman again.

"He's been," said the woman shortly. "Nothing that Doc can do now. It's just a matter of time."

The woman reached out and took the fragile hand of the man on the bed. She stroked it gently—lovingly, and Emily couldn't help but cringe inwardly.

"Suppose you wonder how I can still love him," she mused aloud. "Well, I haven't always loved him. Sometimes I hated him—with such a passion that I could have killed him. I wanted to at times because of the way he was hurting the children."

She was silent for a while, and then she went on. "But one day I was reading my Bible, trying to find some sense to life, when I came across a verse that says that we're forgiven just as much we are able to forgive. Well, that stopped me right there. I knew—I knew that if I was to ever have peace with God, I had to forgive him." Her eyes rested on her husband's wasted form. "Even if he had caused me pain and suffering," she continued. "At first I thought I'd never be able to do it. And I couldn't have—in my own strength. But God helped me. I did forgive—and with that forgiveness I learned to love again.

"Oh, not like at first. Not like I loved the young man who won my heart long ago, but rather like a mother—pitying and caring. He was not just hurting us—but himself. I sometimes think that he has suffered most of all."

She stopped again. "And so, though I still feared him—though I could no longer respect him, I didn't hate him either. I loved—but in a different way."

Emily felt she understood. In a way she loved him, too—this broken, degenerate man.

"He'll not make it this time," the woman went on quietly, "an' it grieves my heart. For I know he isn't ready to go. He hasn't prepared to meet his Maker. There isn't one thing more I can do to help him. He's made his own choices—and he must face the consequence. I have prayed over and over that he be given one more chance—one more chance to start over. And God has answered that prayer—time and again. Now I realize that he will not change—no matter how many chances he is given." This time her reserve broke and her voice caught in her throat. "It's a hard thing to accept the truth—but—I have to give him up now. There's no use putting my children through any more pain."

There were tears falling as she stroked the still hand of the man on the bed. Emily's heart ached for both of them—for the woman in her pain and for this man who, spiritually, was already dead. She stirred in her chair and said she would see to the fire.

"God," Emily prayed when she was alone, "I've asked often

for this family to be relieved of their suffering and pain—but I didn't mean this way, Lord. Isn't there another way? Is she right? Has he had his last chance?"

Emily put wood on the fire and paced the small kitchen before she was ready to once again take her place beside Annie Travis.

All through the long night they kept their vigil and into the next day. At two o'clock he breathed one last struggling breath and lay still. Emily knew he was gone. She knew that Mrs. Travis was aware of the fact also. There were no tears. The woman simply stood to her feet and drew the sheet slowly over the face of her husband.

"It's over," she said sorrowfully. "You can send for Doc Andrew. He will need to prepare a death certificate."

Emily nodded and left for town. "Oh, God," she prayed, "if he only had made his peace with you. I didn't want it to end this way. I had so hoped and prayed . . ." But with a heavy heart Emily had to face the truth that there would be no more chances for Wilbur Travis.

––––––––

The postmaster handed Emily a letter. She gazed at it curiously, not recognizing the handwriting. *Maybe it's from one of the officers of the church telling of some coming event,* she pondered as she started for home. *It certainly isn't from anyone I know.*

Emily tossed the letter on the table and removed her coat and bonnet. Walter sauntered up to greet her, and Emily picked him up, thankful for the warmth and companionship of the friendly cat. It was so much nicer than coming home to an empty house. She put another stick of wood in the stove and pushed the teakettle forward, knowing it would soon be time to put her supper on. When she had made her simple preparations, she sat down at the kitchen table and tore off the end of the envelope.

Emily could see that the note was not more than a few lines in length. She let her eyes fall quickly to the end of the message.

The letter was signed simply, *Shad.*

Emily's heart began to pound. *What does Shad have to say to me?*

Dear Emily, he wrote, *I'm sure this letter will come as a bit of*

*a surprise to you. You may have forgotten all about me—but I
assure you, I have not forgotten about you. Aunt Moll has kept
me posted on your welfare and your work.*

*I missed my yearly trip to the farm and also the annual Au-
tumn Picnic. I would have loved to be there—but I have been
unusually busy.*

*I plan to visit the farm next weekend. Could I possibly see
you? I have some things I'd like to discuss, and a letter doesn't
seem appropriate.*

*You can send your answer home with Aunt Moll. She will be
in to do her grocery shopping on Thursday as usual, and she
promised me she would drop by. A simple yes or no will do—
though I do hope with all of my heart it will be a yes.*

Sincerely,
Shad.

Emily was both puzzled and exhilarated. *What does it all
mean?* she wondered. *Shad is coming home, and he has much
he wants to talk about. Where has he been, and what has he
been doing? How come Mrs. Reilly hasn't mentioned him? It
doesn't sound as if there's been any kind of rift between the
Reillys and their nephew.*

And so her thoughts churned round and round in her mind.
Emily was glad it was Thursday. She was sure she couldn't
have waited one more day for some insight into the unusual
letter.

When Mrs. Reilly called to drop off Emily's eggs and milk,
she had a little smile about her lips. "Did you get a letter?" she
wanted to know.

Emily nodded. "I did. But it was rather—rather strange.
Shad didn't say where he was or where he's been. It was all
somewhat mysterious. What's been happening, anyway?"

"Now, Emily," began Mrs. Reilly, "Shad made me promise
long ago that I would say nothing until he felt it the right time.
I guess he feels that the time is now—he's coming this weekend, you know."

Emily felt her heart pounding, but she was still puzzled. "I
know. He—he asked me to tell you whether he could—could see
me or not."

"And what is your answer?" inquired Mrs. Reilly.

"Well, of course I will see him," responded Emily quickly and
then blushed. "I mean—I often wondered about him, how he
was doing and all."

Mrs. Reilly smiled again. "When?" she asked.

"When—when will he want to see me?"

"Well, as soon as he can, I expect. He's arriving Friday. To-morrow. Around four, I should think. He can pick you up and bring you out to the house."

"No," said Emily impulsively. "Tell him I'll meet him about—about five—by the fishing hole. He'll know the one I mean," she finished in a rush.

Mrs. Reilly smiled again and leaned to kiss Emily on the cheek. "Shad will be pleased, I'm sure. And after you've had your little talk, come for supper," she invited. "In fact, plan to come for the night. We might want to spend Saturday together."

Emily puzzled even more as the woman left the house, but she had little time to dream about what might happen on the morrow. If she was to while away her Saturday visiting the Reillys, she had to prepare for Sunday lessons now. She at once set to work, though she did find it terribly hard to concentrate.

Chapter Twenty-seven

Partners in Service

Emily did manage to collect her thoughts enough to have her Sunday school lesson and her little sermon ready. She even had a bit of time to spare and carefully washed her hair and brushed it until it was shining.

She pressed her best skirt and tied a new ribbon on her favorite blouse, then polished her worn walking shoes with the remainder of her black polish.

I don't quite know why I'm fussing so, she told herself. But deep down inside, Emily did know. Shad was coming home. She didn't know why he wished to see her, but for the moment it was enough that he did.

Emily held herself in check until four o'clock and then she could stand it no longer. It would take her only about thirty-five minutes to arrive at the spot on the creek bank—but it would do no harm if she was early. *Shad won't know of my impatience. He won't arrive until five,* she reasoned.

With burning cheeks and pounding heart Emily set out.

It was a beautiful summer day. Lazy clouds drifted loosely across the sky, looking like wandering sheep feeding in a meadow of blue. *That one looks like a horse at full gallop,* she noted. *And that one like a rose with silvery petals. Oh, now it's changing into a frog, ready to make a giant leap.* Emily laughed at her own imaginings and tried to slow her hurried pace.

"It's not proper to be so eager to meet a young man," she scolded under her breath and forced herself to slow down.

The wild roses filled the summer air with the sweetness of their blossoms, drawing the honey bees to fill their cups at the waiting storehouse. Emily smiled as she watched them dipping into one flower after another.

Emily was intent on reaching the creek and sitting beneath the shade of the poplar trees so she might quiet her impatient heart and control her emotions before Shad arrived. But to Emily's surprise, Shad was already there and waiting in the very spot where she expected to gain her control.

"Hello," she greeted him shyly. "It's been a long time."

Shad stepped forward and took her hand in his. "It has," he said, looking deeply into Emily's shining eyes.

He released her hand and led her to the place where he had spread his jacket on a fallen log.

"Sit down," he invited, his voice filled with eagerness. And Emily was only too glad for a chance to sit.

"You haven't changed," remarked Shad rather shyly, and then added softly, "I'm glad."

Emily felt the color rise in her face. *You haven't changed either,* she was going to say. He still made her heart beat faster, her cheeks flush. *But no. No, that isn't right. There is something different about you. I'm not quite sure what it is yet, but—you seem—you seem more—more . . .* her thoughts went on.

But Shad was speaking.

"Boy, I have practiced this little speech over and over, and now that the time has come to make it—I don't know where to start."

Emily looked at him with questions in her eyes.

Shad ran a hand through his thick hair and laughed nervously. "Well, I guess the best place to start is at the beginning. So much for prepared speeches."

He laughed again and reached for Emily's hand. She did not withdraw it, even though she wondered at his action.

"Remember when we first met?" asked Shad, and Emily nodded slowly.

She didn't suppose she would ever forget.

"Well, you—you impressed me. The way you took my teasing. Your seriousness over your call to the ministry. But at the same time—to think of you as the—the preacher in town made me—well, I felt mixed-up and angry.

"You see, my father had been a preacher—and at one time I thought that I would be a preacher, too, and then my mother got sick. Really sick—but there was no money for a doctor. We watched her get weaker and weaker every day."

Shad paused, the memory still very painful on his face.

"And then, without warning, we lost Dad. He had been the strong one—but he was gone—suddenly—with a heart attack. There was no money, no pension, no place for us to live. We had to move into a tiny two-room shack, and I watched as Mother's health continued to fail."

Emily's eyes misted. She could well imagine the pain of the young boy.

"Well, I decided if that was the way God took care of His preachers, I wasn't going to be one. And I told Mother so in no uncertain words."

He paused again.

"Uncle George and Aunt Moll heard of our situation. They came and got us both, and we lived with them until Mother's death. As soon as Mother was gone, I headed for the city and a job that would care for me in my old age.

"I had a good job—when I met you. But I wasn't happy. And there you were, a little bit of a girl, struggling with the work of running a church. I knew that if I—and other young men like me—hadn't shirked my responsibilities, you wouldn't need to carry all that weight alone.

"It bothered me. But I tried not to let it show. Instead, I had the crazy idea of wooing you away from your calling.

"Well," he smiled softly at Emily, "that didn't work either. You put me in my place, in quick order. And I also realized that if it had worked, I would have been terribly disappointed in you. I guess I wanted you to be stronger—more committed— than I had been.

"But I still couldn't get away from the fact that you had been true to your calling and I had turned my back on it. It bothered me—day and night.

"At last I decided to do something about it. I wasn't happy anyway. I might as well do what I had been called to do.

"So I made things right with the Lord and set off to do what I should have done in the first place."

"You mean—you mean—?" asked Emily.

"I quit my job and went off to train for the ministry."

Emily's eyes grew big.

"You're a minister?"

"Not quite. I still have some more schooling ahead."

"Oh-h," murmured Emily, her voice barely audible.

His grip on her hand tightened.

"What will Aunt Moll say?" wondered Emily.

Shad laughed. "Aunt Moll has already said everything there is to be said," he told her.

"She knows?"

"She has always known. Aunt Moll has sent regular packages of cookies and toilet articles. She said that they were more than happy to have Mother's prayers answered and her son in the ministry—where he belongs." He blinked quickly several times. Emily tightened her grip on his hand.

"Aunt Moll never said a thing to me," she said in a puzzled tone.

"That's because I asked her not to."

Emily was shocked, and her expression told him so.

"I wanted to be sure," he explained. "Sure that I was going into the ministry for the right reasons. Because I had a call— not because I had a crush."

Emily felt her face flush again.

"And do you have a call?" she asked softly.

"I do. I'm sure of it now. God has confirmed it in a number of ways. I don't feel worthy to serve, but I am willing to give my life to it. He will need to take me—and use me. I'm nothing in myself."

Emily smiled. "That's the best news I've ever heard!" she exclaimed. "No wonder you didn't want to share it in a letter."

Shad released her hand and stood to his feet. For a moment he watched the swirl of the creek water. A dragonfly dipped for a water bug. Above them baby robins quarreled in the nest over who would get the proffered worm.

"That isn't what I didn't want to write in the letter," he said slowly.

Emily's eyes widened. Shad reached for her hand and helped her to her feet.

He was very close to her. She could feel her heart pounding. She felt she should move back to get some room, some perspective, but she was rooted to the spot, not wanting to move away.

"What I couldn't write in the letter is the—the fact that I care for you, Emily. Deeply. You have both my respect and my— my love. I was hoping—praying—that you might find it in your heart to honor me with permission to call—to write when I'm away—and perhaps, if God wills it . . ."

Emily's breath caught in her throat. She wondered if she was hearing him correctly.

"Could you—would you, Emily?" he asked huskily.

Emily wanted to answer but she couldn't find the words.

"I know this is sudden—that I have no reason to think you care at all for me—except—except the look in your eyes long ago when you told me that you'd pray. Have you prayed, Emily?"

Emily nodded, still silent.

"Has God answered?"

"Oh-h, oh, yes," murmured Emily with deep emotion.

Shad reached out to take Emily by the shoulders. He looked searchingly into her hazel eyes.

"And the answer?" he prompted.

Emily swallowed. Tears formed in her eyes as she looked steadily into Shad's. "It—it would seem the answer is yes," she whispered. "God has called you again into His ministry. And—this time you are choosing obedience. I—I have never had a prayer answered more—more fully." And Emily's eyes shone with the marvel of answered prayer.

Shad smiled and pulled her into his arms.

"I'm so glad God answers prayer," he whispered, and Emily blushed.

"Oh, but I didn't pray for this," she protested hastily, drawing back, her face red at the thought that Shad might think she'd prayed for his love.

But Shad quickly silenced her. "I did," he said softly as his arms closed about her, holding her tenderly, his cheek against hers. "I did. If God so willed."

And Emily smiled softly to herself as her arms lifted slowly to encircle his neck.

JANETTE OKE

JULIA'S LAST HOPE

Her dreams for her
family seemed to be
crumbling around
her. But what could
she *do*?

Books by Janette Oke

Another Homecoming*
Celebrating the Inner Beauty of Woman
Janette Oke's Reflections on the Christmas Story
The Matchmakers
The Meeting Place*
Nana's Gift
The Red Geranium
Return to Harmony*
Tomorrow's Dream*

CANADIAN WEST
When Calls the Heart	When Breaks the Dawn
When Comes the Spring	When Hope Springs New

LOVE COMES SOFTLY
Love Comes Softly	Love's Unending Legacy
Love's Enduring Promise	Love's Unfolding Dream
Love's Long Journey	Love Takes Wing
Love's Abiding Joy	Love Finds a Home

A PRAIRIE LEGACY
The Tender Years	A Quiet Strength
A Searching Heart	

SEASONS OF THE HEART
Once Upon a Summer	Winter Is Not Forever
The Winds of Autumn	Spring's Gentle Promise

WOMEN OF THE WEST
The Calling of Emily Evans	A Bride for Donnigan
Julia's Last Hope	Heart of the Wilderness
Roses for Mama	Too Long a Stranger
A Woman Named Damaris	The Bluebird and the Sparrow
They Called Her Mrs. Doc	A Gown of Spanish Lace
The Measure of a Heart	Drums of Change

DEVOTIONALS
The Father Who Calls	Father of My Heart
The Father of Love	Faithful Father

Janette Oke: A Heart for the Prairie
Biography of Janette Oke by Laurel Oke Logan

*with T. Davis Bunn

JANETTE OKE'S

Women of the West

THE CALLING OF EMILY EVANS

JULIA'S LAST HOPE

ROSES FOR MAMA

Published by Bethany House Publishers
A Ministry of Bethany Fellowship International
11400 Hampshire Avenue South
Minneapolis, Minnesota 55438

ISBN 0-7394-4380-1

Printed in the United States of America by
Bethany Press International, Minneapolis, Minnesota 55438

Dedicated to the memory of
a dear friend,
Ramona J. Middleton, M.D.,
who went to be with the Lord
on February 16, 1990.
She was so much more than a doctor
to the many who knew and loved her.

JANETTE OKE was born in Champion, Alberta, during the Depression years, to a Canadian prairie farmer and his wife. She is a graduate of Mountain View Bible College in Didsbury, Alberta, where she met her husband, Edward. They were married in May of 1957, and went on to pastor churches in Indiana as well as Calgary and Edmonton, Canada.

The Okes have three sons and one daughter and are enjoying the addition of grandchildren to the family. Edward and Janette have both been active in their local church, serving in various capacities as Sunday school teachers and board members. They make their home near Calgary, Alberta.

Contents

Chapter One

The Unexpected

No one in the household was prepared for the news. Julia Harrigan was in the east parlor, her back turned to the warm rays of the Saturday morning sun. It promised to be another delightful spring day. She hummed softly as her hands worked a dainty hem in a new tablecloth and smiled as the smooth fabric, fine linen imported from England, slipped through her fingers. She did love fine things.

From the dining room came the contented sound of Hettie's low, rich singing as she cleared away the remains of the morning breakfast.

A gentle squeaking sound coming from the porch told Julia that her two daughters were seated in the double porch swing. She imagined their yellow-gold hair reflecting the morning sun, their wide, frilly skirts fanned out across the whiteness of the painted seat. Then the swing became silent, and Julia heard footsteps cross the veranda as the girls moved on to some other activity, chattering as they went.

Again Julia smiled. Life was good. God had certainly blessed them.

"Papa was wrong," she whispered, giving the needle an extra thrust for emphasis. "John Harrigan *can* support me in the manner to which I am accustomed."

Julia almost chuckled at the thought of her father's concern. She looked about her. The east parlor walls were papered with soft yellow roses, the furniture was white wicker, padded liberally and covered with yellow chintz. Everything about the room spoke of comfort and a family of means.

Beyond the doors, rich walnut furniture highlighted the dining room. Deep, skillfully patterned carpet covered the floor, and fine china graced the table.

The large, bright entrance hall featured a winding staircase that led to comfortable and homey bedrooms above. Pastoral pictures, gentle in expression and presenting a sense of harmony and peace, lined the hallway.

In fact, everything about the house spoke of quietness and calm. Julia had always dreamed of having a home that would convey to her family and guests strong feelings of tranquillity. Knowing this, John gave her every opportunity to create a peaceful atmosphere in their home.

Raised in the East and educated in a fine school, Julia had been brought up to be a woman of gentle spirit. But when she met the young John Harrigan, a rugged westerner, she did not hesitate to make her choice known. Even her father was amazed at the way she put her dainty foot down.

"I want to marry him," she insisted.

"Think, girl!" her father roared. "You are used to finery and ease. Do you think this rough woodsman will be able to provide it for you?"

"I really don't care," she responded. "Surely there is more to life than tea parties and silk dresses."

"Yes, there is more to life. There is poverty and need and hungry, unkempt children. But I do not wish it for an offspring of mine."

She pleaded then. "Oh, Papa. Please—I beg of you, don't send him away. I would rather have little with this man by my side than a fine mansion and someone I don't love."

In the end her father gave in, though reluctantly.

"I am thankful that your dear mama isn't alive to see you leave for that godforsaken wasteland," he whispered as he kissed her goodbye after the wedding ceremony. "She would never forgive me." His heavy sigh told Julia that he suffered because of her going.

"Come and see us someday, Papa," she pleaded. "I will write to you as soon as we are settled." And she kissed his cheek where the tears had left dampness.

So she and John moved West, settling in a remote village tucked in the Rocky Mountains. John took a job as overseer in a large lumber mill.

Julia stopped her needlework to concentrate on those early years of marriage. They had been difficult, requiring both her and John to make many adjustments. Thinking back, she was glad her father had not made a trip west to visit them at the time.

Then their lives took an unexpected turn. John's uncle came to them in need. Born and raised in the wilds, Uncle George was a salty, rough man, crude in his manners, and Julia felt uneasy around him. But he was John's kin, and when he took ill, Julia suggested he move into the spare room in the small house they rented.

By the time he died, Julia had changed her mind about Uncle George. At his simple funeral service she cried harder than any of the other mourners. She would miss him, she knew. She had learned to love him in the time that she had waited on him.

"You mustn't weep so," John cautioned as he placed his arm around her shoulders. "You must be extra careful."

Julia looked at her increasing waistline. Not wishing to harm their unborn child, she stopped her crying, straightened her shoulders, and blew her nose in her linen handkerchief.

"I will miss him," she said softly. "He really had a special sweetness about him."

"I never thought I'd hear you call Uncle George sweet," John teased. "Salty was the word you used to use for him. Remember how uncomfortable his quick, sharp tongue used to make you?" John pulled Julia into his arms. "But Uncle George surprised us, didn't he? Underneath all that, he had a sweet spirit. We both will miss him."

And then the unexpected. The old trapper, miner, lumberman, prospector, somehow, somewhere, had hit pay dirt. Stashed away in a local bank was a large sum of money from a gold strike. No one knew about it until after his death, when John and Julia learned that he had left it all to them "as thanks for all you have done in caring for and loving a grouchy old man."

Julia cried again. John was less emotional about the windfall. He set to work immediately to build Julia the kind of home he felt she wanted and deserved.

He spared no expense. By the time the home was ready for occupancy the money was exhausted, but Julia was the mistress of a fine manor, the only one in town that had indoor plumbing and a generator to supply electricity.

By the time they moved into the house their family had increased. The child they had looked forward to turned out to be a girl with a twin sister. Julia was ecstatic. Having been an only child, she could think of no greater gift to give a child than a sibling playmate.

"They will be kindred spirits," she bubbled. "It will be great fun to watch them grow. Do you think they will be alike?"

John looked at his sleeping daughters. One baby stirred— the one they had named Felicity. In her sleep she moved a small fist and managed to get it to her mouth. She slurped and smacked awkwardly, frowning in frustration when her hand slipped from her lips.

The other baby, Jennifer, slept peacefully.

"I'm guessing they will be different," John answered, smiling down on their precious newborns. "Look at them. They are already showing their different personalities."

"I think I will like it that way better, don't you? It would seem rather eerie raising two of the same person—so to speak. Oh, John, do you think we will be good parents to them?"

"With God's help, we will figure out how to raise them," John assured his lovely wife.

The years passed quickly in the big white house. The small lumber town changed very little. A few people came and went, depending on the prosperity of the mill; but most of the people in Calder Springs had lived there for many years.

The Harrigans' morning routine seldom varied. John left the house to go to work at six-fifteen and returned after the mill whistle blew at five-thirty in the afternoon.

Julia never considered living anywhere else. She grew accustomed to the sights and sounds of the small town. The sharp, stinging wind off the icy mountain slopes in winter, the heavy mist curtain of autumn, the fine tints of green as spring slowly spread over the hillsides, the hum and bustle of the summer morning, the lingering acrid smell of the smoke stacks all year long.

John had picked a suitable site for their manor. It was close enough to town so Julia could easily walk on a nice day, yet far enough from the dust and clamor to give her the peace and tranquillity she loved.

There wasn't much entertainment in town, but Julia had never needed outside excitement or activity to make her happy. Julia and John were heavily involved in their church, and that, plus a few community and social events, was enough for both of them.

Julia held a simple but deep faith. Never had John met any-one with the strong personal commitment to God that Julia possessed. She was like a child in her trust of the Savior. John's pride in her was evident in his eyes and in the way he smiled at her.

The community developed a proprietary attitude toward the Harrigans, as though the family in the fine house belonged to the town. Their gentility added refinement to the whole settle-ment. "The Harrigans live just over yonder," folks would boast to any newcomer who would listen. "Hardly a stone's throw from our door. Such a fine family, the Harrigans. Such a proper lady she is—but totally without airs. Greets you on the street like any ordinary soul. Even has ladies in for tea. Fine folk."

Some may have envied Julia Harrigan her fine lace curtains and thick rich carpets, but there was no malice toward her. Ju-lia did not flaunt her finery, and no one could have accused her of snobbery.

Julia rethreaded her needle and snipped off the fine cord with a click of her teeth. "Oh my," she whispered. "I forgot again."

John had warned her about snipping the thread with her teeth, afraid that she might damage them. Julia always in-tended to use her scissors, but she usually forgot until too late.

She wriggled in her seat, impatient at herself, and let her eyes move to the window. It was a lovely day. She should take the girls shopping.

Before Julia had time to lay aside the piece of linen, she heard a step in the hall. Her eyes filled with curiosity, then alarm, for she recognized the footsteps as John's—and John should be at the mill.

Julia's eyes traveled to the wall clock. Twenty minutes to eight. What could have happened to bring John home at such an hour? Letting the tablecloth fall to the chaise lounge beside her, Julia started to stand. But before she could get to her feet, John was in the room.

Julia took one look at him and fear pierced her.

"John! Are you ill?"

He stared at her blankly, making her wonder if he had heard her question. Then he shook his head slowly as he groped for the back of the chair.

Julia looked at his ashen face. She wished to go to him but her body wouldn't move.

He was still shaking his head.

"No. No, I'm fine," John said, but his voice did nothing to put Julia at ease.

"Then why are you home—at this time of the morning?" Julia probed.

"They sent us home. All of us. They called a special meeting this morning. For everyone. They made an announcement. Then they sent us all home."

Nothing he said made any sense to Julia. She fumbled to touch the linen. Perhaps the feel of it would make the world real again.

John raised a hand to smooth his dark brown hair.

He looks tired, Julia suddenly noticed, and wondered why she hadn't seen it before. *He needs a break. He's been working too hard.* Just as she was about to suggest it, John raised his head and looked directly at her. Julia saw a plea for understanding in his eyes when he finally broke the news.

"They announced this morning that the mill is closing."

Chapter Two

Twosome

"Oh, Fel! Don't talk silly," Jennifer said softly, her deep blue eyes imploring her sister.

"Only *you* think it's silly to talk about boys," Felicity answered with an impish giggle. "All the girls at school—"

"Well, the girls at school are silly, too," Jennifer interrupted. Her face flushed slightly. "You know Mama wouldn't like us—"

Felicity tossed her blond curls. "Oh, pooh! Mama's not so stuffy as all that. I'll bet she talked about boys when—"

"Stop!" Jennifer exclaimed, her face growing more red. "Mama was always a lady—"

"But ladies talk about boys, or men. It's just your notion that they are a forbidden subject," insisted Felicity, a new impatience edging her voice.

"I never said they are a forbidden subject," argued Jennifer.

"Well, you act like they are. Every time someone mentions one of them, you scold or change the topic. All the girls think—"

"All the girls think what?" Jennifer prompted Felicity, determined to know the end of her twin's unfinished sentence. Jennifer's eyes narrowed. She didn't like the direction of the conversation.

Felicity lowered her eyes and toyed with a frill on her full skirt, wishing she hadn't made the comment.

"Well?" said Jennifer. "What do the girls think? That I'm stuffy? Conceited? Arrogant?"

Felicity's head came up. If the girls at school even hinted any of those things, she would have defended her twin sister with all her strength.

"No! Nothing like that. They just think you're—well—sort of sober."

"Sober?"

"Yes, sober."

"Sober?" Jennifer repeated, as though unable to believe the accusation.

Felicity nodded again, still fidgeting with the frill.

"What's wrong with being sober?" Jennifer asked.

"Nothing. Nothing at all," Felicity quickly responded.

"Then why—?"

"It's just odd for a girl your age—our age—to be sober all the time."

Jennifer considered the charge. Perhaps she was a bit sober for her age, but most of the things the girls discussed did not interest her, and statements that sent other girls into spasms of laughter weren't even funny to her. After thinking for a few minutes, Jennifer shrugged her slim shoulders.

"Maybe I am odd," she said softly.

Felicity gave her a comforting nudge. "Oh, you are not. You just don't like boys." Then, as an afterthought, added, "Yet."

Jennifer's head came up and defiance tilted her chin. "I like boys," she declared. "I just don't see the point of making silly statements and giggling over them, that's all."

Felicity shrugged. This conversation was going nowhere, and she didn't like to be boxed in. Responding to the restlessness within her, she reached one foot to the porch floor and gave the swing another push. It had been moving much too slowly to suit her.

"Do you think Mama will let us get that green organdy for new Sunday dresses?" she asked.

Jennifer was used to Felicity's quickly changing moods and her jumps from one topic to another. She picked up on both immediately.

"Oh, I hope so," she said with shining eyes, lowering her foot to add her push to the swing. "I have never seen such a pretty color."

"Blue looks better on us," stated Felicity, pulling at a strand of her long hair.

Jennifer nodded. It was true. But the green was so beautiful—so rich looking—and they had so many blue dresses.

"Do you think Mama would take us today?" asked Felicity,

her face brightening with the thought. "It's such a beautiful morning."

Jennifer widened her eyes in support of the idea; then she placed a hand on Felicity's arm as though to restrain her from a sudden dash to the parlor.

"Mama's hemming the new tablecloth," she reminded her sister. "She wants it finished by next Sunday when the preacher's family comes for dinner."

Felicity sighed. It would not be right to ask Mama to stop her work and walk to the shops just to buy their green material.

"What should we do then?" asked Felicity, boredom touching her voice.

"I suppose we could clean our room," Jennifer suggested, giving her twin a brief sideways glance.

"We've cleaned our room," Felicity groaned.

"We've picked up our things and made our beds," Jennifer corrected. "But you know what your closet looks like—and Mama said—"

"Oh, bother!" exclaimed Felicity. "Why bring that up again?"

"Because it's still not done," Jennifer scolded.

"Just because *your* closet looks like it's never been used—"

"That's because I keep it tidy as I go," lectured Jennifer. "You could do that too if you just took a bit of time."

"Time!" Felicity exploded. "Who has time to stop and—?"

"I do. And so do you. It's much easier to hang it up or put it away when it's still in your hand than to pick it up later."

Felicity glared. She put out a foot, stopped the swing with a jerk, and stood up. "You sure know how to spoil a nice day," she fumed.

Jennifer did not look offended. She knew all about Felicity's moods, and this one was harmless. Soon Felicity would be asking her to join in some exciting caper. Jennifer stayed seated, her hand resting lightly on the wooden arm of the swing.

"I will help you if you wish," she offered.

Felicity expected that. Jennifer was always helping someone after she had already done her own work. Felicity didn't stop to analyze the situation or even to consider herself privileged. She shrugged. "Let's get it over with then."

Jennifer stepped from the swing and followed her sister to the offending closet in their bedroom.

Jennifer took charge. She moved everything from the closet floor and placed it in a heaping pile before her sister. "Here," she said. "Sort it out. Make a pile of the things that aren't worth saving. I'll hang your clothes properly."

Felicity didn't argue. She dropped to the floor and began to rummage through her possessions. Felicity was a collector. She treasured things. How could she throw away all these items that represented a part of her life? She looked dismally at the dried wild flowers, still stuffed in a little glass vase, long since void of water. Harley George had given her the field flowers at the school spring picnic. Felicity blushed as she thought about her stammered response. And now Harley was gone. His parents had moved away. How could she throw out his flowers?

Felicity's eyes moved to the news clippings carelessly tossed in a hat box. They told about a young man from Europe who had visited their area to challenge the local mountain peaks. Jennifer and Felicity had stood on the station platform along with a number of other local youngsters and watched him and his party as they unloaded their gear. He had been so dashing! So adventuresome! For a moment Felicity had longed to be a boy—or to make him realize she was a girl. She fingered the clippings and wondered where adventure had taken Erik Eriksen after his visit to Canada.

Felicity reached for a hair bow. She wouldn't think of wearing it now. It was much too childish, but it had been a favorite. She looked at the stain on one end. Claude Singer had dipped it in the inkwell—just to get her attention. All the girls had liked Claude—but hers was the only ribbon he had dipped.

With a big sigh, Felicity scooped her treasures to her, knowing she would be unable to discard any of them. "What we need is separate rooms," she announced.

Jennifer stopped her sorting and shifting of dresses and poked her head out the closet door.

"What do you mean?" she asked. They had always shared a room even though the big house had three additional bedrooms. They had never wanted their own rooms—had never wanted to be apart. The thought frightened Jennifer now.

"There isn't enough room in this dinky closet," insisted Felicity.

"It's the same size as mine."

"Yes, but you—" Felicity stopped. How could she express the fact that Jennifer didn't have treasures without sounding harsh?

"I what?" demanded Jennifer.

Felicity fumbled for words. "You—you don't have—have as many things to put away."

"That's because I throw out the junk," Jennifer stated.

"It's not junk," Felicity insisted.

Jennifer sighed. She knew Felicity was more sentimental about things than she was. At the same time she knew that Felicity was often more impatient with people. It was people and their feelings that mattered most to Jennifer, and now it was Mama she was thinking of. Mama had asked Felicity to clean her closet, and Mama would be upset if it was not done. And Felicity might even be assigned a second chore if the first was not completed in the allotted time. Yet Jennifer hated to get caught in the middle. She had to gently maneuver, suggest, and involve Felicity, although Jennifer would have preferred to work on the mess herself. But that wouldn't set well with Mama.

Jennifer felt trapped.

"I have a little extra space on my shelf," she sighed. "Why don't we put everything you want to keep in a small box and set it in my closet?"

Felicity looked relieved.

It took some skill to fit them all in the box, but they managed to do so. Felicity still had her treasures. Jennifer stacked a few of her own hat boxes to make the extra one fit on her shelf. Finally the task was done. Felicity's closet looked as neat and tidy as her own, Jennifer thought. And there hadn't been a scene over the doing. She felt relief as she closed the closet door and suggested to Felicity that they get some lemonade to take with them to the back porch.

As they passed the east parlor they heard voices. "That sounds like Papa!" exclaimed Felicity.

Jennifer glanced at the hall clock. "He shouldn't be home at this time of day," she reminded Felicity.

Felicity tossed her head and hurried toward the door. What did it matter what time it was? It was always nice to have Papa home. Perhaps he had some delightful surprise. Perhaps—

The two girls arrived at the parlor door just in time to hear the stunned voice of their father say, "The mill is closing."

Chapter Three

Changes

"Closing? What do you mean?" Julia asked, her voice calm and even.

John's voice was not as calm as he answered her. "Closing! Shutting down! Finished!" he declared, his words tight and clipped.

Julia understood then. Not about the mill, but about John. John was worried. She had to do something to help him. She crossed the room and laid a hand on his tense arm.

"It's okay," she whispered. "It will be all right."

John sank into a nearby chair. He shook his head as though to contradict his wife's statement of assurance.

She sat beside him, her hand stroking his sleeve.

"Everything will be all right," she insisted.

"You don't understand," he argued.

"Yes, I think I do," she responded.

He looked directly into her eyes. "What did I say?" he challenged her. He had never spoken to her in such a manner before.

Julia swallowed hard. Then, with a voice as steady as she could summon, answered, "You said the mill is closing. Is going to shut down. Is finished." She found it difficult to keep her chin from quivering, her eyes from filling with tears.

"You must be in shock, just as I was. You still don't understand. But when—"

"I am not in shock," she said firmly. "I am in my right mind. The mill will close. That means you will be without a job."

She held his eyes evenly, daring him to challenge her again. "I know we will be fine," she insisted, and gave his sleeve a tiny tug, hoping to bring them both back to reality. "You can get another job. You have fine references."

"Jule—all I know is lumber," he reminded her, his voice patient again in spite of their circumstance.

"And that is enough," Julia said.

"The mill is closing, Julia." He shook his head as if to clear it. "I knew we didn't have as much lumber as we should, but this . . ." His voice trailed away; then he looked directly at Julia. "If the timber supply is gone, there will not be another mill opening up to take its place."

Julia would not be deterred. "There are still mills in other towns. There will always be mills. The world can't get along without lumber."

"The other mills already have workers."

"If there is no job in lumber—you can learn something else. You have a good mind—and a strong back. There will be other jobs—somewhere."

"Yes," he admitted, "I could—if it wasn't for the house."

"We can sell the house and buy another," offered Julia with a shrug of her slight shoulders. She hoped that John did not read the agony in her eyes. She loved their house. Their home.

He shook his head slowly, pain showing in his eyes. "I'm afraid you don't understand. Without the mill, the town will die. There will be no sale for the houses, any of them. The property will be worthless—useless. It will become a ghost town."

His words made Julia's breath catch in her throat. Her hand on his sleeve trembled slightly and her eyes misted. Then her chin lifted and determination returned to her eyes.

"God has always provided for us," she declared fervently. "He will not forsake us now—when we need Him the most. Although the news is—is crushing, He will show us what we must do. Of that I am sure."

Her words, spoken with such conviction, eased the tension in John's face. "Oh, Jule," he whispered softly and drew her into his arms.

"You'll see. Everything will work out." She stroked his hair and pressed her cheek against his.

Neither of them saw the two girls standing in the doorway. And neither heard them retreat as they turned as one and left for their own room.

Jennifer broke the silence. Her face was ashen, her eyes filled with fear. "What will we do?" she whispered hoarsely.

Felicity had thrown herself face down on her bed and was sobbing uncontrollably.

Jennifer hastened to her and placed a protective arm around her sister's shaking shoulders.

"Shh, shh. It's all right."

"I don't want to move away," sobbed Felicity. "I like it here. My friends—"

Jennifer stroked her sister's long blond hair. "We might not have to move," she soothed.

"You heard Papa," sobbed Felicity.

"You heard Mama," responded Jennifer. "God will show us what to do. He knows all about the mill. Perhaps Papa will find another job—"

"You heard Papa," Felicity countered. "The mill is all he knows."

"You heard Mama," Jennifer repeated. "Papa could learn another trade."

"We would still have to move," Felicity argued, her sobs growing louder.

"Stop! Stop! Listen to me," Jennifer commanded, shaking Felicity by the shoulder. "Mama and Papa will hear you and they will feel even worse than they do now. We've got to think about them right now. Please stop!"

Felicity could not stop, but she did quiet down a bit. Her sobs became softer, her body more relaxed.

Jennifer walked to the window. She lifted a trembling hand to brush aside the pale blue curtains and look out over the scene below. Her eyes scanned the street, the neighboring houses, the small town with its church spire and school yard, the mountainside that rose in the distance. She loved it here too. Tears welled up in her eyes. She would hate it so if they had to leave. Why did the mill have to close? Why couldn't things continue as they always had? They had lived here for as long as she could remember. Surely there was some way for them to continue living the life they had always known. Her hand relaxed, and the curtain fell back into place. Jennifer squared her shoulders and turned to Felicity. "If we have to go—we must make it as easy for Mama and Papa as possible."

Felicity brushed at her tears and nodded her head.

"You can take your treasures with you," continued Jennifer, trying to console her brokenhearted sister.

A fresh torrent of tears ran down Felicity's cheeks. "But I—I can't take my friends or—"

"But if everyone has to move—perhaps our friends will be going with us," Jennifer said to her sister.

"Where?" Felicity sobbed.

"I—I don't know. To wherever we have to go. To another mill. Their papas work in the mill too," Jennifer reminded Felicity.

Felicity began mopping up. She wiped her eyes and blew her nose noisily. Jennifer was glad that the worst of the storm was spent. She crossed to her sister and laid a loving hand on her shoulder.

"We'll be all right," she assured Felicity again, wishing with all her heart that she felt as confident as her words sounded.

Felicity nodded. She pushed herself up from the bed and straightened her skirts. Then she went to the dresser, picked up a hairbrush, and brushed her hair into place. "I'm going to go wash my face," she told Jennifer. When she returned a short while later she showed no trace of her tears.

Jennifer wished that she could dismiss the incident as easily. Inside, she still felt knotted, twisted. In spite of her brave words to Felicity, she did not feel assurance about their future.

"Let's ask Mama if we can go get that green—" began Felicity.

Jennifer stopped her with a quick shake of her head. "Not now!" she exclaimed. "Papa has no job."

Felicity looked surprised, as though she had already forgotten their circumstance, but then her eyes softened and she nodded her head in agreement.

"I guess that would be unthinkable," she finished lamely. "Well then, let's ask if we can go to the drugstore for a soda," she continued. "Surely we can still afford that."

Jennifer gave her a dark look, and Felicity stared back at her.

"Felicity Harrigan," said Jennifer sternly, "we are thirteen years of age. Surely we can be understanding when our parents are in trouble."

Felicity shrugged. "Okay, okay," she said impatiently, "so what are you going to do to make things right, Miss Know-It-All?"

"I—I don't know it all," stammered Jennifer. "I—I just know that we can't be asking for things when Papa is without a job. There will be no money—"

Felicity's eyes brightened. "That's it!" she squealed, and threw her arms around Jennifer's shoulders.

"That's what?" questioned Jennifer.

"Jobs! We are old enough to have jobs. We can help Papa."

Jennifer held herself in check for a moment; then she hugged Felicity in return.

"Of course!" she agreed. "Of course. We can find jobs."

"Let's not tell them," suggested Felicity; "not until we each have found a place to work."

"But—" began Jennifer.

"We will talk to Hettie. Tell her that we are going up town for a soda and she can tell Mama."

"But—" began Jennifer again. She would not lie—even to conceal their plans of helping the family.

"And we *will* get a soda," continued Felicity, walking to her dresser and opening a drawer. "Here," she said, producing some coins. "I have enough for a soda. It's from what Papa gave me last week."

Jennifer had never known Felicity to keep any of her spending money. But there were the coins in her hand. It reminded Jennifer that she too had money stashed in her drawer. But even as she thought of it she decided to leave the money where it was. Who knew how soon her papa would find another job? Perhaps her money would be needed for things other than sodas.

"Okay," she finally conceded. "Let's go see Hettie."

As they proceeded to the kitchen, Jennifer's mind was troubled. Never before had they made their own plans and gone off to the drugstore without asking permission from their mother. Jennifer hoped that Felicity's idea—as good as it seemed—did not get them both in trouble.

Chapter Four

Sharing

The news of the mill's closing had traveled fast. The whole town was in shock. As Felicity and Jennifer sipped a common soda at the drugstore they heard the somber, low voices of men and the frightened, shrill voices of women. It seemed to be the topic of all conversations.

"What on earth will we do?" they heard one woman ask. "We were just getting back on our feet after all of those medical bills. Now this."

Her friend tried to be reassuring, but her own voice broke as she answered, "I guess we'll have to go elsewhere. Start over."

"Start over?" questioned the first, her voice quivering. "We're too old to start over."

"What you plannin'?" a man asked his neighbor.

"Don't know. Just don't know," answered the second. "Right now my wife is sick. I came to pick up some medicine. Doc says the change might be good for her. The smoke here has always bothered her."

The first man nodded. "Maybe it will," he agreed, but there was doubt in his eyes. What good was a change if there was no money with which to buy the needed medicine?

"Came at a bad time," said a third man.

"For everyone," agreed the first, his eyes heavy with the worry of it.

As they listened to the people talk, Jennifer and Felicity sensed more than ever the seriousness of the situation. Their problem was not an isolated one. The whole town was affected, just as their father had said. What would happen to all of them? Was there anything two young girls could do?

It was Jennifer who shook them from their despair.

"If we are going to find jobs, we'd better hurry," she whispered to Felicity. "Everyone our age might soon be looking for work."

Felicity stopped flirting with the young man stocking the drugstore shelves and jumped to her feet. Jennifer was right.

"You take this side of the street and I'll take the other side," she ordered Jennifer and then quickly reversed her decision. "No, you take the other side, I'll take this side." It would be wonderful if the druggist needed more help to fill his shelves, she was thinking.

But the druggist was not interested in another clerk—not even a soda jerk. He smiled at Felicity and shook his head sadly.

"Don't know how much longer I'll be here," he admitted. "Not the right time to be hiring."

All of the merchants along the little street said much the same thing. No one was hiring. Felicity pushed back her hair from her warm face and trudged on. She hoped that Jennifer was having better luck. When the girls met at the end of the main street, however, Jennifer's report was no more encouraging than Felicity's.

"We'd better get home before Mama starts to worry," said Jennifer.

Felicity reluctantly agreed. Besides, she was thirsty, and they had spent all of her money on the soda.

"We mustn't say anything about the mill closing when we get home," Jennifer warned. "Mama and Papa will want to tell us at the proper time."

Felicity nodded and waved to a friend across the street.

Everything was quiet when the girls reached home. They found Hettie in the kitchen serving late-morning coffee to Tom, her husband, who worked the gardens and was general caretaker around the manor. Both looked unusually serious but brightened when the girls walked in.

"You lookin' for a snack?" asked Hettie. Although she had never had children of her own, Hettie had a knack for understanding them. She always knew what the girls wanted and needed.

"Do you have more lemonade?" asked Jennifer, hoping that her voice sounded unconcerned and normal.

"I sure do," answered the older woman, patting Felicity's golden head as she passed her.

"And you, missie?" she asked Felicity.

"The same," responded Felicity without much enthusiasm. Tom lifted his head as though curious, but made no comment.

"Cookies?" asked Hettie. "Got some fresh gingerbread."

"Just lemonade," said Felicity.

"So what has taken the starch outta you?" asked Tom, his hands cradling his coffee.

"We just shared a soda," Felicity answered. "Where's Mama?" She almost asked for Papa as well, but caught herself in time.

"In the garden," Tom answered.

The two girls thanked Hettie for the lemonade and left for the garden. It seemed important to see their mother. They had to know how she was.

Julia was attacking the rose bed with all of the energy in her slim body, singing hymns in her rich soprano as she worked. Jennifer and Felicity exchanged relieved glances and smiled at their mother as she turned toward them.

"Where have you two been?" asked Julia, halting her song long enough to pose the question.

"Didn't Hettie tell you?" asked Felicity.

"Since when is Hettie your messenger?" Julia responded, stepping back to study the two faces before her.

"We just went to the drugstore," offered Felicity.

"I have no objection to your going to the drugstore—when you have permission to do so," Julia replied evenly.

Both heads dropped.

"Sorry, Mama," murmured Jennifer. She had known they would get themselves in trouble.

"You know the rules of the household," went on Julia. "Permission is always needed to leave your own yard. I don't think that is too much to expect. Do you?"

Two heads shook as one.

"In the future, you will see that permission is granted—first," stated Julia.

This time the two heads nodded.

Julia turned again to her rose beds, and the girls went back to the house and sat in the swing. Jennifer squirmed on the wooden seat, but Felicity had already forgotten the scolding.

"I cleaned my closet," she called to her mother.

Jennifer sucked in her breath.

Julia lifted her head. "I'm glad to hear that," she responded.

"It's as clean as Jennifer's," went on Felicity.

"Good," said Julia.

"Do I get a reward?" asked Felicity.

"Indeed!" said Julia, and Felicity's eyes sparkled.

"You may join us for dinner tonight," Julia finished.

"But I always—" began Felicity, then felt the nudge of Jennifer's toe.

"Exactly!" responded Julia, and turned back to her roses, singing as she worked.

After dinner, John lifted the family Bible from the bureau and turned the pages absentmindedly. He knew he had to tell the girls about the mill, but he wasn't quite sure how to do it, what to say. True, changes were in store for all of them—but what changes?

He knew Julia was right. Of course God would care for them—just as He had always done. But God had assigned the care of the family to the father of the home, and John felt as if he were failing his family. Even though he was not responsible for the closing of the mill, he still felt the guilt. He wanted to supply for the needs of his family as he had done in the past.

Though he tried to appear confident, his shoulders sagged. He had spent the afternoon with other men from the lumber mill, and the conversation always came back to the same stark truth. There would be no work in this small town once the mill closed. And there would be no sale for property—no matter how fine it might be. The little town of Calder Springs would soon be a ghost town.

Julia reached for John's hand and tried to encourage him with one of her confident smiles—though deep within her heart she felt little confidence.

John found the place where they were to continue their scripture reading and cleared his throat. He read the story of how Jesus fed 5,000 people with one young boy's lunch, and Julia found herself wondering just how many times in the future Christ would need to multiply the loaves in her cupboard.

The girls listened attentively to the scripture verses. Even Felicity seemed to be concentrating on what her father read.

John closed the Bible and laid it aside. He cleared his throat, and Julia knew he was searching for words.

"Before we pray," he said at last, "we—I—there has been

some news that has come to us—your mama and me—today that we need to tell you about because it affects all of us."

Jennifer looked down at the bows on her shoes. One was crooked. She bent to twist it to its proper position. Felicity stirred restlessly beside her. Jennifer straightened and gave her sister a silencing look.

"We—we may be having some changes in our lives," John continued, and Julia nodded pleasantly, as though changes were always nice.

"The lumber mill has run out of trees to process in this area and is going to move on to—to somewhere else."

Jennifer could not bring herself to look into her father's eyes. Felicity stirred again, and Jennifer placed a cautioning hand on her arm.

Julia remained silent, allowing John to say what he had to say in his own words—his own time.

"That means there will no longer be work for me here," he finally managed.

If he expected an explosion of some sort, he was mistaken. The room was silent.

He waited a moment and then went on. "We might have to give up our home here and move to another town," he added.

The girls sat rigid.

"Do you understand what I am saying?" John asked the girls. They both nodded.

"We will be fine," Julia put in, giving the girls one of her special smiles.

"What will we do till Papa finds work?" Felicity asked, directing her question to her mother. Julia's eyes clouded.

"It won't take Papa long to find work."

"But everyone uptown says they can't hire now. They don't know how long—"

Jennifer gave Felicity a jab.

Felicity stopped short, her eyes filling with horror.

John and Julia studied the two faces before them.

"You knew?" asked John.

Felicity nodded.

"They went to the drugstore today," explained Julia. "I should have realized—the whole town must be buzzing."

"How much did you hear uptown?" John asked.

"Actually," Jennifer replied slowly, "we—we knew before we went uptown. That's—that's why—"

"We went uptown to try to find jobs," blurted Felicity. "But everyone said they would be moving soon and couldn't hire anybody. Everyone."

Julia's eyes filled with tears. "You went uptown looking for work?" she asked.

"We just wanted to help until Papa found work again," Jennifer apologized.

John looked shaken. "That was good of you," he managed to say. "But I hardly think my little . . ." He hesitated when he saw their disapproving looks. "My two young ladies," he corrected. "I hardly think that my two young ladies need to look for work—quite yet." He managed a weak smile.

"So how did you hear the news?" Julia asked.

Felicity spoke again. "We heard Papa's voice and wanted to see him, so we went to the parlor, but he was telling the news about the mill, so we left again."

"I see," sighed Julia.

"Let's pray together," John said, reaching for his wife's hand, as he always did for family prayer.

They bowed together. John had a difficult time voicing his concerns for the future and skirted the issue with a general prayer. He needed time to talk to the Lord alone about his worries. Maybe after he had worked through the situation he would be able to discuss the future more openly with his family.

Julia's hand tightened on his. She understood his tension.

Two weeks. Two weeks of work remained for every mill worker in town. After that the mill would be no more. The machinery would be dismantled and moved to a new location.

Two weeks. Two weeks to make plans—to bolster oneself for the many changes that were sure to follow.

Some men handed in their notices, drew their wages, and left, hoping to find jobs elsewhere before the rush. Others stayed and put in the few hours that would earn them one last paycheck. Then what?

Chapter Five

The Plan

"Hettie, is the parlor set up for tea?" Julia asked her house-keeper.

"Yes, ma'am," the woman nodded.

"Where is Rose?"

"She's in the kitchen making extra sandwiches."

"Good. Did she get all my invitations handed out?"

"All but the one for Mrs. Pruett. She's gone to see her mother."

"Good," said Julia again. "Did Rose say how many we can count on coming?"

"Said most folks seem right anxious to be here," responded Hettie. "We expect most all of them."

Julia nodded. Her stomach was churning. She had never set out on such a venture before. She wasn't quite sure how to go about it now—but something had to be done.

"Did Rose tell everyone two o'clock?" Julia asked anxiously.

"I believe your invitation told them that, ma'am," Hettie reminded her.

"Oh, yes. Yes, of course," Julia responded, her cheeks slightly flushed.

Hettie busied herself with the tea service.

"Oh, Hettie, I am so nervous about this," Julia admitted, lifting trembling fingers to her cheeks. "What if it all goes wrong?"

"Well, now, what could go wrong? You are simply having neighbor ladies in for tea—and while they are here you will discuss your—our—problem and see if anyone has any ideas how it might be remedied. Nothing difficult about that. Neighborhood ladies always talk about neighborhood problems."

Hettie made it sound so simple. "We'll need to get right to it," Julia said, casting a nervous glance at the clock. "It won't be long until the ladies will need to go home. We only have an hour or so until school will be dismissed."

"You can talk about a lot of ideas in an hour," Hettie said to comfort Julia.

Julia hoped so. She also hoped the women would be on time. Just as she was about to begin pacing, the doorbell rang. Hettie ushered in Mrs. Wright, the preacher's wife.

"Oh, I am so glad you were able to come," said Julia, taking the woman's hand. "I may need your help. I don't know how to do this—this sort of thing."

Mrs. Wright held Julia's hand firmly. "Don't be nervous," she whispered, "just pretend you are leading the missionary women's group at church. You always do such a nice job."

"Thank you," Julia returned, managing a smile.

The doorbell continued to ring until fourteen ladies were gathered in the spacious Harrigan parlor. Hettie and Rose busied themselves serving tea and dainty sandwiches, followed by flaky pastries. Julia studied the clock and then the neighbors before her. The news about the mill hung heavily about each of them. An unfamiliar seriousness shadowed their faces, a darkness veiled their eyes, and their shoulders sagged under the invisible load. In spite of their attempts to be casual, Julia knew they felt every bit as anxious as she did.

She rose to her feet and cleared her throat.

"You all know that I have invited you here for more than just tea today," she said candidly. "Though it is a treat to have the fellowship of good neighbors, we all share a common burden at this time. I—I don't know if there is anything—that we—as women—wives—can do about the situation our husbands are in—but I thought maybe—if we put our heads together—we might come up with something."

All eyes focused on Julia. All ears listened carefully.

Julia shifted her weight from one foot to another.

"Now then—we know this is a lumber town. That we have no other industry to keep us going. But is there—is there any other possibility? I mean—what might this town be able to do for—for commerce?"

They searched one another's faces. Each woman seemed to be looking to a neighbor for an answer, but no one was finding it.

"We must think," said Julia with such urgency that her brow puckered and her hands twisted before her.

"Without the mill I don't see much hope," ventured a somber-faced woman.

Several in the circle shrugged in agreement.

"Let's look at what we *do* have," Julia suggested. "Hettie, would you bring that chalkboard, please?" With the easel beside her, Julia continued. "What do we have here?" she asked the women.

Blank looks clouded faces.

"We can't farm," said one woman frankly. "These mountains hardly leave room for a small garden."

"But we do have gardens—all of us," replied Julia, and she wrote "Gardens" to get things started.

"We have some wild berry patches scattered here and there," one woman ventured, and Julia added that to her list.

"We have more'n our share of mountains," offered a timid young woman.

"Mountains," said Julia, writing the word in big letters. "Lots of people love mountains. Now—what do people go to mountains for—besides lumber?"

"Restin'," answered an elderly woman almost hidden in a corner.

Julia stopped with her chalk suspended. An idea was beginning to form. She wasn't sure if it was crazy—or feasible. But she had to share it with her neighbors.

"Do you—do you suppose we could make our little town into a—a resort town?" she asked breathlessly.

"Don't have much for a hotel," commented the banker's wife.

Julia shook her head. It was true. The only hotel in town was in sorry shape. It was used mostly as a boarding place for unmarried, often transient mill workers. The owner had never bothered to "fancy up" the place.

"Well, maybe we could—could use our own homes," Julia ventured.

Eyes moved about the room. They traveled over Julia's thick carpets, rich velvet draperies, expensive paintings, china cups, and silver service. No one spoke but each of the women knew what the others were thinking. Julia Harrigan had the only house in town that visitors might pay to stay in.

"Well, we might not be able to handle many at a time," Julia went on, "but the train will continue to pass through. If we could just advertise—then we could—could set up attractions and tours and cottage industries."

"Such as?" probed one woman.

Julia lifted her chalk again. "How many of you can knit?" she asked. Eleven hands went up. "Crochet?" asked Julia. Nine responded. "Sew?" All hands were raised, though some hesitantly.

"See—it's not impossible. And we can cook—and bake—and grow our gardens and make jam from those wild berries. We could make this a real tourist town if we tried."

By now Julia's face was shining with the possibility. Others seemed to catch the spirit.

"Do you really think—?"

"Would there be enough—?"

"How could we advertise—?"

Questions began to flow. Julia had no ready answers, but she did have interest. Would it really work? Could it?

"We need to think about this some more," she said. "I know the children will be returning from school soon and you need to be home—but let's think about this and meet here again next Tuesday.

"And spread the word to your neighbors," Julia suggested. "If—if it seems workable, we will form committees. There will be much work to do. It will take all of us—working together."

It was a different group of ladies who left Julia's house than had gathered a short time earlier. Dull eyes now had a sparkle. Worried brows were smooth again. Dark shadows had disappeared from faces. Where only despair had been, there was now hope. Frail, fragile hope—but hope nonetheless.

———

"Hettie, do you think Mama's plan could work?" Jennifer asked a few days later.

"Why not?" responded the older woman. "Your mama is a capable woman. When she puts her mind to something, it is likely to happen."

"But people around town are saying it's a crazy idea—just a silly dream," Felicity dared to state.

"An' who's sayin' that?" asked Hettie, her eyes flashing.

Felicity shrugged. "I don't know. I just heard—"

"Well, you don't listen none to such talk. You hear? Folks should at least give your mama a chance to prove herself."

"I sure hope it works," said Jennifer slowly. "I like it here."

Hettie sighed as she lifted a pan of corn bread from the oven. She liked it too, and if the town folded, as folks said it was sure to do, she and her Tom would be without work along with everyone else.

"Well, your mama has been doing all she can. She has sent off a number of letters to see what kind of interest there might be in a tourist town here. We have about as nice a location as one could want. Beautiful mountains, pretty lakes, nice fishing streams. Your mama has summed it all up in her letters."

"But tomorrow is Papa's last day of work," Felicity reminded Hettie.

"Not quite. A couple dozen men will be working for a while yet, tearing down the mill. Your papa still has work until that is done and the machines are shipped out of here. He says that it will take him another two or three weeks to get all that done."

"But by then everyone else will have moved away," pined Felicity.

"Not everyone," replied Hettie.

"Well, most. Some of our friends have left already."

"Some folks don't have much faith," said Hettie.

Jennifer lowered her head. She wasn't sure just how strong her own faith was, but she wouldn't admit as much to Hettie.

"Here's your milk and corn bread," Hettie offered. "Stay here in the kitchen with it so you won't bother your mama. She's busy with her letter writing."

"What's she writing about now?" asked Felicity.

"She's still trying to find someone who would be interested in buying the hotel and giving it a face-lift."

"That old thing?" said Felicity. "Who'd want that?"

"Well, if this becomes a tourist town that 'old thing' could be worth a lot of money."

Felicity shrugged and lifted her milk glass. She wasn't convinced.

Julia and her committee worked doggedly. A number of the ladies had reconsidered Julia's idea and decided that her plan, exciting as it sounded, was just not feasible. They had families that needed to be fed and clothed *now*—they could not wait for some future venture to pay off. Julia's committee now consisted of just eight ladies—eight determined ladies bent on saving their town, their homes, and their dreams.

Chapter Six

Baring the Heart

Julia straightened her bent shoulders and pushed back a wisp of wayward hair. She had always loved gardening. Had always filled her flower beds with summer flowers. Had always planted a garden to supply her family with fresh vegetables. But the plot she worked over now was much bigger than any she had taken on before. She was thankful that Tom had prepared the soil for planting. Already her back ached and her knees felt bruised from kneeling.

She stood up and removed the glove from her right hand. *I'm almost half done with the planting*, she told herself, hoping to feel a sense of accomplishment. But all she felt was weariness. "I have over half of it to do yet," she sighed, unable to keep from stating the negative way of looking at it.

She lifted a hand to remove her garden hat and tossed the hat to the wooden bench under the lilac bush.

"I need a break," she admitted. "I think I'll see if Hettie has a cup of tea."

Julia went directly to the kitchen, stopping only long enough to get rid of her gardening shoes. Hettie hated to have dirt tracked into her spotless kitchen.

"My, you look exhausted," Hettie said in alarm when Julia stepped through the kitchen door.

Julia smiled. "Guess I'm not good for much when I can't even plant a garden," she admitted with a chuckle.

"You've always had a garden—just not a whole farm, that's all," Hettie replied in defense of her employer.

"Well, I decided it was time for a cup of tea," Julia admitted and crossed to the kitchen sink to wash her hands.

"It's a shame Tom can't help more," went on Hettie.

"Poor man! I shouldn't have had him doing all that spading. How is his back?"

"An embarrassment," admitted Hettie. "He feels so bad that his back gave out and you have to do the plantin' yourself."

"Now you tell him not to worry about that," Julia said firmly. "Besides I plan to get myself some help. As soon as the girls are home from school I'm going to teach them to plant. Their young backs can bend much more easily than mine."

Hettie nodded as she bustled about the kitchen preparing the tea.

"Oh, Hettie," Julia moaned, her voice low and worried. "I won't mind the work one bit—if it—if it just works out."

Hettie placed the pot of hot tea on the kitchen table and took the chair opposite her mistress.

"You're still worryin'?" she asked.

"Well, I try not to—but—frankly—I have no idea if anyone will ever want to come to our little town for a vacation. If it doesn't work—I've got these poor women believing in a dream that can never be. It would be better if—"

"Now you stop your fussin'. At least you're tryin'. No one will fault you if it doesn't work out."

"I've prayed and prayed," continued Julia, "and I'm still not sure I'm doing the right thing."

"Well, if it isn't, you can still do as the others. Quit and move." Hettie made the comment with a bit of contempt for those who had so easily given up.

"Oh, Hettie—if you only knew the times I would have gladly quit and moved. Even now I—I would be glad to go if—if only it wouldn't be so hard on John."

Hettie's eyes looked up to study Julia's face above the teapot she held.

"Do you know the first thing that came to his mind when he told me the news?" Julia asked. "The house. Leaving the house. I hadn't known how important it was to him until then. If—if it wasn't for that—I'd move tomorrow. There are other houses."

The creases in Hettie's forehead deepened.

"Oh, I know," Julia hurried on. "I love this house too—but for me it—it isn't the house that brings happiness. It's the ones you share it with."

Hettie nodded and passed Julia her tea.

"You see, I've always lived in a big house. Bigger and more

elegant than this one. We—we rattled around in it. After Mama died there was just Papa and me and the servants—and Papa was rarely home. Do you know what, Hettie? I used to love walking along streets where the houses were small and crowded together and children played in tiny yards and mothers leaned over fences to chat with one another. I listened to the laughter and the chatter—and even the childish squabbles—and I envied those people until I was ashamed of myself."

Julia stopped to stir sugar into her tea, tears forming in the corners of her eyes.

"It wasn't that I didn't enjoy all the nice things in our big house," she went on. "It's just that it—it wasn't as important as having a family to love. But Papa—Papa always felt that fine things were so important—and he taught me to appreciate nice things too. But if I have to do without one or the other—things or family—things don't seem very significant."

Hettie passed her mistress a linen handkerchief and Julia wiped her eyes and nose.

"John never had a big house—or nice things. His folks pioneered on the prairie. He spent his first years in a sod shanty. He was twelve years old before they even had a wood floor, he told me. His mother had to carry water from the stream and carry chips for her fire. She did her laundry in a big tub—on a metal scrub board. Even after they moved into the wood house—with real glass panes in the windows—she still had none of the things that make life easier."

"Many women did that," recalled Hettie, thinking of her own mother.

Julia sipped the sweet tea from her china cup.

"For our first few years—I did it too," admitted Julia, thinking back. "It really wasn't so bad. A lot of work—but I had the time to do it. Although John never let me carry the wood or the water. He always got up early to carry in the day's supply before he left for work. It's funny, but I have never felt as loved and cared for as I did in those first few years."

Embarrassed by her own comment, Julia stirred on her chair. "I—I don't mean that I don't feel loved now," she explained quickly. "John still looks after me in every way—but we shared and planned in a different way then. We only had each other. John—John looked after me, and I—I cooked and—and did his laundry and cleaned his house. We didn't have you for the kitchen—or your Tom for the gardens—or Rose to help with the cleaning and serving. I guess there is a different feeling when you do the caring for each other—with your own hands."

Hettie nodded that she understood as she poured Julia more tea.

"You know, Hettie, if my girls don't have all the nice things— if they have to rough it just a bit with—with the man each chooses to marry, I won't feel sorry for them. If they really love each other—if they work together to make a home—even a small, simple place that is their own little haven—if they care enough to seek the happiness of each other—then I will consider them blessed.

"I have been blessed—more than I realized," Julia continued. "I have had both. A lovely home and a loving family. Maybe I have had more than my share. Maybe I haven't had the sense to be as thankful as I should have been. God forgive me if I have taken it all for granted."

Hettie was about to defend her young mistress again, but Julia kept talking.

"Well, no more. I have sorted out many things in the last few weeks. This I know. God is still in charge of my life. He knows what I need and what is just pleasant baggage. If I must forfeit the baggage—I will not pout. But since it is important to John, I will do my best to hold things together—for him—and for the girls."

Julia stood up and brushed her hands over her coarse gardening skirt.

"Now, I must get back to the planting," she said, "if we are to have that big garden we will be needing."

"But shouldn't you—?"

"I will only plant a couple more rows before lunch," Julia answered Hettie's unfinished question. "Then I will wait for the girls to get home. It will be good for them to know how to plant a garden. I had to learn on my own. They should know how to do such things—and they might even learn to love it."

Julia smiled at Hettie and moved toward the door.

"Thanks for the tea." Then she hesitated, one hand outstretched to the doorknob. "And thanks for the listening ear," she said softly. "I needed to talk. I guess I still miss my mother."

After the door closed softly behind Julia, Hettie allowed her own tears to fall.

Jennifer and Felicity were thrilled to learn that they could participate in the planting.

"I will make the rows and you can drop in the seeds and cover them," instructed Julia, and both girls squealed with delight.

"Now change into one of your play dresses and meet me in the backyard."

The girls soon rejoined their mother, eager to get started. Julia was already stretching the cord from one stake to the other to mark a new row. She liked things neat and orderly and would have been ashamed to have a garden with vegetables growing in crooked lines.

"Can we take off our shoes, Mama?" called Felicity.

"Your shoes?" exclaimed Julia.

"Please," begged Felicity. "The Carlsons all had their shoes off when they worked their garden. We saw them. The dirt doesn't get in the shoes then."

"But your stockings will get filthy," Julia argued.

"You take off your stockings too," Jennifer explained to her mother.

Julia frowned. "Isn't it awfully hard on your feet?"

"Janie says it feels great," answered Felicity.

"Very well," agreed Julia. "If you must—then remove your shoes."

Both girls hurriedly took off their shoes and stockings. But Felicity and Jennifer had never run about barefoot before, and their tender feet did not find the lumpy garden dirt as pleasant as did Janie Carlson, who spent most of her summer enjoying the outdoors without shoes or stockings.

Jennifer winced as she made her way across the soil, and Felicity gave her a deep frown. "They'll get used to it," she whispered hoarsely.

Jennifer nodded. This was a new adventure, and if she spoiled it, Jennifer knew that Felicity would be cross.

"Now," explained Julia, "come here, both of you, and I will show you how to scatter the seed. One of you will plant, and the other will cover. Then you can change jobs."

After a mild argument, the girls decided that Felicity would plant first. Both girls bowed over the open row while Julia showed them how to plant evenly, sparingly, so that the seed would grow properly. Then Julia demonstrated the careful attention needed in covering the seeds.

"This is important work," she told the girls. "It must be done carefully and well if we are to have a good garden."

The planting began. Felicity traveled along the row on her hands and knees, dropping the seeds with careful precision. Jennifer followed, raking the soil gently back over the seeds, then patting it down to bed them.

It wasn't long until Julia saw that Jennifer was limping, but she said nothing. The work carried on. Then Jennifer was at the edge of the garden, sitting on the grass as she replaced her stockings and shoes. Julia still made no comment, but she heard Felicity whisper, "Softy!"

"You wait," answered Jennifer. "You're on your knees, crawling along on your skirt. Wait until you have to walk on this stuff."

The three worked on. Julia expected the girls to plead for release, or at least to find an excuse to take a break from their work, but to her surprise they seemed to enjoy the task. Though Felicity too donned her stockings and shoes after a few trips across the garden soil.

"How long did Janie say it takes to get used to it?" Julia heard Felicity ask Jennifer.

"She didn't say," whispered Jennifer.

When Julia had designed her final row, she leaned on her hoe and watched Jennifer scatter carrot seeds and Felicity cover them with dark, warm soil.

"You've done a good job," she informed the two. "It has gone so much faster with all of us working together."

Jennifer straightened and rubbed her back. "Are we done?" she asked.

"For now," answered Julia. "We will plant the rest when the weather is a bit more certain. We don't want frost to catch our new plants."

Felicity finished covering the last few seeds. "When will they start to grow?" she asked impatiently. "A couple of days?"

"Oh my, no!" laughed Julia. "But perhaps by next week some of them will be showing."

Felicity's face fell at the thought of such a long wait.

They put away the garden tools and went in to prepare for Hettie's evening meal. John would soon be home, and Julia wanted his womenfolk to greet him as usual in clean and orderly fashion.

Chapter Seven

Adjustments

Jennifer and Felicity made frequent trips to the garden. Julia was amazed at their interest. Wild whoops greeted the first glimpse of fuzzy green. Their hard labor was bearing fruit.

"The girls are growing up," mused Julia. "They still sound like children when they express their glee, but they are able to find enjoyment in doing a task—even a hard one."

Julia decided that the girls should be given additional responsibilities to help run the household.

"You know that I have sent off letters advertising our home as a place for summer guests," Julia said to the girls at breakfast one morning.

They both nodded in reply, remembering the many times their mother had instructed them not to talk with their mouths full.

"Well, we will all have more work to do when guests arrive," Julia continued.

"Who's coming?" asked Felicity, for the moment forgetting that her mouth was not empty.

"Well, no one—yet. I mean—I do not know of anyone yet. But it is still early. The advertising has hardly had time to be seen. But when—when we do have guests, we all will have to help. There will be extra cleaning, and laundry, and jobs in the kitchen."

Julia saw concern, then interest, then excitement in the twins' eyes. "What do we have to do?" asked Felicity candidly.

"Well, I thought I might make a list of chores, and each of you can pick the ones you'd like to do."

"A whole bunch?" asked Felicity, a frown appearing. Jennifer's elbow nudged her.

"Not a whole bunch. Some. And it will depend on how many people are here," explained Julia.

"I'll collect the rent," offered Felicity, her eyes shining, and Julia and Jennifer both shared the joke.

"It won't be rent, really," explained Julia. "They will only stay for a short time—so it will be—fees, I guess. Lodging fees."

"I'll wait for the list," said Jennifer.

"Will there just be big people?" asked Felicity, her eyes holding Julia's.

"Perhaps not. I have said that we have three bedrooms and so could take families," Julia answered.

Felicity and Jennifer exchanged nervous glances. "Will we need to share our things?" asked Felicity.

"Your own private possessions, no. But the porch swing and the playhouse, perhaps. Tom is going to build a sandbox and a teeter-totter. We want the children to have something to do. The parents will enjoy their stay more if their children are happy," Julia explained. "Then perhaps they will want to come again—and tell others who might also enjoy visiting a quiet mountain town."

———

John supervised the dismantling of the equipment at the mill and watched as it was loaded on boxcars and moved down the tracks to be set up at another location. It wasn't until he stood watching the train roll from view around the bend of the mountain that the reality of it all settled in. Work at the mill had come to an end.

There was nothing to do but draw his final wage and go home. He had decisions to make. Difficult decisions. He had been holding them at bay—begging for time—but he could delay them no longer. He had to face reality and find a way to provide for his family. He was proud of Julia. He hadn't known that she was made of such "strong stuff." She had rallied the town women, determined to fight to save her beautiful house on the mountainside. The house meant a lot to Julia, John reasoned. She was used to fine things. But John had the sickening feeling that no matter how hard she tried, she would end up brokenhearted. There was no way enough people would be drawn to Calder Springs. They had Banff, already becoming a major tourist attraction. And farther up the Rocky Mountain chain was Jasper. It too was growing in popularity. People already knew about Banff and Jasper, and there were only so many people with money to spend at resorts. There would be no additional dollars to spend in their little town, John figured.

It might have been different if they could have built up a clientele slowly, but no one in the town had money to cover their needs while they waited. The town would die. The rest of the people would be forced to move out—just as some had already done.

John sighed deeply, his shoulders sagged. It was hard for him to see Julia lose what she loved so much. It was hard to face the fact that the girls—who had been born to plenty—might now have to do without.

He himself knew all about hardship. He could live simply. But his family? Except for the first few years of their marriage, John and Julia had lived well. And the girls had never known hardship.

It sometimes bothered John that it was Uncle George's money that had built the grand house, not money he had earned through his own hard work. But he had never begrudged Julia the house. She deserved it. He thanked God for the miracle that made it possible. He always thought of Uncle George's money as a miracle.

John recalled his secret dream of one day owning a business of his own. He had never told anyone. Not even Julia, for he deemed the dream impossible—selfish. Uncle George's money had been a temptation—but only for a brief moment. He would not have considered using it to fulfill his own ambition. Julia's house was always uppermost in his mind.

Still, on occasion, he thought about that little business. A woodshop. A place where he could take the rough wood that came from the forest and shape and polish it until it shone like glistening dark gold beneath his fingers. He loved the touch of wood—the smell—the pattern of its grain.

If they could have sold the big house—even for a fraction of what it was worth—they might have had a possibility of starting over. As it was, they would lose the house, lose everything. John's jaw twitched and his eyes hardened. It would be tough giving it all up. He tried to shrug off his dismal mood.

"As Jule says," he reminded himself, "God didn't pack up and move off with the mill. He's still here—still looking after us."

John headed for the office to pick up his check. Time was passing quickly and he'd be late for the evening meal if he didn't hurry.

———

Julia stopped by the bedroom where the girls were preparing for supper.

"How about wearing your blue gingham dresses tonight?" she asked them.

Two sets of eyes lit up. "Are we going out?" asked Felicity.

"No."

"Are we having guests?" asked Jennifer.

"No—it will just be us." Then Julia answered the question that she could read in their faces. "They're Papa's favorite dresses," she explained.

Jennifer turned to study her mother. Julia also was wearing one of John's favorite dresses.

"Will Papa be feeling sad tonight?" she asked.

Julia tried to keep her voice steady, her chin from quivering. "He—he may be. Just a bit. The mill is gone now. Papa hated to see it go. This was a hard day for him."

Jennifer's face grew serious. Felicity looked more buoyant. "Should I tell him my joke?" she asked.

"I'm not sure he will be ready for jokes," Julia said softly. "Just try to be cheerful—and as agreeable as you can be. No fusses."

Both girls nodded.

Julia closed the door quietly behind her as she left the room.

"I think I should tell him my joke," insisted Felicity.

"What joke?" asked Jennifer.

"A man had twins and they were both the same size and had the same color hair and the same color eyes, so how did he tell them apart?"

Jennifer looked dubious. She slipped her blue calico over her head and then asked the question Felicity was waiting to hear, "How?"

Felicity whisked on her own blue dress, her eyes sparkling in anticipation of the punch line.

"The boy wore britches and the girl didn't!" she exclaimed, then laughed uproariously at the humor of her story.

Jennifer did not even smile. "It's silly," she declared. "Silly and stupid."

But Felicity was still laughing—so hard that she could not tie the bow of her sash.

"It's silly," Jennifer said again.

Felicity's face sobered. "You're just cross 'cause you didn't think of it," she challenged.

"Am not," Jennifer shot back. "I'd never tell such a silly joke."

"You never tell any jokes at all," Felicity threw at her. "You are so—so sour—and—and dull. You never even laugh."

"I laugh when things are funny."

"No, you don't. You never think anything is funny."

"I do too," Jennifer declared. "When Papa tells a funny joke—I laugh."

"Papa doesn't tell jokes."

"He does too."

Felicity shook her head. "He hasn't told a joke since—since—"

"Well, he used to tell them. And he will again when—"

Jennifer stopped as her tears began to fall. Would Papa ever tell jokes again? Would he ever laugh and play with them? Would he ever tease Mama good-naturedly? When would their world get back to normal again?

"See! You don't even know how to laugh. You just cry," Felicity taunted.

Jennifer slapped her.

———

Julia was not at the door to greet John when he arrived home. She was in the bedroom settling the dispute between her daughters. Both girls were in tears, and Julia herself felt ready to cry. She had wanted a warm, serene welcome for John on this most difficult day. Hettie had fixed his favorite dinner, and Julia had groomed herself to please him. The girls were to have presented themselves in their father's favorite dresses, hair carefully combed, happy faces inviting him into the warmth of the family circle. But it had all gone wrong.

"Poor John. Poor, poor John," wept Julia.

Chapter Eight

Hard Work

The scene that greeted John as he entered his home that night did more to lift his spirits than Julia could have imagined. Weeping daughters and a distraught wife reminded him in a very real way that he was still needed.

His eyes lifted to Julia's tearfilled ones as he wordlessly asked the reason for the fuss. Julia shrugged weary shoulders and her tears increased. He nodded her from the room, followed her out and shut the door softly behind them.

"What's the problem?" he asked, turning Julia to face him.

Julia blinked back her tears. "It's just—just a little spat over some silly joke." As soon as she said it she realized that it was really much more than that. "Oh, John," she sobbed, leaning against his broad chest. "I thought we could have a special night to—to—" She couldn't say "celebrate." The day's events hardly called for a celebration. "To show our thanks that we are here—together," she finished lamely. "I wanted your favorite dinner, a happy family, the girls in their prettiest dresses—but the girls—the girls—" Julia burst fully into tears and buried her face in his shoulder, the sobs shaking her.

John held her and stroked her back to ease her tension. He still didn't understand what the trouble was all about.

When the tears began to subside John spoke again. "Should I discipline the girls?" he asked.

Julia jerked to attention, her eyes opening wide. "Oh my, no," she quickly responded. "That would spoil our dinner."

John pulled her close again.

"It's so strange," Julia murmured against him. "I thought they had become—so—so—grown up. They worked so hard—

and so well in the garden with me. Why, I've been thinking that they are now young ladies. I was all set to enjoy their company—their help—and then—all of a sudden—this." Julia sniffed.

"Have you forgotten their age?" John asked, patting her shoulder. "They're only thirteen. I don't think anyone knows at that age whether she is an adult or a child. Remember?"

Julia shook her head. She couldn't remember. She had been forced to go from childhood to adulthood when her mother died.

"I do hope you are not implying that I'm going to have to live with this—this fluctuation—for some time," Julia said as she wiped her eyes and blew her nose on a lace handkerchief. A sparkle of humor had returned to her eyes.

John nodded.

"Oh my!" exclaimed Julia. "We'll never know from one minute to the next whether we have children or adults!"

"Would you like me to talk to them about this incident?" John's arm tightened.

"No, I will," Julia said softly, straightening her shoulders. "You wash for dinner. Hettie will be anxious to serve us before the meal gets cold."

John kissed Julia on the forehead. Then he released her so she could speak to the girls.

Julia found two contrite young ladies sitting solemnly on their beds. Their tears had ceased, though the traces remained.

"Wash your faces and prepare yourselves for dinner," Julia said in a calm voice. "And after you have apologized to each other, you may join your father and me in the dining room—where I will expect you to conduct yourselves as young ladies. Understood?"

Both girls nodded.

Julia left the room and went to inform Hettie that she could serve dinner.

The meal turned out to be a joyous occasion in spite of the preceding event. Felicity did not tell her joke, but John told a few. The family needed something to laugh about. Even Jennifer smiled.

After the evening meal and the family devotional time, the girls led their father to the large backyard where they proudly pointed out the growth in the family garden.

"See, Papa, this is one of the rows I planted!" Felicity said excitedly. "It's peas."

"I planted the row beside it," Jennifer added, her voice more controlled.

"My peas look a little bigger," Felicity boasted. "Don't you think so, Papa?"

John was not to be drawn into such a foolish argument. He eyed the rows of peas. "They all look healthy to me," he observed. "I can hardly wait to taste them."

They returned to the house. The girls were sent to bed, and Julia picked up her handwork. John settled himself at the small desk in the library and drew out his account book. He had one more paycheck—and a number of bills to pay. Would the money go far enough? Would there be any left over to care for their needs in the days ahead?

John figured and refigured, but the numbers always came out the same. After the bills were paid, there wouldn't be much left. He pushed the book aside and left the room, snapping off the light with an impatient gesture.

Julia was still in the parlor, her handwork spread across her knees, her fingers fluttering silently as she turned a skein of white thread into an exquisite doily.

John's thoughts were miles away, but he tried to act interested in Julia's project. "What are you making?" he asked.

Julia lifted the doily for him to see. "It's for our tourist craft shop," she answered, an edge of excitement creeping into her voice. "All the ladies are making things. We're working hard to get it stocked as quickly as possible."

So, John thought, *Julia has not given up her dream.*

"We are getting quite a selection of items," Julia continued. "You should see the lovely lace collars Mrs. Shannon has made. And Mrs. Clancy has specialized in calico aprons—beautiful things. Mrs. Adams is working a quilt. She has already made two crib quilts. One in pinks, the other in blues, and—"

"It's been a long day," John interrupted. "I think I'll head up to bed." It hurt him to hear how hard the women had been working on a dream that would never be any more than that. John wondered whether he should be honest with them or let them continue to work and hope. The work did keep their spirits up.

Julia laid aside her crocheting and lowered her hands to finger the fine silk of her gown. Her eyes sought his.

"Is your last paycheck enough to cover the accounts?" she asked.

John nodded, and Julia sighed in relief.

"The garden will be ready shortly," she hurried on. "And I have another piece of material on hand for new dresses for the girls. Hettie is good at making stews and soups so the—"

"We're all right," John tried to assure her.

"Mr. Brock says there is plenty of wild game in the woods," Julia felt compelled to add.

John had often hunted in the local woods and knew that animals were plentiful.

He reached a hand to her, and she stood. "We're fine," he said again.

Julia was unconvinced. Looking directly into John's eyes, she pleaded, "If there is some way—any way—that we can cut back—make do—you will tell me, won't you?"

John saw the seriousness in her face and he loved her for it. He leaned to kiss her forehead. "I'll tell you," he promised, and then closed his eyes against the pain of the dreadful thought. He would do almost anything rather than tell his Jule that she had to find ways to cut back.

Spring passed into summer. The eight women on Julia's committee continued their industrious labors. Each week they placed more items on the shelves in their little craft store. Julia laid aside her plans to use the new linen tablecloth herself. Instead, she pinned a price tag in one corner of it and placed it on the merchandise shelf.

Soon they would be receiving requests for accommodation in their new resort town. Those who had extra bedrooms had them ready and waiting—with outdoor-fresh linens on cozy beds, newest towels hanging on door racks, and shining windowpanes behind freshly laundered curtains.

But with every mail delivery, letters requesting accommodation were conspicuously absent. In spite of brave smiles and determined brightness, morale began to sag. They tried not to let it show—but it was there, dogging their footsteps, causing them to add more water to the soup pot, less meat to the stew.

For Julia it meant more feverish involvement. Her efforts increased. More letters written. More doilies crocheted. More hours spent coaxing and caring for her garden.

John walked the streets, pretending that he would soon find

work—but deep in his heart he knew that the town had no jobs to offer.

Jennifer and Felicity were like yo-yos. One day the enormity of the family's situation would have them down. The next day, something as small as a smile from a boy could have them up again. For Julia every moment was as fragile as spun glass. She never knew when something might snap—when she might snap. The strain was almost unbearable.

Two more families moved away. The residential streets looked deserted. Houses were boarded and left. No children played skip-rope in those front yards, no weekly laundry fluttered on wire clotheslines, no smoke curled lazily from the chimneys.

Julia hated to pass the empty houses. Where there had been neighbors, now there was only emptiness, nakedness, pain. She avoided looking at them and hurried past as quickly as her clicking heels would carry her.

Downtown was even worse. The butcher had packed his cleavers in wooden crates and thrown his stained, worn apron in the garbage can. "Can't stay any longer," he muttered. "Got a wife and family to feed."

The library closed, as did the bakery, the tailor, the blacksmith. Even the doctor shook his head sadly, packed up his wife and two small sons and left for places unknown.

"Go see Charlie," he told his grim-faced patients. "He can at least give you some shelf medicine."

But Charlie Rennings, the druggist, shook his head. He didn't know enough to become the medical advisor for the town. Nor did he know how long his little drugstore would endure.

The grocer stayed. His shelves were not filled with the same variety of merchandise as in the past, but he still stocked the basics—flour, sugar, salt, coffee. He hoped the women were right—that the tourist trade would come to their small town. Yet, he wondered if people could hang on until then.

There was still the railroad and the post office. Surely they won't abandon us too, the people reasoned. But had they admitted it to one another, their dreams were often haunted by the prospect of days without trains.

And then one day late in July it happened. Julia hurried past the closed-up buildings to do her meager shopping. On the way home she stopped at the post office, and there it was, a white envelope bearing a return address of Toronto. Julia hastened from the building and took refuge on a bench by the railroad track.

Her fingers trembled as she tore open the envelope and withdrew the single sheet of paper. She had difficulty reading, for tears blurred her sight.

At length she calmed herself enough to scan the brief letter. It was a request for accommodation—"for myself, my wife, and three children," the letter stated. Julia's tears spotted the ink before she arrived home to show John.

Chapter Nine

Hope

The Harrigan household was not the only one in town to welcome the good news. The remaining families were all excited about the prospect of their area becoming a tourist town. Activity increased everywhere. Women worked extra long hours to add handcrafted merchandise to the little shop. Men wielded paint brushes and hammers, cleaned up board fences, and repaired broken walks. Boys were sent to mow the lawns of vacated neighborhood houses. Girls swept the walks.

"No one wants to come to a ghost town," Julia told her committee at their weekly meeting. "We must do all we can to make it look as if the town is still alive."

Heads nodded, but every woman in the group knew it would be hard to disguise the fact that most folks had already deserted Calder Springs.

The women agreed that Julia would take the first house guests.

"We want them to get a good impression so they will tell others," Mrs. Greenwald announced to all who would listen.

No one disagreed.

"The rest of us need to be ready at all times for business." The group had been encouraged by a second letter that came soon after the first. The Greenwalds too had the promise of summer guests.

"Too bad we can't do something about Main Street and all those boarded-up buildings," sighed young Matilda Pendleton. The empty town was adding to her discouragement. She was about to suggest to her husband that they board up their own house and move elsewhere, but she did not make her confession to the ladies of the committee.

"We should have asked permission to use some of the buildings for our crafts," said Mrs. Clancy. "It would have kept them in better repair—and we could have arranged a small space at the front that would have kept Main Street more—more active and entertaining to our guests."

"Couldn't we still do it?" Maude Shannon asked. "There's nothing but a few boards covering those store fronts. My Jim would be glad to pull nails. Says he can't stand to even walk down the street."

Julia was tempted to voice her approval, but propriety overcame the notion.

"It's a wonderful idea—to use the buildings, I mean." Then quickly added before the ladies bolted to send their husbands forth with hammers in hand, "But we'll need the owners' permission. Mrs. Clancy—your husband is town clerk. Could he give me the names and addresses of the owners of those buildings so I might write letters asking permission?"

"I'll ask him," Mrs. Clancy offered.

"I'll get them in the mail right away," Julia promised. The ladies finalized plans for the arrival of the first customers, drank tea, and departed to fulfill their various duties.

The big day finally arrived. Julia sent Tom to the train station to fetch the guests. Mr. Clancy had a fine buggy that had been washed and polished for the occasion. They had talked of using Mac Pendleton's team of blacks to pull the buggy. They were the prettiest horses Julia had ever seen. But they were also the most spirited. Tom shook his head emphatically when Julia suggested them.

"Not iffen I'm drivin'," he stated flatly.

Julia was about to suggest that Mac do the driving when she remembered that the black team had bolted even with Mac at the reins, giving him the ride of his life and scaring the townsfolk half to death.

"We'll use our own bays," Julia said instead, and Tom nodded with relief.

Everyone in town waited anxiously for the whistle of the afternoon train. Julia was a bundle of nerves. John knew better than to hang around. He took the hedge trimmers and went out to prune neighborhood hedges—to keep the town looking "lived in."

Felicity and Jennifer hovered around, their eyes big with the excitement of the hour.

"Did you raise the windows in the guest rooms?" Julia asked. "We do want them to smell that fresh mountain air."

"Yes, Mama."

"Did you fluff the towels?"

"Yes, Mama."

"Did you smooth the beds?"

"Yes, Mama."

"Did you dust the furniture one last time?"

"Yes, Mama."

"Did you check the flowers to be sure they are fresh?"

Felicity sighed. "We did all that—you did all that—over and over."

Jennifer's jaw dropped when she heard Felicity's sassiness, but she had to admit to the truth of the words.

Julia did not scold Felicity. She too knew the words were true. Without comment she moved toward the kitchen.

The girls headed for the porch swing. "Now she will go and pester Hettie with her questions," Felicity whispered to Jennifer. "Did you polish the silver? Did you prepare the tea trays? Did you—?"

"Don't be mean," ordered Jennifer. "She's just tense. This is very important, you know. If it doesn't work . . ." Jennifer left the sentence unfinished.

Felicity shrugged. She knew it was important. But she also wondered at times if all this fuss would really help.

"Maybe it wouldn't be so bad to move," Felicity said carelessly.

Jennifer frowned.

"Josie says she likes the new place where they live," Felicity defended.

Jennifer was well aware of what Josie had said in the letter she had sent after her family moved. It had made even Jennifer a bit envious.

"Well, Mama and Papa don't wish to move," Jennifer stated.

"But why?" Felicity dared to ask.

"I guess they like it here," Jennifer said with a shrug.

"I like it here too," Felicity began, and then sighed. "At least I used to."

"And they like the house—and the mountains—and the

neighbors." Jennifer tried hard to think of as many reasons as she could to dispel Felicity's doubts—and her own.

Felicity looked around her. The house was nice, the mountains were pretty. But neighbors? Felicity's eyes widened. "We hardly have any neighbors anymore," she argued. "All of our friends have already moved."

"We still have Millicent," Jennifer reminded her.

"Pooh!" cried Felicity, jumping to her feet. "Millicent is—is dull. She—she talks with her mouth full and she—she scratches in public and she—"

"Shh," admonished Jennifer. "If Mama hears you she'll send you upstairs."

"I don't care," Felicity stormed. "I miss all my friends. I miss the shops and the ice-cream parlor and the—"

Jennifer placed a restraining hand on Felicity's arm and tried to hush her once more.

Felicity shook it off, tears forming in her eyes.

"It's not fair," she cried. "It's just not fair."

Jennifer took charge. "Do you think Mama and Papa like it?" she challenged. "Do you think they wanted the mill to close? The people to move away? Do you think they like having to make do? To open our home to—to strangers? Do you think they are never scared—or lonely? They lost friends too."

Felicity's noisy sniffling abated. She shrugged her shoulders and wiped her nose, then settled back on the swing and continued to mope. Jennifer said no more. She reached out her foot and started the swing in motion. They sat together in silence for some time before Felicity spoke again. This time her voice was low, her tone confidential.

"Jen, I'm going to hate living in a ghost town."

"That's why Mama is working so hard," Jennifer reminded her. "So that it won't be a ghost town. So that it will—will come alive again. With tourists and—and interesting people and—"

"Jen," said Felicity, halting Jennifer's flow of words, "do you think it will work?"

Jennifer stopped short, thought for a minute, then answered honestly, "All we can do is try."

"But what if—what if we don't like the people who are our guests?" asked Felicity.

"We—we need to make them feel . . ."

"At home?" prompted Felicity.

"No. No, better than that. Like they're special, Mama told

the ladies. We need to make them feel like—kings and queens, Mama said. Then they will go home and tell their friends—and the town will be okay."

Silence again.

"What if—what if they are—grouchy—and—and stupid?" asked Felicity.

"What if they are nice—and exciting?" Jennifer countered.

"Do you think they might be?"

Jennifer shrugged. "Why not?"

Then she continued with a statement she knew would intrigue her sister. "Maybe they will even have handsome sons."

Felicity could not keep the laughter from her blue eyes, and it spilled over to her pouting mouth and curved it into an enchanting smile. Then the giggle came. Jennifer had hoped that it would. In spite of Jennifer's usual propriety she joined her sister in a moment of mirth.

"Do you s'pose our first guests will have a son?" giggled Felicity.

"We'll just have to wait and see," teased Jennifer, and they leaned against each other and laughed some more.

———

John was torn. He wanted Julia to keep their lovely house. He wanted her hard-fought battle to be victorious—the venture to succeed, the town to be revived, but he had to admit that things looked grim.

Funds were very low. If it weren't for Julia's big garden—if Tom and Hettie hadn't agreed to work for room and board—if Rose hadn't moved away with her family, if they didn't get free firewood from the old mill site—if—

But John tried to be positive. The first guests were soon to arrive. Julia was sure that many more would follow. She was even concerned about where they would house them all once they started coming. She had already sent letters to former shop owners, asking for the use of their buildings in exchange for proper upkeep. With the shop doors opened, their simple space filled with baked goods, canned wild jams and jellies, handcrafted doilies, quilts and aprons, perhaps—just perhaps, folks would enjoy a stroll down Main Street once again.

In the meantime, he would keep it looking as neat as he could. Snip, snip, went his clippers. From vacated yard to vacated yard, he snipped his way. The Martins, Browns, Carltons, and Schnells. All neighbors just a short time ago. Now gone. He didn't even know where many of them had relocated. He hoped they had found work. He knew the pain of being unable to provide properly for a family.

Snip. Snip. What if the venture didn't work? How long could he let Jule pursue her dream before he stepped in? Would it crush her? Snip. He could never build her another house like the one they had now. Should he suggest sending her and the girls back east to her father while he tried to get established again? The thought made John cringe.

"If only I knew what to do," he sighed for the hundredth time. "If only I could be sure."

And then, through the sharp, clear afternoon air, reverberating from mountain peak to mountain peak, came the distinct, distant cry of the coming train.

Chapter Ten

Guests

Julia met her guests at the front door. Hettie stood a few steps behind her, her starched white apron glistening in the afternoon brightness, her nervous smile well in place.

"Good afternoon, Mr. Hammond, Mrs. Hammond," Julia said, her tone and smile indicating more confidence than she felt. She held the door open for them and allowed them to enter the spacious entrance hall.

Mrs. Hammond smiled, almost, and nodded. Mr. Hammond did not even acknowledge Julia. He was busy studying the curved stairway, the oriental rugs, the art on the walls.

Mrs. Hammond soon joined him, her eyes traveling carelessly over her surroundings. Julia shifted uneasily from foot to foot and cast a nervous glance Hettie's way. Julia's home had never before been so openly and critically appraised.

Mrs. Hammond moved forward just enough to peer into the main parlor and give it a quick assessment. Her children followed her. Julia was certain they acted out of nosiness, not interest. Their rudeness annoyed Julia. After all, this was still her home. But instead of being rude in return, Julia turned her attention to Hettie.

"Hettie, will you show the Hammonds to their rooms, please?" Then, trying another smile, Julia turned to the Hammonds. "I'm sure it has been a long train ride. You will wish to freshen up before tea. It will be served in the main parlor in fifteen minutes. Thomas will bring up your luggage."

Tom was not used to being called Thomas. His stern face showed that he did not like it now. But he said nothing, only nodded and picked up two of the many suitcases and turned to follow Hettie and the guests.

Julia paused long enough to breathe a quick prayer. This was going to be much more difficult than she had imagined. The Hammonds dressed and bore themselves as though they were accustomed to elegance, to opulence. "Used to being pampered and served too, I imagine," Julia said under her breath. "They will take my lovely home for granted and expect it to be at their disposal."

She shook her head and lifted her chin. "In which case—we shall pamper them and serve them, and they shall—shall be made to feel at home. No, not at home. I will never let them feel that my home is theirs. They are only guests here."

With renewed determination Julia went to the kitchen to prepare tea while Hettie finished helping the Hammonds get settled.

The guests were not in the parlor in fifteen minutes. Julia flitted about impatiently. The tea was getting cold. She sent Hettie to the kitchen to boil water for a fresh pot. "But don't make it until they actually show," Julia suggested.

After thirty-five minutes Mr. Hammond appeared. He had changed his traveling suit to something unlike anything Julia had ever seen. It looked very casual—very rugged—and very expensive. "Does he think he's on a wilderness safari, or what?" she muttered to herself.

"Mrs. Hammond will be right down," he growled. "I should like a cup of tea while I am waiting. Hot tea," he emphasized. "We detest tepid refreshments."

Julia went to tell Hettie to make another pot and to be sure it was as hot as she could make it. Then she returned to the parlor.

Mr. Hammond fidgeted while they waited for the pot to steep. "You should have had ample time to prepare," he complained, pulling out an ornate pocket watch and studying the time. "We allowed you more time than you asked for."

Julia bit her tongue to keep from expressing the impatient retort forming in her mind. "Yes, of course," she replied softly. "We did want to be sure that the tea was fresh—and hot, so we held back from making it."

Hettie relieved the uncomfortable situation by appearing with the fresh pot of tea. Julia poured her guest a cupful and placed it on the table near his elbow.

And he left it there until it cooled to lukewarm before taking a swallow.

When Mrs. Hammond appeared they went through the process all over again.

At last the children joined their parents. There were two girls about the same age as the twins and a boy of about five. Julia studied them. They looked snobbish, whiny, and undisciplined.

"Mama," began the oldest. "You said I wouldn't have to share a room with Miranda."

"We have already been through that," the woman argued. "I had no idea this would be such a tiny place."

Julia's indignation rose. She was about to remind the woman that the information she sent stated that the house had three bedrooms available for guests, but just then Julia's attention was averted to the boy. He had lifted the whole plateful of sandwiches and was racing across the room with them.

Julia caught her breath, sure that the child was going to dump the whole plate on her fine blue carpet, but Hettie intervened. Before the boy knew what had happened, she deftly removed the plate from his hand. He seemed about to howl in protest, when Hettie asked, "Would you like a cream puff?"

His disapproval quickly changed to delight.

"I'll serve you on the back swing," Hettie continued. "Come. I'll show you the way."

Julia breathed a relieved sigh and watched the boy and Hettie disappear.

The Hammond girls caught her attention again.

"Fredrika used all the closet and all the drawers for her things."

Julia could well imagine it. Tom had carried up more suitcases than she had been able to count.

"You must learn to share," admonished the mother. Julia guessed that the concept was totally foreign to the two girls.

"But—" began Fredrika.

"Now—no buts. We are not in a hotel, you know. We will be making do for a few days. Your papa wanted to get off to some quiet place. Away from civilization."

The look the woman gave her husband told Julia that the two were not in agreement about their destination. The man ignored his complaining wife and fussing children as he stirred cream and sugar into a second cup of hot tea.

Making do, thought Julia. *Making do—away from civilization.* Though seething, Julia maintained her composure.

"More tea, Mrs. Hammond?" she asked politely.

"The last cup was a tad cold," the woman snipped. "I do hope that shan't be the norm."

Julia went to the kitchen to make a new pot. She detested fussiness, and they were being impossible.

"I do hope that young ruffian is behaving himself in my backyard," she mumbled to herself. Just then the kitchen door burst open and Felicity entered, her eyes wide.

"Mama," she exploded, "that boy is trying to tip over the swing!"

"He's what?"

"He's trying to tip it over. He's swinging hard, and he said he's going to go so high that it flips right over."

"Oh my!" exclaimed Julia on her way to the back porch.

Tom was there by the time Julia arrived. He couldn't reason with the young boy, and he couldn't discipline the guests' child, but he could thwart his action. Tom's big, broad hand held the swing firmly so the boy, push as he might, went nowhere.

Julia thanked Tom and returned to the kitchen. Felicity and Jennifer followed her.

"How long will he be here, Mama?"

"He kicked a flower pot all across the yard."

"He ate four cream puffs all by himself."

"He says he's our boss and we are his servants."

"How long will he be here, Mama?"

Julia sighed, and her eyes pleaded for the girls to be patient. Jennifer caught the message and nudged Felicity. Both girls fell silent.

Julia drew her two daughters close. "I didn't know that it would be this hard," she admitted. "But we must do it. We must help Papa. Do you understand?"

Both girls nodded.

"It won't be long. In fact, they are so unhappy with our accommodations that they might not even stay. It wouldn't surprise me in the least."

Seeing hope in the girls' eyes, Julia hurried on. "But we must try to keep them—to convince them. We must. Your papa—the—the other committee members—they are counting on us. Do you see? We must do the best we can—the very best—to endure."

Julia spoke the last word softly but with such determination that the girls knew how difficult the ordeal was for her. They nodded their consent.

"Can we go to our room?" asked Jennifer.

They had been told to wait on the porch in case the children needed entertaining. Julia could not ask that of them in the present circumstances. She nodded, and the girls left for the sanctuary of their room.

Oh, if only I could run and hide in my room, thought Julia, but she couldn't, so she picked up the pot of hot tea and the plate of sandwiches and returned to the parlor.

"My, it takes a long time to make a pot of tea in the wild," complained Mrs. Hammond. She refused the sandwiches, saying, "My waistline. One must not overindulge."

In spite of the difficult start, things did settle down over the next few days—or perhaps the residents of the big white house just adjusted.

Mr. Hammond was determined to make his visit a wilderness adventure. He spent most of his hours walking mountain paths pretending, Julia surmised, to be the first man who had set foot on them. To the family, he talked incessantly of his "discoveries," much to the annoyance of his wife and the boredom of his children.

The young boy, Hadley, was directed to the vacated mill site, where he spent hours running over sawdust piles and investigating the small empty buildings the mill had left behind. He roared and ran and hooted and climbed, returning home for mealtimes in a dirty, dishevelled state. But at least he was out of everyone's hair, and all those with whom he shared the house, including the Hammonds, seemed thankful for that.

Felicity and Jennifer offered friendship to Miranda and Fredrika, but the city girls turned up their noses and continued to bicker and whine. No amount of coaxing or enticing could persuade them to do otherwise, and soon the Harrigan girls gave up and left them in their own misery.

Mrs. Hammond took possession of the porch swing, demanding pillows to soften the wooden seats. Her back was bad. She had to put her feet up as well, and needed more cushions for them. Snuggled in the softness, she read penny novels and devoured so many imported chocolates that Julia figured they must have completely filled one of the mysterious suitcases. *My waistline, indeed!* thought Julia.

Along with the busy days for Julia and Hettie, John and Tom were also pressed with responsibilities. The garden needed constant care. They had a wood supply to maintain, lawns to mow, and shrubbery to trim—not only at the Harrigan house, but also at empty neighborhood homes.

In addition, Mrs. Hammond never stopped making suggestions as to how the Harrigans could make her and her family more comfortable.

"Surely, you must have attic space. If your youngsters used it, my girls could each have her own room. They are not used to being crowded together, you know."

"If this porch was screened in, it would be much more pleasant."

"The gardens would be more becoming if there were more flowers and fewer vegetables."

Julia tried to let it all pass. She ticked off each day as she left the kitchen at night. In the meantime she and Hettie devised little ways of meeting the demands.

They kept water boiling at all times. Two teapots were put into service, so there was always a hot pot at teatime.

Hettie made hearty lunches for Hadley so the whole family did not need to wait for him to return from his exploring before sitting down to dinner.

Mrs. Hammond was undisturbed on the porch swing, additional cushions borrowed from the committee members.

Men loitering in front of the train station told Mr. Hammond enough stories of bears and mountain lions to convince him that the area was truly wild and dangerous. He would have many stories to tell when he returned to the city.

And the two bickering girls—they were ignored as much as possible.

Eventually the two weeks ended, and the suitcases were repacked. Mr. Hammond took one last walk, hoping to see an elusive grizzly bear. Mrs. Hammond wriggled free of her cushions, stood up, and ate her last chocolate as she left the porch. Miranda and Fredrika whined over who would get the window seat on the return trip, and Hadley roared up and down his sawdust trail one last time before being force-cleaned for the train journey. Then they were on their way.

The whole Harrigan household breathed a sigh of relief. It was over. They had made it.

"I never would have survived without you," Julia admitted to Hettie. "I was so close to giving up."

Julia drew the payment from her apron pocket. It really wasn't much for all the work involved, but it would help—and it was a start.

"I hope the Greenwald guests are easier to manage," Hettie stated.

"Oh my! I had forgotten. They arrive tomorrow, don't they?"

Hettie nodded. The committee had decided that each member would have a turn at keeping guests. Mrs. Greenwald was to host a young couple starting the next day.

Julia looked about her disrupted home. She was eager to restore it to its proper state. The whole place needed a good cleaning.

Hettie knew her thoughts. "We'll get to it," she assured her mistress.

"I'm sure we will," Julia stated, "but first let's have a cup of tea."

"Hot?" asked Hettie, a twinkle in her eyes.

"Very hot!" said Julia, laughing.

Chapter Eleven

New Visitors

Only Julia and three other committee members had the room and the desire to keep overnight guests. The other ladies hoped to make their living by selling goods from their craft shop. Julia was beginning to wonder if each of the four ladies would even get one turn at playing hostess.

Mrs. Greenwald's young couple quickly became bored with the small town and left before their time was up. Mrs. Clancy's first clients made other plans and did not show up at all. That meant Mrs. Clancy would have the next people on the list. Eventually an elderly couple wrote for accommodation.

Julia had received permission from four shop owners to use their facilities. The women, along with their husbands, got busy preparing the space to display merchandise. They expressed some disappointment at the meagerness of their stock as they tried to make so few items fill such big shelves.

"It will be much better next year," Julia encouraged. "We will have all winter to prepare things for the stores."

Although the women looked a bit more hopeful, Julia knew they were all wondering where they would get the funds needed to buy supplies to make the items.

"These will have to do for now," Julia continued. "It does look much better to have some of the boards off the shop windows along Main Street."

Summer was drawing to a close when two letters arrived. A family of three wanted a quiet accommodation for a two-week period and a "genteel" couple requested two rooms for an undetermined number of days. Julia hastily called a committee meeting for that afternoon.

"We don't have much time," she told the group. "Both parties plan to arrive next week."

The Adams family was next on the list, so the committee decided they would get the guests staying for the more certain period of time. Julia was given the genteel couple.

"Will you need help getting ready?" Julia asked Ruth Adams.

"Thank you, but I'm as good as ready right now. After all, I've been waiting all summer."

"Is there anything you need?" asked Julia. "Vegetables? Linens?"

"I could use some new potatoes—and perhaps a few carrots," the woman admitted.

"I'll send the girls over with some," promised Julia.

Next Julia asked for a report from the craft shop.

Matilda Pendleton shook her head. "We haven't had much business this summer. One couple bought three or four things to take home to family, and some men from the train looked in. One bought a lace collar for his wife. That's all."

It was a discouraging report but Julia tried to make the best of it.

"Well, that's a start. We're getting a good stock of summer jams and jellies now. Once word gets around, the train crews might do a lot more purchasing."

The other women didn't look too hopeful.

Julia sensed their discouragement and brought the meeting to an end. "Hettie, I think we could all use some tea," Julia prompted. As the ladies gathered around the serving table with cups of steaming tea and lemon tarts, their spirits were lifted in friendly chatter.

———

"Do you think it will be like the last time?" asked Felicity when the family gathered for family worship in the evening.

"Impossible!" John answered. "The world couldn't contain two such families." He rolled his eyes and put a horror-stricken look on his face to entertain his daughters.

Felicity laughed and Jennifer smiled at John's antics.

Julia hoped John was right but she feared that two such families just might exist. She breathed a quick prayer that she might not be called upon to endure them both in one summer.

"This will be a new family," John reminded them. "They may be 'different'—but that's what makes this venture exciting. We never are quite sure what kind of folk we will be entertaining."

"I hope they don't have a boy!" exclaimed Jennifer, remembering the last one.

"If they do, we'll need to tie down the flower pots," put in Felicity.

"And chain down the swing," added Jennifer. "And—"

"They don't have a boy," said Julia. "The next guests are just a couple."

"Old?" asked Felicity.

"I don't know. The letter just said 'genteel.' "

"What's genteel?" asked Jennifer.

"Well, that means they have good manners—good breeding. They are used to fine things," Julia explained.

Felicity rolled her eyes at her sister. "Oh-oh," she said. "The children-should-be-seen-and-not-heard kind."

John and Julia laughed.

"Well, it could be that you will need to keep down your chatter for a few days," Julia admitted, "but that shouldn't be too hard."

"I keep forgetting," said Felicity. "When I am serving in the dining room or putting fresh towels in the bath, I keep forgetting that I am not to talk—just serve."

"I know," Julia smiled. "It's difficult to shift roles, isn't it?"

John fidgeted. He hated to see his family become servants in their own home. His girls were hardly more than children and they were serving the table, doing dishes, cleaning bathrooms, and making beds. Julia had tried to assure him that the experience was good for them, but John would rather have had them learn their duties under different circumstances.

"Enough chatter for now. We all have things to do if we are to be ready for tomorrow," Julia went on. "Let's be quiet while Papa reads the Scriptures."

The girls settled themselves to listen to the scripture lesson that John had chosen for the evening reading. Then each one prayed, asking God to keep them within His will. Felicity went a step further. "Dear God," she prayed, "bring us good guests—not like the last time. Thank you that they don't have wild boys or grumpy girls. Help us to do our best to care for them and might they pay good money for all of us to live on. Amen."

The buggy did not carry many suitcases when Tom arrived with the guests the next afternoon. Each visitor had one small piece. Tom looked pleased as he carried the two cases to the second floor bedrooms.

"Do come in," Julia greeted the couple. "You must be weary after your long train ride. Hettie will show you your rooms and the hall bath where you may refresh yourselves. We will have tea in the main parlor in fifteen minutes."

The gentleman nodded, giving Julia a kind smile, and took his wife's arm to follow Hettie. The woman climbed the stairs with hesitation, causing Julia a moment's concern. But she completed the climb with no apparent ill effects. Julia put aside her worry and went back to the kitchen.

In fifteen minutes, just as Julia had arranged, the couple entered the parlor. They made no demands. Mr. Williams led his wife to a chair and helped her be seated. He pulled another chair up close to hers and seated himself.

"Cream and sugar?" Julia asked.

"Just sugar for me," replied the woman, "but Mr. Williams will have a bit of both."

Julia served the tea and passed the dainty sandwiches.

"My, you have a lovely home. So pretty. Not—not stark and cold like—like some places," the woman observed as she helped herself to a sandwich.

"Thank you," responded Julia. She enjoyed having her home receive proper respect.

"I love the pictures," the woman went on. "That one in the hall, of the stream and the children. I could almost taste the water the boy is offering to the girl."

Julia enjoyed the compliment. The picture was one of her favorites.

"Who is the artist?" the woman asked.

"He was an acquaintance of my father," Julia stated. "The picture was a wedding gift."

"Then I don't suppose you want to sell it?" the woman asked, her brows arched over her lifted teacup.

"No," said Julia, shaking her head. "I think not."

Julia passed the cupcakes. Mr. Williams accepted one, but Mrs. Williams politely turned down the sweets.

"I would like another cup of that lovely tea, though," she murmured. "Quite the nicest cup of tea I have had for some time."

Julia smiled. "I suspect that our cold, clear spring water has something to do with that."

"Yes," agreed the woman. "Yes, I suspect so." Then she turned to her husband. "Do you suppose we could get our water from the spring?" she asked him.

"We will drink nothing but spring water while we are here," he promised.

"I mean for our tea."

"Yes, dear. For our tea."

"But shouldn't we pay them if we are going to use their water?" she asked.

"My dear, we will pay them," he tried to assure her.

"But I didn't see you pay."

"We pay when we leave," he tried to reason.

"Are we leaving already? Goodness! It seems that we just got here," she said, rising to her feet.

Julia could not understand the strange exchange. She wondered if she should leave the room and give the man an opportunity to calm his disoriented wife.

The man stood also. "No, dear, we are not leaving yet." He eased her back into her seat. "And you are quite right," he hurried on. "We do owe this lady for her fine tea, made of fresh spring water. Here. I will pay her. See! Right now." He reached into his pocket and drew out a bill, which he handed to Julia. His wink told Julia to take the money without comment.

Julia accepted the bill with a trembling hand. "Thank you. Thank you, Mr. Williams," she managed.

Mrs. Williams settled back in her chair.

"That's better," Julia heard her say.

Mr. Williams set aside his cup. "I do think my wife needs some rest," he explained. "If you will excuse us, I will take her to her room."

Julia nodded. "Dinner will be served in the dining room at seven," she said.

Mrs. Williams allowed her husband to take her arm, help her out of her seat, and steer her toward the staircase.

"Wait!" Julia heard her say when they reached the hall. "I want to see the picture."

After several moments Julia heard the footsteps continue on.

Julia wasn't sure how to plan for dinner. Would the couple like company? Should the family join them? Or would they prefer the serenity of being alone?

During the Hammonds' visit, the twins had eaten in the kitchen and Julia and John had taken their meal in the dining room after the guests finished. But the Hammonds had been a family of five. They had almost filled the table themselves. Mr. and Mrs. Williams would not do so. Should the Harrigans join them? Julia pondered the question. She finally decided that the guests, at least for their first meal, should be served alone.

Mr. and Mrs. Williams appeared at the dining room door promptly at seven. Jennifer was given the task of serving the table. Julia oversaw the meal from the kitchen, and Felicity began clean-up at the big kitchen sink.

"She sure doesn't eat much," Jennifer said on a trip to the kitchen.

"I noticed that," replied Julia.

"Do you think she doesn't like our food?" asked Felicity.

"She keeps saying 'this is so good' and 'that is delicious,'" said Jennifer, "but she doesn't even eat it. Just takes a bite or two and lets the rest sit on her plate."

"Perhaps she doesn't have a very big appetite," Julia commented. "She does seem rather frail. Maybe she has been ill."

"He eats well," said Jennifer. "He had two helpings of everything."

"Good," Julia responded. "He is very thin. He needs to put on some weight."

Jennifer disappeared to clear the table and returned a moment later with a frown on her face.

"What's wrong?" asked Julia.

"She asked how long I have been working here. When I told her I live here, she said 'poor child' and patted my arm. Then she said she did hope it wouldn't be too long until I'd be able to leave. What did she mean, Mama?"

"I have no idea," said Julia.

"Did her husband know what she meant?" asked Felicity.

"I—I don't know. I had the feeling he was trying to—to hurry her. He suggested a walk in the garden for some fresh air. He asked me for permission. When I told him to go right ahead, she patted my arm again and said, 'Such a nice, sweet girl. I'll talk to the people in charge.' And he hurried her away."

"That's strange," said Felicity.

Julia agreed, but she said nothing to the girls.

"If they have finished eating, clear the table and reset it," she instructed Jennifer. "Felicity, go call your papa from the garden. We will have our dinner now."

Chapter Twelve

Strangers

The next morning when Julia came down the stairs, Mrs. Williams was sitting in the hall studying the painting of the quiet stream and the children.

"It is so peaceful," she murmured with a sweet smile flickering on her lips.

"Yes," agreed Julia. "Yes, it is." Julia's eyes shifted to the hall clock. "My, you are up early," she continued. "Were you unable to sleep?"

"Sleep?" asked the woman. "Oh no, I don't sleep. James sleeps. He sleeps for both of us. I don't sleep now."

"I see," said Julia. "Would you like a cup of tea or coffee while you wait for your breakfast?"

The elderly woman took on the look of a child being offered a forbidden treat. "Oh, could I?" she whispered, glancing around as if expecting someone to spoil their plan.

"Certainly," said Julia. "It will take just a few minutes. Would you like me to bring it to the parlor or into the dining room?"

"I thought you meant with you," the frail woman said with some disappointment.

Julia recovered quickly from her surprise. "If you'd like to come to the kitchen, that would be fine," she offered.

"I just love kitchens," she giggled like a schoolgirl. "So—so cozy with the fire burning."

Julia offered an arm.

"They'll never know, will they?" the elderly woman chuckled. She took Julia's arm eagerly and tottered along to the kitchen.

She is frail, Julia observed. *And confused. She must have been very ill. I must speak to the girls. We will all need to be patient and kind with her.*

Julia seated her guest in a kitchen chair at the gingham-covered table and hastened to start the morning tasks. She had just added wood to the fire when the back door opened and Hettie entered. Her eyes widened for an instant at the sight of their guest. Then she smiled and set to work on breakfast muffins.

"Mrs. Williams wanted to join us in the kitchen," Julia explained. "What would you like, Mrs. Williams? Tea or coffee?"

"Oh, I'm not allowed coffee," the woman said. "It's not good for my—for my something. I can't remember what. But I could have some this morning. You wouldn't tell them, would you?"

Hettie cast a questioning glance toward Julia, then went on stirring the muffin batter.

"Tea sounds good," mused Julia. "I think we should all have a cup just as soon as the water gets hot. Don't you agree, Hettie?"

"Right, tea sounds good to me."

Julia had no idea what the "something" might be to which Mrs. Williams was referring, but she would take no chances, just in case there was indeed a "something."

"We'll have a good cup of tea with fresh, clear spring water," Julia went on.

Mrs. Williams looked as though she had never heard of such a thing as spring water. "I—I like mine with hot water, please," she said timidly, then quickly added, "If it's not too much trouble."

"Oh no. No trouble at all," Julia assured her. "We'll certainly make it with hot water."

"And a tiny bit of cream."

Julia nodded. The woman had asked for sugar the afternoon before.

As soon as the tea was ready Julia served her guest, then busied herself with breakfast preparations.

"Whose turn is it to set the table?" she asked Hettie.

"Felicity's," Hettie answered. "Jennifer did dining room duty last night."

Julia nodded. She would have remembered if she had stopped to think about it. Her mind was dwelling too heavily on the woman at her kitchen table.

Felicity soon entered, yawning as she tied her crisp apron over her dress.

"Good morning," piped the woman. "Are you still here?" Felicity stopped in her tracks. Her eyes traveled from the woman to her mother and then back to the woman again.

"Yes," she said hesitantly. "I'm still here."

"Would you like some tea?" asked the woman, patting the chair beside her.

"No—no thank you," replied Felicity. "I must set the table."

"Is it time to eat again—already? Oh my, I do hope it's not that awful stew."

She had been served no stew at the Harrigans'.

Julia saw the merriment light up Felicity's eyes. "Felicity," she said before her daughter could think of some teasing response, "use the blue napkins."

Felicity nodded, and Julia hoped she had averted a problem.

I must have a talk with the girls, Julia told herself. *It is obvious that Mrs. Williams is ill. We must all be careful.*

"Mrs. Williams, would you like another cup of tea?"

Just as Julia finished her question, the door flung open and a wild Mr. Williams burst through.

"Have you seen—?" He stopped in mid-sentence when his eyes fell on the woman at the kitchen table. He slumped into a nearby chair and covered his heart with his hand. "Oh, thank goodness!" he exclaimed. "I was worried sick when I didn't find her in her room. I—I never oversleep like this. It must have been the long train ride or—"

"She's fine," said Julia. "Just having a cup of tea. Would you care for some?"

Mr. Williams first shook his head, but then he changed his mind. "Yes, I think I will after all." He still looked pale and shaken. Julia poured his tea and set it before him.

Mrs. Williams smiled contentedly, apparently pleased that her husband had joined them. She patted his hand. The fear was beginning to leave his eyes, but Julia noticed that his hand still trembled when he lifted the cup to his lips.

Jennifer entered the kitchen. She was wearing a green calico dress that matched her sister's. Mrs. Williams looked at her out of the corner of her eye and gave her a conspiratorial nod.

"Are you done already?" asked the woman.

"Done?" asked Jennifer.

"I think she has you confused with Felicity," Julia explained in a whisper. "Felicity was just here and is now setting the table for breakfast."

Mrs. Williams motioned for Jennifer to come closer to her. Then she laid a hand on the girl's arm. "Don't worry," she whispered. "I promised to work on it—and I will. All you will need is a disguise of some kind."

Jennifer looked at Mr. Williams for some explanation. He appeared both anguished and embarrassed. Jennifer reached down and took the frail hand in hers. "Thank you," she said simply. "You're very kind."

The door opened again and Felicity came into the kitchen. "Jen," she began, "where did you put the blue sugar and creamer?"

"On the bottom shelf of the buffet."

Felicity saw Mrs. Williams look from one twin to the other, then back again. Suddenly her face lit up in a big smile. "That is so clever!" she exclaimed. "I never would have thought of it. It's the perfect disguise. They will never catch you—when you are two. They won't know which one to chase. You'll be able to get away for sure." She clapped her hands in childish glee and laughed with uninhibited pleasure.

Mr. Williams moved to his wife. "Come," he said. "You've had enough tea. Let's take a little walk before breakfast."

He helped her up, and she went without protest. "So clever," she chuckled as she left the room. "I would never have thought of it. I wonder how she does that."

––––––

That afternoon as Julia and Hettie were preparing supper, Mr. Williams tapped on the kitchen door.

"Mrs. Harrigan—could I see you for a moment?" he began hesitantly.

Julia nodded and wiped her hands on her apron. Then she took the apron off and laid it on a kitchen chair.

"Let's go to the porch swing," she suggested, leading the way.

Julia welcomed a few moments to sit quietly in the shade, but she knew she could not relax completely. Mr. Williams had something important on his mind.

"I'm—I'm sure you have noticed that Mrs. Williams can—can get a bit confused at times," he began slowly.

Julia nodded. "She's a very pleasant person," she said to ease his anxiety.

"Yes. Yes, she is. A dear, good woman. She always has been." His eyes took on a distant look before filling with tears.

"She has not been well. Has been very sick, in fact," he explained.

"I thought as much," Julia said softly.

"I—I brought her here hoping that the—the quietness would be good for her."

"We'll do all we can to make it so," said Julia.

"All of you have been most kind," the man continued. "You—you just don't know how—how beside myself I have been. I—I hardly know how to—to care for her."

"It must be very difficult for you," Julia agreed.

"I just wanted you to know—to understand," he continued.

"Of course," said Julia. "Please, please let us know how we can help. If there is anything you need—"

"We are very comfortable," he quickly assured Julia. Then he paused. "But there is one thing—"

Julia waited for him to go on.

"Would it—would it be possible for your good husband to put a—a lock on her door?"

Julia tried to hide her surprise.

"This morning I was so frightened. This time it was only the kitchen, but what if—what if she had wandered off down one of the mountain trails? I don't know what I would have done . . ."

Julia understood the man's concern. "Of course," she said. "John will put a lock on the door as soon as she wakes up from her nap."

"Thank you. Thank you!" the man exclaimed. "Now I must get back. She doesn't sleep well."

He hurried off, and Julia gave the swing a slight push and let the motion sweep away some of the anxiety from her heart.

"The poor soul," she said softly. "What an awful burden. I wonder how long this has been going on?"

———

The family accepted Mrs. Williams with her strangeness. Indeed, they decided to do more than accept her. They decided to try to help her.

"Do you think they like to be alone so much?" Jennifer asked at their evening prayer hour.

"I don't know. He certainly wants peace and tranquillity for her."

"But if we sat quietly, and talked quietly, do you think it might be good for her to have company at meals?"

"I will talk to Mr. Williams," Julia promised. "We'll let him decide."

"In the meantime," said John, "if she wants to sit in the hall and look at the painting—or in the kitchen to drink tea—then we'll let her."

"She *is* friendly," stated Felicity.

"And she's not bossy," added Jennifer.

"She always says 'thank you,' " Felicity recalled.

"I like her," Jennifer concluded.

"It's a shame we can't help her more," said Julia. "She seems so sweet."

"Maybe they will stay longer if they like it here and it's peaceful and quiet. Do you think so, Mama?"

"Perhaps," said Julia.

"We'll try to make her feel at home," Jennifer decided.

They included the Williams couple in their prayers that night.

———

Three days later Julia was startled by a knock at the door. Two men in dark uniforms showed Julia their credentials.

"Are you Mrs. Harrigan?" asked the larger of the two.

"That's right," Julia nodded.

"May we come in?"

Julia moved aside and motioned them in. She led the way to the parlor.

The smaller man took charge.

"Mrs. Harrigan, I understand that you keep boarders."

"Short-term guests," Julia corrected.

"Do you ask for references?" he asked.

"No."

"So your guests at present are strangers?" Without waiting for her answer he continued. "We understand that you have a Mr. Williams and his—his companion here."

"Yes."

"You know nothing about them?"

"Just that they wanted a quiet place to—for Mrs. Williams to regain her strength."

The men looked at each other.

"Are they here now?"

"Why, yes. They are—are resting."

"So you know that the woman has been ill?" asked the larger man.

"Yes. Mr. Williams said she has been ailing," admitted Julia.

"What else did he tell you?"

"Nothing."

"Then you don't know that she has been assigned to an asylum?"

Julia drew in her breath sharply.

"And that she is absent without permission? That Mr. Williams spirited her away to avoid the authorities?"

"What? I—I can't believe it. They seem like—like such a fine couple—"

"In fact," the man continued, "Mr. Williams is indeed Mr. Williams, but Mrs. Williams is Miss Margaret Whistler."

"But—why—why would—?"

"Apparently they were childhood sweethearts and then the war and circumstances separated them. When he returned she had been terribly ill, and the fever—well, she has been in the asylum for years. He kept visiting her, determined that she would recover. She didn't. He kept asking for her release, but they wouldn't grant it. Finally he just took it upon himself to run off with her."

Julia could not hide her amazement. "Mr. Williams? There must be some mistake. He seems so—so—"

"Shrewd? Oh, he's shrewd all right. Downright clever. He planned the whole escape himself. Outsmarted everybody. Folks at the hospital got so they trusted him—and then he took off. Now it is costing a small fortune to find them and take them back."

"But surely—surely you don't have to take them back. He cares for her. He seems most solicitous. He—"

"Oh yes. He cares. He means well. We've been told that he even has the foolish notion of a hasty marriage. Thinks that will give her 'security'—help her get well again. It just doesn't work. We've tried to let others out. They do all right for a few days or possibly weeks—and then they need to be locked up again."

"Locked up?" gasped Julia. It sounded so cruel. "What do you mean? She is such a—a sweet, agreeable person. Perhaps a bit confused, but perfectly harmless. She—"

"No one confined to an asylum can be considered harmless,"

said the man. "She might seem fine today—but who knows what her confusion will cause her to do tomorrow? She might start setting fires, or she might take a knife to someone or something."

Chapter Thirteen

A Twist

Julia's eyes widened with shock. "Not Mrs. Williams!" she gasped.

"Miss Whistler," corrected the smaller of the two men.

"Why I—I just can't believe it. I mean—"

"We're going to be taking them back," said the bigger man.

"Oh my! I do wish—You don't think they would be fine if someone watched out for them? I mean—"

"Sorry, ma'am, but we can't take those chances."

"Of course," murmured Julia.

"Now if you'll just go get your boarders, we'll be on our way."

"House guests," Julia corrected. All the way up the long flight of stairs and down the hallway Julia mumbled. "What a shame! What an awful shame." She raised her calico apron to brush away the tears.

She hesitated before the door of the bedroom occupied by Mr. Williams. She had decided to speak to him first. He could talk to his wife—to Miss Whistler. He would know the best way to break the news to her.

Julia sniffed away her tears and lifted a trembling hand to knock. There was no answer so she knocked again. Still no answer.

"Mr. Williams? Mr. Williams," called Julia, softly at first and then louder. Still no answer.

"That's funny, I didn't see them go out."

A noise behind Julia caused her to wheel around. The small man was eyeing her with suspicion.

"They . . . they don't seem to be in," Julia faltered. "I didn't see them go out, but perhaps—"

The man pushed past Julia. He opened the door without knocking and entered the room with one swift motion.

Julia peered over his shoulder. The room was empty. The bed neatly made. The two small suitcases missing.

"He's—he's gone. But how—?"

"Tricky little—" The man bit off the rest of his remark, perhaps remembering that a lady was present. Then he confronted Julia. "You really knew nothing of this?" he quizzed.

"No, I had no idea. They didn't say—I mean, he said they would stay until—"

"Well, I guess I'll just have to accept your word," he interrupted, implying that he still doubted her.

"My word can be taken," she said firmly. "God has set a standard. We are not to lie—even to protect someone—someone we have grown fond of. I tell you the truth, Mr.—Mr.—"

"Is there any place you know of where they might be?"

"No," said Julia.

"No place where they liked to go?"

"No."

"Is there any way out of this town?"

"Just the railroad."

"When did the last train go through?"

"Why, it was the one you arrived on, I believe," answered Julia.

The man looked surprised. Then he mumbled something Julia couldn't understand. She guessed they were more words he didn't want her to hear.

"Slipped out right under our noses," he growled.

Julia turned to hide the relief in her eyes. Then she noticed something on the dresser. She crossed the room and picked it up. It was a letter addressed to her.

Dear Mrs. Harrigan,

You have been most kind to Margaret and me, and I am sorry we cannot stay as long as planned.

I have left the amount we owe you in the top drawer of this dresser. I have also left what I believe is an appropriate amount for the picture from the hallway.

Julia's eyes widened, but she said nothing to the man standing behind her. She read on.

Margaret found it so restful. I could not deny her the privilege of ownership. I do hope you understand.

I have also left money for some provisions. We made a lunch for ourselves from your kitchen pantry, not wishing to bother any of the household.

Again, thank you for your kindness.

James W. Williams, Esq.

When Julia looked up she realized the man had been reading over her shoulder.

"So they stole—"

"They did not," cut in Julia. "They paid for—for everything."

The man turned and left the room without another word to Julia. The next time she heard him speak it was to his companion, who apparently had been stationed at the open door. "Let's get going" he said, "before the trail gets cold."

Julia shuddered. *Such a foolish way to talk. I think he's been reading too many cheap who-done-its.*

Julia knew she should bid her uninvited guests good-day, but she turned instead to the drawer mentioned in the letter and opened it slowly.

A neat pile of bills was tucked in one corner. Julia lifted them. Little slips of paper were bundled with the bills, held by small clips. The first one said, "Board and room, five days, two people." Julia counted the money. The payment was exact. The next one said, "Lunch payment." Julia counted again, finding that the amount was more than ample. "My! I wonder if he emptied the whole cupboard," she exclaimed. The last bundle said, "Painting." When Julia counted the money she determined that Mr. Williams had indeed been generous.

"The poor dears," she cried. "The poor, poor dears."

Julia heard stirring behind her and turned her head. Hettie stood there, her eyes filled with questions.

"Who were those men?" Hettie began. "I saw them leaving the house, waving their arms and turning the air blue with their talk. I was scared that—"

"They were from some asylum," Julia explained.

"Asylum?" Hettie gasped.

Julia nodded.

"What did they want with you?" asked Hettie, still stunned.

"No—no. Not me. Them." Julia waved a hand toward the vacant room.

"Them?" Hettie exclaimed, following Julia's gaze. "Them? Why?"

"They—they escaped."

"Escaped?"

Julia began to laugh helplessly. She waved the money at Hettie and picked up a corner of her apron to wipe her eyes.

Hettie looked at her, her face perplexed, her eyes filled with concern.

"Oh, Hettie. It's really—it's really quite funny. He outsmarted them. Again. That funny little man. Mr. Williams. He—he's as sharp as—"

Hettie was still shaking her head, wondering if Julia herself needed an asylum.

Through spurts of laughter Julia told Hettie the story. "They came here to get Mr. Williams. He had been a visitor at the asylum where Mrs. Williams—no Miss Whistler—that was her real name—was a patient. They weren't married at all. Well, Mr. Williams tried to get her discharged, but she never seemed to get well and so they kept her in the asylum. He loved her, and when they wouldn't discharge her to his keeping—well— he just stole her away. They are really—how do you say it—on the lam—the run. And those two men thought they had caught up with them here—but when I came up to call Mr. Williams— he was already gone."

Julia was laughing again, great tears rolling down her cheeks. Hettie couldn't tell if her tears were from laughing or crying. Julia didn't know either.

"It's sort of sad," Julia stopped to say. "Sad—and sweet. Imagine—the old gentleman loving her enough to risk everything. He left only a note—and the money." Then Julia's face brightened. "Well, I'm glad," she said firmly. "I'm glad they got away. The men from the asylum implied that I knew all about this. That I helped them escape. Well, I didn't. But I'm not sure I wouldn't have—had I known."

At the sound of Hettie's gasp, Julia hastened to explain. "Well, why not? I mean, they are hurting no one. Why shouldn't they be free to live their own lives? Wouldn't it have been wonderful if we could have had the minister marry them? Just think! We could have given them a little reception!"

Hettie did not respond enthusiastically.

"Don't you think—?"

"I think they are total strangers," said Hettie slowly but firmly. "I think they were fugitives. We don't know much at all about their circumstances—but—if she was in an asylum, then there must have been a need for her to be there. A reason."

Julia sobered. Hettie was right. "Well, they seemed so—so blameless—so sweet," Julia ventured.

Hettie nodded.

"They left the money," Julia said again, showing Hettie the bundles. "He was very, very generous. He figured the cost of the rooms exactly. And he left money for the picture, the one from the hallway. The one she would sit and look at," Julia explained. "He even left money for the food they took with them."

"So that's where it went," Hettie said. "I went to get dinner and couldn't find—"

"Did they take much? He certainly left adequate payment."

"I haven't checked closely. I just couldn't find some things I was looking for. I couldn't understand—and when I saw those two strange men I started to worry."

Julia's eyes darkened as she remembered the two men. She tucked the bills in her apron pocket.

"Well, as you say, perhaps she should be back at the asylum. Perhaps there is a reason for her being there. But—well, quite frankly, I'm glad they got away. I wish them the best—wherever they are, and I hope they are able to outsmart those two bloodhounds—forever."

Julia closed the dresser drawer and wiped her hands across her apron.

"Now, perhaps we should check the pantry. We might need to do some shopping before dinner."

Chapter Fourteen

Summer's End

Julia hung a small mirror in the hall where the painting had been. She missed the quiet scene, but she would not have taken it back from the woman who had found so much joy in it. "I do hope it brings you many hours of pleasure," Julia whispered as she adjusted the mirror.

Julia went to the kitchen to help Hettie prepare tea for the committee meeting. Jennifer and Felicity were already there. Felicity was bent over a rolling pin, working on pie crust, and Jennifer was whipping the filling.

The scene startled Julia. The girls had matured so much over the past weeks that she could not get used to it. At the start of summer she had two children. As it drew to an end, she was the mother of two young ladies. Julia recalled her words to John. She had told him that helping with the household chores would be good for the girls. Now Julia wasn't sure she wanted them to grow up so quickly.

"Hettie is letting us make dessert," Felicity explained, and Julia understood that both girls considered it a privilege.

"I'm sure it will be delicious," she responded.

"It's one of Papa's favorites," said Jennifer. "Lemon."

"And we are having fried parsnips and carrots," continued Felicity, "with ham."

"He'll be pleased," Julia responded.

"We want him to know that we are doing just fine," Felicity went on. "Hettie says that—"

"Fel, you talk too much," Jennifer cut in.

Julia wondered if Hettie shared the conviction. Her eyes were masked, her lips pursed.

"Well, we *are* doing fine," Julia stated, trying to believe her own words. "The money that Mr. Williams paid us certainly helped. We'll get by."

"As soon as it snows, Tom is going hunting," said Felicity.

"Hunting?" Julia had never known Tom to be a hunter.

"Hettie says moose or elk—or even deer—is just as good as beef if you know how to cook it."

Julia made no comment, but she wondered if pantry stocks were lower than she had guessed.

"Papa and Tom are taking in some of the garden things," Felicity added. "We don't want an early frost to get any of it."

Julia nodded. They could not afford to lose anything. She decided to change the subject. "We should learn today when school will begin. Are you excited?"

Jennifer showed some interest, but Felicity just shrugged. She was enjoying her time in the kitchen.

Julia turned to the trays on the kitchen table.

"I see you are ready with tea," Julia said to Hettie.

"Just last-minute things to do. You go ahead with your meeting. The girls will bring it when you need it."

Julia looked again at her two growing daughters. Then she went to the parlor to make sure the chairs were in proper place and to greet the ladies as they came.

"Do we have any reports?" Julia asked the committee members after everyone was settled.

"There hasn't been much to report," Mrs. Clancy answered after a brief silence.

"The last family bought a few items from the shop," said Matilda Pendleton. "I have the money here." She reached into her pocket and took out three envelopes.

"Mrs. Shannon, this is for one of your doilies. Mrs. Greenwald, they took one of your stuffed toys. And Mrs. Harrigan, they bought your linen tablecloth."

Matilda distributed the envelopes. Julia felt guilty. Some of the committee members needed the funds much more than she did. They had had very little money come in over the summer. Julia wondered how they were managing to live.

"Perhaps we should put the craft sales money into a pot and divide it equally," Julia suggested.

"No," Mrs. Clancy objected, shaking her head. "That wouldn't be fair. Some folks do more work—and some folks put more money into their projects—and some folks do nicer work."

The others agreed.

Julia felt her cheeks flush. There seemed to be no way to help her neighbors. "Did everyone have a good garden?" Julia continued. "Some of us may have surplus if anyone is in need."

The ladies seemed pleased with the produce from their gardens.

"Our men are planning to go hunting as soon as the snow falls," Julia said. "Perhaps we can share wild meat—"

"Jim has been hunting already," said Maude Shannon.

So had some of the other husbands, they learned.

"Then no one is short of supplies?" Julia asked.

"Supplies, yes. Vegetables and meat, no," answered Mrs. Clancy.

"We don't have much flour or tea. Salt is getting low. Baking things are in short supply," said Mrs. Adams.

"I'll check what I have," Julia promised. "Perhaps we have a bit to spare." Heads dropped slightly. Julia knew the women were not used to charity, so she hastened to explain. "We can work out some means of exchange. Perhaps grocery items in exchange for a lace collar or linen handkerchiefs. I can put the items back into the craft shop and sell them next year."

The women brightened. That seemed fair.

"Perhaps I can make arrangements with Mr. Perry at the store. I will leave money on account, and you can make your purchases and leave the payment for me to pick up." Julia referred briefly to the notes she held in her hand. "Now, Mrs. Clancy, have you a date regarding school opening?"

"Still no word," Mrs. Clancy answered. "I wrote—I even put through a wire—but nothing."

"Oh my," said Julia. "It is late—"

"I know, but there's nothing more I can do about it."

"Of course," Julia replied. "Thank you for doing all you could."

"I—I'm afraid I have some bad news too," announced Mrs. Wright, the pastor's wife. All eyes turned toward her.

"We—we just received word that we are to be moved to another parish."

Shocked looks, shadowed faces turned toward Mrs. Wright.

"Who will come to take your place?" asked Julia.

"That's the difficulty," said Mrs. Wright. "They won't be sending anyone. They want to—to close the church."

"Close the church? But we need the church, especially now. How can they close it?" Julia asked.

"Well, they feel the congregation is too small to—"

"But there are still eight or nine—maybe even a dozen families in town," Julia interrupted.

"Yes," agreed the woman, studying her embroidered handkerchief. "But only three families come."

It was true. Only the Adams family joined the Harrigans and Tom and Hettie at church on Sunday mornings.

"When will you leave? When will the church close?" Julia asked.

"The end of the year."

"Surely we can do something before then to make them change their minds. We've lost so much already. We can't give up our church too. What if attendance increased? Would they leave it open?"

"I—I don't know. They might."

"We need the church," Julia said again to her neighbors. "We need a minister here for the difficult times—now more than ever. We can't let the church go."

Some nodded, others looked away, unwilling to meet Julia's gaze.

"We'll see what we can do between now and the end of the year," Julia assured Mrs. Wright. Then with a trembling voice she announced tea was ready.

———

That night, after they had gone to bed, Julia told John the news.

"John, we can't let the church go. We just can't. We need it. Our children need it. The whole town needs it. What if—what if someone were to get sick or—or die?"

John nodded in agreement. "So how can we save it?"

"We have to increase the attendance."

"Jule, folks have moved, and there is still nothing to bring them back."

"I'm not talking about them," said Julia. "I'm talking about the ones who are still here. There must be thirty or so still in town. That would be enough to keep a church open, don't you think?"

"It would if they all went to church, Jule, but they don't. The church has been here for years, and so have they, and they only go on special occasions. How can we change that?"

"They need the church," Julia insisted. "More than ever, they need the church. I don't know how they ever manage to get along without it—without God. Especially now that things are so hard. How do they get by without prayer, John? What do they do when they need answers?"

John just shook his head in the darkness.

"Well, it has dawned on me that I haven't been doing my job," said Julia softly. "Here I am, trying to save their homes, their possessions, their—their way of life—and I haven't even been thinking about saving their souls."

There was silence in the room.

"What do you plan to do?" John asked at last.

"I—I don't know. I wish I knew. I need to do some praying. A lot of praying. Perhaps God will show me. Show us."

Silence again. John, too, was thinking on Julia's words.

"I don't know why I didn't realize it earlier," went on Julia. "For—for some reason I—I guess I thought that believing—going to church—trying to live right—was enough. It's not, John. Not when your neighbors don't know—don't understand about—about God."

John drew her close. "We'll pray, Jule," he said softly, "for the people who are left. Maybe there is still something we can do for them. We might not be able to help them find work, but maybe we can help them find God."

Julia nodded her head against John's chest. Tears trickled from her eyes onto his pajamas.

"I—I hope we're not too late," she whispered in the darkness.

―――――

Julia stopped at Mr. Perry's store the next morning. She pushed open the squeaky door and stepped inside.

"Good morning, Mrs. Harrigan," the elderly bachelor greeted her.

"Good morning, Mr. Perry."

"So how is the committee doin'?"

"We haven't had a very good summer," Julia admitted. "I hope things will improve next year." Julia let her eyes travel over the shelves. Stock was very low. She remembered when the shelves had been crowded with merchandise. Sudden fear gripped her.

"You—you wouldn't be planning to move, would you, Mr. Perry?" she asked, keeping her voice as even as she could.

Mr. Perry let his eyes travel over the shelves. He understood her concern.

"Me? Never. Not me," he hastened to explain. "I got no place else to go. This here spot is mine—bought and paid for. Don't have much laid aside—but it's enough. Don't take much for me to live on. I can order in the supplies I'm needin' and pick them up at the train. Live cheaper here than any other place I know. 'Sides," he finished softly, "I like it here."

Julia was glad to hear that.

"Just don't need to keep as much stock on the shelves no more. Folks ain't buyin' like they used to."

"Perhaps it will pick up again," Julia said, her fears relieved. She produced her money from the sale of the linen tablecloth and explained her mission. "The money won't go far—not nearly far enough, but it's the best I can do—for the present."

"Be glad to accommodate," Mr. Perry said. "Very nice of you, Mrs. Harrigan."

Julia picked up the few items she needed and left for home. She was relieved to have the matter cared for, though it had been difficult to leave behind so much of her income when her family needed it so badly.

Well, the others need it more, she told herself as she walked home in the warmth of the autumn sun. *God will supply—in plenty of time—as the need arises.*

Two days later Julia heard loud knocking at the front door. She hurried to answer, for it sounded urgent. There stood Mrs. Clancy, her face red, her chest heaving from overexertion. Although she was out of breath, she started talking before Julia even had a chance to invite her in.

"The wire just came through," she panted. "The wire about school starting."

"Oh yes," said Julia. "Come in. Let's hear the news."

Mrs. Clancy did come in, but it was clear that she did not intend to sit down for a visit. She waved the wire beneath Julia's nose.

"Right here," she stated.

"When?" asked Julia. "When will the children be going back to school? The girls will be excited. I can hardly wait to tell them."

"See for yourself," said Mrs. Clancy, and she pushed the telegram in front of Julia for her to read.

IN REPLY STOP NO TEACHER FOR SCHOOL STOP TOO FEW PUPILS STOP

"What?" She looked at Mrs. Clancy. "What does this mean? It doesn't make any sense."

"They aren't starting school at all," said Mrs. Clancy. "They think our youngsters don't matter. We won't be having school this year. What do we do now, Mrs. Harrigan? What do we do now?"

Chapter Fifteen

Winter

John talked about sending the girls away for school, but both he and Julia knew there was no money for such a venture—important as they believed it to be.

"We'll borrow some books from the schoolhouse," Julia decided, as though it were a simple matter. "They are good students. It won't set them back to study for one year on their own. Next year we may have our school back."

John nodded. It seemed all they could do for the present.

Julia assigned daily portions for study. She spent three hours every morning going over lessons with the girls.

At first it seemed fun, even exciting, but the excitement soon wore off. Julia tried to think of ways to make the lessons interesting, but she had too many other things on her mind.

Winter came early. Julia was thankful that John and Tom had already dug the potatoes and pulled the remaining carrots. They could ill afford to have vegetables under the snow rather than in the root cellar.

On each of the first days of snow, John and Tom shouldered their rifles and took to the forested hillsides, hoping to bring home meat. Day after day they tramped through the frosted world, but each time they returned discouraged and empty-handed.

Jim Shannon was the first to have success in winter hunting. He brought a large venison roast to the Harrigans. Julia was glad for the meat. They had been dining on vegetables for a number of days.

"Portion it out, Hettie," Julia advised. "We don't know how long it will be until we get more."

Hettie followed instructions, reserving enough meat for stews and pot pies for several days.

John worked hard to build up the wood supply; then he left on an extended hunting trip. On his fourth day he returned with a yearling elk. It was an answer to prayer for Julia. But after dividing it among the townsfolk, she realized that the remaining portion would not last long.

But then Mac Pendleton got a small buck, and Jim Shannon shot another.

Julia began to relax. *With so many men hunting we are sure to have something for the stew pots,* she reasoned.

How to save the church topped Julia's list of concerns. *We need the church so people will have a chance to hear the Gospel,* she kept telling herself. She organized a ladies' afternoon meeting and sent out personal invitations for Sunday services. Then she arranged special events for the children during Sunday school.

The response was not good. Few people seemed to notice. They enjoyed her afternoon meetings, and some of them even sent their children to the Sunday school classes. But they seemed no more interested in the church than they had in the past.

"Frankly, I don't know what else to do," Julia confided to John. "Do you suppose a club program would help?"

"I'll talk to the pastor," John promised. "Perhaps he'll have some ideas."

But Pastor Wright had no ideas either. "We have tried and tried to get the people interested," he sighed. "There just doesn't seem to be any concern for spiritual things. Most folks who supported the church moved when the mill closed."

"Well, we'll just keep working—and praying," John promised. "Perhaps it's not too late."

John talked to some of the men, trying to convince them that letting the church close was as bad as having the mill shut down. But the blank stares he got in response told him the men had no idea what he was talking about. They did not understand why anyone would worry about religion when just getting food on the table consumed all their energies. They did not consider spiritual needs as important as physical needs.

Julia appealed to the women at her committee meetings, but she too received only blank stares in response to her pleas. The women didn't seem to feel that church was important.

Try as they might, John and Julia couldn't get anyone interested.

"Don't you care? Don't you even care?" Julia wanted to say, but their attitude answered the question for her.

––––––––

The families eventually decided that the children should study together. They divided them into groups—the first three grades, the second three grades, and those above. The groups were assigned to the parents whose children formed them. The mothers took turns supervising the studies each weekday morning.

Jennifer, Felicity, and Millicent Shannon were the only members of the top group. That meant the Harrigans had to supervise four mornings each week. Julia took the heavier share because Maude Shannon had children in the other groups also. Julia chose a small back room for the class area and tried to brighten it up with books, maps, and a world globe. John moved a table into the room and placed three chairs beside it.

"I hope this works," Julia heard Felicity say to Jennifer on the first morning of school. "I'm not sure what Mama will do with Millicent."

"She'll be okay," Jennifer responded.

"She's not too bright, you know," said Felicity. "She always has trouble in school."

Julia soon discovered that Felicity's assessment was accurate. Millicent was not very smart. Julia had to give most of her time and attention to Millicent, leaving her own two to study by themselves. Millicent did make some progress with the coaching, but Julia was concerned that her own girls were not getting the help and encouragement they deserved.

When Christmas came, Matilda Pendleton suggested that everyone get together.

"We should," Julia agreed. She could well imagine that the young woman was bored with the lack of excitement in town.

"Where?" asked Mrs. Shannon. "There aren't many of us, but we still won't all fit in a house."

"What about the schoolhouse?" suggested Mrs. Clancy.

"It's boarded up," sighed Mrs. Pendleton. "The whole town is boarded up."

"We can tear off the boards easily enough. Surely they owe us something for all the years we paid our taxes."

"Do you think we should?" another lady asked.

"Why not?"

"She's right," others replied.

"We won't hurt anything," went on Mrs. Clancy. "Just take off enough boards to get in, have our dinner together, and then board it up again."

It seemed harmless, even sensible.

"Do you think we should wire for permission?" asked Julia.

"No time," replied Mrs. Greenwald. "They'd have to have a meeting to consider it and by then Christmas would be over."

"The building should belong to the town, anyway," argued Mrs. Clancy.

Julia conceded. After all, Mrs. Clancy's husband was town clerk. They should know who had rightful access to the town buildings.

So the residents of the small community met together on December 24 to celebrate Christmas. Reverend Wright offered the table grace and read the Christmas story. Though this was new to some, they didn't object. Then they shared their potluck dinner, sang a few carols, and visited until the large pot of coffee ran dry.

John and Julia walked the few blocks home through the falling snow. Behind them they could hear the laughter of Felicity and Jennifer with the younger children as they shuffled along.

"They must miss children their own age," Julia commented. Then she heard Felicity yell, "Tommy Shannon, I'll get you for that!" and squeals and laughter followed the threat.

"But they do seem to be having fun," John remarked. "Children always manage to have fun. It's too bad grownups have to take life so seriously."

There was a certain wistfulness in his voice, and Julia slipped her arm through his, hoping to drive away his sadness.

"John," she said, "we *are* doing all right, aren't we? I mean, we have enough to eat. We are together. We are making it through the first year—the worst year. Things will get better, won't they?"

John squeezed her hand, but he had no ready reply.

At the end of the year the Wrights packed their belongings, boarded the train, and left. Julia had been unable to save the church.

"I won't board up the building," Rev. Wright said firmly.

"Even if there is no minister, the church must be open for the people."

Julia was thankful for that. At least she could still slip into the building for a few moments of prayer.

Julia felt heavy with sorrow as she watched the Wrights depart. The townspeople needed the Gospel. How would they hear it now that their church had been taken from them?

"Honestly, Hettie," Julia admitted later that day, "sometimes I come desperately close to giving up."

The older woman patted Julia's hand and suggested tea. It was the only cure Hettie had to offer for the world's ills.

Winter dragged on with cold winds blowing off the mountain peaks, threatening to freeze everything in its path. Snow fell, burying their world in harsh whiteness. But on a few days the sun shone with such brilliance that the whole valley glistened like strung jewels, and there were days when the climbing temperature made folks think spring might be early.

In February, Mac and Matilda Pendleton announced that they could no longer endure the lonely settlement. They loaded their few possessions, padlocked the door of their cottage, and climbed aboard an outgoing train.

"We just keep dwindling and dwindling," Mrs. Greenwald commented. "Soon there won't be anybody left but us and Mr. Perry."

Mr. Greenwald was in charge of the local train station. He would be needed as long as the train stopped at the town. Julia still had nightmares of the train being withdrawn. She would awaken in a sweat of terror, repeating, "No. Please, no. That is all we have left!"

Julia was not the only one who had fears about the train. "If they ever take the train, that's it! The town won't survive overnight without that train," she had often heard people say.

"Well," Julia said to Mrs. Greenwald, "we still have the train. No one has threatened to take it—yet."

"One can scarcely keep a family here with no doctor, no school, no neighbors—nothing," Mrs. Greenwald replied.

Julia would have added church to the list, but the Greenwalds did not consider the church a real loss.

Julia and John felt the urgency to do something. They needed spiritual nurturing. Their children needed biblical training. Their neighbors all needed it too, though none seemed to realize it.

"We'll just have to start our own Bible study," John decided. "We'll gather those who are interested and have our own simple service."

"Where?" asked Julia, eager to get started.

John thought for a few minutes. "Not in the church. People have shied away from church in the past. Perhaps—perhaps if we have it here, like you do the committee meetings, folks might get the notion to come."

Julia nodded, her eyes beginning to shine. "Do you really think it might work?"

"Might. We'll never know 'til we try."

The next morning after breakfast, Julia set to work writing invitations for a Bible study hour and sent Jennifer and Felicity to deliver them.

Only the Adams family and Hettie and Tom came to the first meeting. John read the Scriptures and discussed the lesson. Those who wished to pray did so, and the meeting ended.

Julia kept her initial disappointment to herself, but she didn't remain disappointed for long. As the remaining winter weeks passed, a few others began to join them for worship. Mrs. Greenwald came first. Julia wondered if she came out of boredom or curiosity. Then Mrs. Shannon came, and soon she was bringing her children. Julia decided they needed a lesson for the children, so she started a children's class. Soon the news got around and other children began coaxing their parents to allow them to attend. The class grew, and Julia assigned the younger ones to Jennifer and Felicity. Excited about being involved, the girls prepared lessons on Noah and Daniel with great care.

The group grew and interest deepened. There was actually participation—excitement. Julia and John began to pray more sincerely. Perhaps this was why God had kept them in town— to win their neighbors.

But it was hard, slow work. They prayed daily for the wisdom, the strength, the commitment to keep going. They made it through the winter. Spring came, bringing warm breezes that melted the snow. Spirits lifted. Folks began to talk of gardens. Children played in the warm sunshine. They had survived the first winter with no disasters. No serious illnesses. Surely they could make it through spring and summer with ease.

Julia began her letter writing again, promising visitors a quiet and restful vacation in the beautiful Rocky Mountains. The women laid aside their winter handwork to care for household chores. The children were given a week's break from their studies, more to give their mothers a rest than anything else. And then they settled in to prepare for another season, with renewed faith and courage.

Chapter Sixteen

Another Chance

"We know better what to expect this year," Julia said at their first committee meeting of the tourist season.

Actually, no one had gotten much experience the year before. Each family had hosted only one vacationing family. Julia had cared for two—if she counted the little old man and woman trying to outwit the authorities.

"We will take turns as before," Julia continued. "I had the last ones, so we will move down the list. We have a number of items in our shops now. Many more than last year, so perhaps business will improve for those not taking guests."

As Julia spoke, she remembered that some of the ladies had used their merchandise to buy flour and sugar at the store. Still, there would be some revenue from the sale of goods.

"And we have the jams and jellies from last year's picking," Julia added.

"I used a few jars of mine," said Mrs. Clancy, and Mrs. Greenwald admitted that she too had dipped into her supplies.

"Fine," said Julia. "Our families come first. If we need our produce to feed them, then we must use it, that's all. We'll pray for a good berry crop this year. All our children are a year older. They will be better pickers this year than last."

Maude Shannon shifted uneasily. She was to have another child in a few months. She wouldn't be picking many berries for a while. But that wasn't what worried Julia as she looked at Maude. It was the lack of a doctor. She wondered if Maude planned to go away to have the baby. She wondered whether the Shannons had family she could stay with. And what about the five other Shannon children? The townsfolk might have to care for them for a few weeks.

Julia pushed the thoughts from her mind for the present and continued her meeting.

"We all need to plant good-sized gardens. That kept us going last winter. And it will help us feed our guests and see us through another winter as well. Is anyone short of garden space? I'm sure we could find some way to—"

"We dug our neighbor's potatoes last year," interrupted Mrs. Greenwald. "They were gone. No use letting them go to waste."

"We used our neighbor's garden too," admitted Mrs. Adams, blushing.

Julia had not thought about the gardens of those who had moved away. It was only common sense that someone should benefit from the produce.

"Perhaps," she said, choosing her words carefully, "it would be wise to plant those gardens again." Julia paused, then went on. "It would keep them free of weeds, make the yards look more presentable for our summer guests, and give each of us additional garden space."

As she spoke, she wondered if it was wrong to use the neighbors' yards without permission. *Lord, show me if this is wrong. I don't want to encourage anything that displeases you,* Julia prayed silently.

"We can't care for them all," stated Mrs. Clancy, "so I suggest we use the closest and the best."

"Jim is willing to use that old tractor left behind by the mill to work up the land," said Maude Shannon. "He's already been talking about it."

Julia tried to mask her surprise, then reasoned, *This is a case of survival. Perhaps we should take advantage of everything at our disposal. If we save the town, if our venture is successful, then those who left will be able to return to their homes, their gardens.*

"We must set some guidelines," Julia voiced tactfully. "I think we should call a meeting with our husbands to draw up some plans as to what is proper—and what is—is stepping over boundaries."

"Like?" said Mrs. Clancy.

"Well, like, we can plant and care for garden plots—it will be better if the yards are cared for. But if we use a garden, we must also pull the weeds. And if the owners return, the garden spot, along with its produce, belongs to them. And we can use things that have been deliberately left behind, having no value to the owner, such as the old tractor. But we must be careful not to take possession of other people's property or gain from their losses."

Julia hoped she had made a point. She would suggest to John that he call a meeting of all town residents before they ran into a serious problem of "borrowing" items left behind by vacating neighbors.

The new Shannon baby arrived. Mrs. Greenwald helped with the delivery in the absence of a doctor, but it was Jim Shannon who kept calm and cared for the mother and child. The baby boy was fine, and the entire settlement breathed a sigh of relief. Many prayers went up, thanking God for the child's safe arrival—even from lips that wouldn't normally have admitted to prayer. The neighborhood ladies organized help for the family for the first few weeks. Then life returned once again to its familiar routine.

The first paying guests arrived in July. The next came a week later. Both families spent a few dollars in the shops along Main Street.

The next guests didn't come until mid-August. Julia did not get her first turn until near the end of the month when a young couple came to take advantage of the quietness of the mountain village.

"We wanted a place where we could just be by ourselves," the young woman confided.

"We will see that you have all the time alone you desire," Julia promised her.

The Harrigans ate meals in the kitchen while the young couple was served in the dining room. Jennifer and Felicity took turns serving.

"It is so romantic," Felicity crooned the first night. "Just the two of them, with the candles and the silver. Mama, do you think they would like us to move in the Victrola so they can listen to soft music?"

Julia smiled at her romantic fourteen-year-old. "Perhaps," she said. "Why don't you ask them?"

The couple turned down Felicity's offer of dinner music. "We really don't care to linger," the young man explained.

The couple spent their first few days wandering town streets and mountain trails. Then he went for walks alone and she sat on the back porch swing, whiling away the hours with no handwork, no reading, nothing to keep herself entertained. To Julia she looked very bored, very listless, and very lonely.

"Would you like something to read?" Julia asked. "We have a number of good books on the library shelves and you are welcome to borrow them."

The young woman smiled and shook her head.

"Are you tired of walking?" Julia questioned.

"I've already seen everything there is to see."

Julia nodded. It didn't take long to see everything.

"Your husband likes to walk?"

The woman shrugged. "I guess so."

"Would you like to join us in the kitchen? We're making blueberry jam today. The girls have just returned with full pails of wild berries. Perhaps—"

"I don't think so—thank you," the young woman responded.

Julia had run out of ideas, so she left the girl alone.

Jennifer served the table that evening. "I don't think Mr. and Mrs. Alberts are very happy," she said as she brought the empty soup dishes into the kitchen and prepared to serve the main course.

"Why do you say that?" asked Julia, turning to look at her.

"They haven't said a word to each other all evening," Jennifer explained. "They just glare at each other or look at their plates. They aren't even eating much—and he is usually ravenous."

The next day Julia sent Jennifer and Felicity off to the berry patch. The young woman was on the porch swing alone again, and Julia approached her, tea tray in hand.

"Anna, I thought you might like some tea," she ventured.

The young woman didn't answer.

"It is such a beautiful day," Julia continued. "I love it when the breeze is just strong enough to stir my hair and bring the scent of flowers."

Still no response.

Julia set down the tea things and poured a cup. "Have you been married long?"

"Almost a year."

"Well, you hardly get to know each other in a year. I remember when we had been married for just a year. I was wonderfully happy. I was deeply in love with John. Still, I wasn't sure if John really knew me. Really understood me," Julia sighed. "It's funny, I wasn't even sure at times if he really loved me.

"There is so much to learn about each other," Julia went on, passing the sugar and cream. "It takes far more than a year to get in step with one's mate."

Julia offered the young woman a piece of shortcake.

"John is a good man. A wonderful man. But at first—well, I guess we didn't know how to express our love. Or else we just forgot to. I learned something then. I learned that it is basically up to the woman to set the tone for openness and closeness. We just understand a bit more about expressing love, I guess. Boys are taught not to show emotion—to be masculine. I'm not saying that's right—it's just how it is.

"Well, women don't have that problem. We are free to say how we feel. To show others we love them—by doing little things, saying little things. Women can find lots of different ways to say 'I love you.' "

Julia paused to think a moment. Then she went on. "Sometimes I feel sorry for men. We teach them one thing—and then expect quite another."

Julia sighed and stirred her tea.

"You know, I was secretly hoping that I would have a son. I wanted to—well, to break the rules. To raise a boy free to express love and tenderness. I don't mean I'd want him to be a sissy. It takes a strong man to be tender. John is that, but he still has a hard time expressing it. He just—he just holds me—comforts me—but he can't seem to say how he really feels. If I didn't know him so well, I wouldn't understand."

Julia raised her cup and sipped.

"But I didn't have a son. I had twin girls—and how I thank God for them. John and I wanted more children, but, well, God knows best. I am blessed indeed. Two girls—and a wonderful husband."

Julia fell silent, allowing the young woman some time to ponder.

At length Anna raised her head and looked into Julia's eyes. "You know, don't you? That something is—is wrong between—" She could not go on. Her eyes filled with tears and her head lowered. She bit a quivering lip between even white teeth.

"I guessed," said Julia softly. "Would you like to talk about it?"

"It's just—just—well, it isn't what I expected it to be," the young woman finished with a burst of tears.

"It never is," responded Julia.

Anna's head came up. She looked surprised.

"We expect romance, flowers, love songs," said Julia; "instead, we get dirty dishes, laundry, and silence."

"But I thought—"

"And he thought," said Julia. "I suppose he expected things like welcome-home kisses, favorite pie, and slippers. Instead, he got broken plumbing, mounting bills, and complaints."

Anna dug for a handkerchief.

"If only there were some way to prepare for reality rather than romance," Julia went on, "marriage would have a much better chance."

"Are you saying there is no romance?"

"Oh my, no! There is romance. Our problem is that we want it *all* to be romance. And we want fulfillment—a perfect relationship—immediately. In reality we must first know each other, learn from each other, protect and support each other. We must build together. Work together. Marriage is hard work. The hardest task we will likely ever undertake. And then when we are well on the way to accomplishing some of those things— then we experience the real romance—the excitement of fulfillment and shared love. More exciting than we ever dreamed."

Julia's face was shining as she spoke the words.

That's how it had been for her and John. She loved him more—was more sure of his love for her—at the present than at any other time in their marriage, and they had enjoyed many good years together.

"I guess I thought—I guess I wanted it all—romance, fulfillment—right from the start," Anna said. "Why—why can't it be that way? I mean—I loved him—"

"And I'm sure he loved you. *Loves* you. But it takes time to work through the sharing of that love—to figure out how love works."

Julia leaned from the swing and plucked a flower from the nearby bush.

"See this rosebud?" She held it out to Anna. "It's perfect. So new, so full of promise and color. Someday it will be a full flower. Beautiful, fragrant. But just suppose I want it that way now. So I take the petals and force them to open up, to be mature—now. What will happen?"

Anna waited.

"I'd spoil it," Julia said. "I would crush and bruise it, and it would just wilt and die. It takes time to reach full-flower," Julia continued. "We must nurture it, not rush it. It will happen if we are patient—and loving."

The young woman blinked away her remaining tears.

"Here," said Julia, handing the rose to Anna, "there is a vase in the hall for it. Place the rose in your room and give it care. Watch it unfold—slowly—naturally—fully."

She patted the young girl's shoulder and moved to gather up the tea things.

Anna smiled. "Thank you," she whispered. "I—I will try. To be patient—and loving. I promise."

"That's all we can do," responded Julia. "Try. Try with all our might." She walked away with a prayer that the young man might also be willing to try.

Chapter Seventeen

Heavy Thoughts

John was not sleeping well. His mind was troubled in spite of his faith in his God, in his Jule. Things were not going as planned. The summer had turned to fall and they'd had only one paying customer. All of the reserve money was gone.

The garden had been good again. John breathed a prayer of thanks for that. But even so, they needed many items that the garden could not produce. John wondered how they would manage to purchase them.

There was also the matter of the girls' education. Another school year was drawing near. The girls needed more than Jule could teach them in home lessons. They were quickly becoming young women, and John and Julia wanted them to have a proper education—perhaps college if they were interested.

John shifted under the blankets, unable to find a comfortable position. Beside him, Julia breathed evenly. He was glad he wasn't keeping her awake with his tossing.

Oh, God, he prayed silently as he had many times before, *show me what to do. Please, show me what to do. It would break Jule's heart to leave here—this house. I could never offer her a house like this again. But we can't go on living like this—no income to speak of—nor much hope of any—and so many needs for the family.*

Help me, too, when I talk to Jule about our future. Give me the right words. Oh, God! I need you so much!

John lay in the darkness thinking about their circumstances. Perhaps he could find work at another mill. His old boss had written him on a number of occasions urging him to leave Calder Springs and join him at the new mill site. Perhaps some position would still be open—though John was sure they had found a foreman by now. Still—any job would be better than no job.

John rolled onto his back and stared at the ceiling. *The moon must be bright tonight,* he mused. Then he thought about how easily his mind slipped to other things. He let his gaze go to the window. Light sifted in around the edges of the full velvet drapes. He was tempted to rise from bed and take a stroll outside to see the mountain valley by full moonlight.

It must be pretty out there tonight, he thought. The cry of some night creature interrupted his thoughts. It was followed by the hoot of an owl. John visualized the scene. The owl, hungry and in need of food for its growing family. The small nighttime animal being caught off guard. The speed of the owl, as with one silent and powerful swoop it split the air, grasped the victim with outstretched talons, and, hardly slowing its speed, continued on to its nest.

Tonight John's empathy was with the owl. He knew the desperation of trying to provide for a family.

"We do what we have to do," he muttered.

Julia stirred. John wanted to reach out and take her in his arms—not for her comfort, but for his. But he did not want to wake her. She too was carrying a heavy burden and needed her rest. John turned so he could watch her in the moonlight, and his thoughts began to mellow.

It's a marvel we have made it this far—and with no debts. I don't know how she does it. Keeps food on the table—and the girls cared for.

Then John remembered noticing the girls at the supper table that evening. Their dresses were getting tight and short. Julia had let out all the seams and let down all the hems. There was no more room for growth—but the girls kept growing.

"They will soon be done with their growing," Julia had assured him with a careful little laugh. "They are as tall as I am now. Girls don't grow much after they reach their age."

John hoped Julia was right. She had no more bolts of material in the upstairs sewing room from which to sew new dresses.

The clock in the downstairs hall chimed three o'clock. John changed his position once more. He had to get some sleep. But sleep wouldn't come. *It's no use,* he finally sighed. *I might as well do something useful.*

John slipped out of bed and headed downstairs. The moon bathed the hallway and the stairs with enough light for him to find his way. He went first to the kitchen for a drink and then to his desk in the library.

He drew out a sheet of writing paper, dipped his pen in the ink well, and began a letter to his former boss. He would tell Jule his thoughts at the first opportunity.

"Look!" cried Felicity, as they dressed the next morning.

Jennifer looked, though she didn't seem too concerned.

"Look how tight this bodice is getting. I feel so—so conspicuous in it. Doesn't it bother you?"

Jennifer nodded. Ill-fitting dresses bothered her too. But she didn't see any sense in fussing about them. There was really nothing her folks could do.

"Jen, do you really think Mama is going to make it?"

"What do you mean?" asked Jennifer, hoping she wouldn't need to answer the question.

"Do you really think this will ever be a resort town?"

"I don't know," answered Jennifer. "Mama has worked awfully hard to make it one."

"I know, but some things are impossible—even for Mama."

Jennifer smiled. It was one of their shared jokes. They never spoke of it to any other person. That would have been disrespectful. But through the years, they had joked with each other about their mother's need to fix things. "Let Mama do it," they would tease. "Just give it to Mama," "Bet Mama could fix it," and "Have you shown it to Mama?" as though there was not a thing in the world Julia couldn't manage, either by coaxing or by coercion.

"Well, we mustn't give up yet," whispered Jennifer. "Mama hasn't."

Felicity shrugged. "I think some of the other ladies have almost given up. Did you see Mrs. Shannon yesterday?"

Jennifer nodded. She had noticed the strained, hopeless look in the woman's face.

"Maybe she was just tired. She has so many children to care for—she must feel like the old woman in the shoe."

Felicity tied the bow at the waist of her dress. She had already forgotten about Mrs. Shannon. She studied herself in the mirror. "You know," she said to her twin, "I get more and more thankful for big aprons."

Jennifer laughed. Hettie's big aprons worked well to hide one's appearance, but they were not very becoming to young figures.

"We'd better get down to breakfast," Jennifer said with a quick glance at the clock. "Mama will be calling us if we don't hurry."

———————

The day's mail brought a letter. The Harrigans were to have more house guests. Julia breathed prayers of thanks all the way home from the post office.

"We needed this one so badly, Lord," she explained. Then added, "But of course you knew that. Thank you, Lord. Thank you."

She hurried home to share her good news. "Hettie," she cried as soon as she entered the hall. "Hettie, good news. We have another family coming. A couple with two grown daughters. Next week. We only have a couple days to prepare."

Hettie appeared, wiping her hands on her apron. Julia had to repeat her words.

Felicity and Jennifer were called from the garden to hear the good news. John and Tom were off hauling more firewood so they would have to wait to find out.

"When are they coming?" asked Felicity.

"Monday," replied Julia, her eyes aglow.

"How long will they stay?" asked Jennifer.

"They are a bit undecided. They may stay for two weeks or more—if they like it here."

Felicity and Jennifer exchanged glances. They loved Calder Springs, but it didn't have much to offer folks who were used to excitement.

"We must get ready. Hettie, check the pantry. We'll have to make a trip to Mr. Perry's store and buy what we need on credit."

Then Julia had another thought. "Let's plan the daily menus, Hettie, and only purchase for one day at a time—that way if they leave sooner than expected—" Julia left the sentence unfinished. There was no sense in purchasing supplies and then ending up with no income to pay for them.

Hettie smiled at Julia's burst of energy. She was glad they

were to have guests, but she still secretly wondered how long they could hang on.

"How far did you get with the weeding?" Julia asked the girls.

"There aren't many weeds," Felicity replied. "We have been over that garden so often this summer."

"Then let the rest go. I want you to freshen the three guest rooms. Open the windows wide and turn back the bedding. Do the floors and the dusting and clean the bathroom."

Felicity was tempted to remind her mother that they had been through the procedure enough times to know what to do, but she held her tongue. Julia was excited. She had to vent her emotions by taking charge.

The girls turned to do as bidden, Felicity chattering to Jennifer as they left.

"I think I'll run down and tell John," Julia said to Hettie as she followed her to the kitchen. She removed her uptown slippers and put on the gardening shoes from behind the door. Then she reached for her gardening bonnet and hurried off.

"John! John!" called Julia as soon as she was within earshot. John spun around, afraid something was wrong at home.

Julia quickly dispelled his fears. "Good news," she called, waving the white envelope.

John walked toward his wife, brushing the sawdust and bits of clinging bark from his shirt as he moved.

"A letter," called Julia. "We are having more guests."

She was so excited that John decided to say nothing to dampen her spirit. He knew, however, that it would take many more guests to meet the family's growing needs. He forced a smile. "When?" he asked.

"Monday!" exclaimed Julia. She was out of breath from hurrying.

"Here, sit down," John urged her, indicating a fallen log. "Catch your breath—then tell me all about it."

Julia sat—but she did not wait to catch her breath.

"Next Monday," she hurried on. "A couple—and two girls—grown girls. They plan on a couple of weeks—but may stay much longer—if they like it. They'll like it. It's so—so beautiful here." Julia let her eyes travel over the scene before her. She gazed at the sweeping valley with the silver curve of the river, the shimmer of the distant lake, the slopes of nearby mountains rising up to join rugged crags and rocky peaks still covered by glacial ice.

John smiled. Jule did love her mountains.

"That's great!" he responded, trying to make his emotions match his words.

"Isn't it? I've been praying and praying—and here is our answer. Oh, John. This—this venture has been so difficult at times—but it has been a time of—of growing too. I have been shown over and over how God answers prayer. He never lets us down, John. Just when I think we can't make it any more, He answers my prayer again. And—He's never late. Though at times I think He's going to be."

Julia's eyes glistened. John turned away to gaze at the distant peaks. His eyes were threatening to spill over as well, but for a different reason. *Oh, God,* he prayed silently, *I wish I had Jule's faith.* His arm tightened around his wife's shoulders.

"Well, I must run," Julia said suddenly, standing swiftly to her feet. "I just wanted you to know about the letter. I left Hettie busy in the kitchen so I'd better get back and lend her a hand."

"Don't travel back as fast as you traveled out," John cautioned.

"Promise," she whispered. She gave John's hand a squeeze and started up the path that led home.

Chapter Eighteen

Sunday

A dozen or more were now meeting for weekly worship. John and Julia had talked about moving the group to the church but feared some might drop out if they did. It was less formal—less threatening perhaps—to have the Bible study in the comfort of the Harrigan parlor with coffee and scones served afterward.

Julia had a hard time keeping her thoughts on the lesson John had prepared. They kept shifting to the house guests who would be arriving on the morrow. She needed to tell the neighbors her news, but she wasn't sure how or where to begin. She must not let them see her excitement. They too needed additional funds to get through another winter. Julia did not want to gloat over her good fortune when their needs were still unmet.

Yet she must speak of it. No stranger got off the train without the whole community knowing of it. It would not do for the Blakeneys to arrive without the townspeople knowing ahead of time. Besides, Tom would need to borrow the Clancy's buggy.

Julia shifted in her seat and forced her attention back on the lesson.

Forgive me, Lord, she apologized. *But I am so troubled about this, even though I know I shouldn't be. Though I might not know how to say what I need to say, I know you will help me when the time comes.*

"What do you think Jesus meant by these words?" John was asking the group. Julia flushed, having no idea what words her husband was referring to.

I do hope he doesn't call on me! she thought.

Julia was relieved when Mrs. Adams spoke.

"I've been sittin' here, puzzling over them," she admitted. "But perhaps He means, what we try to keep—try to hang on to—can still slip from us. What we honestly, openly, give to Him, He somehow keeps for us—and might even one day allow us to have back."

"Isn't He talking about our lives too?" added Mr. Adams. "If we refuse to give our life to Him, try to hang on to it for our own pleasures and self-seeking, we will eventually lose it. We will have no future with Him in heaven. If we give our life to Him, He cares for us in the way that only He can, and will also reward us with eternal life."

"I think you are both right," said Mrs. Shannon. "He's talking about our lives—but the same principle applies to other things too. We can never hold tight to anything. We haven't the strength—nor the power to keep it. Nothing—nothing in this life is safe from destruction and decay. Take our town here— our jobs. Even our lives. We can't save anything by our determination—no matter how we try."

A feeling of doom was seeping into the room. Julia could feel it. Could sense the fear—the anxiety. She was about to speak when Tom, in his slow, drawling voice came to the rescue.

"But does it matter? I mean—I love this town. I've lived most of my life here. But life goes on. Change isn't always bad. Sometimes change is for our good. Sure, it might sadden us for a time, but if He is in charge—if we really let Him take charge— does it really matter? He is with us wherever we go."

Julia shifted again. Tom was right. They musn't fret so. They must develop more faith in the leading of God.

"But how do we know?" asked Mrs. Adams. "How do we know when to trust—to hang on—and when to let go—to move on? I mean, I have prayed and prayed and still don't know what God wants us to do."

Julia looked around the group. She could sense that John didn't want to be the one to answer, and *she* certainly didn't feel prepared. She was still struggling with the question herself.

It was Hettie who spoke. "Don't you think," she said slowly, feeling her way, "that as long as one doesn't feel—well, compelled to move on, that it isn't time yet? I mean, don't you think we'll know when it's time—if He decides that we should?" Hettie stopped and fiddled with the worn Bible in her lap. "I'm no speaker—you all know that. I never can say what I want to say, but it seems to me—if we are truly committed to Him—He'll tell us when to stay put . . . and when to move on."

"But what if you sorta feel that it's time to be movin'?" asked Mrs. Adams.

Julia felt that she must speak. She cleared her throat and looked directly at the woman across from her. "Then—you must," she said softly. "If you feel that God is urging you—no matter how gently—then you must follow."

"My Victor has been offered a job," Mrs. Adams said in little more than a whisper. Victor stirred restlessly in his chair beside her.

"We didn't want to—to desert the—the rest of you."

"You won't be," John assured the couple. "We would never want to hold you back. If you believe this is God's answer—for you—if He is providing for your family in this way—then you must go—with our blessing."

Mr. and Mrs. Adams exchanged glances, both looking relieved.

"And that goes for all of you," said Julia. "We have banded together to try to help one another—but if any of you feel you must move from Calder Springs—then please—please don't stay here for the sake of the rest of us. We must all be free to do our own choosing." There were somber nods and somber faces all around her. Silence ruled for several minutes.

After a while Mrs. Greenwald spoke. "Mr. and Mrs. Adams have been church people for years," she reminded the group. "They know when God speaks. But what about the rest of us? Like me and—well, I won't mention any other names, but how do we know when God speaks, when we have never asked for, never looked for, His leading?"

The stillness hung heavy in the room. "I wouldn't have known—a few years ago," said Victor Adams. "A person needs to walk with God, to pray and read the Word, before he can know when God speaks and where He is leading. You might need to take that important first step toward God—accept Him as Savior—before you can hear Him speak to you, Mrs. Greenwald."

Mrs. Greenwald nodded in assent.

John was quick to seize the opportunity. "Would you like to come into the east parlor?" he asked. "We will show you how you can take that first step—to become a child of God."

She nodded again, her eyes misting.

"Victor and Ruth, will you join me?" John invited. "Julia, do you want to come?"

Julia decided to look after her other guests. After all, what if someone else expressed an interest in taking the same step of faith? "I had better stay here," she whispered to John.

Hettie and Tom went to get the coffee and scones. Julia addressed the remaining congregation. "We will all miss Victor and Ruth when they leave us," she began. "I don't know when they are planning to go—but maybe we can have a potluck dinner for them before they do. I am going to be quite busy this week. I just received a letter, and I have guests coming in—for a few days at least. The length of their stay is still indefinite. But I am sure I could find time to bid our dear friends goodbye.

"And I did mean every word of what I said a few minutes ago," she continued. "We want the best for each family here. If that means a move elsewhere—then we—you must be free to go. School should be starting, and we have no school for our children again. I don't know how much we can teach them. So all of you—do what you can, what you must. Those of us who remain behind, we understand."

Hettie set down the cups and saucers, and Tom placed the large coffee pot on the table beside them. Julia nodded to Felicity and Jennifer to start serving. Soon the room was a hum of chatter. Julia slipped out to the parlor to join John and the others.

She was met by a glowing Mrs. Greenwald, who dabbed at tears with a white lace-edged handkerchief.

"I've wanted to do that for a long time," she admitted, "but I didn't know how to go about it. And I was scared to death to go to the parson. I was afraid he would want an account of every sin I ever committed and there are—were—so many of them."

Julia knew that their former pastor would have demanded no such thing, but folks often had funny ideas about preachers.

"I had no idea that I could go directly to God—in Jesus' name—and ask forgiveness," the woman went on.

"That's how we each must do it," said Julia, giving her a warm embrace.

"Well, it's a big relief, I'll tell you that." Mrs. Greenwald turned to give Mrs. Adams a hug as well.

They rejoined the group in the main parlor. Julia noticed people watching Mrs. Greenwald. Folks were curious as to what had happened and if it had really "worked." If Mrs.

Greenwald was conscious of the attention, she did not let on. She hugged each of her children, then turned to greet her neighbors with a shining face.

"I don't know why I didn't do this years ago," she told them, and they could see the new strength in her face.

———

"Oh, what a wonderful day," Julia said to the family at dinner. "Imagine! Mrs. Greenwald is the first convert of our worship services. I don't think she ever would have gone to church. Here I was praying to keep the church open, and there she was with a hungry heart but too stubborn—or afraid—to go to the services. God knew what He was doing all the time in closing the doors of the church."

"But, Mama," spoke Felicity, "what if there are others who would go to church, but won't come here?"

"I—really don't know," Julia admitted. "Maybe I said it all wrong. Maybe God didn't speak to Mrs. Greenwald *because* the church closed its doors. Maybe He had to use our group because the church *had* closed. Maybe that was the only way He could get our—my—attention. Suddenly I realized that I had an obligation. Before, I had left it all to the church. To the minister. I shouldn't have. If I had been as concerned when the church was still here as I am now—well, the church might still be open."

It was a sobering thought for Julia. She knew she had failed in her Christian commitment. She had waited too long to express concern for her neighbors.

"Well, we still have a big job to do. There are those in town who might move any day—so our time may be short. We need to share our faith with them—as God gives us opportunity."

"Jen talked to Millicent," Felicity announced.

Julia's head came up. "I didn't know that."

"She had a whole bunch of questions," said Jennifer. "I tried to explain to her—what it means to serve God."

"She's scared," continued Felicity. "Says she doesn't want to go to hell when she dies."

"Did you—do you need some help with your answers?" John asked Jennifer.

"I—I'm not sure she understood all I said. I told her that God doesn't want anyone to go to hell—that's why He sent His Son Jesus to die on the cross. Then I tried to explain how we confess the bad things—the sin—and ask Him to forgive us—then thank God for sending Jesus. Then we ask God to accept us as His children and help us live the way He wants us to—by faith."

"It sounds as if you did a good job of explaining it," said John, pleased with Jennifer.

"She said she wanted to think about it some more," went on Jennifer.

"She should think about it carefully," John agreed. "It is not a decision to be made lightly."

John pushed back from the table. "I don't think we should wait until our family worship time to remember these people in prayer. Let's stop and pray for them right now."

Each person at the table said a brief prayer for Mrs. Greenwald, that God would help her grow in her knowledge and understanding of Him, and for Millicent, that she might understand the meaning of the step she was considering, and that she might make the right choice.

Chapter Nineteen

The Blakeneys

On Monday morning Julia tried to get her mind back on preparations for her coming house guests, but her thoughts insisted on returning to the previous day. The eternal significance of Sunday's events made the coming of visitors much less important to Julia. She prayed that Mrs. Greenwald's decision would be strengthened as days passed, and that Millicent too would come to understand the importance of the decision she was considering and be bold enough to make it. She also prayed that Jennifer would have the wisdom to answer Millicent's questions.

Julia made one last round of the house to check that all was in readiness. She placed fresh fall flowers in the bedrooms and on tables throughout the main floor and sent Tom off to the station to meet the train.

Julia's heart pounded as she awaited her new guests. To help ease her tension she went to the kitchen to see Hettie. *Perhaps a chat, a cup of tea, or both, will calm my nerves,* she thought.

"Is the kettle hot, Hettie?" she asked as she entered the room with a swish of her skirts.

"Sure is." Hettie moved to get the teapot and the cups. She could sense that Julia was agitated. It was not a usual thing.

"Are the girls around?" asked Julia.

"I sent them to the store for the things I'll need for the guests," answered Hettie.

Julia took a seat at the kitchen table.

"Did they open the windows to let fresh air into the bedrooms?" she asked, though why she asked she didn't know. She had seen the curtains stirring in the light breeze when she made her last check of the rooms.

Hettie nodded. She too knew that Julia had just checked the rooms.

"Why do I feel so nervous?" Julia asked. "It's not as if this is our first experience with guests."

"They're likely the last guests of the season," Hettie answered. "We need the money badly."

Hettie was right. It seemed reason enough for a case of the jitters.

Hettie set the tea cup in front of Julia and asked, "You want cake or cookies?"

"Yes, please," Julia surprised Hettie by saying. Julia never took sweets with her tea, saying it was not good to have too much sugar.

"Which?" asked Hettie, and Julia looked puzzled by the question.

"Cookies or cake?" repeated Hettie.

Julia shrugged her shoulders, and Hettie placed some sugar cookies on a plate.

"I will need to be at the door to greet them," Julia murmured.

"No hurry. We'll hear the whistle long before they arrive."

Julia took a cookie from the plate. "There seems to be so much to think about all the time that my head fairly swims," she admitted.

"Like?" prompted Hettie.

"The girls mostly, I guess," answered Julia. "Some days I wonder if this is fair to them. I said to John once that learning household chores would be good for them—and it is. But shouldn't they have a chance to learn other things too?

"I think of my own youth," Julia continued. "It was so different. I took lessons in piano, tennis, riding, French. I went to a fine finishing school. My girls won't know much more than how to scrub floors, make beds, bake cookies, and hoe gardens. Is that enough, Hettie?"

"They still have time," Hettie comforted.

"Do you think—?"

The train whistle blew before Julia finished her sentence, and she forgot her question, her tea, and her half-eaten cookie.

"They're here!" she said excitedly. She rose quickly from her chair.

"No. No, it'll take Tom a bit of time to get them here. The train is just pulling in."

Julia brushed her skirts, lifted trembling hands to her hair, and sat down again. But she couldn't stay still for long. After one more sip of tea she left the kitchen for a final check of the house.

"Is this all there is to your town?" Mr. Blakeney asked Tom as the horses trotted along Main Street.

Tom hardly knew how to answer. If the Blakeneys expected a hustling, bustling town, they had not read the brochure carefully.

Tom cleared his throat to answer, but Mrs. Blakeney cut in. "It is just what we wanted, isn't it, Thaddeus?" Her shrill voice made the words into a command rather than an observation.

The man only sniffed.

The two younger women stared directly ahead, no questions on their lips or in their eyes, no apparent interest in the town at all.

They passed the yard where the Shannon children played. As the team approached, the game stopped and four pairs of curious eyes looked at the passengers in the buggy. One lifted a pudgy hand to wave, and Tom dipped his head in reply.

"I do hope we won't be harassed by curious neighbors," said the older woman.

Tom noted all of the boarded-up houses. It was obvious they were empty. Not much harassment from neighbors there.

Julia was waiting at the door, Hettie close behind her. Mr. Blakeney bowed stiffly, but his wife was too busy looking around to notice Julia's welcome. She studied all she saw.

"It should do just fine," Julia heard her say to her husband. When at last she turned to Julia, she gave an order. "Show us to our rooms." Then to Hettie she said, "You will draw a bath for Miss Priscilla at once. She is very weary from the journey."

She turned then to Tom. "The suitcases will be needed immediately. I will point out to you which ones go in which rooms."

Julia, who normally sent Hettie up with the guests, led the party up the stairs herself. She indicated the three available rooms with the shared bath in the hallway. Hettie was already in the bathroom filling the tub.

"Priscilla, you may choose," the older woman said to one of her daughters.

The girl surveyed each room, then looked them over a second

time, studied them more closely a third time, and finally settled on the room that overlooked the valley.

"Your father and I will take the room across the hall," Mrs. Blakeney informed the young woman. The third room was thus assigned to the second daughter, who moved into it without a word.

"Tea will be served in the main parlor in half an hour," Julia told her guests.

"So long?" asked the woman.

"I—I thought we must allow your daughter time to properly enjoy her bath," Julia explained.

"She will have tea in her room," Mrs. Blakeney replied. "The rest of us will be ready in ten minutes."

"As you wish," Julia answered. *No wonder I have been nervous about these guests,* she thought. *They are going to be more than demanding.*

"In ten," she repeated and went to help prepare tea.

Felicity and Jennifer were in the kitchen putting away the items they had brought from the store. Hettie had not returned from drawing the bath for Miss Priscilla.

"Come," said Julia to the girls, "give me a hand with the tea things. Hettie has been waylaid running a bath for our guest."

"I thought you said they had grown children," said Felicity.

"They are. At least twenty, I think."

"Then why—?" began Felicity, but she was stopped short by one look at her mother.

"Because, it seems the dears are used to being waited on hand and foot," Julia replied. "I'm afraid we are in for some trying days."

The girls exchanged nervous glances, then busied themselves arranging the tea tray and preparing the plate of sweets.

"And I think it might be wise if you said 'ma'am' and 'sir' when addressing them," advised Julia. She had never before asked her children to act as servants—only as equals—caring for the needs of others.

Both girls showed their surprise.

"Well," Julia apologized, "we do need the money, and the longer they stay the more money we will make. You both need new dresses badly."

It was the first time Julia had mentioned to the girls their need of clothes.

"We'll try to remember," said Jennifer.

Hettie puffed into the kitchen, her face red.

"Dear little Miss Priscilla," she scoffed. "Miss Prissy, if you ask me!"

Julia had never seen her housekeeper so upset.

"First it's too cold—then it's too hot. Huh! Goldilocks herself had nothing on that one."

Julia tried to suppress a smile, and Felicity had a hard time stifling her giggle.

The sharp ring of a bell startled them all.

"What's that?" asked Julia.

"I'll go see," said Felicity, hurrying off to find the source of the noise.

It was not hard to do, for the bell rang persistently. Felicity found the answer in the parlor. Mrs. Blakeney, sitting in Julia's favorite chair, was shaking the daylights out of a copper bell.

"Is something wrong?" asked Felicity.

"We are ready for our tea," said the woman.

Fearing she would burst into laughter, Felicity did not dare answer. She turned and headed back to the kitchen. At the parlor door she remembered her mother's instructions and turned to say, as evenly as she could, "Yes, ma'am." Then she closed the door carefully, remembering to not let it slam, and hastened to the kitchen.

"You're not going to believe this," she said, her eyes big. "There Mrs. Blakeney sits, like a queen or something, ringing that noisy bell. There it goes again."

Julia picked up the tea tray and left the kitchen. Jennifer went to help her serve. The days ahead might indeed be trying.

"Miss Constance will let you know when Miss Priscilla is ready for her tea. She likes it weak—with both cream and sugar. And she prefers cake to cookies," said the woman as she accepted her cup of tea.

Julia nodded.

"We like to dine at seven," the woman went on. "And we will have breakfast served in our rooms when—"

"No," Julia interrupted, firmly but softly. "Breakfast is served in the dining room at seven-thirty or eight, whichever you prefer."

Though taken aback, the woman recovered quickly. "Eight will be fine," she said a bit sharply.

Julia turned to leave, and Jennifer followed. *Perhaps I should have humored her,* Julia thought. *We do need the money,*

and she is a paying guest. But no. It has gone quite far enough.
We simply can't cater to them all day long.

As soon as the door separating the parlor from the dining
room closed behind them, Jennifer whispered, "Good for you,
Mama."

Julia allowed herself a weak smile. She hoped she hadn't
done the wrong thing.

When they reached the kitchen, Felicity was waiting for a report. Jennifer was happy to fill her in.

"She just sits there and gives orders," she concluded.

"Oh, to have Mrs. Williams back again," breathed Felicity,
and the others laughed.

"She was strange but sweet," admitted Jennifer.

"I wonder where they are—and how they are," said Julia,
setting the tea tray on the kitchen table and taking the cups to
the sink. "Jennifer, get the smaller tray and set it up for Miss
Priscilla. Felicity, get the flowered sugar and creamer from the
sideboard. She might be calling any minute."

"I wonder what kind of a bell *she* has," Jennifer commented
as she completed her task.

"Likely a gong," replied Felicity, and the two girls laughed together.

It was some time before Miss Constance rapped on the
kitchen door to say that Miss Priscilla was ready for tea. Apparently she liked a long, leisurely soak.

"I'll send it right up," Julia promised.

"No need for you to run up with it. I'll take it."

Looking up in surprise, Julia looked into eyes full of deep
sorrow. Her heart went out to Miss Constance. She wanted to
step forward and pull the young woman into her arms. But the
moment quickly passed, and Julia turned her attention to the
task at hand. She added steaming water to the teapot, set it on
the tray, and passed the tray to the young woman.

Miss Constance left the kitchen, her back straight, her chin
up.

"My," remarked Julia, when the door had closed, "have you
ever seen a sadder looking face?"

"Is she the maid?" asked Felicity.

"No," answered Julia. "The letter said the Blakeneys have
two grown daughters."

"So, why do they pamper one and work the other?"

"I don't know," admitted Julia, shaking her head. "Of course, it may not be that they work her. Perhaps she just offered to carry the tray, this once, to save us the steps."

"Sure different from the rest of the family," observed Jennifer.

"She's awfully quiet," said Felicity.

"She was quiet in the parlor too," Jennifer added. "I never heard her say one thing over tea. Did you, Mama?"

"No, I guess I didn't," admitted Julia.

"The mother—now, she prattled the whole time," Jennifer explained to Felicity. "I don't know who she was talking to. No one was listening. But she talked without stopping."

"They are even more strange than poor Mrs. Williams," said Felicity. "That's what I'm thinking."

"Remember, girls," cautioned Julia. "Don't judge too soon—or too harshly. We really don't know anything about them yet."

Chapter Twenty

Getting Acquainted

As the week passed, Julia discovered that the twins had accurately summed up the Blakeney family on the day of their arrival. Mrs. Blakeney *did* talk all the time, and no one listened. In fact, Mr. Blakeney paid little attention to any of the women. He was stiff, bored, and not very courteous. Miss Priscilla whined or primped, and Miss Constance ran all errands not assigned to the "servants."

Julia wondered at the strange family arrangement but never mentioned her thoughts to her daughters. The girls openly discussed the situation, however, concocting stories to explain the circumstances.

"I'll bet she's a stepdaughter," said Felicity.

"But whose? His or hers?" asked Jennifer.

"She must be his daughter. He doesn't talk to anyone, but Mrs. Blakeney would talk to Constance if she were her daughter."

"She *does* talk to her—Constance just doesn't listen," Jennifer reminded Felicity.

"You're right. Mrs. Blakeney *does* talk."

"Maybe Constance was adopted."

"She looks too much like Priscilla."

"She does, doesn't she? Though I am sure Priscilla would die if you told her that."

Felicity mimicked the airs of Priscilla. "You're right. Priscilla sees herself as much prettier."

"She is a little prettier," admitted Jennifer, "though I think Constance might be just as pretty—maybe even prettier because she isn't as pouty—if she weren't so stern."

"And wore her hair a little softer."

"And chose prettier dresses."

"That's enough," Julia cut in. "This is none of our business. Let's be kind," she reminded her offspring.

The girls washed the remaining dishes with fewer comments.

"It *is* strange," Hettie remarked after the girls slipped off to the porch swing with glasses of lemonade.

"It certainly is, but you know how some families are. For one reason or another they favor one child over the others."

Hettie too had seen it happen.

The back door opened, and the twins entered the kitchen, their glasses still full.

"Is it windy out?" asked Julia.

"No," grouched Felicity. "Miss Prissy has the swing." The girls often called the young woman by the name Hettie had used on the day she arrived.

"She wants some lemonade too. With cookies," Felicity continued.

Jennifer placed two glasses and some cookies on a tray and left with it.

Julia turned to Felicity. "Was her mother with her?"

"No."

"Constance?"

"Constance *was* there, but she had to run back to the room for Miss Prissy's shawl."

Julia was glad Jennifer had included lemonade for Miss Constance too. She felt sorry for her.

"Is Miss Prissy all settled?" Felicity asked when Jennifer returned.

Jennifer nodded. "She even said, 'Thank you kindly.' "

"Miss Prissy?"

"No. Not her. Miss Constance. 'Thank you kindly,' just like that. I've hardly heard her speak before."

"Mama," said Felicity, "how old do you think she is?"

"Well, I don't know," responded Julia, rolling another circle of pie crust dough. "Perhaps twenty-one or twenty-two."

"And Miss Prissy?"

"A couple years younger maybe."

"Miss Prissy looks bored to death," observed Jennifer.

"I suppose Miss Constance would be bored too if she didn't have all those books to read," Felicity stated. "But she is bound to run out soon. I wonder what she will do then?"

"We have a fine library. She is welcome to read any of our books," said Julia.

"She sure is different from her sister," Jennifer said as she stirred the lemon slice in her drink. "She doesn't say much, but she always makes her own bed, hangs up her clothes, and opens her window to air the room. Miss Prissy would never do that."

"But Miss Prissy talks more," said Felicity.

"If you call giving orders talking," Jennifer stated.

"Or whining," added Felicity.

"Now, girls. We have talked about this before," scolded Julia. "I don't want you saying nasty things about people."

"Even if they are true?" asked Felicity.

"Even if they are true," replied Julia.

The next day Jennifer and Felicity left the kitchen carrying pails. They found Miss Constance alone on the porch swing reading. She looked up when she heard them approach. Her eyes rested on the buckets.

"Do you milk cows?" she asked.

"Oh no," laughed Felicity. "We buy our milk from the Shannons."

"Do you carry it home like that?" she continued her probing.

"No, Tom gets it," answered Jennifer. "We are going to pick berries."

"Berries? Here?"

"No. Not in our garden. Wild berries."

"Where?" asked Miss Constance.

"It's a ways from here. In the woods. We know almost every patch around, I guess. Mama sends us out for berries, and she makes jams and jellies."

"Would you like to come?" asked Felicity.

Jennifer gave her a nervous look. Millicent was going along, and Jennifer had hoped to talk with her about the questions she had been asking.

"Oh, could I?" Miss Constance asked. "I have never picked berries before."

Felicity and Jennifer exchanged glances. "I'll get another pail," said Jennifer.

"I'll get it," said Felicity. "You go with Millicent. We'll meet you at the patch."

Jennifer gave her twin a grateful look.

"Do you have some walking shoes?" Felicity asked Miss Constance.

"I'll get them. And leave a note for Mother."

Felicity returned to the kitchen for another bucket. "I can't believe it," she told her mother. "Miss Constance wants to go with us. She has never picked berries before."

"Perhaps she will enjoy the outing," said Julia, who always found a quiet stroll through the trees relaxing.

Felicity took the pail and waited on the porch for Constance. She didn't have to wait long. The young woman hurried toward her a few minutes later, her cheeks pink with anticipation. Felicity had never seen her show any excitement before.

Felicity led the way down the winding path through the tall timber. "It's a bit of a walk," she explained. "I hope you don't mind."

"Oh no," said Constance. "I love walking."

The comment surprised Felicity. She had not seen the young woman walk anywhere.

"Walking is about the only way to get around here," Felicity explained. "We don't have roads for teams or motor cars."

"It's nice and quiet," responded Miss Constance.

"Is that why you came?" asked Felicity.

The girl hesitated. At last she replied, "We came for Priscilla. She needs a quiet place."

"Has she been ill?"

"You might say that," Miss Constance answered after another pause.

Felicity looked at her walking companion. *Surely Priscilla is not another escapee,* she thought. *She seems so—so normal—in a grumpy kind of way.* Putting her thoughts aside, Felicity responded, "I'm—I'm sorry to hear that."

Miss Constance was looking off in the distance, breathing deeply of the smell of pine and spruce. "Are there any bears here?" she asked.

Felicity hesitated. She didn't want to lie, but she didn't want to scare her companion either. After a short battle in her mind, honesty won. "Yes," she answered. "That's why we talk or sing when we walk—or rattle our pails or something. If they hear us coming they don't stay around."

Miss Constance laughed. It was the first time Felicity had heard her express any feeling of happiness. It sounded a little tight and strained, as though she was out of practice, but it was definitely a laugh.

"I think I'll like it here," she said.

"Are you staying longer than two weeks?"

A strange look crossed the girl's face; then she nodded slowly. "I expect so. Unless Priscilla just can't bear it."

Felicity wondered at the remark, but didn't question Miss Constance.

They beat Jennifer and Millicent to the patch and were busily filling their pails with plump, juicy berries when the other two girls arrived.

"How are they?" called Jennifer.

"Delicious!" answered Miss Constance. Stains on her lips proved that she spoke from firsthand knowledge.

Jennifer and Millicent found their own spot for picking and fell to work without conversation. Occasionally a bird flew over and loudly scolded the pickers for usurping the patch. They paid little heed to the chattering. Squirrels added their complaints from nearby trees. Chipmunks dashed into the patch and helped themselves, as if afraid there would be no berries left for them if they didn't hurry.

Hearing Miss Constance sigh, Felicity turned to look at her. She was sitting quietly, her hands motionless in her lap, her face upturned, studying the scudding clouds.

"It's getting hot," observed Jennifer. "I'm thirsty."

"Me, too," said Millicent. "Let's get a drink."

"Did you bring water?" asked Miss Constance, returning from her reverie.

"No—we just go to the stream over there."

"There's a stream?"

"You can hear it if you listen carefully," said Jennifer, tipping her head.

"Oh yes. I hear it. I didn't realize what that sound was. Can we go?"

"Sure. But take your berries with you. Some animal might get into them if you leave your bucket behind."

Miss Constance laughed again, a little freer now, as if she were beginning to find pleasure in life.

———

That afternoon at tea Mrs. Blakeney announced they would be leaving. Julia was disappointed. She had hoped for a bit more income from the family—even though they did keep her running with their multitude of orders.

"Send one of the young girls to help me pack in the morning," Mrs. Blakeney ordered.

Julia promised she would.

"Do you need them both?" she asked, trying to be helpful.

"Oh, I think one should be able to handle it just fine—unless she is dreadfully slow," said Mrs. Blakeney. "I just have the two suitcases."

"And your daughters?" asked Julia, unable to believe that Miss Prissy, who hadn't lifted a pretty pink finger since her arrival, would actually pack her own luggage. Unless, of course, poor Miss Constance would be packing for her.

"The girls! Oh, they aren't leaving," answered Mrs. Blakeney as though Julia should have known.

Julia stared at the woman, who kept talking without even a pause.

"It will work just fine. I know Priscilla is bored, but she must endure that. She knew it would be this way. Constance will see to her."

Julia still had not thought of anything to say.

"Mr. Blakeney and I will be getting back to the city. There are so many events to attend to. I just can't be away very long at a time. You understand. Things are always so busy in the city. Especially when one is a social leader, so to speak. I will try to find time to pop out now and then to see how the girls are doing."

Chapter Twenty-one

Decisions

"Mama! Mama!" Jennifer cried as she rushed into the kitchen. "Millicent decided. Millicent decided!"

Julia stopped slicing bread. "That's wonderful!" she exclaimed, knowing exactly what her daughter meant. She took Jennifer into her arms.

"She said she thought about it and thought about it—and then she decided to ask God to forgive her sins—and to make her ready for heaven."

Felicity joined in the celebration. "That's great, Jen," she bubbled, getting in on the hugs.

"We should pray for her and help her in every way we can," said Julia.

"She promised to come to all the Bible studies."

"Does she have a Bible of her own?" asked Julia.

Jennifer shook her head.

"Then we must find one for her," said Julia. "I'm sure we have an extra one we could give her."

"Where is Papa?" asked Jennifer. "I want to tell him the news too."

"He and Tom are helping Mr. and Mrs. Adams get ready for their move. You may run and tell him. But Jennifer, do it discreetly. Millicent should be allowed to share her own good news with others. Do you understand?"

Jennifer nodded and was off to find her father.

"My! What excitement," said Julia. "But we do have guests to attend to. Felicity, would you get the cream for the tea tray? And fill the sugar bowl again, please."

"When are they leaving, Mama?" asked Felicity as she went to get the cream.

"On tomorrow's train. But the young ladies are staying on—for I don't know how long."

"I'm beginning to like Miss Constance," stated Felicity. "If she were given half a chance, I think she could be downright pleasant."

"Well, then," Julia said, "let's give her a *whole* chance. What do you say?"

Felicity grinned in reply.

They served the tea to Mr. and Mrs. Blakeney. As usual, Miss Priscilla stayed in her room. Miss Constance chose to take a bath after her outing to the berry patch rather than have tea in the parlor.

Mrs. Blakeney spoke to Julia over her cup of tea. "I have been admiring those silver candlesticks in the dining room. I have never seen any quite like them. I told Mr. Blakeney that you surely didn't get them here."

"No," smiled Julia, amused at the woman's forthrightness. "They came from the East. They were a wedding gift."

"So, you are from the East?"

"I was raised in Montreal. My papa still lives there."

Mrs. Blakeney nodded her head toward Mr. Blakeney as though to say, "I told you so."

"I like the candlesticks very much," continued Mrs. Blakeney. "How much are they?"

Julia fumbled for a response. Her first impulse was to tell her guest the candlesticks were not for sale. But Julia remembered the painting from the front hall. She would never have sold it had she been properly asked. Yet it was gone and life continued, and the money had helped them through a difficult time. She was sure life could go on without the silver candlesticks as well. She turned to her guest.

"They are really—quite expensive," she answered.

"I judged that," responded Mrs. Blakeney, as though Julia had insulted her.

"I hadn't considered selling them, but if I were to consider it—I would ask—" Julia thought quickly. *If Mrs. Blakeney really wants my candlesticks, she will not have them for one penny less than they are worth.* Having thought it through, Julia named a rather outrageous sum.

Mrs. Blakeney did not flinch. She turned to her husband.

"You see," she said smugly, "I told you they could be had. Pay her." Then she looked at Julia. "I shall want to take them with me tomorrow," she said. "See that they are wrapped carefully."

Julia assigned the task to Hettie. She didn't have the heart to bundle the candlesticks herself. Later, as she fingered the money paid for the purchase, Julia had the sense to thank God for meeting their needs. Then she blinked away the sentimental tears.

"You asked her for how much?" John choked as he and Julia talked in the darkness after retiring.

"She didn't even blink," replied Julia, with some resentment.

"She gave it to you?"

"Well, not exactly. She ordered her husband to give it to me, and he did."

"You have the money?"

"I put it in the strong box in your desk drawer," said Julia.

"Well, the money will certainly help, but I'm sorry you had to let the candlesticks go," John sympathized. "I know they were important to you."

Julia allowed the silence to snuggle in around them and then she said, "Not as important as my family." She paused a moment before proceeding. "And that brings me to another subject I've been thinking about, John. It has to do with the girls. They need more schooling, and I don't think I—we—are able to teach them much more. They need a real school."

"I've been thinking too," John cut in. "And I've been meaning to talk to you, but it's been difficult to find a minute alone when we aren't both exhausted."

Julia tilted her head so she could see his face, but in the darkness she could barely discern the outline.

John continued. "I wrote a letter a while back. To Mr. Small. He has been in touch two or three times since the mill moved, you know, asking me if I wanted a job. Well, that was some time ago—but I thought it wouldn't hurt to ask if he still has anything open."

Silence again.

"Others have done it. Gone out for seasonal work, I mean. I could come and go on the train while you and the girls stay here. Maybe we could afford a tutor if I had a paying job. It wouldn't be for long—"

That's what has been troubling John, thought Julia. *He knows we are short of funds even with my few guests. Yet he is hesitant to seek work because it will mean splitting up the family.* Julia's heart constricted. She didn't want to split up the family either. The thought of it frightened her. Yet she had been about to propose the same thing. Julia forced her thoughts back to what John had been saying.

"Have you heard from him?" she asked as evenly as she could manage.

"Not yet, but I just sent the letter a few days ago."

Julia reached for John's arm in the darkness. She needed an anchor.

"I was thinking," she said slowly, "that maybe we should send the girls away for a year of school."

"But that would cost a fortune," John began. "Even with me working and money from the guests—how could we afford—?"

"By sending them to Papa," Julia interrupted.

"To your father? Way back East?"

"He would love to have them, and it wouldn't cost us much. Papa would insist on having them as family, and they could attend the same finishing school I did. It's nearby and it's a good school."

"Have you talked to the girls about this?"

"Oh no. No. I'd never do that without talking to you first," said Julia, a bit offended.

John relaxed somewhat, but Julia could still feel the tension in his body.

"It means a lot to you, doesn't it?" he asked at last.

Julia thought a moment. "Well, yes and no," she said finally. "If you mean 'it is important to me that the girls go to the same school I attended,' then no. No, that doesn't matter. In fact, I had never even considered it before there was a need to find schooling—somewhere. But if you mean 'it is important to me to have them educated,' then yes, it is. And Papa is the only answer I can come up with."

John lay in the darkness thinking. "Do we have to decide right now?" he asked softly.

"No. Not tonight. But it is time for the first term to start. They will already be late—even if we send them now. We shouldn't delay if—"

"Let's try to have an answer about this by the weekend."

"Besides," said Julia slowly, "Papa always coaxes in his letters for some of us to come."

"But what about their clothes?" John asked. "They are hardly fit to attend a fashionable school in the East."

"I've thought of that," Julia admitted. "We could send the money from the candlesticks with them, and Papa could see that they are properly dressed."

"They need so many things. Would that be enough?"

"If it isn't, Papa will see to the rest."

"Julia, you know I don't want your father to have to dress my family."

"Oh, John!" exclaimed Julia. "He has so few pleasures. Would you deny him that as well? After all, they are his family too."

John reached out in the darkness and drew his wife against his side. "Of course they are," he murmured into her hair. "Of course."

Mr. and Mrs. Blakeney left on the morning train. According to Hettie, Miss Priscilla carried on "something awful." Miss Constance took their leaving in stride, though she didn't look happy about the situation.

"Whatever will I do without Mama?" wailed Miss Priscilla.

"I will be here," said Miss Constance.

"But you always have your nose in a book," accused Miss Priscilla.

"Perhaps you would do well to stick your nose in one occasionally," said Miss Constance without sympathy. And Miss Priscilla cried more loudly.

The community gathered for a potluck dinner on the Harrigan lawn to say farewell to the Adams family. Mrs. Adams wept as she bid her friends goodbye.

"I will miss you all so much," she sniffed.

"You must write," said Julia. "We will want to know all about your new home—Victor's job. The church you find. We are going to miss you too."

The neighbors helped load the Adams' belongings onto the outgoing train, and the family climbed aboard. Mrs. Adams clutched her small valise and the hand of one child. Mr. Adams carried the bulging suitcase and gripped the hand of the second child. And then the train was hissing and straining, ready to be off. Mr. and Mrs. Adams waved through the window to those who had been part of their lives for so many years.

———

With Mr. and Mrs. Blakeney gone, the Harrigan household soon settled into a new routine.

Miss Priscilla kept more and more to her room, and Miss Constance continued to insist upon waiting on her. As Miss Priscilla became more recluse, Miss Constance became more friendly. She even came to the kitchen when it wasn't time to pick up a tray for her sister. At Julia's invitation, she also joined them for tea. On one of those occasions she had begged them all, "Please don't call me Miss. Just call me Constance."

"I like her," Julia remarked later to Hettie and the girls. "We must be especially kind to her. I have a feeling she has not had an easy life. Though she has never indicated . . ." Julia let her remaining thoughts go unspoken and turned her attention to the other sister.

"We must watch out for Miss Priscilla too. It would be unthinkable for us to let her lie in her room and fade away if she is ill. I wish we saw more of her so we might judge her condition a bit more accurately." Julia decided to find some reason to call on Miss Priscilla often enough to keep an eye on the situation.

When Julia made her first visit she found Miss Priscilla sitting up in bed, nibbling cookies, and filing her nails.

"Is there anything I can do for you?" asked Julia politely.

The young woman sighed, "Just make the weeks go faster."

"I'm afraid I can do little about time," Julia smiled. "Though I have found that keeping oneself occupied makes time *seem* to pass more quickly."

Miss Priscilla scowled. "And how is one to be 'occupied' in this forsaken town?"

"Well, there are some nice paths to walk. There are little shops along Main Street. We still have one mercantile in town. And handwork can be interesting."

Miss Priscilla rolled her eyes.

Later in the day, however, Julia saw the young woman go for a walk down a forest path.

Chapter Twenty-two

Discoveries

"But we don't even know Grandfather!" Felicity wailed.

"I know," said Julia, tears in her eyes. "But he is a very gentle man. You will learn to love him just as I do."

"Couldn't you come with us, Mama?" pleaded Jennifer. "It's been ages since you have seen him."

"No," replied Julia. "Perhaps someday, but not just now."

"Do you think they will take us at that school?"

"I am sure they will. You are both good students—and fine young ladies."

"But what about—our dresses?" asked Jennifer, looking down at her ill-fitting, unstylish gown.

"We have money for shopping," replied Julia.

"What do you think, Papa?" asked Jennifer, turning her eyes to John.

"I think your mama is right. You deserve a good education— your grandfather has been yearning to get acquainted with you. He lives all alone in that big house. This seems like a perfect opportunity."

"But what about Christmas?" whispered Jennifer.

"It—it will be difficult for us. But by then you will have made friends—and will be feeling at home with Papa. And we do have the mail. We can send our gifts," said Julia, trying hard not to let her true feelings show.

"Well—it is exciting," declared Felicity. "I mean, we have never been East—never been out of our town much. Are you sure we'll know how to act?" She giggled at the thought of making some ridiculous social error.

"You are your mother's daughter," John assured her. "You

would not be more of a lady had you been raised in a palace."
John meant every word. He had no fear that his daughters
would embarrass themselves with bad manners.

Felicity knew he was right. Their mother had taught them to
behave properly. The idea was becoming less frightening and
more appealing.

"Oh, Jen—let's!" she cried suddenly, and threw her arms
around her twin.

Jennifer allowed a slow, crooked smile to curve her lips. "All
right, let's," she finally agreed, and the girls rushed to embrace
their mother and father.

A letter came for John from Mr. Small. He was pleased that
John had at last agreed to seek employment with him again. "I
have work for you as soon as you are available," he wrote. "Just
let me know the date of your arrival and the accommodation
needed. If you need an advance for moving expenses, I will forward it immediately."

Mr. Small apparently assumed the whole family would be
moving.

The news relieved John's tension somewhat, but he knew the
solution was only temporary. He still needed to figure out a way
to reunite his family.

Julia kept her mind off the coming separation by keeping
herself busy. There was much to do to get the girls ready, and
she had only a few days in which to do it.

John purchased the train tickets and got the luggage ready.
Julia surveyed her closet and chose four gowns she could alter
to fit her daughters. It left her short—it had been some time
since she had been shopping for herself—but she had no place
to go anyway, and the gowns were much too fancy to wear in
the kitchen.

Julia sewed for two days, taking only a few hours for sleep.
She remodeled, patched, made over, and made do. She had little to work with, but when she finished the girls had suitable
garments to wear on the train. After that it would be up to
Papa.

Julia had wired him, and his return message revealed that
his excitement more than matched that of the girls.

In her previous letters, Julia had written nothing about their hardships. *It would only worry him,* she told herself. *And he would surely send money—and that would nearly kill John.*

Julia had told him the mill had moved. And he knew Julia was hoping to keep her lovely home by sharing it with guests, and was indeed striving to make their entire town attractive to tourists. But Julia provided no further details.

As Julia worked anxiously to prepare her daughters for a time with their grandfather, her tears often fell on the material. She hoped with all her heart that the three would fall in love. She hoped her father understood her great love for him as she sent to him her most precious possessions. She hoped too that her girls would see in him all of the goodness, kindness, and wisdom she had always found. Julia prayed and prayed as she stitched. Her papa, whom she loved dearly, had not yet made his peace with God.

The time is getting short, Julia often reminded herself as she had reminded him in the past. But whenever she wrote to him of her concern, his return letters responded to every part of her letter except the paragraphs about his spiritual condition.

Perhaps Jennifer . . . Julia thought. *She shared her faith with Millicent. Perhaps she will be able to explain her faith to her grandfather—in her own simple way.* The thought made Julia pray even more diligently.

The day of the girls' departure came all too quickly for Julia. Felicity had thrown all fear and concern to the wind about five minutes after hearing of the plan. Jennifer accepted the idea more slowly. But by departure time, she too felt only excitement.

"You will write often?" Julia said as both a question and a statement. The girls had lost track of how many times she had reminded them.

"We promise," they replied in chorus.

"And to me too?" John added. He would be leaving the next day for the lumber camp.

"We promise," the girls repeated.

"I will miss you so," Julia said, her voice catching in her throat.

"We will miss you both too," they assured, but their attention had already turned to the train. They were eager to get aboard. The girls took turns embracing their mother and father.

"One more kiss," said Julia, kissing the two soft cheeks, "and one for each of you to give Grandfather from me."

And then in a flurry the girls were gone. It all happened too quickly for Julia. One minute she was holding her two daughters; the next minute the train was chugging away, leaving her empty and alone. She watched the white handkerchiefs waving from the windows until they were out of sight.

Then she turned to John and let the tears flow freely. He held her tightly, wishing with all his heart that he didn't have to leave the next day.

Julia soon straightened and looked into his eyes.

"We have done the right thing?" She worded it as a statement, but she pronounced it as a question.

John patted her shoulder. "We *have* done the right thing," he declared, and Julia found comfort in his reply.

―――――――

The next morning it was even more difficult for Julia to let John go, but she tried not to cling to him. She did not want him to sense her great reluctance.

"I will try to get home for a weekend just as soon as I can," he promised.

"I have Hettie and Tom," Julia assured him. "I won't be alone."

"And the two guests," John reminded her. "They will keep you busy."

He was right about that. If Miss Priscilla had her way she would certainly keep Julia busy. Although the guests meant more work, Julia was grateful to have additional people in her house. It would not seem quite as empty.

"I will write," John promised, "every day," and he kissed her tenderly.

Julia could not answer.

"And you will be in my prayers—constantly," he continued.

Julia blinked hard to keep tears from spilling. She nodded her head and hoped John understood the depth of meaning in her silent communication.

"And remember—if you need me you can send a wire."

Julia nodded again, still unable to speak.

The train whistled, and Julia knew she had to let him go.

"I love you," she managed to whisper as he kissed her one last time. Then he too was gone.

Julia walked home alone. She did not hurry. She wanted to be in control of her emotions by the time she reached her kitchen. Hettie would have a strong, hot cup of tea waiting. Although the tea wouldn't do much for her emptiness, Hettie's company would help some.

Chapter Twenty-three

Deceived

Julia burst into the kitchen, tray in hand, cheeks flushed and her eyes snapping. She stopped at the kitchen table and set down her tray, fearing she would drop it in her agitation. But even after setting it down, she still gripped its edges.

Hettie waited for Julia to say something, but she just stared at the wall, her lips tightly drawn.

"What is it?" Hettie finally asked.

Julia lowered herself into a chair as if her legs would not hold her a moment longer.

"Miss—Miss Prissy!" exclaimed Julia, using the unflattering name for the first time. "She's—she's with child," said Julia, her eyes flashing.

Hettie nodded.

"You knew?" cried Julia.

"I suspected," said Hettie as she continued to peel potatoes.

"Well—well, I never! Who would have thought of such—The very idea—using my house—my Christian home—as a—as a hideaway."

Julia put her head in her hands, her shoulders trembling.

Hettie went on removing potato peels.

"Well, I won't have it!" Julia declared suddenly. "Not in my house. I will not hide a woman who—who lived immorally and came sneaking off to me to hide her sin."

Hettie said nothing.

"She—she—oh, I'm so thankful the girls aren't here to see this," Julia wailed.

Hettie still made no reply.

"Why did she pick us? Why did she come here? There must

be other places. But no. She had to choose us." Julia waved a shaking hand to show her disdain.

Hettie shifted her position, easing her weight from one foot to the other. Without lifting her eyes from the task before her, and without raising her voice, she responded, "Maybe she didn't choose us."

Julia's head came up. "Well—I mean—I know her mother chose us. Her mother runs everything in the family. If she spent more time training her daughters and less time being a— a social leader this—this—disgrace might not have beset her family."

"I didn't mean her mother," said Hettie slowly.

Julia looked puzzled. "Well, it certainly wasn't the father," she said. "I doubt he's ever made a family decision in his entire life."

Silence hung about them for a minute. Julia's face showed more and more impatience. "What are you trying to say, Hettie?" she asked at last.

"The woman is a sinner—just like you said," Hettie answered softly.

Julia's face flushed again. She was about to begin another discourse denouncing evil when she noticed a flicker in Hettie's eyes. "So what are you trying to say," Julia again demanded.

"How did our Lord feel about sinners?" asked Hettie, dropping the peeled potato in the pot. She picked up another and rinsed it in a pan of water.

Julia's eyes grew big. Her head dropped. Her trembling hands fluttered to her breast. "Oh, Hettie," she repented, "I just never thought . . ."

There was silence again while Julia did some soul searching. At last she lifted her head, her eyes tear-filled, her voice low.

"Do you think God sent her here for us to—to help—to love?" she asked.

"Could be."

After another long silence Julia nodded. "Yes, Hettie. It could be. And I nearly failed. Miserably."

"You would have gotten to it—sooner or later," Hettie comforted.

"I was about to send her away," Julia admitted.

"You might have thought of sending her away, but I doubt you could have done it."

"Oh, Hettie. I'm ashamed. So ashamed of my—my quick response. I was so angry. I felt so—so used."

"And so you were," said Hettie.

"Well, if God sent her to us, then we must do our best not to let Him down. We must somehow—somehow convince her that God can forgive—even this."

"It won't be easy," said Hettie, rinsing the pot of potatoes.

"You don't think she will be able to understand that God can forgive such sin?"

"No. I think it won't be easy to make her see that anything she takes a fancy to do, God would dare oppose," said Hettie. "She's a selfish, headstrong young woman if I ever saw one."

Hettie's thought was new to Julia. She paused to reflect on it. The assignment ahead would not be an easy one.

Chapter Twenty-four

Loving

"Are you still lonely?" Felicity asked Jennifer as they prepared for bed. When Jennifer failed to answer, Felicity responded to her own question with sisterly insight. "Me too."

Then the room was quiet again.

"It *is* nice to—to make Grandfather so happy," Felicity said.

Jennifer nodded and went on brushing her long hair.

The girls had settled into the new household quickly, at least by outward appearances. It hadn't been much different from their own, though Grandfather's larger house was more impressive and formal than their home in the mountains.

School was exciting. The girls were relieved to learn they were not far behind in their studies—and were every bit as refined and mannerly as their city peers.

But in spite of their doting grandfather's warm welcome, the acceptance of the other girls, and the shopping trips and entertainment, the empty feeling remained. They missed their parents. They missed home.

Felicity picked up her brush and swept it casually through her hair. "You know what I've decided?" she asked Jennifer.

Jennifer shook her head, afraid to trust her voice.

"I've decided to get married."

Jennifer's hand stopped in mid-stroke. She gave her twin a quizzical look. "You're *not* serious."

"I *am* serious. The only way to solve Mama and Papa's money problems is for one of us to marry a wealthy man. Since I don't suppose you will—I will."

"That's foolish talk," said Jennifer, no longer concerned. The idea was too preposterous to even consider.

"It's not foolish," Felicity shot back with a toss of her head.

"And where will you find this wealthy man?" asked Jennifer. "We go to a girls' school. We go straight to church and home again. Grandfather entertains people his own age. Where do you expect to meet anyone?"

"I'll manage it. Just wait."

Jennifer was unconvinced. "By the time men are wealthy, they are also old—and already married."

Felicity considered the comment. "There are young ones—who inherit," she insisted.

"Well, you certainly don't know any."

"I will. You'll see."

Jennifer laid aside her brush and went to turn down her bed. "Well," she flung at her twin, "if you find a young man—wealthy, a Christian, willing to marry you, and Mama and Papa decide you are old enough to marry—*then* you will have my blessing."

Felicity flipped back her long hair. "What makes you think I need your blessing?" she snorted. "I am doing this to save Mama and Papa and you talk like—"

"Mama and Papa do not need 'saving.' "

"Well, they need—need something—or we wouldn't be here while they are there," said Felicity, nearly in tears.

Jennifer felt like crying too. Loneliness crowded out her courage, making her feel deserted and desperate. "Let's not fight," she pleaded. She knew she could not stop her tears if she tried to say more.

Felicity turned her back. She did not want Jennifer to see how difficult it was to hold her own tears in check.

"You don't think it's a good idea?" Felicity finally managed to ask.

"No. And I don't think Mama and Papa would either. You are much too young even to be thinking of marriage."

"Other girls marry at our age."

"Other girls have not given it proper consideration."

"Then what *can* we do?" asked Felicity.

"Pray," Jennifer replied. "Just pray. And while we are at it—we must pray for Grandfather. Even though he's been taking us to church, I don't think he is a—a real believer."

Felicity had the same fear. "He's sweet, though, isn't he?"

Jennifer wiped her eyes with the sleeve of her white nightgown.

"He's very sweet," she agreed, then added, "and he must miss Mama something awful."

———————

John pushed his chair away from the table in the cook shack and turned to leave for his own sleeping quarters. He shared the stark, simple shack with five other men. It was not the kind of arrangement he enjoyed.

It was noisy, crowded, and often filled with smoke. Although he was determined to endure the inconvenience, to live with the simplicity, and to forgo his need for privacy, he continually longed for Julia.

John slowly strolled the short distance from the eating area to the shack. He wanted time to think—to pray. It was nearly impossible to pray with the raucous laughter, coarse jokes, and smoke-filled air pressing in on him. He stepped off the beaten path and lowered himself onto a fallen log. The night sky was clear, and stars were beginning to appear. John was weary. It had been a long, hard day of heavy work in the woods. He was a cutter now, not an overseer. Mr. Small had told him that would soon change, but for now John was working alongside the other men on the cutting crew. Actually, he figured the hard labor was good for him. The physical exhaustion kept him from thinking too many painful thoughts and made it easy for him to sleep at night despite his many concerns. And of course he was glad to have a paycheck coming regularly.

John turned his face toward heaven as his chest tightened with loneliness. Jule. The girls. Even the familiarity of his small town. He missed it all very much.

"God," he whispered into the darkening night, "I'm glad I didn't need to leave you behind too."

He sat silently, unable to go on. Even his prayers were painful. He watched the moon rise over the nearby pines. A cloud covered it for a moment. Then it reappeared, bigger and brighter than before. In the forest a wolf howled and another responded. They were on the hunt. They needed to survive. John felt a kinship with the wolves. He too was fighting for survival. For himself—but mostly for Jule. For the girls. He had to survive—for them.

———————

Julia placed a late summer rose in a small vase on the breakfast tray she had prepared for Miss Priscilla. Constance had gone for a walk down one of the numerous wooded paths. Julia had assured the girl that her sister would be fine. Julia was quite able and willing to care for Priscilla's needs. Constance had looked relieved—anxious for a few moments alone. Priscilla was getting increasingly restless and difficult.

"I think a short walk would be good for Miss Priscilla too," Julia suggested.

"So do I," responded Constance with a weary sigh, "but she absolutely refuses."

Julia said no more. She had tried everything she could think of to make Miss Priscilla feel more comfortable—more content—more loved. But Miss Prissy was not an easy person to love. Determined to show her love no matter how difficult the task, Julia prayed more fervently for the strength to do so.

Julia lifted the tray. She did not look forward to the trip to Miss Priscilla's room. Along with the tray she carried another letter from Mrs. Blakeney. The woman had not made a single visit to see her daughters. Constance had told Julia that each letter from their mother apologized, but explained that she was too busy to come.

"That's the way it has always been with Mama," Constance said with little emotion. "We have long since become accustomed to it."

But Miss Priscilla did not seem used to it. She chafed and fussed and made life miserable for everyone whenever another promise was broken.

Julia rapped softly on the door.

"Yes," called Miss Priscilla, and Julia opened the door and walked in.

"Good morning," she said cheerfully. "Did you—?"

"Just set it down!" snapped Miss Priscilla. "I am famished. Where is Constance? She should have been here with the tray hours ago."

Julia let the words pass. She knew Miss Priscilla had awakened only a few minutes earlier. She and Hettie had been checking the room regularly.

"You have another letter," Julia said.

"From Mama?" Miss Priscilla brightened for a moment, and then turned glum. "I suppose she will tell me all about her most recent parties. I hate it. I hate hearing about all I am missing."

"You must like parties," Julia said as she poured coffee.

"I don't suppose you understand either. Constance never did.

She just sat at home and read her old books—or worked in the flower beds or went to Ladies' Aid or something. Just like—like an old spinster."

Miss Priscilla spat out the last word. Julia guessed that spinster must be the most disagreeable term the girl could think of.

There were many things Julia wished to say in response but she held her tongue. "She seems happy," was all she said.

Miss Priscilla ignored the comment. She ripped open the envelope bearing her mother's letter and started to read. Her face suddenly brightened. "She's coming!" she cried. "She has her ticket. She is due on Thursday. That's tomorrow."

It was the first time Julia had ever seen the girl excited—rejoicing—over anything.

"We must wash and set your hair," Julia urged. Miss Priscilla had recently been refusing proper grooming. "Go ahead and eat your breakfast. I will come back and do it for you," Julia promised.

While working on Priscilla's hair, Julia encouraged her to come to the downstairs drawing room to greet her mother and have tea when she arrived.

"She won't do it," Constance warned later. "That would spoil the effect. She wants Mother to feel guilty for leaving her here alone—in her condition—and all that."

———

Mrs. Blakeney arrived the next day as promised. Right up until train time, Julia expected to receive some last-minute excuse. She was sure some social engagement would keep the woman away.

But she arrived. Bag and baggage. Julia heard her coming long before Tom opened the door for her.

Constance had been right. Priscilla refused to greet her mother in the parlor. Mrs. Blakeney went straight to Miss Priscilla's room. When Julia took up the tea tray, Miss Priscilla was sprawled on her bed, her hair a tangled mess around her pale face, and her eyes drained of all excitement or eagerness. She moaned each time she shifted position and fretted and scolded until Julia wanted to shake her.

"My poor baby," soothed Mrs. Blakeney, smoothing the girl's hair. "Constance—I trusted you to take better care of your sister. Look at her. Her nails look like they haven't been attended to in weeks and—"

Julia set down the tray and quickly left the room. She grabbed a shawl on her way through the kitchen and headed to the garden. "I wish—I wish there were potatoes to dig—or carrots to pull—or something!" she hissed. "I need to work off some steam."

But the garden had all been cared for by Tom. Winter was approaching. Julia's thoughts turned from the spoiled Miss Priscilla to her own dear daughters and the long winter without them.

Mrs. Blakeney stayed for only a few days. Julia wondered if she found her daughter too disagreeable to endure. Before she left she purchased a porcelain pitcher and bowl and a small gilt-edged mirror from Julia. Julia didn't allow herself the pleasure of tears as she tucked the generous payment into the safe-keeping box in John's desk drawer. They needed the money. They could live without treasures.

Another month passed and Julia had another guest. His name was Dr. Martin Waters, and he came from some spot unknown to any of them. Mrs. Blakeney had hired him to be on guard until Miss Priscilla's baby came, to deliver the infant, and then to leave discreetly. This information came out little by little, for he had been given strict orders to keep silent about his mission.

Dr. Waters was very aware of his own presence, and he made certain that others were too. He wore flashy clothes, twitched his carefully trimmed mustache, and cast furtive glances as though fearful someone were following him. His steel blue eyes flashed impatience with the least provocation, and Julia sensed that he was very short-tempered.

Julia felt uncomfortable around him, but there was little she could do. Although difficult to endure, he was a paying guest.

Miss Priscilla seemed to like the idea of having a little male company, and she began ordering Constance to brush her hair and manicure her nails again. Dr. Waters, a man of about forty, was not without a measure of masculine appeal, and his silence and manner made him mysterious and intriguing.

Miss Priscilla may as well have saved herself the trouble,

however. The doctor seemed to be interested in nothing except his fee—which likely would be sizable.

Dr. Waters kept mostly to himself and ignored the majority of Miss Priscilla's moans and groans and cries of complaint. He did care for her solicitously, however, handing out little pink or white pills with abandon. Julia feared for the unborn child, but dared not be too open with her comments.

"I just hope this whole ordeal is over quickly," she confided to Hettie. "It seems that our efforts to show love and understanding have been in vain. Miss Priscilla has not softened one bit. In fact, I fear she is even more disagreeable than ever. I don't know how poor Constance stands it."

"I think she has had years of practice," responded Hettie. "It's a clear case of the older, rational, responsible sister needing to care for the younger, spoiled, irresponsible one."

Julia felt that Hettie had summed up the situation well.

Julia did not get her wish for quick release from their circumstance. Miss Priscilla, in spite of her great impatience, failed to deliver on time. The days dragged by and everyone in the house became tense and edgy. Miss Priscilla fussed and scolded, screaming at anyone who entered her room and at anyone who did not come when she called.

Julia found it more and more difficult to keep her promise. The young woman was nearly impossible to love.

Chapter Twenty-five

Delivery

A sharp rap on the bedroom door awakened Julia. Then she heard a voice. "Mrs. Harrigan. Mrs. Harrigan. It's time. It's time."

Julia could make no sense of the words—or their urgency. She sat up in bed trying to get her bearings, trying to figure out who was calling and why.

"Mrs. Harrigan," the voice came again, sounding desperate. "Please come. Please hurry. It's time."

"It's Constance," Julia said. Then reality flooded over her. *The baby. It must be Priscilla and the baby.*

Julia arose swiftly and snatched a robe from the wardrobe. The generator had been turned off so they had no electricity. Julia didn't take time to light a lamp. She hastened to the door, tying the robe as she went.

Constance was about to rap again when Julia jerked the door open. "It's time," Constance said again, her hand still in midair.

"Does the doctor need anything?" asked Julia.

"Oh my!" exclaimed Constance, "I didn't think to call him." She turned and hurried down the hall toward the doctor's room.

His bedroom door opened before Constance reached it, and the man came out. He looked disgruntled to have his sleep disturbed—but Julia was thankful to see that he was prepared to take charge. His sleeves were rolled up and he carried his official-looking black bag.

"Is the kettle hot?" he asked.

Of course the kettle is not hot. It is one o'clock in the morning, Julia thought. But she kept her snippy answer to herself and said instead, "I'll see to it right away."

Julia closed her ears to the sounds coming from Priscilla's room and hurried down the stairs, through the house, and to the kitchen.

———

It was after eight when Constance came running to the kitchen to inform Julia that the delivery had gone well and that a baby boy had arrived.

Julia felt the excitement a new baby always brought to her. She wanted to run upstairs immediately to see the child.

"The doctor wants to know where to put him," Constance continued, and Julia's thoughts came back to earth with a jolt.

This is not a wanted baby, Julia reminded herself. *No one has prepared for his coming. Even I did not think to make any arrangements.*

"Why—why—" she stammered, "won't he be staying in Miss Priscilla's room?"

"Priscilla doesn't even want to see him," replied Constance, her voice breaking. "She wants him out of her room at once. She has turned her face to the wall."

"But—but surely—" But then she put everything together. Miss Priscilla had hidden for four months. She had never intended to return home with a child.

"I'll—I'll fix something. Bring him to my room."

"But—but I thought perhaps I could keep him in my room," Constance explained as they hurried through the house. "I—I don't know a thing about babies, but if you would be kind enough to—And if we had a bed—"

"I don't have a baby bed," Julia said, an edge to her voice. *Why hasn't Mrs. Blakeney made provisions?* Julia wondered. *She has been quite thorough in everything else. After all, the baby is her flesh and blood.*

"Can we use a—a box—or a drawer—or something?" Constance asked, and Julia scolded herself for her angry thoughts.

Poor Constance, she thought instead. *This has all been so difficult for her, and now she must be a nursemaid to a baby as well.*

"We'll find something," she assured the girl.

Baby boy Blakeney was eventually dressed in a white gown with pink ribbons, bundled in used pink blankets, and laid in an emptied, towel-padded dresser drawer. Julia could have wept as she looked down on him.

"You poor little soul," she whispered. "You didn't ask to come into the world. And you certainly didn't get much of a welcome. What will happen to you? Whatever will happen to you? If only I could have had you to love—" Julia brushed away tears and went back to the kitchen to prepare hot tea for Miss Priscilla.

They had nothing for the new baby. Tom fashioned a nipple of sorts from the finger of a new glove. It was all Mr. Perry had in his store that would make any kind of feeding arrangement. Julia fixed a bottle of milk and fed the hungry baby.

Constance took over the care of the infant as Julia instructed her. There were no diapers, so Julia told Hettie to tear up an old flannel sheet. There wasn't even time to put in a proper hem.

Julia had never before felt so disturbed over the birth of a baby. Her heart cried, *It's not right. It's not fair. He wasn't at fault.* It seemed so totally wrong that a child should be born un- wanted—unwelcomed—unloved.

But when Julia looked at Constance's face as she held the baby and coaxed him to drink from the makeshift bottle, she was forced to change her opinion.

I've been wrong, Julia concluded. *He may have been un- wanted—but he is not unloved. Constance has already fallen in love with him.*

And it was true. Never did a baby get more tender care than Constance gave her new nephew.

"What do you call him?" Julia asked Constance one evening.

"Mother said he is not to be named," responded Constance with a sigh.

Julia could not disguise her surprise.

"But—secretly—I call him Peter," the young woman con- fided.

"Peter. I like it." Julia waited for Constance to finish feeding Peter and give him to her to hold.

———

"He seems to be doing well, doesn't he?" Julia said on one of her daily visits to see the baby. She lowered the small garment she was stitching for Peter and watched him sucking hungrily.

"He's a little piggy," laughed Constance in a way Julia had never heard her laugh before.

Constance kissed the top of the downy head. "I think he has grown already," she said. "Eight days old—and already bigger."

Julia smiled. "I can see it too. The way he eats, I guess he should." Then Julia added with a chuckle, "We are going to have to buy more gloves. I do hope Mr. Perry has another pair or two. We have already cut all the fingertips off the pair we bought."

Constance looked up. "Oh, it shouldn't be much longer," she said. "The doctor says Priscilla will be ready to travel soon."

Julia lifted her eyebrows in surprise.

"Will the doctor be traveling with you?" she asked.

"Oh no. He plans to go straight back to—wherever. He says his contract does not include escorting us home."

"I see," said Julia, but she still had many questions.

———

"I will be leaving tomorrow," the doctor announced at dinner the next evening.

Even Priscilla had joined them at the table. She still looked pale, but Julia believed that it was as much from shutting herself in her room, away from fresh air and sunshine, as from her recent delivery.

"I shall need clean garments and blankets for the baby and enough feedings to last for a twelve-hour trip."

Three heads lifted and three pairs of eyes studied the man's face.

"What do you mean?" asked Constance.

The doctor looked blank at her question. "I need clothes and food for the infant," he repeated. "Enough for a twelve-hour trip. Why is that confusing?"

"But you won't be taking the baby."

"Indeed, I will. I have instructions from your mother—"

"My mother doesn't understand the situation," Constance interrupted. "She made those plans long before—"

"I have my orders—and I plan to fulfill them," the doctor said adamantly.

"But you *can't* take the baby."

"I *must* take the baby—according to contract," the man declared.

"But—"

"Oh, Constance. For goodness' sake don't fuss," broke in Priscilla, tossing her napkin on the table and standing up. "You know the plan—the arrangement. Mother has it all cared for."

"But Mother doesn't know Peter!" cried Constance, also rising.

"Peter? Peter?" screamed Priscilla. "Who called him Peter? You know Mother said he wasn't to be named. What right do you have—?"

"I *love* him!" Constance shouted back at her screaming sister. "I *love* him."

Priscilla looked at Constance. Surprise and anger flashed across her face. Then she began to cry. Hot tears washed down her cheeks and made trails in her face powder.

"That's—that's—just like you!" she shouted at Constance. "You can't even be trusted to—to care for a baby. You know that Mother said he—"

"I *will* care for him. I will!"

"You will not bring that—that baby home. Do you hear? You will not!" Priscilla shouted.

Julia trembled. She had never witnessed such a quarrel. She wanted to cover her ears and flee, but she was rooted to the spot.

"Of course I won't take him home!" Constance shouted back at her sister. "I wouldn't dream of taking him to where—to that place. I will keep him here—for a while. I have money. I can find us a place."

"You're a fool!" yelled Priscilla. "You're a—a pigheaded, selfish fool." With that final burst of anger she fled the room, sobbing loudly.

Constance dropped back to her chair and reached for a napkin to press to her cheek. Her shoulders trembled, but Julia knew she felt that she had won the battle.

At length she lifted her head and looked at Julia.

"Is it—can I stay—for just a while? Just until I am able to make arrangements for me and—and Peter?"

"Of—of course," whispered Julia.

A stirring at the table reminded Julia they were not alone. She had forgotten the doctor.

"I'm afraid it's out of the question. I already have all of the papers in order for the adoption."

"But you can't."

"I can—and I will," the man said. "I have a legal document. Signed and binding. You will not interfere." He pushed back his chair and stood up.

"I want the child ready by nine o'clock," he said with authority. Then he looked directly at Julia. "Mrs. Harrigan—I expect you to see to it."

He stalked from the room, and Constance buried her face in her hands and sobbed.

The next morning when Julia went to check on Constance and Peter, she found a note.

> Peter had his morning feeding, and all his things are packed and ready to go. Give him one last kiss for me. I have gone for a walk. C.L.B.

Julia opened the door softly, brushing away tears. Peter lay sleeping in his makeshift bed. Beside him was a suitcase that belonged to Constance. In it, neatly folded, were all of the garments Constance and Julia had made over the past several days. The borrowed clothing that had belonged to Julia's two baby girls lay in an orderly stack on the bed.

Julia lifted the small baby from his bed to prepare him for his journey.

"She loves you—so much," she whispered to the sleeping child, her tears falling onto his blanket. "I only hope—only pray that your new mother—whoever she might be—will love you half as much."

Julia lifted the small bundle and kissed the soft cheek. The baby squirmed but did not waken.

"One from me—and one from Aunt Constance," whispered Julia as she kissed him again. She paused a minute to gain a measure of control before she took the baby to the waiting doctor.

Julia was pacing the kitchen floor, her brow furrowed, her lips moving in silent prayer when the door opened and Constance stepped in. Julia took one look at the young woman's face and moved to embrace her. They clung to one another for several minutes, neither one speaking. Shared tears were their only communication.

"You must be starved," Julia whispered. "You have been gone all day. Sit down. Hettie saved you a plate."

Julia pushed the teakettle forward on the stove and checked the warming oven that held the waiting food.

"Draw your chair closer to the fire," Julia urged. "It's cold out. You must be chilled through and through."

Constance wiped her eyes, blew her nose, and then did as Julia suggested.

"I walked with them to the train," Julia said hesitantly. "He was—fine. He never even awakened when the whistle blew."

Constance turned her face.

"The—the twelve hours will soon be up," Julia went on. "Just think of it. Somewhere—right now—there is a very excited woman—and man—waiting for that little one. Can you just imagine how they feel?"

Julia saw the sagging shoulders tremble.

"There was a time when we thought of adopting a baby boy. But we were told there weren't many children available for adoption. And because we already had two healthy girls it might be a long wait."

The young woman made no effort to respond. Julia stepped closer and placed her hand on the trembling shoulder.

"Constance, I am not trying to make it harder for you. I just want you to think about the other couple. How they might have prayed—longed for a baby. Little Peter could—will—make them very happy. He is such a sweet little thing. He will be loved. We'll pray for that. We'll pray that he has wise and kind and loving parents."

Constance wept again, but soon she looked at Julia and whispered, "You are right. He is better off with—with both a mother and a father. I loved him—will always love him—but I couldn't have given him the home he deserved. Oh, Julia, I need to learn how to pray so that I might pray for him. I know you know how. I have watched you—with me—with Priscilla. No one could have been as kind or as patient without—without a deep faith in God. Please—please tell me what I must do to find God in that way."

Through tears that blurred her vision, Julia led Constance in reading Scripture portions that explained how to believe in the Son of God.

———

Priscilla and Constance left the next day. Constance seemed reluctant to leave, but Priscilla was impatient to be gone.

"I suppose that poky old train will be late," she fussed, but the train was right on time.

"I will write," Constance promised.

"I will be waiting," said Julia.

"Thank you. Thank you so much—for sharing your faith—for understanding—for your love," said Constance.

Julia hugged her again and blinked back another onset of tears. She turned from Constance to Priscilla. The train was coming toward them, chugging heavily as it pulled up the incline toward the station.

"Priscilla," said Julia. "I—I'll continue to pray for you." Julia tried to give the girl a parting embrace, but Priscilla accepted only a token hug and then stepped back quickly.

"Constance, grab that big bag," she ordered, "it's much too heavy for me."

Julia turned back to Constance who welcomed the warmth of her farewell embrace.

"Don't let her upset you," whispered Constance. "She was affected by your love much more than she lets on. She said as much to me. And now that I know God—I will be able to help her. I will keep working and praying and—who knows?"

Chapter Twenty-six

Family

Winter's snow arrived early, making Julia feel buried and confined in the big, empty house. If she had not had Christmas projects to keep her mind and fingers busy, she felt sure she would have gone out of her mind with loneliness and sorrow.

John came home for Christmas, and Julia clung to him as if he were her only link to sanity. "I have been counting the days ever since you left," she moaned, "but they ticked by so slowly."

John pulled her close and brushed his lips against her hair.

"You've lost weight," Julia fretted.

"Not much."

"But you *have* lost weight. Aren't the meals—?"

"The meals are fine. They feed us like—like lumberjacks," John said with a grin.

Julia lifted a hand to rub his cheek. "It's so good to have you home."

But strangely, having John home made her ache even more intensely for Jennifer and Felicity—or perhaps it was because of Christmas. Julia's thoughts kept returning to the girls.

It will be such a special Christmas for Papa, she kept telling herself. She pictured the big house on St. Pierre. The staff would have decorated the halls with boughs of cedar and holly. The tree would be standing in the wide front parlor, hung with ornaments too numerous to count. Cinnamon and nutmeg would fill the house with irresistible aromas. Julia remembered it all. It would be as it had been during her childhood. Having the girls this year gave her papa a reason to celebrate Christmas.

"Oh, if only we could be there too," grieved Julia. "Then— then I would be so happy."

But they were not there. Julia mailed her parcels with teary eyes and a loving heart. Then she busied herself baking John's favorite desserts, hanging the familiar streamers, and carefully placing the glass balls on the tree John brought home to her.

On Christmas day Julia set the table for seven. She had invited the Clancys and Mr. Perry for dinner. She had wanted to have everyone who was left in town, but the Shannon children had the measles and could not go out, and the Greenwalds had guests of their own.

John and Julia managed to get through the day. Julia tried to be cheerful, tried to keep her mind on her guests, but her thoughts kept slipping to her family in the East. *I wonder what they are doing now. I wonder if the girls are thinking of us. I wonder—*

And then the guests went home and the day was over. Julia was glad she had worked so hard to get ready. As bone-tired as she was, at least she would be able to sleep.

———

Julia was hard pressed to keep busy as the winter days came and went. The household needed many things, but she had no materials with which to work. Julia chose to be frugal. She stretched John's paychecks as far as possible so they could lay aside sufficient funds to reunite the family.

In February Hettie took sick. Julia worried more than she admitted. There was no doctor and no longer even a druggist in town. What few medications remained were shelved in Mr. Perry's back room.

"I really have very little to offer you," Mr. Perry told Julia when she asked for his help.

"I just don't know what to do," Julia sighed. "I have heard of poultices for chest colds and steaming for head colds—but this is neither. I don't know what is wrong with her."

"Well, keep her warm and quiet—that's about all I know," said Mr. Perry. "And chicken broth. My ma used to swear by chicken broth."

"And where am I to get a chicken? I have tasted nothing but wild meat for two years now."

The man nodded his head but said nothing more.

Julia picked up a few tablets said to bring relief from aches and pains and then trudged home through the snow.

It was several days before Julia saw any improvement in

Hettie's condition. By then Julia was exhausted from work and worry.

"I'll sit with her," said Tom, entering the room. "You get some sleep."

Julia did not argue. She went to her room and fell on her bed without even removing her clothes. "Dear God, may she be all right now," she whispered, and then she slept.

In March the Clancys moved away.

"There's no need for a town clerk when there's no longer a town," Mr. Clancy said simply.

"I've been thinkin'," Mrs. Greenwald said to Julia a few days later. "No need to keep those shops open when there is nothing much in them. Might as well sort out what is left and board up those windows before everyone is gone and there's no one to help us."

Only the Shannons, the Greenwalds, and Mr. Perry were left.

"What about the summer trade?" asked Julia.

"Perhaps Mr. Perry will lend a shelf or two in his store," Mrs. Greenwald continued, and Julia didn't argue.

The few remaining hand-crafted goods were moved to Perry's store, and the men of the community nailed the boards back on the shop windows.

At last Julia began to feel that spring might actually come again. She took every opportunity to be outdoors, even though it was too early to plant a garden, too wet to walk in the woods, and too desolate to stroll downtown. Julia mostly puttered at home or hurried to the post office to see if she had a letter from John, the girls, or her father.

John's letters always sounded cheerful. True to his word, Mr. Small had found John a position as overseer so he no longer had to put in hard, heavy days as a cutter. He told Julia how the town was growing, with more and more homes lining the crooked streets.

"They have even put in electricity," he wrote in one letter. "Of course that is thanks to the lumber mill." He spoke often of missing his family and how happy he would be when he had saved enough money so he could come home again.

The girls' letters always told interesting incidents of life in the big city. They had learned to love their grandfather. They enjoyed school and the young ladies who had quickly become their friends. They wrote about their interests in music and sports, and they told Julia about shopping trips and visits to exciting places. But they also spoke of their eagerness to be back with their parents again. Julia could often detect little cries of loneliness.

Her father's hasty notes were filled with comments about the girls. He praised Julia for raising such fine young ladies, talked of their accomplishments in school, gloated over how well Jennifer was doing on the piano and how sharp Felicity was in mathematics. It was always a joy for Julia to read her father's letters—but they did make her even more lonely.

After Tom plowed the garden, Julia set out with her packets of seeds, glad to have something to do, something that would actually show growth—advancement. At the same time she wondered, *Why am I doing this? I am planting a garden big enough to feed the town—and there is only Hettie, Tom, and me.*

What about your summer guests? she argued with herself.

Guests? Perhaps a few—but never enough. Never enough to earn a suitable income, and never enough to eat all of these vegetables.

But Julia planted on. She felt compelled to do so. It kept her feeling busy—profitable.

"We are leaving, too," Maude Shannon told Julia toward the end of spring. "Jim just doesn't want to struggle here anymore."

Julia didn't even raise her head. She had expected it.

"Do you want the cow?" asked Maude.

"I'll ask Tom. He would have to care for her. I will let him decide."

"I'm sorry to leave you like this," Maude went on.

Julia managed a half smile. "That's all right," she said. "We have always said that whenever a family feels they should move—that it's time to go—then they should do so."

"Might you go too?" Maude asked.

Julia shifted. She had thought of it. Had wondered. Had even hoped John might suggest it.

"No," she finally said. "No, I don't think so. Not now at any rate."

"Do you have folks coming?" Mrs. Shannon asked.

"You mean summer guests? No, not yet—but it's still early. Most folks don't come until late summer or early fall."

"Well, I should get going. I've got a lot to do," Maude said. "Packin' and all. Thanks for the tea, Julia."

Maude started to leave but then turned back to Julia. "I was wonderin'—before I go, could you—could you sorta say a prayer for me. I'm—I guess I'm scared and—and worried and I need some faith if I'm gonna get through this. I need God, Julia."

With a sense of humility, Julia took her neighbor's hand. "Of course, Maude. Of course. He's here. You only need to reach out to Him."

After praying with Maude, Julia followed her to the kitchen door and watched her go. Julia then turned to her garden. A few weeds were showing again.

———

John arrived home unannounced. He surprised Julia by walking up behind her and pulling her apron string as she hoed her garden. Startled, Julia whirled to see who would tease her in such a way. She could not believe her eyes. Throwing herself into his arms she wept on his shoulder.

"Why, I didn't even know—hadn't even received your letter—" she said when she could speak again.

"There wasn't any letter," John admitted. "I just—well I just had to see you, so I begged for a few days off."

"The Shannons have gone," Julia told him.

"I noticed. I saw the empty yard—the boarded-up windows."

"It's an empty town," said Julia, shaking her head. She turned her face to keep John from seeing the tears building up.

John led Julia to the porch swing and motioned for her to be seated. He eased himself down beside her. "Jule," he began slowly, "I've been doing a lot of thinking." He paused to choose his words carefully. He did not want to hurt the woman he loved so dearly.

"You have—have given it everything you could, but, Jule—I don't think it's going to work. Not here. I'm afraid we are going to have to give up, Jule. To let the house go."

John waited, holding his breath. He had never given Julia

orders before. He expected a cry of protest, but Julia remained silent.

"We can't go on like this, Jule. I can't stand being without you—without the girls. I think—"

"What are you saying?" asked Julia, her voice trembling.

"We need to be together. To be a family again. I know it will hurt you to lose the house, but—"

"The house?" gasped Julia. "You think I can't give up the *house*?"

John looked at his wife, a puzzled expression in his eyes.

"John, I don't care about the house. Oh, I—I've loved it, of course—but without my family—the big, beautiful house has become a—a mammoth tomb. Empty and lonely. No, John, it isn't my love for the house that has kept me here—trying to—"

"Then what?" asked John.

"You. You, John. I thought you couldn't bear to give up the house. I didn't want to lose it—for you, John."

"You mean—?"

Julia nodded her head vigorously. "You worked so hard to give me everything—to have things perfect for me. I thought— I thought it would—would crush you to—to give it all up. I tried to hold it for *you*," sobbed Julia, burying her face against her husband's shoulder.

"Oh, Jule, Jule," John soothed her. "I just want—I just want you. I want us to be together. I can't stand this—this being apart."

"That's all I want too," sobbed Julia.

John kissed her wet cheek. He held her close, his own tears joining hers. Then he smiled and lifted her chin. "You'll come with me? Move? Now?" he asked.

"Oh yes!" cried Julia, her eyes beginning to shine.

"What of Hettie—and Tom?"

"Hettie's father just wrote. He wants them to live with him. He's not been well. Hettie was fussing about it because she wouldn't leave me."

John's arm tightened around Julia. "I found a little house," he enthused like a child. "It's—it's not much—nothing like this one—but it does have a mountain view."

Julia sensed his teasing. "Is there room for all of us?" she asked.

John nodded. "It will be crowded. The girls will have to share a room."

"They've always shared a room," Julia reminded him. "Oh, John—I'm so—so filled with—with joy—I fear I might burst. I can hardly wait another minute."

John kissed her again, his face sobering. "I was so afraid," he admitted. "So afraid you might not want to go off to another lumber town. That you wouldn't be able to leave—this." He nodded toward the large white house.

Julia shook her head with confidence. She was surprised that her long-troubled mind felt peace at last.

"It's time," she whispered. "I feel—feel free to go now. I didn't feel this way before. This—release. Why?"

"Perhaps because you were still needed here," John answered.

Julia thought of Constance and of Maude Shannon. "Yes, perhaps that *is* the reason," she said. "Maybe I *was* still needed here."

"And now?" asked John.

Julia placed her arms around his neck, her face aglow. "Now," she said, "now God is giving us new challenges. New adventures. Oh, John! I'm so thankful we can face them together."

"Let's go wire the girls," John suggested, and Julia hastily agreed.

"Perhaps Papa will bring them home to us!" she exclaimed, thinking ahead to the great reunion of their family. Tears of happiness glistened on her cheeks as she laid her head against John's shoulder.

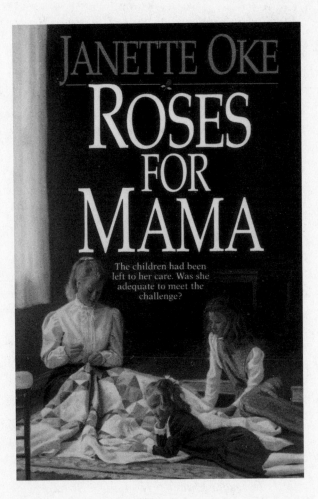

JANETTE OKE

ROSES
FOR
MAMA

The children had been
left to her care. Was she
adequate to meet the
challenge?

Books by Janette Oke

Another Homecoming* / Tomorrow's Dream*
Celebrating the Inner Beauty of Woman
Dana's Valley†
Janette Oke's Reflections on the Christmas Story
The Matchmakers • Nana's Gift
The Red Geranium • Return to Harmony*

CANADIAN WEST

When Calls the Heart   When Breaks the Dawn
When Comes the Spring   When Hope Springs New
Beyond the Gathering Storm
When Tomorrow Comes

LOVE COMES SOFTLY

Love Comes Softly   Love's Unending Legacy
Love's Enduring Promise   Love's Unfolding Dream
Love's Long Journey   Love Takes Wing
Love's Abiding Joy   Love Finds a Home

A PRAIRIE LEGACY

The Tender Years   A Quiet Strength
A Searching Heart   Like Gold Refined

SEASONS OF THE HEART

Once Upon a Summer   Winter Is Not Forever
The Winds of Autumn   Spring's Gentle Promise

SONG OF ACADIA*

The Meeting Place   The Birthright
The Sacred Shore   The Distant Beacon

WOMEN OF THE WEST

The Calling of Emily Evans   A Bride for Donnigan
Julia's Last Hope   Heart of the Wilderness
Roses for Mama   Too Long a Stranger
A Woman Named Damaris   The Bluebird and the Sparrow
They Called Her Mrs. Doc   A Gown of Spanish Lace
The Measure of a Heart   Drums of Change

Janette Oke: A Heart for the Prairie
Biography of Janette Oke by Laurel Oke Logan

*with T. Davis Bunn   †with Laurel Oke Logan

JANETTE OKE'S

Women of the West

THE CALLING OF EMILY EVANS

JULIA'S LAST HOPE

ROSES FOR MAMA

Published by Bethany House Publishers
A Ministry of Bethany Fellowship International
11400 Hampshire Avenue South
Minneapolis, Minnesota 55438

Printed in the United States of America by
Bethany Press International, Minneapolis, Minnesota 55438

ISBN 0-7394-4380-1

To Mother,
Amy Marie Ruggles Steeves,
from one of your bouquet of eight.

JANETTE OKE was born in Champion, Alberta, during the depression years, to a Canadian prairie farmer and his wife. She is a graduate of Mountain View Bible College in Didsbury, Alberta, where she met her husband, Edward. They were married in May of 1957 and went on to pastor churches in Indiana as well as Calgary and Edmonton, Canada.

The Okes have three sons and one daughter and are enjoying the addition of grandchildren to the family. Edward and Janette have both been active in their local church, serving in various capacities as Sunday school teachers and board members. They make their home near Calgary, Alberta.

Contents

Chapter One

Angela

Angela Peterson wiped her hands on her dark blue apron, then reached up and tucked a wisp of blond hair into a side comb. It was a warm day, and the tub of hot water over which she had been leaning did not make it any cooler. She stretched to take some of the kink from her back and lifted her eyes to the back field where Thomas's breaking plow stitched a furrowed pattern. He would soon be in for his dinner.

Angela bent over the tub again and scrubbed the soiled socks with renewed vigor. She wanted to finish before stopping to put dinner on the table, and this was her last load.

"I hate washing socks," she fretted, then quickly bit her tongue as she recalled a soft voice: "Remember, never despise a task—any task. In doing any job, you are either creating something or bettering something."

Mama had always said things like that. Usually Angela grasped the truth of her words quickly, but sometimes her statements made Angela stiffen with a bit of rebellion. After giving the words some thought, though, she always came to understand their plain, common sense. As each year slipped by, Angela went back to the words of her mother more and more. Mama had not just spoken her thoughts to her children; she had lived the lessons before them. And Mama had been a living example of all the things that make a lady.

As usual, thoughts of Mama were followed quickly by thoughts of Papa, and Angela felt her eyes lifting up and up, as though Papa were suddenly standing before her. He was of Scandinavian stock. He was so tall—her papa. So tall and strong, with broad shoulders, sturdy forearms, and a straight, almost stiff back. His eyes were blue, like deep, icy water. "Like the fjords," Mama would say, then smile softly, and her children knew she considered the fjords something very special even though she had never seen them herself.

Angela smiled at the thought, then turned her attention back to the dirty sock on the washboard. The wind had strengthened and she had to stop again and brush silky strands of hair from her face. From across the valley came the sound of a ringing bell. The school children were being called in to resume their morning classes. And Angela resumed her scrubbing on the sock before her, wrung it out, and tossed it in the rinse tub. She swished a slender hand through the soapy water to locate the next one and sighed with relief when her hand came up empty.

Her back ached as she straightened, but she had no time to dwell on the discomfort. Another task called for her attention. Thomas would have heard the ringing school bell too—his signal to come in for dinner.

Hurriedly, Angela rinsed the footwear and pegged it to the line.

I'll leave the emptying until after we eat, she told herself as she hastened to the kitchen.

The house the Peterson family inhabited was not large, but neither was it crowded, even though five people lived there. On a bluff overlooking the valley, it was protected on three sides by poplar trees. From the front, the wide veranda looked out over open countryside way over to the slim spire of the town church, the only thing belonging to the town that they could see from their yard. Angela pictured the rest. The wide main street with narrower streets leading off to this side and that; the board sidewalks; the hardware store filled with hammers, shovels, and yard goods; the drugstore with its window display of hard candies; the grocery with barrels and bins of kitchen stock; the meat market with its sawdust-covered floor. Angela had never liked trips to the meat market. She didn't like the smell of meat until it was simmering in the big frying pan or sizzling in the roaster in the oven.

Angela had just enough time to put the left-over stew on to heat and set the table before she heard steps across the side porch. She turned to the loaf of bread she had placed on the cutting board and placed thick slices on a plate. Thomas was washing up at the blue basin and wiping dry on the wash-worn towel suspended from the roller.

Angela put the bread on the table and hurried back to the stove. The coffee still hadn't boiled and the stew was not yet bubbling.

"I'm sorry," she murmured softly over her shoulder, "I'm a bit slow. The washing seemed to take me longer today."

"I saw," Thomas responded. "The line's full. You need more clothesline?"

Angela shook her head and looked at Thomas, who had taken his place at the table. His face was shining with a just-washed look, but his hair was still tousled from the morning breezes.

"I don't think so—it just seemed that most everything was dirty this week. Don't know when Louise had so many dresses in the wash, and Derek had extra overalls, what with his mishap with the puddle and all. Then there was extra bedding with Sara having Bertha sleep over—and, well, it all just added up I guess."

Thomas nodded and leaned a muscled arm on the table.

Angela stirred the stew again and looked at Thomas. "You want it now—or hot."

"Hot," he answered without hesitation. "The horses need time to feed anyway. And I don't mind sitting a spell myself."

Angela left her spot by the stove and went to take the chair opposite Thomas.

"How's it going?" she asked simply.

"Looks good. Lots of spring moisture. Low places a bit wet yet."

"You going to try some of your new seed?"

Angela had never understood Thomas's love for experimenting with the crops, but she allowed him his pleasure. And she was interested in anything he was doing. Thomas was a very special person in her life—though she had never thought to tell him so.

Thomas nodded, a new sparkle coming to his eyes. "I don't have much, but I plan to plant a bit right out there beside the garden plot."

"Is it warm enough to plant the garden yet?" asked Angela.

"I'll get it ready for you—but I'd give it a few more days. I don't like the feel of the wind today. It could blow in another storm."

Angela could smell the stew and quickly rose to check. A look into the pot showed her that it was bubbling. She stirred it again on the way to the serving bowl she had placed on the table. She could hear the coffee boiling, too, but it was Thomas who moved to lift the pot from the hot stove. Without comment he filled their cups and returned the pot to the back of the stove.

"Mrs. Owens was planting her garden yesterday when I went in to town," Angela commented as she placed the empty stew pot on the cupboard and took her chair at the table.

"Mrs. Owens plants a couple times each spring," replied Thomas, lowering himself to his chair. "She always gets caught by frost. 'No patience,' Papa used to say."

Angela smiled. It was true.

Thomas led them in the table grace.

"I'll be patient," Angela said as she lifted her head.

Thomas passed her the stew and waited while she spooned some onto her plate. Angela knew that Thomas was ravenous after a morning in the field, but he would not serve himself before she was served any more than Papa would have cared for himself before looking after Mama.

"When Derek gets home from school have him check that south fence," Thomas said. "I don't want to take any chances on the cows visiting the neighbors. Grass is still in pretty short supply and grazing might look better to them on the other side of the wire."

Angela nodded.

They talked of common things. Farm life. Neighbors. Needs. They sipped their second cup of coffee, enjoying the flavor and the chance for a rest. Then Thomas lifted his eyes to the wall clock and hoisted himself from his chair.

Angela knew he had given the horses their allotted time to feed and rest and he was ready to resume plowing. She stirred in her chair. She had dishes to do, the wash water to empty, and clothes to iron as soon as the spring breeze had dried the garments hanging on the line. Before she knew it another day would be gone and it would be time for the children to come home from school. They would arrive in a flurry of excitement over the day's events and be looking for a glass of cold milk and a cookie or two and a listening ear as they recounted the day's events.

She watched Thomas lift his cap from the corner peg and

leave the kitchen with long strides. "Don't forget about the fence," he called back over his shoulder.

Angela cleared the table and stacked the dishes in the dishpan. She would take care of the wash water first. But when she went out into the yard she found that Thomas had already emptied the tubs. They were hanging in their proper places on the side of the back porch and the washstand was folded and put against the house. *He is very thoughtful,* Angela mused as she turned back toward the kitchen. The tubs were heavy, especially when they were full, and she was thankful the job had already been done.

As she walked toward the kitchen she felt the clothes on the line and removed a few pieces dry enough for ironing. She would get started on that task after doing the dishes.

Chapter Two

Family

"Guess what?" Louise called before she had even opened the kitchen door.

Angela lifted her head from her ironing, her eyes brightening. She always enjoyed this time of the day when the children came bustling into the kitchen, words tumbling over words as they shared the day's adventures. She didn't have a chance to reply before Louise hurried on.

"Marigold likes Derek."

Angela turned her eyes to Derek. The boy said nothing, but a red tinge began to flush his cheeks. His eyes fell.

"Louise," reprimanded Angela gently, "don't tease."

"Well, it's true. Isn't it, Sara? She tried to sit beside him and everything."

Sara nodded, her pigtails bouncing and a mischievous grin lighting her face.

Poor Derek, thought Angela. *So shy—and now this.*

"Lots of girls like Thomas, too," she countered. "I've watched them at church and at picnics. They try to get his attention in all sorts of ways. There's nothing wrong with having friends."

"But," argued Louise, trying to keep her announcement controversial, "Thomas is growed up."

"Grown up," corrected Angela. "Grown up."

"Derek is still just a kid."

"Kids need friends, too," said Angela in Derek's defense.

"Well—not that kind. Not the kind Marigold wants to be. She smiles silly smiles and rolls her eyes and says, 'Oh-h-h,' like that, and all sorts of silly things."

"Derek is not responsible for the way Marigold acts," Angela said firmly. "He is only responsible for himself. Mama always said that true breeding is shown in how we respond to the foolishness of others," she finished, her voice softer.

Louise lowered her eyes, and Angela noticed the stiffness in her shoulders. She had seen such responses before and they concerned her. There was an attitude of resentment there, as though Angela had somehow managed to spoil a bit of Louise's fun.

Angela's eyes clouded as she placed her flatiron back on the stove and added a few sticks of wood to the fire. It was time to change the subject before doing more harm.

"Get your milk from the icebox," she instructed the children. "Louise, you can get the milk and Sara the glasses. Derek, the cookies are in the blue tin."

All three moved to do as bidden. "Get the big glasses," Louise called to Sara. "I'm really thirsty."

"As soon as you have finished, change your school clothes and care for your chores," Angela went on.

There was silence for a few minutes and then Louise lifted her head and stared at Angela.

"Why do you always say that?" she asked.

"Say what?" asked Angela.

" 'Change your school clothes and care for your chores,' " said Louise, mimicking Angela.

"Because it always needs to be done," Angela responded simply.

"Don't you think we know that? We've been doing it ever since—ever since we started off to school—and I'm in fifth grade now."

Panic began to stir in Angela's breast. Louise had never openly challenged her before, and she wasn't sure how to handle it. Nor, for the first time in her life, was she sure how Mama would have handled it. Was there something in her past that would give her direction? She groped around in her memories for a few minutes and came up empty. She could not remember *ever* having challenged Mama, and none of the others were old enough to defy her Mama when—

"That's naughty," Sara was saying to Louise. "We're s'pose to 'bey Angela."

Louise said nothing, but her eyes challenged Angela further.

Derek shuffled uncomfortably. He hated discord.

"She's not our mama," Louise said in a defiant whisper.

"Well—she—she has to take care of us," Derek managed in a weak voice. "And—and you know what Thomas would say if—if he heard you talking sass."

Louise flipped her braids.

"And Thomas is not our papa," she responded, repeating the challenge.

Derek's face paled. Angela was afraid he might burst into tears or flee the room. She moved over to place a hand quickly on his narrow shoulder. She could feel him trembling under his coarse woolen shirt.

"We don't got a mama and papa anymore," cut in Sara insistently. "Angela and Thomas are all we got."

The comment hung in the air for a moment. A sharp pain stabbed Angela's heart when she realized that this fact did not seem to bother Sara to any great degree. She wondered if young Sara could even remember the father and mother she had lost.

"Louise," said Angela as softly as she could, "go to your room, please. We need to have a talk. I will be in just as soon as Derek and Sara have had their milk and cookies."

Dear God, what will I do if she refuses to obey me? Angela wondered, but to her relief, Louise only gave her an angry look and moved toward the bedroom.

Angela tried to calm her trembling soul as she poured the milk. She had an ordeal ahead of her and she wasn't sure how to handle it. None of the children had ever challenged her authority before. What was she to do—and how often in the future might she need to face the same crisis?

Oh, God, she prayed. *Help me with this. What should I do? I've noticed—I've noticed little hints of tension—but this—this open defiance—I have no idea—*Her voice trembled as she spoke to Derek, "Thomas would like you to check the south fence. He doesn't want the cows getting out. I'll have Louise and Sara help with some of your other chores so you won't be working after dark."

"What do I have to do?" asked Sara.

"Well, you can feed the hens and gather the eggs as usual; then you can help Louise fill the wood box."

"What if Louise doesn't want to?" questioned Sara as she dipped her cookie into her milk.

Angela hesitated. *What if Louise didn't want to?* "Louise is a part of this family," she finally said. "We all must share in the work. I'm afraid she will have to do her share of chores—whether she wants to or not."

Angela delayed her visit to the bedroom as long as she could and then went slowly toward the closed door. She had no idea what she might face when she opened it, and she prayed silently with every step she took. Would Louise still be tossing her blond braids and looking at her with angry eyes? Would she be prostrate on the bed, sobbing for the mother they had lost? Would she have left the room through the opened window and fled to who-knew-where?

But Louise was seated calmly on the chair by the bed reading from her favorite book. She had changed into her chore clothes and her school garments were neatly hung on the pegs on her wall. Her bed was not wrinkled from a bout of crying and her face was not flushed or tear-streaked. She looked quite composed.

"Louise," spoke Angela as she closed the door softly behind her, "I think we need to talk a bit."

Louise nodded.

"Perhaps I do—do tell you over and over again—what I expect you to do. I—I still need to tell Sara. She hasn't—well, hasn't heard it as often as you—and I guess—well, I guess when I am telling one—it is just easier to include all of you."

Louise nodded, no defiance in her eyes now.

"I'm sorry," Angela said softly. "I—I'll try to—to remember that unless—unless it is a new chore—that you are responsible enough to know—to look after your usual duties."

Louise nodded again.

Angela waited for a moment. She didn't want to spoil the calm, but she knew Louise had to be given further instructions.

"Tonight there are some more things to do," she ventured. "Thomas needs Derek to—to check the fence, so Derek won't have time for his usual chores. That means you and Sara must carry the wood and maybe even feed the pigs."

Angela waited. There was no angry stiffening of Louise's back. She simply nodded.

Angela sighed with relief, tears threatening to spill over. She sat down on the bed near her younger sister and took her hand.

"Louise," she said as gently as she could, "you know that when Mama died she—she asked me to care for all of you. I—I told her I would. Now Mama—Mama felt strongly that caring was—was more than putting food on the table—and seeing that your clothes were washed and mended. Mama wants you—each of us—to grow to be strong, good, dependable. Part of that—that growing process comes by sharing chores—and learning obedience. Now I know it won't always be easy to—to have an older sister be your—your authority but—"

Louise stirred on her cushioned seat.

"But that's the way it is," continued Angela. "Not by our choosing, but that's the way it is."

Louise lowered her head, the tears forming in her eyes trickling down her soft cheeks. She sniffed, lifted her eyes, and nodded. That was all. Just a slight nod of her head. But Angela knew that for now it was enough. She gave her sister a hug and stood up.

"Your milk and cookies are on the table," she began, then quickly bit her lip before she followed the statement with what chores needed to be done afterward.

Louise got to her feet and dried her eyes.

She is still such a child, Angela thought as she watched her. Her heart ached for the young girl.

In typical youthful fashion, Louise gave her big sister a smile, seeming to have already forgotten the battle of a few moments before, and bounded off to the kitchen for her snack.

And don't run, Angela almost called after her. *A lady does not—*

But Louise was not a lady. She was still a little girl of eleven. Playful and careless. And with so very much to learn. "Oh, God," breathed Angela as she sank down onto the bed again and lifted a trembling hand to her face. "How am I ever going to be able to teach them all they need to know? All that Mama would want them to know? Will I ever be able to make a lady out of Louise? Of Sara? Will I be able to teach them about you? Will Thomas be able to fill in for the father Derek needs? Oh, God, we need an awful lot of help."

Chapter Three

Memories

"Something bothering you?"

Angela turned her head to look at Thomas through the soft darkness settling in about them as they sat on the veranda. She had hoped her worries had not shown, but she should have known that Thomas would realize she was anxious about something.

"It's Louise," sighed Angela. "I think she is missing Mama. It's almost as if she misses her more now than—"

Thomas nodded in understanding, then swatted a mosquito that had landed on his bare forearm.

"In what way?" he asked.

"Tonight when I spoke to her about her chores, she—she said I wasn't her mama." Angela couldn't keep the tremor from her voice.

"Did she do her chores?" asked Thomas.

Angela wondered if he was about to waken the young girl out of a sound sleep to make sure she had done her work properly.

"Oh yes. Her fuss didn't last long—then she was sweet as can be. But—well—it just troubles me. What are we going to do if she decides she doesn't want to do our bidding? I mean—if Papa was here—he required obedience with one stern look. But what if—?"

"She hasn't done this before, has she?"

"No. But I'm just scared that it might be the first of many. She is growing up, you know—and she has always—well—had a mind of her own."

"You want me to talk to her?"

"Oh no."

"Do you want me to punish her? Give her an extra chore or—"

"Oh my, no," cut in Angela quickly. "She doesn't need more punishment. She's already lost her mama."

After a moment of silence, Thomas answered through the spreading darkness, "We have all lost our mama."

"I—I know," Angela said with a trembling voice, "but I think it is harder on the younger ones."

There was another short silence, and Thomas, again, was the one to break it. "It has been three years," he said softly. "They should be sorta—well—getting used to it now."

"That's what frightens me," Angela admitted. "I always—we always thought it would get easier—with the passing of time and all. But it hasn't. I mean, when they were little it was just a case of feeding them and looking after their clothes and—and loving them a lot. Now—now I have a feeling that all those years without Mama to guide them—to show them how to be ladies, to teach them how to treat others, how to show respect and obedience—that's what they've missed, Thomas."

"You've been giving them that," Thomas assured Angela. "Why, at the last church picnic I heard some of the ladies talking about what fine kids they are and what good manners they have and—" Angela was pleased to hear the comment, but she knew that much more than "please" and "thank you" was involved in properly raising children.

"They have proper conduct—on the outside. At least I think they have," Angela agreed. "But on the inside? All the things Mama taught—about thinking of others—about not letting little hurts make one into a snob or complainer—about seeing beauty in simple things—about—about so many things. I'm afraid I haven't been getting some of those lessons across to the girls. I—I'm not even sure how Mama did it. I just know that those thoughts—those feelings are there—deep inside of me— and they came from Mama."

Angela laid a quivering hand over her heart and blinked away tears that wanted to fall. At length she was able to go on.

"I was old enough to understand—to remember those lessons—but I'm afraid Louise and Sara won't remember. Mama was too sick those last months to be able to—to—"

Angela could go no further. Thomas touched her hand briefly in the darkness. They sat silently together, listening to the croaking of the frogs in the pond beyond the barn. An owl hooted into the night. Then a cow bawled somewhere off in the distance and another replied somewhere beyond.

"You're doing a fine job, Angela," Thomas said hoarsely. "I'm proud of the girls and of Derek."

"I am, too," Angela admitted. "But I worry. I want so much for them to grow up to be—to be the children Mama would have been proud of."

"They will," said Thomas with confidence. "They will."

Angela made no reply but her brow still puckered with concern. Would they? Louise was already showing defiance. True, her little bit of fuss hadn't lasted for more than a few minutes, but what would come next? Would she again be telling Angela that she didn't have to accept her authority?

And what of Sara? She was such a carefree, sweet little darling. But she was about as wild and uncontrolled as a prairie mustang. Mama had always wanted her daughters to be little ladies, with clean pinafores, carefully manicured fingernails, neatly braided hair, skirts arranged tidily over properly crossed ankles. Sara never seemed to remember—or care about any of those things, though Angela was sure she had told her about each of them at least a hundred times.

"I do worry about Derek sometimes." Thomas broke in on her thoughts through the darkness.

Angela's head came up quickly. "What do you mean?" she asked. "What's he done? He's never given me a moment's trouble."

"That's just it," responded Thomas thoughtfully. "When I was his age—well, I was giving both Papa and Mama a bit of trouble."

"You—?"

"Don't you remember the number of times I was sent to my room or had to carry extra wood or miss a ball game? Boy, I was always in trouble of some kind."

Angela smiled. It was true. Thomas had been in hot water a good deal of the time.

"Well, Mama and Papa knew how to manage it," Angela said, feeling that it gave strength to her argument. "But how will we—?"

"The same way, I guess," Thomas cut in. "The youngsters need discipline—even if they haven't got a mother or father."

"I'm afraid it's going to be so hard. I mean—I don't mind

cooking and cleaning. I think I have done a fair job of that. But, Thomas—I'm not sure I am quite so good at—at mothering."

She could hear his soft chuckle. "Well, you are a mite young to be doing it," he reminded her. "At seventeen most girls aren't married yet—let alone mothers of half-grown kids."

"Yes—and most young men of nineteen aren't responsible for a family of five, either," replied Angela. "You've been running the farm for three years. Well, four really. You had to take over even before Mama—"

Angela stopped. It was too difficult to say the words, even now. She wrapped her hands in her apron and let the conversation become thoughts.

It had all been so strange. So ironic. They had moved west because her mother had not been well and the doctor said that the cooler, clear air of the region might be easier on her lungs. Her father had sold his productive Iowa farm and loaded everything they could take with them in three wagons.

The trip had been a real adventure. Angela still had many memories of it, but the younger children could remember virtually nothing of the move west.

Thomas remembered, of course, because he was older than Angela. And the stories he told about the trip revealed that, to him, it had been an adventure of a lifetime.

They had found new land—a new life—and their father had set about building a farm again. He put all his strength and energy into building the house and barns. Into erecting straight, even fences. Into plowing land to prepare it for seed. Into clearing rock and planting a windbreak.

The farm soon responded, taking on the well-cared-for look of their previous one. Her father was a good farmer, a hardworking man, and soon the farm was the most productive, most attractive one in the area.

Her mother's health did improve—at least for a while. She seemed to breathe more easily, seemed to have more energy in her slight frame. And then a winter cold put her back in bed and the family watched as she gradually lost ground in her long fight for health. But even from her bed she continued to guide her family. Angela remembered the long talks, the careful instructions. Looking back she realized now that her mother had been grooming her for the task ahead, but Angela had not been aware of it at the time. It was so easy for her to pretend that her mother would soon be well again, that things would return to normal.

But it was their strong, healthy father who left them first. An aneurysm, the doctor had said, shaking his head sadly. "We never know when they might strike—or whom. Sometimes they pick the most unlikely."

So it was Thomas who first had to shoulder the responsibilities of an adult. Thomas—at age sixteen—took over all the farm duties.

Their father had taught him well. He was a hard worker, and a built-in pride drove him to try to maintain things just as his father had always done. The farm had repaid him. Though no one could have thought of them as wealthy, they had never been in want.

Seven short months later, their mother also slipped away from them. At the last Angela had the feeling that Mama was almost eager to join her husband, though she did put up a long, hard fight to live for the sake of her children. The days before her passing were spent in long talks whenever Angela's duties allowed a little free time. The three younger children were all in school. Angela envied them at first. She'd had to give up classes to help at home. Her mother had sensed how she felt and made sure to provide books so Angela could continue learning. But as her mother's condition worsened, Angela had no time for reading or studying.

And then her mother was gone. She was laid to rest beside their father on the green knoll by the little church. Thomas and Angela were now solely responsible for their three siblings. They never questioned their lot. There was a task to be done and they put their time and attention into doing it.

———

Angela stirred. The spring evening was getting cool, and she knew they should go in. Tomorrow would be another long day. She still felt an uneasiness within her. Now she was not only worried about Louise and Sara, Thomas had unwittingly added Derek to her list of concerns.

"About Derek," she said slowly, "what exactly are you worried about?"

"Well, he's just so—so quiet. He never speaks what's on his mind. I'm just afraid he might be dwelling more on Pa—or Mama—being gone than we realize."

Angela had not thought of that before. It was true that Derek was quiet—pensive. He was always most cooperative, but perhaps that was not always a true sign of how he was feeling.

"Maybe he needs more boy fun," suggested Angela. "Remember when you were his age? You were always off fishing. Or playing ball. Or chasing frogs or—or hunting bird nests or something."

Thomas nodded.

"Well, Derek never does any of those things."

"I know," said Thomas. "He's more like a little old man than a boy."

Angela had never seen it that way before. Now she realized Thomas was right.

"What can we do?" she wondered out loud.

"I've been thinking. Maybe I should take him fishing—or something."

Angela unfolded her tense hands and reached out to touch Thomas's sleeve.

"That's a wonderful idea!" she exclaimed. "When?"

"Well, I don't know—exactly. I've got to get the crop in and then—"

"Thomas, I don't think you should wait. Not until you have everything done. You know how it is. On a farm there is always something that needs doing. You'll never find the time if you wait for it all to be done."

"Well, I can't just up and leave the work while I run off to—"

"Why? Why not? The kids are more important than anything else. I know that's what Mama would say. She would want you to go. At least for a couple of days—even an afternoon if that's all you can manage. We need to be—to be putting first things first. I mean—what good is the farm if—?"

"Maybe I can take an afternoon," said Thomas.

"This Saturday," Angela prompted, the idea filling her with excitement. She was sure Derek would be pleased.

"This Saturday? I was planning to plow up your garden Saturday afternoon," replied Thomas.

"It can wait. Like you said, there's no reason to get impatient."

"This Saturday then. Hope the weather stays good. No fun fishing in the rain."

Nothing much had changed. There was still the problem of

responsibility. Angela still faced the need for mothering a brother and two sisters. But somehow just this one small planned action lifted the anxiety from her heart. At least they were planning. They were trying to do more than just feed and clothe their siblings. And it wasn't her alone. She had Thomas to help her, to share the responsibilities. For some reason her load had lifted as she stood and turned back to the lighted kitchen.

"I must take more time to do things with the girls," she said, more to herself than to Thomas as he held the door open for her. "All I have been doing is handing out orders. Do this. Don't do that. They need time to be children."

"Children, yes," agreed Thomas, "but responsible children."

"That's what scares me. It is my job to make sure that's what they are."

"You're doing fine."

"But I need to—to find ways to teach them. Encourage them. Just like Mama did with me."

Thomas let a hand drop to her shoulder. "Don't be too hard on yourself, Angie," he cautioned. "Don't set the standards impossibly high. You're human, too, you know."

Angela was very aware of that as she picked up the lamp to light her way to her bedroom. Thomas had turned to bolt the door behind them. In the semidarkness he looked like her pa standing there. She had never noticed the likeness before. Her pa would be so proud. So proud of his son. But Thomas had been almost raised before they had lost their parents. If only— if only she could bring the others up to deserve family pride, too. If only they would grow up to be responsible members of society. If only they grew up to love God and belong to His family . . .

Chapter Four

Neighbors

There had been disagreement among the people in the community as to what should be done with the Peterson children when they lost their parents. The Blackwells, to the north of the Peterson farm, had never been blessed with a family of their own, but that did not prevent Mrs. Blackwell from expressing very decided opinions about the children.

"They need caring for," she stated, "by adults who are responsible." She suggested that the children be divided among district families and that she and her husband take Sara and Derek. When Thomas stated firmly that they had no intention of parcelling the children out here and there, Mrs. Blackwell changed her mind as to what should be done.

"Iffen they are to be responsible citizens," she maintained, "then they need to do their own caring. I don't plan to be a caterin' to 'em."

And she didn't.

"No use fussin' over 'em. They've made them their jam. Now let 'em eat it."

But Mr. Blackwell apparently didn't share his wife's view. On occasion he was seen delivering a sack of seed potatoes to the Petersons or making sure they had enough coal in the bin.

The Petersons' closest neighbor was a sour man who lived on his own. From outward appearances, he may not even have known the Peterson family existed, or that they were left on their own. He was not old—nor was he young. His face was weathered from being outdoors riding herd on his cattle or supervising maintenance and repairs on his property. He was not popular in the neighborhood, but no one spoke of it much. He was far too rich and powerful for anyone to risk getting on his bad side. Only his hired hand, Charlie, who acted as foreman of the spread, seemed able to get along with the crusty Mr. Stratton. Angela wondered if perhaps it was because Charlie was the only one who had known his boss long enough to be aware of the circumstances that had shaped him.

"Oh, he ain't so bad as all thet," Charlie would say. "He barks a lot, but I ain't seen him bite yet."

Charlie, in his own quiet way, was more help to the Peterson youngsters than anyone else in the neighborhood. In the evenings, after completing his daily rounds, he would slip over to their house. Sometimes he brought things from town, sometimes he gave hints as to how Thomas should plant or plow. Sometimes he just came to chat and to see that everything was going all right. Those first years would have been awfully difficult without Charlie.

The pastor was supportive—but he was a very busy man. He shouldered the burdens of the congregation as well as his own young family.

The Reverend Merrifield had lost his first wife and then married again, a fine widow with a family of her own. The new marriage had given them a family of eight. His Roger, Ernest, and Lucy, and her Peter, Pauline, and Perry. To that number had been added little Priscilla and Pearl. In addition to the confusion of so many in one household, there was also a bit of friction between the oldest sons. One of the conflicts, unknown to Angela, involved her. Both boys spent a good deal of time lobbying for position to get a bit of her attention. Roger was eighteen and Peter seventeen. Most folks thought they should have been out on their own by now, providing the family with income, but they lived at home, doing only odd jobs here and there as they were able to find them in town.

There were families in the church who expressed concern about the Petersons. The Conroys, who were neighboring farmers to the west, spoke frequently about their intentions to give a hand here and there. Occasionally they did, but their own field work and gardens took so much time that little was left for the Petersons. They did, however, faithfully remember the children in their daily prayers. The Conroys had a family of their own to consider. Hazel, nineteen, was a friendly enough girl, but being older than Angela, she had always seemed to feel a bit superior as well, and now that she was making preparations for her coming marriage, she acted queenly indeed. Roberta was Angela's age and might have been a real companion had she not been severely handicapped because of a serious case of measles at age three. Angela would gladly have offered her friendship, but Roberta preferred to play with young children. Ingrid and Bertha Conroy were good friends of Louise and Sara, wanting to spend more time at one another's houses than their own.

The Sommerses also attended the local church, and their daughter, Trudie, was Angela's age. It was accepted by the church members that Trudie was Angela's best friend, but the truth was, Angela was not sure about Trudie. At times Trudie gushed and fussed, at other times she seemed to pass Angela by without even a nod of acknowledgement. Trudie tended to be peacock-proud, tossing her reddish mane with snobbish abandon, and about as flighty as a barn swallow. She was always getting herself into some kind of tizzy about something. But the church folk were often heard to say with deep feeling, "It's so nice that Angela has Trudie."

Angela tried to be friendly to Trudie. After all, she was the only girl her own age with whom to associate. And Angela was in need of an understanding companion. Yet she hesitated to share anything important with Trudie. She was never sure that her secret thoughts or feelings would be kept secret for long.

The Sommerses had three other children. Claude, thirteen, was Derek's age, and was kind and considerate. Angela regarded Claude as one of the finest young boys she knew and was happy to encourage friendship between him and her little brother. But for reasons Angela could not determine, Derek held himself back from forming close friendships.

Then there were Baxter, nine, and Wylie, eight. Sara was constantly being teased and taunted by the school children about one or the other, so Baxter and Wylie were off limits as a topic of conversation in the Peterson household.

The dearest and closest friends of the Peterson family were the Andrewses. Mr. Andrews operated the town mercantile, the store where Angela did the family shopping. He was a soft-spoken man, as good at living out his religion as declaring it. There were few people who could have found anything disparaging to say about Mr. Andrews—they would have needed to embellish it with untruths. He was not interfering, but each member of the Peterson family knew that if ever a need arose, Mr. Andrews was the man to whom they should go.

Mrs. Andrews was a motherly woman who had little to say but whose smile welcomed everyone. And her instincts seemed always to be right. She passed out cookies and hugs with abandon. Even Thomas, big and strapping as he was, accepted his share, and Angela felt that some of her days were made endurable because of the embrace of the kind woman.

The Andrews family had not escaped sorrow. Their daughter Emma had been Angela's best friend before the girl had drowned in a tragic accident when the girls were nine. Perhaps that was another reason Mrs. Andrews used any occasion to hold Angela close for a moment.

There were three others in the family. Frankie, their youngest, was nine, and Agnes a grown-up twelve, but of the Andrews family it was Thane who was the dearest friend of the Petersons.

Thane was the same age as Thomas, and the two boys were as close as brothers. They had spent much of their earlier years fishing or hiking together. Angela remembered many times they had stayed at the other's house. It was Thane with Thomas or Thomas with Thane. But Karl Peterson's sudden death changed that greatly. Thomas was no longer free to be a carefree lad, off on nature hikes or overnight campouts. In that instant he became a farmer, responsible for the welfare of a family. So now it was up to Thane to come their way—and he did—often—bringing sacks of penny candy, a bright red "spinner" for fishing, or new hair ribbons for the girls tucked in his pocket.

And so life went on for the Peterson children, even though some days were heavy with sorrow and others weighted with responsibility. Although the neighbors occasionally reached out a loving or helping hand, for the most part the young people were assumed to be capable of caring for themselves.

Chapter Five

Party

"Angela, wait."

Angela recognized the voice of Trudie Sommers. She turned and pushed back her bonnet to wait for her friend.

The girl was running toward Angela, skirts and ribbons flying out behind her.

"Don't run," called Angela. "It's too hot. I'll wait."

Trudie slowed to a walk, but at a brisk, excited pace.

Angela leaned over and put her parcel of groceries on the grass. Then she straightened again and brushed curls of blond hair from her face.

"I thought I'd missed you," gasped Trudie, finally reaching Angela. "Mrs. Layton said you would be halfway home."

Angela laughed. "I should have been—but I stopped to see the new Willis baby."

"Isn't she a darling?" said Trudie somewhat distractedly.

" 'She' is a 'he,' " Angela smiled.

"Oh yes, well," Trudie replied, then quickly changed the subject. "I wanted to let you know that I am having a party on Saturday night."

"A party?" Angela couldn't remember when she had last been to a party.

"I'd like you to come," Trudie hurried to say.

"What kind of a party?" asked Angela.

"Just some friends. We'll play party games and—and eat," she laughed.

It sounded wonderful to Angela. With all her heart she wished she could go.

"I'd love to but—"

"No buts," cut in Trudie. "Everyone thinks you need to get out and have a little fun. You're only seventeen, you know. Not seventy."

"Yes, but—" Angela stopped. Trudie was right. She did need a little fun. She wondered if she even knew how to have fun anymore.

"I'll see if Thomas will stay with the kids," she said, but then noticed the disappointed expression on Trudie's face.

"I was hoping Thomas would be able to come, too," Trudie said.

Angela was quick to sense the circumstances. Perhaps Thomas was the real target of the invitation. She had seen a number of young women from town watching Thomas. Some were quite bold in their nods and smiles. Angela felt sure that her mama would not have approved of such forwardness.

"I'll see," Angela promised. "I'll talk it over with Thomas."

Trudie's lips formed a smile again. "Good," she responded. "I'll be expecting you." She turned to leave, and Angela hoisted the heavy package and headed toward home.

All the way Angela thought about the invitation. She couldn't remember the last time she and Thomas had been to a party. She wondered if Thomas would accept. He had already taken one afternoon from his work to go fishing with Derek.

"I wonder if Thomas will agree," mused Angela. "And if he does, what will we do with the children?"

The rest of the day was busy for Angela. She forgot about the party until after the children were tucked into bed for the night. As she and Thomas spent a few minutes on the veranda before retiring, she remembered the invitation.

"Oh, I 'most forgot," Angela began. "We had an invitation to a party today."

Thomas laughed.

"It's Saturday night. Just neighborhood friends. Games and food."

Thomas chuckled again. "What makes folks think we have time for partying?" he asked.

"It would be fun to go," Angela ventured.

"You can go if you want to," Thomas said quickly.

"You won't go?"

"I'm not much into partying," he replied.

"How do you know?" asked Angela. "I don't remember you trying it."

Thomas just shrugged.

"Trudie said—" Angela saw Thomas's head lift and knew he was waiting for her to go on.

"Trudie said that she hoped you would be able to come, too."

Thomas shrugged again, but Angela noticed something different about the movement. He was no longer laughing. He seemed to be considering the invitation.

"Will you?" asked Angela.

"Might not hurt—this once," responded Thomas lightly.

"What will we do with the kids?"

Thomas looked surprised at the mention of the children. After a few moments of thought he responded. "Guess it wouldn't hurt none for them to stay alone for a few hours. After all, they aren't babies anymore. You and I were almost running things by the time we were their age."

The suggestion troubled Angela. She found it hard to believe that the children were old enough to be left alone. Still, she must not coddle them, she reasoned. Papa had always been one to give added responsibility as age increased.

"Maybe so—if we aren't gone too long," she said hesitantly.

And so it was decided that Thomas and Angela would accept the invitation to the Sommerses' party. They gave careful instructions to the three children about what would be expected of them "on their own."

"Why can't I go?" fussed Louise.

"The party is for—for older people," responded Angela, trying to keep her voice firm yet gentle.

"Well, I don't think it's fair," Louise continued, but a stern look from Thomas made her fall silent.

"I'll have a party for some of your friends," Angela put in quickly. "I promise. We'll plan it together."

"When?" asked Louise.

"Just as soon as the garden is planted," replied Angela.

"Sure—you just want me to help with the garden," Louise accused.

"You always help with the garden," Angela returned evenly.

"Well, you want me to do more. More than my rightful share. You think that I'll—"

"Louise," said Thomas sternly, and Louise left the room before saying anymore.

Angela looked at Thomas. "Let her go," she whispered. "She's having a hard time growing up. I—I just don't know quite how to help her."

———

When the night of the party arrived Angela held her breath in case Thomas backed out at the last minute, but he didn't. Angela noticed his fussing over his shoes and hair. He spent more time before the kitchen basin slicking down his wayward cowlick than Angela spent pinning up her own tresses.

Angela tried not to let him see that she was noticing his lengthy grooming, but she did wonder about it.

They walked the road together and cut across the neighbors' field to speed their progress. Thomas had a hard time slowing his stride to accommodate his sister. Angela had never seen him so eager before.

Perhaps he has been missing fun, she reasoned, wondering why he had never shared with her how he felt.

Trudie met them at the gate. She reached a hand to Angela, but it was Thomas who got her full attention.

"I'm so glad you could come," she said, her voice soft and warm, and Angela felt a funny little prick of fear running up her spine.

Trudie out to win Thomas? Could it be? *It was Thomas she wanted all along,* Angela suddenly realized. *She didn't care about me at all. She just wanted me to get Thomas here.*

Angela felt betrayed. Rejected. And terribly annoyed with Trudie—even with Thomas. Thomas was smiling back at Trudie. He even allowed her to take his arm and draw him toward the circle of neighborhood friends. Angela seemed to have been forgotten. It occurred to her that she could just hoist her skirts above the dust of the roadway and make her way directly back home. She was about to do so when she felt someone take hold of her arm. She was hardly in the mood to be civil, much less friendly. Who else besides Trudie might treat her as if she were some mindless dolt—like Thomas suddenly seemed to have become?

"Glad you could come," said a voice at her side, and Angela recognized it immediately. *It's just Thane,* she thought, relieved.

"Thank you," she said, but her troubled thoughts made it difficult to control her voice.

She didn't try to pull her arm away, though. If Thomas

wasn't planning to be with her it would be a comfort to have Thane nearby.

Her eyes still followed Trudie and Thomas. Trudie's silly laugh floated across the yard, and she was hanging on to Thomas's arm as though her life depended on it. The part that bothered Angela was that Thomas did not seem to object.

What if Trudie was successful in wooing Thomas? Who would run the farm? Help raise the children? Angela cast a nervous look at the bubbling girl. Surely Thomas would see through the ploy, would let Trudie know in no uncertain terms that he was not interested.

But Thomas was still smiling at Trudie and responding to her playful glances with animated conversation.

Thane carefully guided Angela toward a small group of young people. Some of them were from church, and before Angela had time to think further about her concerns, she was included in the circle and made to feel welcome. Now and then throughout the evening she stole a glance at Thomas. Each time, Trudie was not far from his side. Angela tried to push aside the nagging fear. Thomas belonged to the family. He was hers. Had always been hers. They had been together ever since their pa and ma had left them. They bolstered each other, encouraged each other, cheered each other. If she should lose Thomas, she wasn't sure she would be able to carry on.

"Care for a sandwich?" Thane was asking.

Angela's thoughts jerked back to the moment and she tried to smile.

"I'm really not very hungry," she managed, shaking her head.

Thane accepted her reply and took a seat beside her. He passed her the sandwich he had just offered her and winked. "If you don't want it, would you mind holding it for me until I'm done with this one?" he asked.

Angela couldn't help but smile. She held the sandwich as she watched the group of merrymakers before her, then took a bite to Thane's approving nod. Everyone seemed to be having such fun. For a moment she felt cheated that she wasn't able to wholeheartedly join them. But her thoughts kept going back to Thomas, then to the children at home.

What am I doing here? she asked herself. *These people don't have a care in the world. Not one of them knows what it's like to*

*have full responsibility for a family. I shouldn't be partying. I
have long since forgotten how.*

Thane was speaking to her. It took a moment for the meaning to make sense to her. Could he get her anything? He was
going to get another sandwich "since you have eaten mine," he
teased. As she shook her head, she noticed the concern in his
eyes.

"Something wrong?" he asked. "You're a million miles away."

Angela managed a smile and stirred restlessly on her log
seat. "I guess I'm just not much good at partying," she replied.
"I—I keep thinking of the kids at home."

"Want me to walk you back?" he asked. "No need for ol' Tom
to leave yet. He seems to be having himself a great time."

Angela could hear the chuckle in Thane's voice. He didn't
seem to have any problem with the way Thomas was carrying
on.

" 'Ol' Tom,' " she said with emphasis, "should remember that
he needs to be up early in the morning to have the chores done
in time for church."

"I reckon Tom won't be forgetting that," replied Thane easily.
"Never known him to miss church—or chores—yet."

Thane was the only one who ever called her brother Tom. Angela didn't know why. Everyone else called Thomas by his given
name. Why Thane chose not to use it—and why Thomas never
seemed to object—she had no idea.

Angela really did want to go, yet she hated to be the one to
break up the party.

"Well," she said, "it has been fun—but all good things must
end, they say." She tried to sound light and carefree like the
others about her.

"You're really going now?" asked Thane.

"I think we should. We have been gone long enough. Would
you mind telling Thomas that I'm ready to go?"

Thane nodded his head and went to speak to him. Angela
was sure that Thomas, when he heard she was leaving the
party, would quickly get her wrap and escort her home.

But it didn't happen that way. Thomas looked her direction
for a moment, gave her a careless wave of his hand, then spoke
to Thane again.

It was Thane who arrived with her wrap. Thomas was still
chatting with a group of young people. Trudie was near him,

though not leaning on his arm as she had been so often during the evening.

"Ready?" asked Thane as he settled the wrap about her shoulders.

Angela allowed Thane to lead her from the group. Laughter followed them as they walked down the lane, and Angela wondered how much longer the party would continue.

"Good thing there is a full moon," Thane observed. "It's easier to see the way."

"Oh, I expect that Trudie calculated well," Angela responded moodily. "She would have been sure to order a full moon."

Thane seemed puzzled by her comment but made no reply. After a few attempts at light conversation, Thane let Angela walk in silence. Occasionally he reached out a hand to help her over some rough ground. She accepted without protest. She was almost as used to Thane as to Thomas. He had always been Thomas's best friend. He spent almost as much time at their house as did her own family. He was as comfortable to be with as Derek. Angela did not pay much attention one way or the other.

But Thane knew her well.

"You're angry about something," he stated when they reached the porch. "Not just worried about the kids—but angry. What happened?"

Angela's chin began to quiver in spite of her attempt to still it.

"Did you see Trudie?" she hissed, squaring her shoulders. "She was—was hanging on to Thomas like—like she owned him."

Thane's answer came with a soft chuckle. "Maybe she would like to."

"Well, she'd better—better back off."

"Why?" Thane asked mildly. "I didn't see Tom objecting."

"Well, he should have. We—we need him here—with us. He—he isn't—"

"Wait a minute," said Thane, taking Angela by the shoulders. "Do I hear you right? Are you saying that you expect ol' Tom to—to just lay life aside and give all of his years to you?"

"Not me," choked Angela. "Not me. The kids need—"

"Angela," Thane broke in seriously, "there might come a day when Tom will choose a life of his own. He deserves that. He has already postponed his own dreams. Is it right to expect him to just forget about all of that—forever?"

Angela shivered. She wanted to lay her head against Thane's shoulder and let the tears fall, but she didn't.

"*I*—I have to," she told him, her voice trembling.

There was silence for a moment; then Thane answered slowly.

"For now," he said. "For now. But may God grant that it might not always be so."

He kissed her forehead gently, and quietly slipped into the night. Angela watched him retreat until he was lost in the shadows; then she turned to the door. Too many emotions were fighting for her attention. She was still angry with Trudie—and with Thomas, though Thane was right. Thomas deserved a life of his own. But what about the children? Who would care for them if Thomas left? And who would share her burden? And what had Thane meant? It would be years before the children were grown and on their own. Angela had no thoughts for anything but the task that still lay ahead of her. She had to raise them properly—for Mama.

Chapter Six

The Game

Angela did not rest well. Thoughts of Thomas deserting the family kept spinning in her head. When she finally fell into a restless sleep, she dreamed she had been split in two and one side was arguing ferociously with the other.

"He can't leave us for some—some pretty face."

"He deserves a chance for a life of his own."

"But we need him far more than she does."

"What if he's not happy here? Do you still think he should stay?"

"We need him. We need him" seemed to be the endless refrain. Angela awoke in a sweat, heart pounding. She wasn't sure which of the two sides had been the real Angela—or maybe they both were.

She was pale and withdrawn as she prepared the morning porridge. The children, in their usual blustery fashion, did not seem to notice that anything was bothering her, which Angela was thankful for. She did feel Derek's eyes upon her once or twice, but he asked no questions.

Thomas seemed even brighter than usual. He whistled his way in from milking the cows and teased the youngsters at the breakfast table.

"Did you have fun at the party?" asked Sara brightly. She tossed back her curls that Angela had formed to go with her Sunday frock.

Thomas answered enthusiastically, "Sure did."

"What did you do?" Sara asked next.

Thomas tipped his head to one side as though thinking

deeply. "Funny thing," he observed at last. "I don't recall doing much of anything."

"Aw, Thomas. Tell us. Don't be mean," pleaded Sara.

Louise was sitting silently by, picking little bites from her toast and eating them one by one. She still was cross that she hadn't been allowed to attend the party.

Derek seemed totally oblivious to the conversation, as though he were sitting all alone at the breakfast table.

Angela was not pleased with the discussion. She wanted, with all her heart, to blurt out that Thomas had spent the entire evening making a fool of himself in the company of Trudie Sommers. But even as the accusation formed in her mind she knew it was unfair. Thomas had been mannerly and proper. He had simply been a young man enjoying an evening with friends. Nobody, not even Papa or Mama, would have faulted Thomas on his behavior. No one, that is, but his frightened sister.

"C'mon," Sara coaxed. "Tell us what it was like."

"Well, let's see," began Thomas, more serious now. "We played a few games. We talked a lot. We sang a few songs."

Angela's eyes widened. There had been no singing while she was there. She loved to sing. She might have enjoyed the party more if she had participated in the songfest.

Thomas hesitated for just a moment. His eyes lifted to meet Angela's.

"That was after Angela had come home to check on you. She couldn't really enjoy the party for worrying that you were all right. We all missed her soprano in the singing. Several people asked about her."

Angela turned back to the stove. She felt cheated. No one had told her they were planning to sing.

"What else?" asked Sara.

Louise had quit picking at her toast and was listening, but Derek still had not joined the conversation.

"Well—we ate. We ate lots. There was popcorn and gingerbread and chocolate cake with some kind of crispy stuff on top. Angela, you should ask Trudie for that recipe. It was good. Um-m-m," said Thomas, giving his head a shake for emphasis.

Angela had no intention of asking Trudie Sommers for anything. Besides, if things went as Trudie was planning, Thomas could be eating the famous chocolate cake with crispy stuff on top for the rest of his life, Angela reasoned.

"Louise," she said almost sternly, "I believe it is your turn to wash the breakfast dishes. Sara, you dry. And Derek," her voice softened automatically, "I need another block of ice from the ice house."

She saw Derek's nod. He shoved the rest of his toast into his mouth, emptied his milk glass and rose from the table.

Angela was about to remind him to excuse himself when his eyes met hers for just a moment. She thought she saw pain in them. She closed her lips on the words and looked away. She could not bear to gaze so openly into the boy's anguished soul.

As the door shut behind Derek, Angela's attention was caught by Thomas's words.

"And Trudie says we should get together more often." Thomas was continuing his report.

With an angry flip of her hand, Angela dropped the roast into the pot with a loud noise. "I'll just bet she did," she said under her breath, but no one seemed to notice her anger.

"Well, I suppose the others might have another party—but me—I told her I appreciated the offer but I had work that needed doing."

Angela wondered if she heard disappointment in Thomas's voice. A feeling of sympathy tugged at her heart. She could not understand herself. How could she feel angry at Thomas one minute and sorry for him the next? She was so mixed up. She hoped with all her heart that the church service would help her get her thoughts untangled.

———

Angela returned from church having regained a measure of serenity. She still felt concern about rearing her siblings. She still felt a quiver of fear that Thomas might leave them for a life of his own, but she had balanced all of that with the fact that God did truly care about the Peterson family. Surely she didn't bear the burden of their welfare alone.

I must remember that, she chastised herself. If there ever was a lesson Mama emphasized it was that God loves them and would care for them. They only needed to trust Him.

The conversation around the dinner table that noon was of the usual sort. They spoke of the things they had heard that morning. They shared little stories about friends. Even Louise laughed at Thomas's silly jokes and joined in plans of "we should" or "could we?"

In fact, it seemed to Angela that things were back to normal again, and she began to wonder why she had allowed herself to get into such a stew.

Their talk turned to childhood remembrances.

"Remember," she joined in, "when Mama fixed us that little picnic and we ate it out in the yard under the bed sheets?"

Thomas nodded, his eyes sparkling with merriment at the memory, but three pairs of eyes looked blank.

"She pinned the sheets up to the clothesline," explained Thomas, "and then Pooch, that big oaf of a dog, came tearing around the corner of the house, afraid of the old sow or something, and ran smack into the side of it. It came down off the line and wrapped all around him and he ran off yapping, with that sheet flapping out behind him, like he thought the world was coming to an end."

Angela and Thomas laughed until their sides ached.

"And remember the time Mama made those cookies with the great big eyes and funny looks?" Thomas added. "Sad faces, happy faces, frowning faces, surprised faces. Then she put them on a plate and offered each of us one. We all picked a happy face. Remember? And then she said, 'Oh, look. You have all chosen a happy face. I guess everyone prefers a face that is happy. No one wants the sad or angry face. Let's change the rest.' And she did. Then she let us eat them."

Angela nodded. Her mama had been so skillful at getting across simple lessons. If only Angela knew how to do it.

"And remember the time she walked with us to the creek to show us—"

"Mama walked?" cut in Sara, her eyes big with wonder.

Both Angela and Thomas turned to look at her.

"What do you mean?" asked Angela.

"I didn't know Mama could walk."

"Of course she could walk."

"All I 'member is her being in bed or sometimes in a chair," continued Sara.

Tears came to Angela's eyes. She had worried that the younger children were forgetting their mother—had not had as many years to glean memories as she and Thomas had enjoyed. But she had not realized just how much they had been denied.

"You don't remember?" she asked.

Sara answered by shaking her head.

"You don't remember having Mama in the kitchen fixing

after-school snacks? You don't remember the walks through her garden? You don't remember taking her hand to see the new calf?"

With each question Sara continued shaking her head.

"I remember a little bit," broke in Louise. "I remember the color of her hair. I even remember Papa calling it 'spun gold.' I remember her apron with the big pockets. And I remember one time when I scratched my knee and she fixed it—then she rocked me and sang me a song—about little birdies or something. I forget that part."

Angela was disturbed that her sisters had so few memories of their wonderful mother. No wonder it was so difficult for her to pass along to them all the lessons of proper conduct and correct attitudes. There was no base there, built solidly by their mama.

"Do you remember Mama?" Angela asked, turning to look at Derek. The boy did not lift his eyes from his plate but nodded slightly. Angela saw him swallow. Her eyes misted as she wondered just what memories Derek had tucked away in his heart.

Angela blinked away the tears and responded quickly lest her emotions would overcome her, "Well, it is important for each of us to remember Mama and Papa. If you don't remember much about them, Thomas and I—and Derek—are going to have to share our memories. From now on we'll play a little game and the three of us will share memories about what they did—what they said—what they were like—so all of us will know them and have memories."

Sara clapped her hands, her eyes shining. She approved of the game. Louise nodded her head.

"Thomas, you start," Angela encouraged.

"Well, let's see. Where do I start? There are so many things."

"Wait," said Angela, jumping up from the table. "Let's write down each one—then we won't be getting mixed-up and telling the same ones over and over. And later we can read them."

Angela returned with a sheet of paper and a pencil.

"The next time I'm in town I'll buy a proper book. For now this will do."

"Let's call it our Memory Book," put in Sara excitedly.

"And we could divide it into how they looked, what they did, and what they said," Louise offered, adding, "That way, Sara and I will get to say something, too."

"Great idea," Angela agreed. "Instead of Thomas going first, you start, Sara."

Sara puckered her brow and thought deeply. "Well," she said at last, "I 'member Mama in her bed with a blue blanket tucked up close around her chin. I thought she was sleeping, but when I tiptoed in she reached out her hand to me—and smiled."

Angela swallowed the lump in her throat. She knew from Sara's account that the incident had happened shortly before their mother left them. Angela wrote quickly, for she knew Louise was anxious for her turn.

"I remember," began Louise, "Mama sitting in her chair, by the fireplace. And she was knitting me mittens. Red ones. Remember? They were my very favorites—but I lost one and—I don't know what happened to the other one."

"I guess you lost them both, huh?" teased Thomas.

"I did not. I just lost one," insisted Louise.

"Derek?" encouraged Angela.

Derek fidgeted with his fork, his eyes downcast. He swallowed a few times and eventually spoke. His voice was low and strained, as though speaking was difficult for him.

"I remember Mama baking pie" was all he said.

Angela struggled with the few words. She found it difficult to control her emotions. Poor Derek. He was suffering far more deeply than she had ever known.

"Thomas, now you," Angela managed to say.

"Well, I'm going to share a memory of Papa," said Thomas. "I remember how big Papa was." Thomas stretched his hand in the air to emphasize his point. "I only reached about to the top of his boots—or that's the way it seemed to me. I was so proud when I got as high as his pockets. He used to tuck penny candies in them when he went to town. I remember when I could reach candies on my own."

Angela wrote hurriedly, pressed to keep up with Thomas.

"Your turn. Your turn," her family finally was shouting.

Angela chose to share one of Mama's simple lessons.

"I remember one day when I didn't want to do the washing," she began slowly. "There were lots of grimy clothes. Piles and piles, it seemed, and I thought I would never finish the wash. Mama said, 'Angela, never let your task become a drudge. You are special. You are unique. No matter what your duty, no matter how distasteful you might find it, inside you can be whatever you decide to be. Outside, your hands might be soiled with daily toil—inside, your soul and spirit can be refined and elegant. You can be just as much a lady leaning over a tub of hot, sudsy water scrubbing farm-dirty socks as you can sitting on a velvet cushion, fanning yourself with a silk and ivory fan.' "

"What did she mean?" whispered Sara.

"Well," responded Angela, "I think she was trying to tell us that work is necessary—but it is honorable. It is what you are—deep inside—not what you do that is important."

"You mean," asked Sara, "I can pretend to be a grand lady while I'm washing the dishes?"

"You don't have to pretend," answered Angela. "You can actually be one."

Chapter Seven

Growing

Angela was pleased with the children's excitement over the memory game. Sunday after Sunday they exchanged their stories. With their memories refreshed by the discussions, Louise and Sara were surprised at how many events even they could remember. And Derek always added his brief account.

"Derek still isn't saying much in our game time, is he?" Thomas mentioned one evening as he and Angela sat on the porch together.

"Just a line—a brief sentence," Angela responded. "I hadn't realized how—how many deep hurts must be buried inside him."

"I guess he was right at the age where he needed Papa and Mama the most. And we—you and I—were so busy trying to keep body and soul together that we missed seeing what it was doing to him."

"Poor soul," sighed Angela. "Thomas, do you think we are doing enough?"

Thomas pondered the question. "I don't know," he said at last. "I just don't know. But I'm not sure what else we can do."

"Do you think the minister might be able to help him?"

"Maybe. I just don't know."

"He is so withdrawn—yet so strangely sweet. It's as though—as though he lives in fear of—of causing someone pain or something. He tries so hard to be good. Yet he—he seems so reluctant to even talk about the folks. I'm not sure he even likes our game—though there have been times when I've thought I have seen some light in his eyes at a memory we have discussed."

"Well, for now I guess we'll just continue as we are. I think—
I think maybe he is enjoying the company of other boys more. I
see him at church joining the group of fellows outside after the
service. He didn't use to do that."

"At least he responds now, a little anyway. Though he never
initiates a friendship, that's encouraging."

Thomas was about to make another comment when their attention was drawn to a horse and rider coming down the lane.

"It's Thane," announced Thomas, rising from his chair to
wave a welcome.

"He hasn't been out for a while," responded Angela.

"His pa has been working him pretty hard in the store. He
says he hardly has time to take a Saturday night bath,"
Thomas laughed.

"I'd better get something ready to eat," Angela said as she
stood up. "He's always hungry."

Thomas laughed again, but he didn't argue with her observation.

Angela left for the kitchen as Thomas descended the porch
steps to greet their visitor.

Angela heard the voices and the laughter as she stirred
lemonade and placed cookies on a plate. Then the voices lowered as though the topic of conversation had become more serious. She stepped out onto the porch in time to hear Thomas
ask, "When did it happen?"

"Almost a week ago. Word didn't get out very soon—even
though Doc knew about it. Guess Charlie asked him to keep it
quiet."

Angela's heart skipped a beat. Something had happened.

"Is something wrong with Charlie?" she questioned, concern
making her voice shake.

"No, not Charlie," Thomas quickly assured her. "Mr. Stratton
has had a stroke."

"A stroke?" Angela thought of the man with his dour face and
his curt nods. She had always been a bit afraid of him. Now she
pitied him. Perhaps if they had been kinder, more neighborly,
the man might have softened a bit.

"Is it serious?" she asked, directing her question to Thane.

He nodded slowly. "According to the report Pa got in the
store, he's in pretty bad shape."

"So that's why we haven't seen much of Charlie for the last

week or so," mused Thomas. "I was wondering why he hadn't been over to check on my spring plowing."

"Guess he's had his hands full just caring for his boss. Won't let anyone else do it, so I hear."

Charlie was withered and poorly himself. He shouldn't have to spend full time nursing another.

I must get over there, Angela said to herself, vowing she would go first thing the next morning.

Thane surprised her by changing the conversation abruptly. "I hear Trudie is throwing another party—she had so much fun at the last one."

Thane gave Thomas a teasing grin and punched him on the shoulder. Thomas reddened slightly but responded good-naturedly. "Jealous, old man?"

"Not on your life," continued Thane. "I have my eye on better things, but if you enjoy the chatter of a—" Thane stopped, suddenly realizing his remark would be in poor taste—"of a pretty little redhead," he finished lamely, "so be it."

For just a moment Angela felt a bit smug. Thane shared her opinion of Trudie. She stole a quick look at Thomas. Would he be offended? Hurt? But Thomas seemed totally unruffled by Thane's little slip. Angela sighed in relief and passed the cookies again.

"I'm planting a bit of that new seed," Thomas was saying. "The handful I tested is germinating well."

Thane turned to Thomas with a glow in his eyes. "Where is it?" he asked. "I'd like to see it."

Thomas ran for a lantern so he could lead Thane to the shed where he did his experimenting. Angela noticed excitement in both of them as they bounded down the steps, deep in conversation all the way to the small building.

Early the next morning Angela wrapped a cake, fresh from the oven, and started off for the Stratton farm. It was a short distance across the stubble field and soon she was knocking on the door of the big house. She had never visited the Stratton home, and she held her breath as she stood before it, remembering the scowling face of the owner. The door opened tentatively at first, and then Charlie poked his head out. When he saw Angela he swung the door fully open.

"Come in. Come in, girlie," he invited.

Angela stepped into the wide front hall. The heavy shades on the windows had not been raised, so it took a minute for Angela's eyes to adjust to the darkness. When she got used to the veiled light she began to make out the objects lining the walls.

The place was much more formal and feminine looking than she would have guessed, having been inhabited by men for so many years. Angela knew Charlie was allowed the privilege of a downstairs bedroom, and Gus, the cook, lived somewhere else inside the big house. Mr. Stratton, according to town gossip, occupied the upper portion. Angela let her gaze lift gently up the long, ornate staircase. She wasn't sure who did the housekeeping chores. Rumor had it that Mr. Stratton would not allow a woman within the walls.

Charlie spoke from beside her, and Angela broke off her daydreaming.

"He's quite poorly," Charlie was saying as he accepted the cake Angela held out to him. "I don't s'pose yer anxious to be seein' him—him being like he is."

"No. No-o," faltered Angela. "I really came to see you, I guess. How—how are you managing?"

Charlie shook his head, sadness in his eyes. "Never thought I'd live to see the day when that big man had to take to his bed," he said simply.

"How are you managing?" Angela asked again.

"Me and Gus take turns. He needs someone night and day."

"Should you—should you get some outside help? Maybe Mrs.—"

"Boss wouldn't like thet much. He's not used to women fussin' around here."

"But if you need—"

"We'll manage jest fine," Charlie insisted. Then he turned their attention to other things. "C'mon to the kitchen. I'll fix us a cup of coffee."

Angela followed. She had never been in a man's kitchen before and she wasn't sure how Gus would keep his. When she saw him in town she had noticed that he was none too fussy about his own appearance. She expected his kitchen to reflect the same casual approach to things, but to her surprise the large, sunny room was in good order.

"My!" she exclaimed before she could check herself, "it is nice and clean in here."

Charlie grinned and then said soberly, "Gus'd have the head

of anyone who messed up his kitchen. He's as fussy as an old woman 'bout it."

He cast a glance at Angela to see if she would take offense at his expression, but Angela paid no heed. She was much too busy gazing around the big room with its spacious cupboards and gleaming stove.

"It's nice," Angela murmured, more to herself than to Charlie. He nodded in acknowledgment and poured a handful of coffee into the pot. After adding some water, he placed the pot on the stove and put a few more sticks of wood on the fire.

"Sit down," he invited. "Sit down and tell me how things have been goin' at yer house. Since this here happened, I ain't been nowhere—or heard nothin'."

"Well, I guess nothing much has happened over our way," began Angela as she removed her bonnet and seated herself in a kitchen chair.

"Thomas started in the field yet?"

"Oh yes. He has most of the plowing finished."

"He gonna try some of thet there new seed?"

"A little. He doesn't dare plant much in case something happens. He doesn't want to lose all his work. He did tell Thane the seed seems to be germinating fine, though."

Charlie shook his head and a bit of a grin pulled at the corners of his mouth. Angela knew he had a fatherly interest in them and was pleased with Thomas's success.

"If he gets him a good, sturdy seed for these parts, he will have done us all a great favor," Charlie commented.

As soon as the coffee boiled, Charlie poured a cup, cut a generous piece of the cake Angela had brought, and started for the door.

"I'll be back in jest a jiffy," he said over his shoulder. "I'll take this on up to Gus and see how things are goin'."

Angela nodded and sat stiffly in her chair as she listened to his lumbering footsteps climb the long stairs. A door opened and she heard voices, but they were too far away for her to make any sense of the words.

Soon Charlie was back, his expression sober. "Gus says there's been no change. We keep hopin', but it don't look good. Doc says he—he ain't likely to come out of it."

Angela didn't know whom she felt sorriest for, the crotchety rancher or his devoted foreman and cook. She knew both Charlie and Gus were suffering over the illness of their long-time boss.

"Is there anything we can do?" she asked Charlie. "I could take a shift with the nursing if—"

"No, no. You got 'nough to do carin' for those young'uns. Me an' Gus'll make out just fine."

"But what about the other work? The cattle and—"

"Got enough hired help around here thet they oughta be able to see to thet. About time thet some of them started to earn their keep," said Charlie with a wave of his hand.

They had their coffee together and Angela excused herself.

"Be sure to let us know if we can do anything," she said as she left. "You know we'd be glad to help out." She could have added, "After all you've done for us over the years," but she didn't. Charlie probably understood.

"I will. I will," promised Charlie. "Thet cake was mighty appreciated. Gus hasn't been doin' his usual meal fixin' lately."

Angela left with the resolve that she would send over more baking in a couple of days and as often as she felt it was needed until things improved at the Stratton household. It was the least she could do to try to lighten their load.

"Come quick! Come quick!" Sara burst frantically into the room and grabbed Angela.

"What's wrong?" demanded Angela, grasping the young girl's shoulders and holding her at arms' length to look into her face.

"Louise!—" shrieked Sara.

"What happened?" Angela cried, shaking the slight shoulders. "Where is she? What happened?"

"She doesn't know."

"Where is she?" Angela repeated with another shake.

"In the bedroom," Sara managed to reply.

Angela released Sara and rushed to the bedroom, her heart hammering within her breast. Louise was there, lying across her bed, sobs shaking her body. *At least she is in one piece,* thought Angela with relief.

"What is it?" Angela asked, dropping to her knees beside the bed and lifting Louise into her arms.

"I—I think I'm—I'm dying," the child sobbed, a fresh torrent of tears running down her cheeks.

"What is it? Why? Are you ill? Did you—?"

"I don't know. I must be," sobbed the frightened girl.

Sara joined Louise in crying.

"Listen, both of you. Stop it. Stop the crying. Tell me what's wrong."

After asking only a few questions, Angela realized that her sister was not dying. Angela lifted herself from her knees to the bed and gathered Louise into her arms.

"You poor thing. You poor thing," she crooned, brushing her hair back from the flushed face.

"It's all right. You're fine. Really. You are just growing up, that's all. I should have known—should have thought—but I didn't. Mama would have known. She would have talked to you and prepared you. I'm sorry. I'm really sorry."

Angela looked from one girl to the other. They had both managed to quit crying. Their faces were still flushed and tear-streaked, and their shoulders still shook with an occasional sob, but they both seemed to be under control again.

Angela patted the bed beside her. "Climb up here beside us, Sara," she invited. "You are a bit young, but there is no help for it now. You might as well hear what I have to say to Louise."

Angela took a deep breath, trying hard to remember what her mother had said in their little chat years ago. She wasn't sure if she did it well, or if she was thoroughly understood by her two young sisters, but she did the best she could. In the end the faces were at peace again. Louise even managed a wobbly smile. Angela was only too glad to finish her mission and escape back to her kitchen.

Chapter Eight

The Unexpected

Thomas had worked hard in the field all day and was still warm and tired when he joined Angela on the veranda where she worked on the hem of a new dress for Louise.

"She's growing awfully fast, isn't she?" he observed, and Angela nodded. *Far too quickly as far as I'm concerned,* she thought.

"Do you think—" Thomas began, but Thane's arrival interrupted the thought.

"What are you up to?" Thomas called to Thane. "Can't your pa think of anything worthwhile to put you to doing?" he teased.

Thane stepped down from his horse and flipped the reins around the hitching post.

"Boy," said Thane, "I'm most ready to drop in my tracks, my pa's been working me so hard. If it hadn't been that I was worried some about my friend Tom, I would have just fallen in my bed and stayed right there."

Angela had heard the friendly bantering many times. She listened now with a slight smile. Thane was good for Thomas. His good-natured teasing helped lift the weight from her brother's young shoulders for a short time.

Angela laid aside the dress she was working on and went to get some refreshments.

"How's the new seed doing?" she heard Thane asking Thomas.

"Great. Just great. If we had more light, I'd show you. Why do you always come out here in the dark?"

"I tell you," responded Thane. "If I didn't come in the dark, I wouldn't get here at all. Pa's been pushing me at the store. He's adding a whole new section on the side. A big storage area and—"

Angela passed out of earshot. She could hear only the murmur of voices and an occasional hearty laugh.

When she returned with the milk and donuts the young men were talking about baseball. Angela passed the refreshments and picked up the garment again. It was too dark now to see well enough to finish the hem. With a sigh she laid the dress down again and settled in her chair to listen to the conversation.

Thane was quick to bring her in. "I hear you've been helping out the Stratton household with baking."

Angela nodded.

"Gus was in town for some supplies and he's been bragging all over town about what a top-notch cook you are."

"Nothing fancy about what I've been sending," said Angela, embarrassed. "Guess if one is hungry enough, anything tastes good."

Thane grinned and winked at Thomas. "Think you and I have tried enough of her cooking over the years to know it isn't hunger that causes a man to come back for more," he said, and Angela knew she had just been paid a nice compliment.

"How is Mr. Stratton?" asked Angela.

"Nobody is saying," responded Thane. "Even Doc is evasive. I don't think things are going well." Suddenly his tone changed. "Have you heard the latest bit of news?" he asked.

Angela shook her head.

"Mr. Stratton has a son."

"A son? I didn't even know he had a wife."

"I guess he doesn't—anymore. But he did at one time. Some of the older neighbors knew her—though they had almost forgotten she ever existed."

Angela's eyes opened wide. "Did she live here?" she asked.

"For a short time, it seems."

"That's why the house is so nicely decorated!" Angela exclaimed, feeling that the mystery was now solved.

"He built it for her. Tried to have it just the way she wanted. But she didn't like the West. She was from some big city back east, and I guess this life just didn't agree with her. She went back home. Took their baby boy with her. Folks say that Mr.

Stratton hasn't seen either one of them since. That was some years ago."

Angela's face clouded. "How sad," she murmured softly. "Really sad. No wonder the poor man looks so gloomy all the time."

"But that's not all," Thane continued. "Rumor has it that the son is heading out this way. Seems that Charlie felt honorbound to let him know of Mr. Stratton's condition, and the fellow has decided to come see for himself."

Angela smiled. Perhaps there would be a happy ending after all. She was glad for Mr. Stratton. She did hope that he was well enough to know and enjoy his grown-up son.

"Gus didn't sound too excited about it," Thane continued. "I think he fears that the fellow is just interested in getting his hands on the Stratton money."

Angela was suddenly angry. Why should Gus go and spoil her dream? Why couldn't it be concern—if not love—that was bringing the junior Stratton to his father's bedside?

"Well," she said defiantly, "perhaps Gus should wait and see before he brands the man as a black-heart. He could at least give him a chance."

"You're right," Thane responded, more serious now. "Maybe we all should."

"When is he to arrive?" asked Angela.

"I don't know. Soon, I gather from what Gus said. He was spreading the word around town, though he was none too happy about the situation."

"That's awful," Angela said, still annoyed. "The poor man hasn't even done anything, and already folks are against him. Fine welcome for someone coming to see his sick pa."

Angela resolved that she would not be one to brand a man before she knew his intent. She promised herself she would take over some more baking the minute she learned of his arrival.

They spent the remainder of their evening talking of other things. After the moon had climbed high into the sky, Thane announced he'd better get on home.

Before leaving he reached into his shirt pocket and withdrew a small brown bag that he handed without comment to Angela. Like a small child, she could not resist a peek. Pink peppermints. Her favorite. She gave Thane a warm smile in thank you. He acknowledged it with a smile of his own, touched his cap, and was gone.

————

Mrs. Blackwell called. Even though she maintained that the young Petersons should be left strictly on their own, she still made it her neighborly duty to drop by now and then to see that they were doing things right. Angela had seen her coming and longed to slip out the back door and escape to the fields where Thomas and Derek were stacking the summer hay.

Instead, she laid aside her soiled apron and pushed the kettle forward on the stove to make a cup of tea.

Mrs. Blackwell was puffing her way up the veranda steps when Angela opened the door and smiled a welcome.

"My, that sun is hot today" was the only greeting the woman offered. She whisked off her heavy black bonnet and wiped her perspiring face.

Angela stepped aside to let her enter the kitchen. She headed directly for a chair beside the table, her eyes traveling hither and yon to survey the room.

"It's cool in here," she observed. "Guess you haven't been doin' any bakin' for a while."

"No," acknowledged Angela slowly, "when the weather is like this I try to do enough in one day to last us the week."

Mrs. Blackwell nodded her head but made no immediate comment. She wiped her face again and sat down heavily on the chair.

"How do you keep it fresh?" she asked forthrightly.

"We have an extra icebox in the shed out back. I wrap it and put it in there."

The woman frowned. Angela knew Mrs. Blackwell had no spare icebox and was probably thinking it wasn't fair that someone so young should have things she didn't.

"S'pose you heard about poor Mr. Stratton?" Mrs. Blackwell asked.

Angela nodded and willed the kettle to boil quickly.

"Such a shame. But then—jest another reminder thet the Lord don't take kindly to sin. One reaps what one sows—jest as the Book says."

Angela was glad she could turn to lift the teapot down from the shelf and not have to comment.

"You use that one for everyday? My, looks to me like your mama would have kept thet for special occasions."

"Mama felt it a special occasion when a neighbor came to call," Angela answered sweetly and gave the woman a nice smile.

Mrs. Blackwell flushed an even deeper red and busied herself with fanning for several moments before she found her tongue again.

"This here Mr. Stratton—has him a son. Did ya ever hear of such a thing? Comin' on out. Seems to me it woulda set better had he been here all those years helpin' his pa out. Might have saved his heart, or whatever the man has, iffen he would've been here. Doc won't say none what's ailin' the fella."

Angela set two china cups and saucers on the table and went for the cream and sugar.

"Well, I'm thinkin' thet he'll likely scoop up what he can get his hands on an' head straight back east to his mama—thet's what I'm thinkin'. He's probably a chip off the old block—as stingy and unneighborly as his pa. I remember the woman—shouldn't you let that tea steep a bit longer?—she was a flighty thing, let me tell you. Pretty as a picture—an' 'bout as flimsy. Couldn't lift her hand in her own kitchen. An' the mister. He tried to give her everything so thet she would be happy here. We knew it would never work. Some of us tried to tell him, but he jest turned a deaf ear. Well, I guess he learned."

Angela set the tea before Mrs. Blackwell and turned for the sponge cake.

"Yer brothers hayin'?" the woman asked.

Angela nodded.

"Wonder iffen it's quite dry enough. You can sure ruin good hay iffen you don't give it time to dry proper."

Angela bit her lip and then boldly suggested that they thank the Lord for the refreshments. Mrs. Blackwell looked surprised, as though tea and cake were hardly worth a prayer.

Angela's prayer was simple and sincere. When she lifted her head she passed the cake to her neighbor.

"Those sisters of yours big enough to be of any use to you yet?" asked Mrs. Blackwell as she stirred the cream and sugar into her tea.

"They have always been of use to us," responded Angela a bit too quickly.

"Work? Work?" hurried on Mrs. Blackwell in explanation. "Are they able to help with—?"

"Oh yes," cut in Angela. "They've had their own chores from when they were tiny—which they see to on their own," she informed the older woman, feeling a bit smug.

"Where are they now?" asked Mrs. Blackwell, her eyes traveling about as though she thought the two young girls should be scurrying about the kitchen.

"I sent them out to pick strawberries for jam," replied Angela.

"It's a bit late for strawberries."

"Oh no. The girls brought in a nice pailful yesterday. I canned five jars of jam with it."

The woman seemed to be at a loss as to what to say next. She took a bite of her sponge cake and turned again to Angela.

"I'm guessin' you've been a bit wasteful in usin' eggs. I have a way of making this same recipe with about half the eggs. Eggs are worth money, you know. Every egg saved means—"

"We have lots of eggs," said Angela softly.

"Still—you can take 'em to town and sell 'em. Trade 'em fer something needed. No sense being wasteful—"

Louise burst through the door. In her hand was a pail filled with bright red strawberries. "We found the best patch—" she began but jerked to a halt when she saw the woman at the table. "Excuse me," she said softly. "Hello, Mrs. Blackwell."

Sara moved in beside her sister, her face flushed and streaks of dirt on her pinafore. But her blue eyes were dancing, and Angela knew she was nearly bursting with excitement over some find. But Sara held her tongue and curtsied slightly. "Hello, Mrs. Blackwell," she said in no more than a whisper.

Angela could have hugged them both. They had remembered their manners. She felt pride swelling within her. Her mama would have been so pleased.

"Wash your hands," she instructed, her voice shaky with emotion, "and you can have a slice of sponge cake and a glass of milk."

Mrs. Blackwell collected her thoughts and spoke again. "Won't thet spoil their supper?"

"They have worked hard," replied Angela firmly. "And growing children must be fed."

She sliced generous pieces of the cake and poured out two chilled glasses of milk as the girls washed at the corner basin.

"You may take it to the back porch out of the sun," she told Louise and Sara as she handed them the food.

Mrs. Blackwell may have felt that Angela did not trust two rowdy children at the same table as a neighborhood guest. But in truth, there was no way Angela would have subjected her two young sisters to the tiresome exchange she was enduring.

Chapter Nine

The Son

"Well, he's here," Thomas announced as he hoisted the box of groceries onto the kitchen table. "Thane said that Gus came into town almost bursting."

"Who's here?" asked Angela, reaching for the bag of sugar.

"The young Mr. Stratton. Don't even know his name. No one seems to know his name."

"Is he—is he like his father?" asked Angela hesitantly.

Thomas laughed. "I haven't laid eyes on him myself, but from what folks are saying, he is pretty citified. Don't expect he'll last long out here."

"Thomas, don't be like the others and brand him bad before he even gets a chance to prove himself," Angela reprimanded gently.

Thomas moved to the corner stand and lifted a dipper of cold water. He drank long and deeply before he lowered the dipper. With a quick movement of his wrist, he splashed the remaining water into the blue basin and returned the dipper to the pail.

"You're right," he said seriously. "We need to give the fellow a chance."

He reached out and ruffled Angela's hair as he headed for the door. "I'm going to be working on that last hay field. Send Derek out as soon as he has his chores done."

Angela nodded and lifted the salt and baking soda from the grocery box. Already her mind was rushing. Should she bake a chocolate cake or a batch of fudge brownies to take to the Strattons? She still felt it was a shame how folks were so willing to think ill of the young Mr. Stratton even before they knew him.

It was fudge brownies that Angela delivered to the Stratton household later in the day. She was not as timid when she stepped up to rap on the door as she had been when she had made her first delivery to the big house. Over the weeks the little trip across the field to see Charlie—or Gus—had become a welcomed break in her routine day.

She looked about her now before lifting her hand to the wooden door. Flowers were blooming in the bed to the right. She wondered who had the time or interest to plant flowers, and then quickly attributed them to Charlie. Charlie, though elderly and crippled, liked pretty things.

Angela knocked and waited, expecting Charlie to pop his head out the door. But the door was opened by a stranger. Angela blinked, then stepped quickly back and felt her face flushing.

She had never before seen anyone dressed quite like he was. His long tailored suit jacket with velvet lapels hung open over a matching vest. A gold chain stretched across his front from button hole to side pocket. A carefully knotted scarf at the throat of his stark-white stand-up collar added a softening touch to the otherwise stiff-looking attire. Softly striped trousers and highly polished boots were the last things Angela noticed before remembering her manners. Her eyes moved quickly back to the man's face.

His complexion was pale and looked baby-soft, as though neither sun nor rain had ever touched it. And his hair seemed as though wind never tousled it. Every shining strand was carefully combed into place. Slight waves hinted at curliness, but Angela somehow was sure they were never allowed to get out of control.

He seemed so foreign to Angela that she felt confused. He did not belong to the world she was used to. She hardly knew how to address him. Her flush deepened.

"H—Hello," she finally stammered. "I—I am looking for Mr. Stratton."

The gentleman tipped his head slightly while she awkwardly tried to tuck in a strand of silvery blond hair that danced playfully about her face in the afternoon breeze. Her blue eyes, wide in astonishment, and her flushed cheeks revealed her confusion.

Then he offered a smile—not a friendly grin like Angela was used to receiving from Charlie but a smile—soft, curving, and controlled.

"I do hope you are a neighbor," he said in a deep, resonant voice. "A close neighbor."

"I—I'm Angela," she murmured and felt even more foolish. "I—I—expected Charlie—"

"Charlie is busy."

"Oh—of course. Well, really I came to see Mr. Stratton and well—"

"I'm sorry," he said, kind but firm. "He really isn't up to visitors. He's quite ill."

"Oh, not that Mr. Stratton," Angela said quickly. "I mean the—the new Mr. Stratton." She knew she had said it all wrong. She tried again. "Mr. Stratton's son."

The door swung open to its full width and the youthful gentleman stepped back and bid her enter with a wave of his hand. The smile had returned.

"That Mr. Stratton would be most pleased to see you." He motioned Angela into the hallway. "Won't you come into the parlor?"

Angela stumbled along in step.

"Please be seated," he continued. "I will have Gus prepare some coffee—or perhaps you prefer tea?"

Angela had never been in the parlor before. Her wide eyes studied it now, going from the gold damask of the sofa and chairs to the rich mahogany of the piano. She wanted to just stand and look, but the man beside her seemed to be asking her something. She turned her attention back to him and shook her head slightly.

"I—I'm sorry," she murmured.

"Tea—or coffee?" he repeated.

"I—I think—tea, please," she managed to answer and then remembered the pan in her hands. "I—I've brought some baking," she said. "To sort of welcome the—the other Mr. Stratton—to the community—as a neighbor—you know." She thrust the pan out toward the stranger.

She had never been so flustered before. Was this young man Mr. Stratton's lawyer? Maybe he had accompanied the son here. If only he would stop looking at her. If only Charlie would make an appearance.

"Please," the young man said again. "Won't you have a chair. I'll only be a minute." As soon as Angela had taken the seat he offered, he left, baking in hand.

Angela arranged her skirts carefully and wiped her palms on her pocket handkerchief. Before she could turn her attention back to the identity of the stranger and to her intriguing surroundings, she heard footsteps in the hall and turned to see Charlie enter the room. She could have hugged him. He crossed to her and took her trembling hand.

"Are you ill, girlie?" he asked, noticing her flushed face and clammy fingers.

"Oh, Charlie," she admitted, "I have just made such a fool of myself. I—I came over here to—to sort of welcome Mr. Stratton's son with some baking and I—I expected you—or Gus—to open the door and it—it quite threw me when this—this total stranger was standing there, and I've been babbling like a silly schoolgirl ever since."

Charlie gave Angela a quizzical look. Then his hand tightened. "He threw ya, did he?" he asked, and Angela detected annoyance in his voice.

"Oh, it wasn't that. I mean he was most polite," she hurried on. "It was just that I expected you—or Gus—or maybe even Mr. Stratton's son, but—"

"Angela," said Charlie giving her hand a bit of a shake, "that *was* Mr. Stratton's son."

Angela looked at Charlie with wide eyes, unable to believe that he was serious. She wasn't sure what she had expected—perhaps just a younger version of the older perhaps, with a gloomy, weathered face, dusty boots, and a buckskin jacket.

"That—?"

Charlie nodded.

"But—but—he is so *young*!"

Charlie nodded again.

"He—he's not much older than—than Thomas!" exclaimed Angela.

"A little," said Charlie.

"But I thought—I mean, I expected—well—someone quite—quite different."

"I apologize that I took so long," said a cultured voice from the doorway. "I couldn't find Gus so I had to make the tea myself. I do hope—" Then the young man spotted Charlie. "Oh, Charlie—" he said and let the words hang.

"Gus is with your father," Charlie explained, then turned back to Angela. "I'll try to get over one of these evenings," he said, giving her hand a final squeeze. Angela nodded and watched him leave the room.

"Cream and sugar?" asked her young host after a few moments of awkward silence.

"No—no thank you. Neither," Angela managed to reply, and then she took charge of herself. *I need not be flustered,* she informed herself. *My mama taught me to be a lady, so I will act like one.* Angela willed her racing heart and trembling hands to be quiet. Soon she sat at tea in the big parlor as though she had done so for many years.

"I must offer my apology," she said shyly. "I did not realize that Mr. Stratton's son would be so young; therefore I did not realize who you were when you opened the door."

He answered with a playful smile, as proper and controlled as his laugh had been.

"I do hope you have not been disappointed," he said.

Angela was quite shocked when she realized she had fluttered her eyelashes in response.

"Now—you must tell me about yourself," he invited engagingly. "You are Angela. Do you have a last name, Angela?"

She laughed a light, silvery laugh and looked fully at the young man before her. "My, I did appear like a simpleton, didn't I?" she admitted, and then hurried on. "My name is Angela Peterson."

"And you live—?"

Angela was beginning to relax and decided to allow herself to enjoy the afternoon tea.

"I could say, just over the stubble field," she replied, "but I guess it would be more proper to say, on the farm adjoining your land to the left. Well, one of the farms on the left. I realize that your land stretches far enough to border several farms on each side."

He accepted the acknowledgment of the Stratton wealth with a slight smile and a nod of his head.

"And you are the Angel of Mercy who has been bearing sustenance to Charlie and Gus since the illness of my father."

It was his compliment to her, but for just a moment her breath caught in her throat. A distant memory had been awakened of a little girl with silvery pigtails flying in the wind, running toward the outstretched arms of a man with hair of the same color. He was a tall man, with broad shoulders and strong arms, and as he swept up the girl and enfolded her against his chest, she heard her father's words, "And how is my Angel?"

Yes, she thought, *Father used to call me that. I had forgotten.* Angela fought to return to the present so she might give the proper response to the young man before her.

––––––––

The Petersons played the memory game again. Angela could hardly wait for her turn so she could tell them her memory of her father's pet name for her.

As usual Sara was given the first turn. "I 'member—remember—I remember," she said, her brow puckered in deep concentration; then her eyes brightened. "I remember when Papa took me to the circus and bought me lots of treats and showed me big elephants and walking bears and—"

"Sara," cut in Louise. "You never went to the circus."

"I did, too," argued Sara, her lower lip beginning to protrude.

"You did not," insisted Louise before anyone else could comment. "There was never a circus here to go to."

"Louise is right," said Angela slowly. "You must have had a dream."

Louise wasn't as gracious to her young sister as Angela had been. "That's a lie," she condemned Sara. "We aren't ever to tell lies."

Sara's pouting lip began to tremble; then a flood of tears followed. "Well, I can't 'member anymore," she sobbed. "Everyone has more to talk about than me."

Angela took the small girl into her arms and soothed her. "Sh-h-h," she whispered. "It's okay. That's why we are playing the game, remember? So those of us who have more memories can share them with you. Sh-h-h."

At last Sara was quieted and Angela knew that it was her turn to make a statement.

"But Louise is right. You must never tell stories as—as truths if they are not. Papa and Mama would never tolerate tales of any kind. You must remember that in the future."

With that understanding, the game went on.

"I remember," said Louise, "when Papa brought a whole big box of apples home from town and he let me have one to eat—

even before Mama made pie or sauce or anything. It was—yummy."

Even Sara laughed as Louise rolled her eyes and rubbed her tummy.

It was Derek's turn. His contributions had been a bit more open recently, his comments a bit lengthier. But both Thomas and Angela knew he was still a troubled boy.

"I remember—" began Derek, and then a frown creased his brow. He swallowed hard, seeming determined to go on. "I remember—the—the day Mama died."

Angela caught her breath. Thomas moved as though to reach out a hand to his young brother, then quickly withdrew it. "Yes?" he prompted.

"I remember—I brought her a bird shell—just a little blue one—it was in two pieces—the baby had already hatched—but I knew she would like to see it."

He stopped and swallowed again. His eyes did not lift from his empty dinner plate.

"I—I tiptoed into her bedroom—I thought she might be asleep—then I—I touched her hand."

There was a pause again and Angela feared that Derek might not be able to go on.

"It was cold," he managed after some time. "I—I whispered to her—but she didn't open her eyes. Then I—I shook her—just a little bit."

The room was chilled and quiet. Not a person moved. Not an eye lifted from their brother's pale face.

"Then I—I shook her harder—and she still didn't wake up. I started to get scared. I shook her again. Then I started to cry, and then—then Mrs. Barrows opened the door and looked at me, and she frowned at me and said, 'Your Mama is gone, boy. Mustn't cry, now. You're a big boy,' and I ran past her and I ran and ran until I was out of breath and—"

Tears were now falling freely down Derek's cheeks. Thomas reached for him, pulled him close, and held him. Angela, through tears of her own, quietly led the two young girls, also weeping, out of the kitchen. As she left she could hear Thomas's gentle voice. "That's right. Go ahead and cry. Just cry it all out. I never heard Papa say that a man couldn't cry when he had good reason."

From the tremor in Thomas's voice, Angela knew he was shedding tears of his own.

"Oh, God," she prayed, "help poor little Derek. Wash his memory of this—this terrible hurt—and touch his soul with your healing. Might he be—be freed from the past now—and be able to go on."

Chapter Ten

A Birthday

"Why don't you go? I really don't have much time for a party," Angela said to Thomas.

It's you who Trudie wants anyway, she was thinking, but she didn't voice it.

Thomas was shaking his head. "Nope. You don't go, I don't go."

Angela was a bit annoyed and a little surprised at his response. He usually was not so stubborn.

"Truth is, I didn't really have much fun at the last one. And I hate to leave the—"

"They were fine last time—remember?"

Angela had to admit that the children had gotten along perfectly well without them for a few hours.

"I really don't see why—"

Thomas cut her short. "You need to get out. You didn't have fun last time because you had forgotten how. You are not a little old lady, Angela. You are seventeen."

"Eighteen," corrected Angela with a deep sigh.

"All right, eighteen," Thomas agreed. "Tomorrow you'll be eighteen. But that's still a long way from eighty, and that's how you're acting. Now get yourself all prettied up and let's get over there—before the party is over and the food is all gone," teased Thomas.

Reluctantly Angela pulled herself from her chair and put aside the sock she had been darning. She didn't feel one bit like partying. Especially not at Trudie's house.

It did not take her long to change her dress and pin her hair firmly into place. She dusted a bit of fine flour across her nose and tucked a clean hankie into her pocket. She knew she wouldn't enjoy this evening, but Thomas seemed to have his heart set on going, and Angela did not want to spoil it for him. After all, Thomas was not old either, and he had certainly missed out on his share of fun.

It could get cool later in the evening, so Angela grabbed a shawl and went to meet Thomas at the kitchen door. She was expecting a bit of a fuss from Louise, who felt she was old enough to be in on the entertainment of the young folks of the community. And Louise didn't care much for her appointed task of the evening.

Angela had posted all three youngsters at the kitchen table to do review lessons. She believed it was important over the summer months to have them study what they had learned the year before. They often argued vociferously, saying that none of the other mothers demanded so much from their offspring, but Angela held firm, and one evening a week was deemed "study night."

Angela was about to release them from tonight's assignment and tell them they could read a book of their choice instead. It didn't seem fair that they had to study while she partied. But when she entered the kitchen all three were working diligently. Louise hardly lifted her head.

"We won't be long," Angela promised, and Derek raised his eyes for a moment and nodded. Louise and Sara kept their eyes on the opened books before them. Angela shrugged. It seemed that Thomas was the only one with any enthusiasm for the party.

Thomas helped her climb into the wagon, and then they were off.

It was a clear evening and the moon was just coming up. Angela decided to forget her ill humor and enjoy the ride. The fields of ripening grain stretched along beside the roadway, promising another good harvest.

Dear God, don't let anything happen to it, Angela prayed silently. *We need it so. The children need new things for school. They grow so fast, I can hardly keep up with them. And Thomas—it's been years since he's had a new suit, and I have let down every hem and let out every seam and he still looks like a little boy on a growing spurt instead of like a man. And I know it must embarrass him some, Lord, even if he doesn't say.*

Angela stole a look at Thomas. He had filled out to be almost the size her father had been. In fact, he reminded her more of their papa every day in appearance and carriage.

Thomas must have felt her eyes on him, for he turned and gave her a grin. "Still mad?" he teased.

Angela dipped her head. How could she be angry with Thomas? He deserved to have a good time. If he wished to party—then she would party. Though she still couldn't understand why he had insisted that she go along.

She gave Thomas a reluctant smile. "No. I'm not mad," she responded, and the smile came in its fullness.

"Good!" was all he answered, and he turned his attention back to the horses.

They rode in silence for several moments, then Angela turned to her brother and asked a blunt question. "Thomas, if you could be anything you wanted—do anything you wanted—would you be a farmer?"

Thomas looked directly at her and his eyes seemed to darken slightly. He appeared reluctant to answer, but he finally began to shake his head slowly.

"Don't you like to farm?"

"Well—it's not—not that I don't like it—really. It's just that I think there is something I would like better."

"I never knew that," Angela replied softly. "But then, I never even thought about it before."

There was silence again. Finally Angela took up the conversation again.

"What is it that you think you'd like better?" she asked.

"Research," he said without hesitation. "With grains and fruits and things."

Angela nodded. She should have known. Thomas was always working with his seeds and hybrids.

"But you do that now," she reminded him.

"Not the way I'd like to. I have no space—no training—no proper equipment. And very little time," he finished with a sigh.

Angela nodded her head. He was right. He did have very little time and he did not have the proper tools or the room to work. More than once his precious plants had frozen and he had been set back in his experimentation. Angela hadn't realized until now what a great disappointment that must have been for him.

They rode in silence again while Angela mulled over the

dream Thomas had just shared. *If it wasn't for the children,* she was thinking, *Thomas might have a chance to work with his seeds. I could find a job or*—But there was no use dreaming. The children needed his care.

"And you?" asked Thomas.

Angela came back from her reverie with a start and looked at her older brother. She shrugged and shifted her shawl in her lap.

"Oh, I don't know. Nothing I guess. At least nothing like that. There was a time when I thought I would like to be a teacher, but not anymore. I would have liked to go to school more, though. Just to learn. I had to quit so early. But then, I guess one never needs to stop learning—from books and—and everything in life. I can read the lesson books the children bring home."

"Is that why you are so—so—"

Angela knew Thomas thought she was too hard on the kids about their studies. He had never fully agreed with her regarding the summer review sessions, but he had always backed her.

"Is that why you are so determined that the three of them make the most of their studies?" he finished at last.

Angela nodded. "It seems such a shame not to get all they can out of their years in school. They are over all too soon anyway—and then adult responsibilities crowd in and take over and there is no more time to learn from books," Angela said soberly.

Thomas nodded.

"Yet," said Angela hesitantly, "I almost let them off tonight. It just didn't seem fair that we were off to a party and they had to sit there at the kitchen table with their lesson books. But they were so intent when we left that I decided not to disturb them." Then Angela changed the subject. "Who's going to be at the party?" she asked.

"The usual, I guess," answered Thomas. Angela wondered why his casual answer didn't match his rather knowing expression.

"Who's going to be there?" she repeated.

"I guess we'll see when we get there" was all Thomas would say as he clucked to the horse.

When they entered the Sommerses' yard and Angela saw the number of teams tied to the fence posts, she thought the whole community must be there.

"Looks like Trudie is throwing quite a party," she murmured.

Thomas tied the team and extended his arm to Angela. She took it and let him escort her around to the back of the house. There didn't seem to be anyone around and Angela was about to suggest that they try the front door instead.

As they rounded the corner an explosion of sound greeted them. "Surprise." "Surprise." "Happy birthday." "Happy birthday." The shouts were coming at Angela from all sides as heads began to pop out from behind every tree and shrub.

Angela drew a quick breath, and Thomas had to hold fast to the hand tucked in his arm.

It was then that Angela noticed the streamers strung in the tree branches. And then an even more amazing sight caught her attention. There were Derek, Louise, and Sara, dressed in their Sunday finery and yelling right along with the rest of the crowd, "Surprise! Surprise!"

"How did you get here?" Angela stammered.

"We cut across the field," Louise called cheerily, and Angela knew she had the answer to their diligent studying. Louise was getting in on the party after all.

The evening was a blur to Angela. She had never been the guest of honor at a party before—and she wasn't sure how much she enjoyed being the center of attention now. Still, she did appreciate all the effort Trudie had put into the event. She determined to be kinder, a little more tolerant of her friend— until she spotted Trudie hovering around Thomas again. *My— what a good deal of time and expense just to get Thomas over here,* Angela mused. Thomas had turned down each invitation to the other parties Trudie proposed, up till now. Angela shook her head. Some girls were so foolish.

Angela noticed that Thomas did not devote his total evening to Trudie. He mixed easily through the crowd, chatting and laughing and teasing. He truly seemed to be enjoying himself.

Derek hung back some, but gradually joined the younger boys. They mostly sat and watched the older ones. Angela decided that perhaps they were studying the older youths so they would know how to behave when it was their turn.

Louise was more socially inclined and made repeated attempts to join in. Angela knew how much her sister longed to be a part of everything that was going on while still feeling unsure of herself. Angela ached for the young girl. "It just takes time," she whispered under her breath. "Don't try to rush it, Louise. You'll be an adult soon enough."

Sara, still a little girl in the eyes of most of the partygoers, was pampered and fussed over. Sara enjoyed the spotlight and seemed to feel that she deserved every nod and smile. She bounced about, chattering and giggling and accepting every goodie offered to her.

They played party games and a few jokes on one another. Then Angela had to cut the enormous birthday cake and serve the pieces to each one present. By the time she had finished giving out the cake, the others had finished eating and were busy chatting and teasing again. Trudie suggested a sing-song, looking at Thomas for his answer.

"Not tonight," he answered. "When I get singing I hate to stop and I have to get the younger ones home."

Louise gave Thomas an impatient scowl.

"Angela can stay," Thomas was quick to say. "I'll leave the team for her and we'll walk across the field."

"I'll drive her home," offered Thane.

"But I—I should—" began Angela.

"Nonsense," Thomas replied. "It's your birthday party. You stay and sing. I'll tuck them in."

Louise pushed out her lip, but a word from her older brother quickly erased the pout. Angela wondered what Thomas had whispered to her.

Trudie looked about as upset as Louise. For a moment she stood silently, her face clouded with disappointment. Then she flipped her reddish hair and crossed to Thomas. She laid a hand on his sleeve and looked up at him with her long eyelashes fluttering slightly. "You can come back after you've tucked them in," Angela heard her say.

"We'll see," nodded Thomas as Angela turned away.

Thomas gathered up the three younger ones and they headed for home, calling their thank yous over and over as they left. They had enjoyed the party; and Angela was glad, for their sakes, that she had consented to come.

The singing began and Angela found herself tucked between the preacher's two sons. They sang heartily, one a bass, the other a tenor, of sorts—he never could quite find the right notes.

Angela found it easy to forgive the missed notes, but the constant shuffling and vying for her attention unnerved her.

"I just turned nineteen," Roger informed her.

Angela congratulated him.

"I'm only six months younger," said Peter from the other side, edging a bit closer and making Angela feel uncomfortable.

They began another song and Angela joined in heartily, glad for a chance to put an end to the conversation.

At the first break, Peter whispered in her ear, "You want anything? Cake or more punch or anything?"

Angela graciously declined.

"Your shawl?" asked Roger, pointing to where Angela's shawl still hung on a nearby shrub.

Angela wondered how he could possibly think she needed her shawl. She felt so crowded that she was overly warm, not cool.

"No thank you. I'm fine," she responded.

"It's a nice evening, isn't it?" said Roger. "I bet the stars would really show up away from the campfire. Would you like to walk around a bit?"

Angela declined that offer as well.

She turned her head slightly to see Thane standing just to their left. It was not hard to catch his eye.

She mouthed the words "I think I'm ready to go," and he must have been able to read her lips. He came immediately to where she was sitting, offered her his hand, and helped her up from her sitting position on the grass.

Angela smiled her good night to two disappointed young men and wound her way through the crowd of young people to thank her hostess.

"When you get home you can tell Thomas—" Trudie began.

Angela nodded in understanding, thanked her for the party and turned to go before Trudie could return to her sentence.

It was a beautiful evening. Even now Angela did not need her shawl. She tossed it carelessly over the back of Thane's buggy seat and sighed deeply as she looked up at the multitude of stars. The moon cast a soft mystic light on the world about her.

"Have fun?" asked Thane.

"I—I guess I did," answered Angela. She would never have thought to be anything but candid with Thane. Besides, he knew her so well that he would not have been fooled anyway. "I certainly got the surprise of my life. Why, I never dreamed that—that anyone would have remembered my birthday."

They rode in silence for a few moments and then Angela asked abruptly, "Has Thomas ever talked to you about—about his—his longing to work with seeds—as a researcher?"

"He shows them to me all the time."

"No, I mean to really work with plants and things—in a big—Where do they work with seeds, anyway?"

"In a laboratory, I guess—or out in small fields or something."

"Well, wherever. He would like to do that."

Thane nodded. He didn't seem at all surprised.

"What would you like to do?" asked Angela. "If you could do anything you wanted to."

"Marry a pretty girl," responded Thane without a moment's hesitation.

"Be serious," protested Angela, giving him a little push.

"Oh, I am," he insisted, but there was teasing in his voice.

"No, really. Tell me. If you could do anything you would like."

"Farm," said Thane, and Angela could not have been more surprised at his answer.

"Farm?" she echoed.

She looked at him, her eyes big in the moonlight. "Are you really serious?" she asked.

"Why do you think I spend so much time out at your place?" he asked, and Angela could hear the teasing again.

"You're joshing," she said.

His voice softened. "You want the truth. The real truth. Okay. I really would farm. I have always loved helping Tom and learning about planting and harvesting and caring for the animals. But that is not the reason I spend as much time as I can at your place."

Angela knew he was serious now.

"Are you surprised?"

"Yes," said Angela. "Yes, I guess I am. Does your—your pa know?"

"About my wanting to farm—or my reason for visiting your place?" Thane was quiet for a minute and then went on. "It doesn't seem too likely that I ever will farm, so I haven't really said anything to anyone."

Angela nodded slowly and then reached out and took Thane's arm. Thane gave her hand a slight squeeze in response.

"It's really strange, isn't it?" Angela said. "Thomas is farming and he wants to leave and do something else. You work with your father in a good business in town—and you want to farm. It seems that life gets terribly mixed up at times." Angela sighed deeply.

"And you?" asked Thomas.

"I—I want you both to be happy," replied Angela with deep feeling.

"But for you?" prompted Thane. "What do you want to do?"

"Oh, I don't know," sighed Angela, but tears formed in the corners of her eyes. "For now—I guess—I guess I just want to care for the youngsters—to try to raise them as Mama would have. And I can't. It's too big a job for me, Thane."

"You are doing just fine," Thane assured her, pressing her hand lightly.

Angela pulled out her handkerchief and dabbed her eyes. Then her chin lifted slightly. She looked ready to take up her task.

"And what about your life?" Thane pressed. "They won't need you forever. Don't you think you have the right to make some plans of your own?"

"I don't know," said Angela honestly. "I try not to think ahead any further than to getting the children raised."

They reached the farmyard and Thane stepped down from the buggy and turned to lend a hand to Angela. He led her to the veranda and up the steps. He still had not released her hand.

"Tired?" he asked.

Angela responded with a shrug of her shoulders.

"I guess I am. I—I'm not sure I'm ready for sleep, but I'd better go in. Thomas might want to go back for the sing-song."

"Is that why you left early?"

Angela laughed. A soft, good-humored laugh. "The real reason," she confided, "was because those Merrifield boys had me smothered."

"I noticed," said Thane, sounding a bit annoyed. "I'd a liked to have banged their heads together—"

"Well, it was time to leave anyway," Angela responded quickly. "Thanks for bringing me home. I'd better go in."

"I—I have something for you—before you go." Thane reached into a pocket of his coat.

"What—?" began Angela.

"A little birthday gift."

"Oh-h-h, Thane!" exclaimed Angela, "You shouldn't—"

"Now don't try to tell me what I should or shouldn't do," he chuckled. "Turn around," he instructed softly, and Angela did as bidden.

He reached his arms over her shoulders to settle something around her neck. In the moonlight she saw it glisten, but it was too dark for her to make it out properly. Thane fastened it without a fumble and then Angela felt something pressed lightly against her hair. Her breath caught. It was as though—as though he had kissed the top of her head like her papa used to do with her mama. But no—surely Thane wouldn't.

"There," he said, his lips close to her ear. "Happy birthday. I do hope that we—that you—will have many, many more."

"Thank you," she whispered back, wondering why they were speaking so softly. "Thank you. I can—can hardly wait to get into the light so I can see—"

He laughed at her. A soft, merry laugh. "Well, off you go then. Sweet dreams."

She stepped away, then back again. Thane had not moved. "Thane," she said, her voice breathless, "thank you so much for—for everything." She reached up on tiptoe and gave him a light kiss on the cheek, then hurried across the veranda and into the house.

Thomas was sitting at the kitchen table reading one of the study books. He lifted his head when she entered the room and she pointed to the cameo that hung from her neck on its silver chain. She lifted it with trembling fingers and studied it closely in the light.

"From Thane," she said softly, her eyes sparkling. "For my birthday."

Thomas nodded, showing no surprise at her announcement.

"Isn't it just—just beautiful?" whispered Angela, and she moved toward the stairs with misty eyes. She forgot all about asking Thomas if he wished to go back to the party.

Chapter Eleven

Harvest

As the days moved toward harvest, Angela found herself extremely busy. Thomas suggested that Louise stay home from school for a few days to help, but Angela would hear none of it. Thomas did not argue.

Angela had very little time to think about neighbors, but one day she quizzed Thomas as he hurriedly ate his dinner in the field. "Have you heard how Mr. Stratton is doing?"

"Which Mr. Stratton?"

"You know the one I mean," she said impatiently.

"Haven't you been delivering your baked goods lately?"

"You know I haven't had time—and Charlie hasn't been over for—for just ages."

"Poor Charlie," Thomas commented, and Angela's eyes opened wide with concern.

"He's on duty night and day, I hear," Thomas went on to explain. "If he wasn't so attached to that crotchety old man, I'm sure he would have left by now."

"I don't know how he manages," agreed Angela. "Nursing Mr. Stratton and running the ranch—"

"Oh, he doesn't run the ranch anymore," Thomas interrupted.

Angela swung her head to look at him.

"The son took over as boss of the ranch," Thomas explained. "About as soon as he got here he made it clear that he would be giving the orders. Charlie was told he was official nursemaid, nothing more."

"How awful!" exclaimed Angela. "Charlie has always been foreman at the ranch."

Angela gathered up the lunch things and started back to her kitchen, pondering the new information as she picked her way home through the stubble field.

If Charlie really had been assigned new duties, he must be feeling pretty bad about it, she reasoned. Charlie had loved the ranch and working with the cattle. Angela always got the impression that the herds were sort of like family, or friends, to old Charlie.

"I should get over there," Angela mused out loud. "Charlie might really be feeling down—and too busy to come calling."

In spite of her already busy day, Angela prepared a cake for the oven and determined to deliver it as soon as it cooled.

It didn't take her long to hurry across the fields separating the Petersons from the Strattons. Soon she was rapping lightly on the door of the big house. She recalled her last visit and her surprise when the young Mr. Stratton had answered her knock. She wondered if he would be the one at the door again today. She flushed slightly as she looked down at her Sunday dress. She had changed from her working frock—just in case. And she had pinned her hair a bit more carefully as well, and fastened on her most becoming bonnet.

But it was Gus who opened the door. He seemed genuinely pleased to see her and with great enthusiasm invited her inside.

Angela, recovering quickly from just a twinge of disappointment, said, "I'm sorry it's been so long. We've been so busy with the harvest and all."

"Of course. Of course," replied Gus, ushering her into the kitchen. "We haven't been expectin' you with everything you have to do. Sit down. Sit down. I'll jest put on some fresh coffee before I call Charlie."

"How is—?" Angela was going to say "Charlie," but she changed her mind, thinking that she would wait and see for herself. "How is Mr. Stratton?" she asked instead.

"He's poorly. Poorly," answered Gus, repeating himself, a little habit he had.

"I'm sorry," said Angela. "It must be awfully hard for all of you."

Gus nodded. "Tough. Tough," he admitted, his eyes clouding.

Gus did not have to leave the kitchen to call Charlie. Angela heard a step on the back stairs and Charlie entered the room looking tired and old. Angela had never seen him looking so down. He had not even shaved.

His eyes brightened when he saw her, and he straightened his bent shoulders just a bit.

"I've been worried about you," Angela admitted, and Charlie gave her a nod.

"I hear he is no better," Angela went on.

Charlie settled himself in a chair across from her at the small kitchen table and rubbed a hand over his unshaven face. A look of shock filled his eyes, as though he suddenly realized how he must look to the young girl.

"Didn't have time—" he began apologetically, but Angela would not let him finish.

"I hear you are nursing night and day. You must be worn out."

Charlie nodded and let his hand drop to the table. Angela wondered how much longer he would be able to hang on.

"I'll go on up for a while and give you a break," said Gus, and he lifted a piece of the fresh cake from the pan and headed for the stairway.

"Bring me some coffee when the pot boils," he called back over his shoulder.

"How are you?" Angela asked as soon as Gus had gone.

Charlie looked confused over the question and Angela wondered if he had been getting any sleep.

"Thomas said you don't care for the cattle anymore."

Charlie nodded, but Angela didn't see pain in his eyes as she had expected.

"The young Stratton does that," Charlie admitted.

"Does he know how?" Angela asked before she could stop herself.

Charlie nodded a tired nod. "He's sharp enough—even though he is a city-slicker. He studies on it—and he asks if he doesn't know. I gotta hand him thet."

"Does he—does he plan to stay then? I mean—I thought—well, I just assumed that he would be going back to—to wherever, as soon as—"

Angela couldn't finish.

"Sounds to me like he means to stay," said Charlie.

Angela felt a tingle pass through her.

"And what will you do?" asked Angela.

Charlie just shrugged. "I'll figure thet out when the time comes," he replied, revealing neither concern nor enthusiasm.

"What you need is a good night's sleep," declared Angela. "Couldn't I come and stay with Mr. Stratton for a night or two and—?"

Charlie shook his head adamantly, stirring for the first time. "We make out fine—and it won't be much longer, I fear. Thet sickroom is no place fer a young lady."

"But—"

"No, ma'am," insisted Charlie, and Angela knew it was useless to argue further.

"I'd best get on home." She stood up and smoothed the skirt of her dress, feeling a little foolish now and wishing she had come over in her kitchen frock.

"Gus might like his cup of coffee now," Angela prompted.

Charlie swore softly under his breath. "I fergot all about it," he murmured, rising quickly and lifting a big mug from the cupboard shelf.

Angela let herself out and started for home deeply troubled. It was clear that Charlie was about at the breaking point. She wished there were something she could do.

She was so absorbed in her thoughts that she did not hear the approaching horse until the rider had reined in beside her.

"Good afternoon, miss."

Angela jumped in surprise.

"My apology, Miss Peterson," the young Stratton quickly responded, stepping down from the horse with one smooth motion. "I didn't mean to startle you. Are you quite all right?"

He took her hand and drew her toward him.

Angela flushed and stepped back. "Oh, I—I'm fine," she faltered. "You—you just caught me off guard for a minute. I was too deep in thought, I guess." She took another small step backward and he released her hand.

They stood there—face-to-face—assessing each other.

Angela watched his eyes move from her bonnet to her shoes and back to her face. He smiled approvingly, and she wondered if that meant she was as pretty as the city girls he knew.

Angela used the time to take a full look at the young man before her. He was even taller than she had realized. He was not dressed in the finery of their first meeting. Instead, he wore western garb—and wore it well. His clothing was newer and more expensive looking than the working clothes worn by most of the local young men. His chaps were still highly polished dark leather, his shirt unfaded from the summer sun. His wide-brimmed hat was not yet stained from rain and snow, nor his gloves hardened into the shape of curled fingers. He removed a glove and reached up to lift his hat from his head. He stood before her, dark hair glistening in the sun, dark eyes softened with concern for her welfare. Angela found him most appealing.

"I was—was just checking on your—your father—and Charlie," Angela said suddenly, taking one more step backward.

He was suddenly the young man she had met before—in spite of his change of outfit.

"I'm hurt," he said. "I was hoping you had called to see me."

Angela had regained her composure, realizing that she probably made a rather striking picture in her Sunday dress and bonnet. She turned her blue eyes directly on the young man and allowed her lips to curl into a teasing smile. "I assumed the boss would have little time for afternoon tea parties," she countered.

The young man tipped his head to one side and his eyes studied her face. Angela felt her cheeks glow under the close scrutiny.

"I must apologize for my appearance," he said at last, "but if you will give me a few minutes, I will rid myself of the dust and filth and be happy to share that cup of tea."

He offered Angela an arm, and for one unguarded minute she was about to accept it.

"Oh, I was only teasing," she admitted. "I—I must hurry home. I've got a thousand things to do."

"What a pity!" His voice sounded as if he meant the words, but Angela still couldn't read his eyes. She felt confused, knowing that he was testing her, yet realizing she didn't understand his meaning.

"Another time then?" he asked. Angela wondered if she sensed an arrogance in the young man.

She tipped her head to one side and looked at him candidly. She was not flirting now. She had recovered from her moment of youthful foolishness. "I'll give it some thought," she replied simply. "I may call on Charlie again."

She turned to go, but he caught her arm, his grasp gentle but definite.

"And what about me?" he asked in a low voice. "What if I should wish to call?"

Angela felt her pulse racing. She hardly knew how to respond. No young man had ever asked her if he could come calling. She cocked her head as though considering—when in fact she was trying to once again gain control of her emotions.

"It hardly seems the proper time to be calling—when—when your father is so—so ill," she responded at last.

"Of course. Of course, I meant later. After he is—well again."

Angela wondered if he was very deeply concerned about his father. He didn't seem to be embarrassed that he had suggested calling when the man lay desperately ill. Nor did she believe for one minute that he expected his father ever to be well again. A shiver passed through her. She didn't think she cared much for the man, after all—even if he did think he was such a fine gentleman.

Angela eased her arm from his hold and gave him one last look. She was about to take her leave when she remembered her mama. Mama would never have allowed her children to respond to poor taste with poor taste. The young man had paid her a fine compliment and she was about to walk away in a huff. *Perhaps his city ways are different than the ways out here,* she reminded herself. *And remember, he has never really known his father. That man—sick in bed—unable to think or speak— that really has been a poor way to meet the man who should have earned his respect and love.*

Angela turned back to the young man, a friendly smile on her lips. "I do think that it is proper to attend the house of the Lord on any occasion," she said quietly. "And it would likely be quite in order for the neighbors to invite one home for dinner following."

He paused a moment as if to sort out her meaning and then nodded. "And where do I find your church?"

"It's the only one in town," she replied.

"Next Sunday?" he asked.

"Next Sunday," she nodded. "The family will be expecting you."

She turned and without a backward glance headed determinedly home.

Her cheeks burned as she walked. What had come over her? She had acted like—just like she had seen Trudie act with Thomas. She had not appreciated it in Trudie and she did not appreciate it in herself.

I refuse to act like a silly schoolgirl, she scolded herself. *If he does show up for church, then we shall all treat him as a dinner guest. But I will not—absolutely will not—flirt with him again.*

Angela's face burned even more deeply as she thought of her coy looks and teasing smiles. "Whatever came over me anyway?" she said aloud with impatience. "I have never—never acted so foolish before. I can't for the life of me imagine what I was trying to do."

Though it was still just a feeling she couldn't quite put into words, Angela was beginning to realize that buried deep within her was a young woman longing for special attention—special love.

Chapter Twelve

Sunday

Angela felt agitated as she prepared for church on Sunday morning. She should have been elated—relieved—as Thomas was, for the harvest was all in the bins and the crops had done well. Thomas was set to relax and be thankful. The family would have their needs met for another year.

Angela was thankful too. It was a relief to know that she could now shop for the needed material from which to sew winter garments. It was wonderful that they would be able to get new footwear for each family member. With thanksgiving she would buy the wool for mittens and heavy socks. But even though Angela knew she should be humming a tune of praise, she fidgeted and fiddled and felt her nerves strung tight.

She had told no one of her invitation to the young Stratton for Sunday dinner—not even Thomas. *Mr. Stratton probably won't be at church anyway*, she told herself, *and I did rather make that the stipulation.*

But just in case, Angela had two young roosters prepared and in the roasting pan and the table was set with Mama's good china.

"I see we are celebrating," said Thomas, and when Angela nodded her head, he smiled. Angela was sure that Thomas felt it quite appropriate to celebrate.

If he should happen to come—and I'm sure he won't, Angela reminded herself, *I will not act like a smitten young adolescent. I will act like the young woman Mama would expect me to be.*

Angela took a bit more time with her grooming, and when she finally appeared and announced that she was ready, the rest of the family was waiting for her.

"Thane's birthday gift looks nice with that dress," said Thomas approvingly as they walked out to the wagon. Angela nodded in agreement, wondering about his rather knowing smile.

It was not a long drive to church, and soon they joined the others gathering for the service.

The Merrifield brothers joined their little procession into the church, and Angela feared they were going to try to crowd in the pew beside her. With a bit of maneuvering she managed to place herself between Sara and Louise, and she smiled a polite greeting to the two young men as they passed on by.

The Andrews family was across the aisle. Angela waved a hand as discreetly as possible to signal that the lovely cameo was resting against the bodice of her pale blue calico. Mrs. Andrews smiled and Thane looked pleased.

Angela turned her attention back to the Sunday congregation.

Trudie came in with a rustle of skirts and a flip of her red hair and seated herself directly in front of the Petersons. She turned to say hello to Angela and to give Thomas a cute smile. Angela again reminded herself that she would not encourage such a manner.

The service was about to start when Trudie turned and whispered to Angela, "Look. Over there."

Angela stole a glance to the side indicated by Trudie's bobbing head, and there was the young Mr. Stratton, planted firmly in a church pew. At Angela's glance he nodded his head slightly and she felt her face flush. She turned her full attention back to the front of the church, relieved that Pastor Merrifield was taking his place behind the pulpit.

Perhaps Angela could have concentrated better on the morning service had not Trudie been so restless. Angela caught her stealing frequent glances in the direction of the young visitor. She seemed to have forgotten Thomas totally.

So that's how fickle you are, Trudie Sommers, Angela said to herself. Then she felt anger stirring within her. *Well, if you think you can just throw Thomas aside because you have discovered a fascinating new face, you are wrong. If I have anything to do with it, Mr. Stratton will not so much as give you a "good morning."* Angela decided then and there that she might do just a bit of flirting, after all, if it would stop Trudie from claiming the attention of the young man.

From then on, Angela had a hard time paying attention to the morning worship service. She chided herself, forcing her thoughts back to what Pastor Merrifield was saying, but at another glance and toss of the red head in front of her, she would lose the train of the message again.

As soon as the service ended, Trudie was at her side. "Did you see him? Did you see him? I wonder who he is."

"You mean you don't know?" asked Angela, as though she had known the young man for years.

"Do you? Do you know him?" Trudie was shaking Angela's arm as she asked the question.

"He's our neighbor," answered Angela matter-of-factly.

"Your what?"

"Mr. Stratton," replied Angela, straightening the sleeve that Trudie had been tugging.

"Mr. Stratton? That's not him. I know Mr. Stra—You mean the son? That young man is Stratton's son?" Trudie was shrieking her whisper into Angela's ear.

"What's his name? Oh, what's his name?" Trudie demanded.

Angela suddenly realized she didn't know, but she wouldn't have admitted it for anything.

"I choose to address him as Mr. Stratton," she answered.

"Oh, you must introduce me, you simply must," Trudie gushed.

Angela stood and nodded to her sisters to allow them to exit the church.

"Very well," she said to Trudie as they walked down the aisle. "I'll introduce you if you wish."

She hoped that by the time they reached the church steps, the young man would have disappeared. But he was making the rounds of the young men, being introduced by Thane. Thane had met the young Stratton on more than one occasion when he came to purchase items from the store. It seemed that the young men of the church were giving the visitor a warm welcome.

As Angela moved down the walk, the young man lifted his hat and stepped forward.

"Good morning, Miss Peterson," he said politely with a dip of his head. Angela again noticed the deep, cultured voice.

"Good morning, Mr. Stratton," she responded, almost shyly. Feeling Trudie tug her sleeve, an impishness possessed her. "I trust you can find your way to our dinner table with no difficulty. We are looking forward to having you." And she gave the young man a warm smile—almost as coy as Trudie would have given.

There was a gasp beside her and then Trudie gave another yank on Angela's sleeve.

"And before my friend tears my sleeve from my dress," she went on, "let me introduce you. This is Miss Trudie Sommers. I believe she would like to meet you."

Trudie's red face did not keep her from stepping forward and taking the young man's extended hand.

Mr. Stratton bid her good morning. Then he turned his attention back to Angela.

"May I drive you home, Miss Peterson?" he asked, and Angela felt her own face flush slightly. She had not even told Thomas they would be having a guest, and now he was proposing that she ride with him instead of the family.

But Trudie was standing by, her mouth open and her eyes wide with wonder.

"I'd like that," Angela responded. "Just give me a minute to inform my brother," and she hastened off to find Thomas.

Thomas was talking with Thane. Angela burst in upon them and blurted out her mission.

"Thomas," she said breathlessly, "I—I've gotten myself in rather a—a strange situation. I invited Mr. Stratton to dinner—if he came to church first—and he is here. He has—has asked me to ride with him, so I will see you back at the house."

Angela turned quickly without reading the two faces before her. She feared that Trudie, if left too long, might turn the tables on the day's plans.

The dinner went well enough. Thomas was courteous to their guest and spoke with him easily. Angela learned more about the young man from listening to their conversation.

He had been raised in Atlanta, his mother's hometown. In fact, he was reared in the same house that his mother had been. He had no aunts or uncles, but he did have grandparents. It sounded to Angela as if they doted on the boy.

"How did they feel about your coming west?" asked Thomas.

"They weren't very happy."

"And your mother?"

"I'm not sure my mother still claims me," he answered candidly.

"Then why did you come?"

"I had to. I had heard so many little remarks about my father over the years that I had to come and see for myself if he—if he was as they described him."

"And is he?"

"I don't know. I have been trying to piece things together. I think that many things might be accurate. But—I may never know. I still don't really know the man."

Angela felt it was a shame that his coming had been delayed until it was too late for both of them.

"Will your mother join you?"

"Oh no. She hated it out here. She would never come back."

Angela moved out of earshot. She felt like an eavesdropper in her own home. There were better ways to get to know her guest. She would wait until he volunteered the information to her.

She did discover his name. It happened as she served the coffee.

"Do you take cream or sugar, Mr. Stratton?" she asked.

"Please—please call me Carter," he quickly replied. "All of you, and I will call you Thomas, if I may," he added, asking permission from Thomas with his eyes.

Thomas nodded, and from then on they referred to their guest as Carter.

It was a pleasant afternoon. Without Trudie hovering near, Angela was able to keep her resolve of not being foolishly flirty with the young man. She acted as a proper hostess, caring for her guest and family.

When he prepared to go, Carter found a few moments with her alone.

"Will you walk me to my carriage?" he asked, and Angela realized it was the first time she had heard the conveyance referred to as a carriage. But then, perhaps his buggy was a carriage. It was certainly fancier than any other vehicle about.

She fell into step beside him and accompanied him to the hitching rail.

"This has been delightful," he assured her. "You are a much better cook than Gus," he teased, and when Angela smiled he looked pleased.

"May I come again?" he asked.

When Angela's brow began to crease he hurried on.

"I know—it doesn't look proper to call when my father is near death." His candor surprised Angela. "But we are neighbors, and I do enjoy your brother and—and the others. And I would honestly like the pleasure of your company again. May I?"

"Perhaps, as a neighbor—and friend—dropping in," said Angela, "but not as a gentleman caller—at the present."

"I understand," he said softly, and he tipped his hat and bid her good day.

Angela did not wait to see him go. She turned back to the house and her kitchen. The days were getting cooler she noticed. It was a good thing Thomas had all of the crop in the bins. Any day now they might be surprised by snow.

Trudie showed up on the doorstep the next day. Angela thought at first that it might be to try to make amends to Thomas for so thoroughly ignoring him the day before, but Trudie was still full of questions about Mr. Stratton.

"Does he plan to live here?" she asked.

"I believe so," Angela replied.

"Oh-h, just think of it," crowed Trudie. "Every girl in the neighborhood will be after him, and I saw him first."

Angela wondered how Trudie came to that conclusion. She was the one who had introduced them.

"I think I'll have another party," bubbled Trudie. "I wonder what he likes to do."

"He says he likes the stage and operas," said Angela, challenging Trudie to match that with her backyard parties.

"Oh-h," Trudie sighed ecstatically, undaunted. "He is so—so sophisticated. I just love it."

Angela was glad when Trudie rose to leave. Her friend was almost to the door before she called back, "Oh, I came to see what you are wearing to the wedding on Saturday. I think I will wear my lavender satin."

Angela knew the dress. It was a lovely, full-skirted gown with generous amounts of ribbons and lace. Angela had always felt that it was not a good color choice for a person with red hair.

"I don't know," answered Angela. She had almost forgotten that Saturday was the day Hazel Conroy had chosen for her wedding. She hadn't even thought ahead to what she—or any other member of the family—would wear, but she knew they would all be expected to be there.

"I heard Hazel invite Mr. Stratton," explained Trudie, "and he said he would be delighted to attend."

Then Trudie was gone, tossing her head and smiling.

As soon as Angela had finished the morning washing, she cast a furtive look at the lowering sky and headed for the barn to find Thomas.

"Thomas," she asked, "do you mind if I drive over to Carson?"

"Today?" he questioned.

"Right now. I had forgotten about Hazel's wedding on Saturday and they have a bigger yard goods store there. I thought I could do my purchasing for the winter things we need, too."

"It's rather late in the day to be heading for Carson."

"I'll hurry. I'll have lots of time to catch the store. When the kids get home, you can put them to their choring." Then she quickly amended her words. "No, you won't need to do that. They know what they are to do."

Angela ran back to the house to prepare for the trip while Thomas hitched the horse to the light buggy.

Chapter Thirteen

The Wedding

Angela coaxed the mare into a trot and settled into the buggy for her ride to Carson. She was eager to cover the miles, but careful not to push the mare too fast. It was bumpy enough at a moderate pace and she did not want to wind the animal.

In a small box at her feet were garments from home. She had Thomas's suit to compare with others in the store. She also had one of Derek's jackets and a foot pattern for each child. She hoped these would enable her to make some sensible choices for her family and be back home again before it got too dark.

The trip took Angela longer than she had anticipated. She kept one eye on the darkening sky as she made her decisions. She did find a suit for Thomas. By comparing the old and the new she was sure that with a minor adjustment here or there, it would fit him just fine. Then she began her search for a proper suit for Derek. That took a bit longer, and Angela was really getting nervous by the time she found what she was looking for. The footwear came next—shoes and winter wear. There weren't many clothes to select from so the choice did not take long. She turned her attention to the fabric, fingering some rich materials with sensitive hands.

She found a delicately patterned calico for Sara. With a bit of lace on the collar, the finished dress surely would please the young girl. It was more difficult to make the decision for Louise. She knew her sister would like something a bit more grown-up, but Angela did not want to rush her into adult garments. Finding the right balance was difficult, but after carefully considering fabric and patterns Angela made a decision and felt pleased with her choice.

She then gave her attention to the material for her own dress. She fingered the fine silks, let the satins drip from her hand, and eyed the expensive laces with longing.

"This is foolish," she finally muttered softly. "Here I am willing to spend the autumn's harvest on a silly notion that I need to dress to attract attention. Well, I don't. I need a good sensible dress for church, not a frilly frivolous dress for partying." Angela deserted the shelves of expensive material and moved to the more durable fabrics.

In the end she chose a blue voile. It was both sensible and attractive. Then with one eye still on the darkening sky she hurried to choose materials for warm winter garments and wool yarn for mittens. Having completed her purchases, she piled them all on the counter.

The total cost was staggering, and Angela was glad Thomas had insisted she bring extra money. She paid the bill and the young man in the store helped her load her parcels into the buggy.

"Got far to go?" he asked, his eye also on the sky. Angela nodded. She had farther to go than she cared to admit.

"Looks like it could snow," the boy went on, and Angela climbed quickly into the buggy and clucked to the horse.

"Thank you for your help," she called to the boy as she turned the mare around and urged her to a trot.

The mare did not need to be encouraged. She, too, was anxious to be home again. She lifted her nose into the air and snorted, then jerked her head in impatience and headed out of town at a brisk trot.

Angela had nothing to do but hold the reins. The wind was blowing now, and she felt the sting of it right through her coat. She tucked herself in a bit more closely and turned her back slightly to the chilling breeze. She would be glad to get home.

When at last Angela pulled into the farm lane she was met at the gate by Thomas, lantern in hand. It had long since grown dark, and she could tell by his pacing that he had been concerned.

"It took longer than I thought it would," she called to him in explanation.

"I'll take Star. You get in out of the cold," he said, relief in his voice.

Angela did not argue. She climbed stiffly down from the buggy. Derek and Louise emerged from the kitchen.

"Did you get the things?" Louise asked excitedly.

"I did," replied Angela and realized she could not speak without causing her teeth to chatter.

"You'd better get in by the fire," advised Derek. "I'll bring in these parcels."

Angela murmured her thanks and hurried into the house. Louise took her coat and hung it on its proper peg, and Angela moved to the warm kitchen stove.

"Sara, bring a chair," called Louise. "She's 'most frozen." Louise sat Angela down and poked more wood into the stove.

"Take off your shoes and stockings," she ordered as she went for the washbasin. "I'll get some warm water to soak your feet."

Louise had never taken over and told Angela what to do before, but Angela obeyed without question. For once, it felt kind of nice to be the one being fussed over.

Soon Derek came in with the parcels and the girls began to coax to see what she had bought.

"No. Let's wait until Thomas comes in," Angela said, shivering. "We'll all look at them together."

Angela was glad Thomas did not take long, though the wait was difficult for the children.

"Now you can look—one parcel at a time," Angela said as she sorted the packages, telling them who should open what.

They all seemed pleased with her purchases. Louise was especially excited over the new Sunday dress material. Angela knew the girl was envisioning herself in the pretty green print.

Thomas took the new suit to his bedroom and soon emerged to model it. It fit him even better than Angela had hoped.

"Derek, you try on yours!" cried Sara, and Derek obliged. He came out grinning. He seemed pleased that his arm no longer showed below the hem of the jacket sleeve. The pants were a bit long. "Growing room," Angela called it and promised she'd take up the hem in plenty of time for the community wedding.

They fussed over the shoes, the warm materials, the wool—everything Angela had purchased. Angela sneezed once or twice as she thawed out beside the stove, but in spite of her discomfort she was glad she had made the trip to Carson.

They played their game again. Thomas started it spontaneously. "I remember," he began, "one time when Pa and Mama went into Carson. They came back with new clothes for each of us, but they also brought me a new bridle for Midget. Do you remember that, Angela?"

Angela nodded. It had been a long time since she had even thought of the pony Midget.

"And at the same time they brought new boots for Sara. They were so tiny. I remember thinking that I had never seen anything as little and cute as those shoes."

"Were they?" asked Sara, her eyes glowing.

"They were. Just little tiny things. Black—with buttons."

"Oh, I wish I still had them!" exclaimed Sara.

"You wore them out, if I recall properly," put in Thomas.

"Did they bring me anything?" asked Louise.

"They brought things for each of us. Let's see if I can remember some of them. Was that the time—no. It was another time they brought you the white muff. It was from Andrews' store, I think. Do you remember it, Louise?"

"The white muff? I do. I do. I remember how I loved to put my hands into it. I would take off my mittens so I could feel it on my hands. It was so soft!"

Angela sneezed again and then turned to Derek. "I remember what they brought you. That spinning top. The one you keep on your shelf. They got it for you on that trip. Do you remember?"

Derek nodded.

"Nobody could ever make it work as good as Papa," he said, and Angela realized again how much the boy missed his father.

"We'd better get Angela to bed," said Louise suddenly. Angela was surprised at the girl's concern until she added, with laughter, "If she goes and gets sick, we won't have any new dresses for the wedding."

————

Angela did not get sick. She worked long hours to get her sewing done. Louise and Sara even volunteered to do some of her usual chores so she could stay at the machine. At last the two suits were altered and three new dresses hung from wooden hangers, just in time for the big day.

Louise couldn't wait to appear in her new gown. She tried it on repeatedly and looked at herself in the mirror. Then she began to experiment with her hair, lifting it up this way, then holding it that way.

Oh, dear, thought Angela, *she is going to insist on wearing her hair up and she's too young for that. Now we'll have another fuss for sure.*

The weather warmed in time for the wedding. Angela was thankful for that as there really wasn't much warmth to the blue voile. There was a good deal of hurrying as they all dressed for the occasion. There was a minor fuss over Louise's hair. She came down with it pinned up in a fashion much too old for her years. Angela caught her breath and was about to comment when the unruly curls came tumbling down around Louise's ears. Louise looked as if she were about to burst into tears.

"Would you like me to help you?" offered Angela. "It is hard to get it to stay until one gets used to pinning it up."

Louise nodded, and in the re-pinning Angela was able to retain much of Louise's little girl look. At first Louise began to protest over the adjusted style but Angela cut in simply with, "This suits you better," and Louise took a second look in the mirror, grinned at her image, and said no more.

Thomas hustled them all to the buggy and headed the team for the Conroy farm.

"How is Hazel going to get everybody into the living room?" asked Sara.

"I have no idea," admitted Angela.

"Well, when I get married I'm going to pick June or July so I can have an outside wedding," went on Sara. "It's silly to try to get married in October. It could have been snowing on our heads."

"She had to wait until the harvest was over," Angela informed her sister.

"Well, there won't be any harvest to worry about in July," Sara insisted.

Thomas laughed and reached out a hand to tousle Sara's hair.

"Don't you dare," cautioned Angela. "It took me a good part of the morning to get those curls and ribbons just right."

Thomas quickly withdrew his hand and laughed again.

Trudie was the first one out to meet them when they arrived. She bounded toward them, her lavender skirts swishing over the grass. She tossed her mane of red hair and gave Thomas a coy look to see if he had taken notice of her. He was busy tethering the horses.

"He hasn't arrived yet," Trudie whispered to Angela, "but Hazel says he promised to come."

Why should Hazel care? wondered Angela. *She is about to be married.*

Trudie opened her mouth to speak again when Angela noticed Roberta. She was in her own special chair—one from which she could not fall. Angela moved toward the girl to speak to her. Trudie trailed along behind until she realized Angela's intentions.

"What if he comes?" she whispered frantically. "He'll catch you talking with her."

Angela gave Trudie a long look and moved on toward the handicapped girl.

Angela was never sure whether Roberta recognized her or just responded as she would to anyone who came near.

"Hello," Angela said.

"Hello." She held out a fragile hand, which Angela took in her own.

"How are you, Roberta?" asked Angela, giving the girl a smile.

"Haz—Haz get marry," managed the girl, pointing to the spot where a small pulpit had been set up under the trees. October or not—it was to be an outdoor wedding.

"Yes, Hazel is getting married," agreed Angela, and Roberta laughed gleefully, kicking her legs and clapping her hands.

Then Roberta turned her attention to the restraints that held her in her chair. She picked at them impatiently. "Out," she said in agitation.

"I can't take them off. You might fall," Angela tried to explain. "If you fall and get hurt, you won't see Hazel get married."

But the girl still picked at the soft straps that kept her safely in her chair.

"My, you have a pretty dress," Angela said in an effort to distract her. The dress was becoming. Angela was sure it had been sewn for this special occasion.

But Roberta would not be sidetracked. "Out," she pleaded again, and Angela was relieved when she saw Ingrid coming to bring the girl a drink and a cookie.

Just before the ceremony was about to start, Angela felt a hand touch her elbow. It was Carter. He had arrived just as he had promised. For a moment Angela wished she were wearing one of the lovely silks or satins she had admired at Carson. But the moment quickly passed. She looked across the yard to where Trudie was standing in her elaborate lavender satin. Angela couldn't help comparing her simple frock with Trudie's.

But my own simple dress suits me, thought Angela. *I am simple—not stunning like Trudie.*

Carter tipped his hat and complimented Angela with his eyes as he gazed on her new gown and her newly trimmed bonnet.

"You look lovely, Miss Peterson," he said at last, and Angela's breath caught. She wished to believe him.

"Why, thank you, sir," she responded, merriment making her blue eyes shine.

Then Angela's eyes met Thane's. He was standing as usual with Thomas. The two always managed to get together. Angela gave a little wave and smiled his way. Thane nodded in response, then returned her smile. But Angela noticed that he did not brighten as he usually did. Was something wrong? She felt her throat tighten. She wanted to ask him the reason for his serious look, but Carter was steering her to a nearby bench. Even then she might have tried to push her way through the crowd and speak with Thane for just a minute, but the preacher was taking his place at the front of the gathering. The ceremony was about to begin.

Hazel made her entrance and all eyes turned to the bride.

Chapter Fourteen

Changes

Charlie arrived at the Peterson door one evening. The wind held a chill, and Thomas quickly bid him enter and warm himself while Angela hustled to put on the coffee. One look at the poor man and she sensed something further was wrong.

"He's gone," Charlie said, lowering himself into the chair Thomas offered.

"I'm so sorry," said Angela, setting the pot on the stove and crossing to Charlie. "When?"

"This afternoon—'bout four."

"You need some sleep. You look worn out. Why don't you just stay here for the night and—?"

"No. Gus will need me."

Angela let the matter drop.

"When will the funeral be?" asked Thomas.

"We haven't made those arrangements yet—and there might be some complications."

"Complications?"

Charlie nodded his head. "The boss said, 'No service.' He just wanted to be buried on his own land. But the new boss says thet's heathen. Says there's no way he's gonna jest stick his pa in the ground without some ceremony."

Angela nodded, new respect for Carter growing in her thinking.

"Sounds reasonable to me," expressed Thomas.

Charlie nodded his head. "Well, I gotta say thet I agree with 'im on thet one. Still, it's hard not to carry out the boss's wishes."

Angela laid a hand on the bent shoulder. She understood how he must feel.

"You've served him well for many years," Angela reminded him. "I guess no one could expect more than you have given."

Charlie stayed long enough to drink a cup of coffee and eat a slice of lemon loaf. Then he bundled up in his heavy coat and headed back across the empty field.

"If things had continued on as they have been, I'm not sure Charlie could have taken it much longer," observed Thomas.

Angela nodded in agreement. "The poor man," she said in a whisper. "He looks like a bearded ghost. He's lost weight, Thomas, and his eyes look sunken from lack of sleep."

"Well, it's over now, I guess."

Angela nodded again and then a new thought struck her. "But not for poor Mr. Stratton," she said. "For him—there is an eternity ahead—and I fear for what it holds for him."

Thomas lifted his head to look at her.

"Oh, Thomas," admitted Angela. "I never once tried to share my faith with him."

"Pa tried," responded Thomas.

"He did?"

"More than once. I was with him one time. I remember. Pa said that the caring for the state of one's soul was the most important job a man had to do in life. Then he invited Mr. Stratton to church."

Angela waited.

"The man cursed at Pa. I will never forget it. It shocked me that a man would speak in such a way. Then he clenched his fist and shook it in Pa's face. Pa never even blinked. I was hoping Pa would punch him." Thomas stopped to smile momentarily at the memory, then went on.

"Pa didn't back down, but he allowed the man some self-respect—even though he knew he was wrong. 'Mr. Stratton,' he said. 'A man's got a right to make his own decisions in life. I'll grant you that. But I'll also continue to pray for you—and if you ever want to discuss the matter—well, you've got a neighbor and friend just over the fence.' "

"He said that?"

"I was so proud of my pa that day," declared Thomas. "I knew right then that it took a bigger man to extend his hand than it did to fight."

Angela picked up the empty coffee cups.

"Thomas," she said. "We have been so blessed—you and I—to

have parents like we had. It just hurts me to think that all the—the memories that we treasure—the—the younger ones can't share. Our folks—through their teaching, built such a strong, sure base for us."

"We share them in our game and in our Memory Book."

"But that's not the same as getting them firsthand," insisted Angela.

"But it is still important," Thomas replied.

Angela crossed to the kitchen shelf that held their Memory Books. There were three scribblers now—all recording the things family members had recalled about their parents. She let her hand caress them gently. They *were* important. In sharing memories, they had grown even closer as a family.

"Yes," Angela agreed. "It's the best we can do." Then she lifted her head and spoke again to her older brother. "Thomas, we must be careful to be kind to Carter. He doesn't even have any memories of his father. Only rumors. And I don't think he and his mother are on very good terms at present, either. I could—could hear it in his voice when he spoke of her."

"I think she spoiled him—then became angry when he wanted to be his own man instead of her little boy," observed Thomas.

"Well, he needs friends. If one doesn't have family—then one needs friends even more."

———

The funeral service was held two days later. Reverend Merrifield conducted the brief ceremony, and Mr. Stratton, Sr., the community's rich man, was laid in the town cemetery with an appropriate stone marking his final resting place.

Most folks from the area attended the service. Only a few, like Mrs. Blackwell, declined.

"I had nothing to do with the man while he lived," she observed sourly, "so I see no reason to have anything to do with him when he's dead."

Mr. Blackwell came into town to get a harness repaired and slipped, unobtrusively, into the gathering.

The three mourners who stood close to the graveside made quite a contrast. Carter towered above the other two. He was dressed in a fine dark suit. His broad shoulders wore it well and his head was bowed just enough to show proper respect for the man who had been his father, but whom he had never known. The two little men who stood beside him wore the same suits they had worn for funerals over many years. The garments were faded and wrinkled—much like the two who wore them. But the faces of the two little gentlemen were etched with genuine grief. Charlie stopped to brush away a tear now and then, unaffected by the crowd of observers.

There wasn't much the Reverend Merrifield could say in comfort to the bereaved, so he spoke to those who remained behind.

"I go to prepare a place for you," he quoted and then lifted his eyes to the neighbors.

"Friends—Christ spoke those words—and so we know them to be true. He has gone to prepare a place for us—for each one of us. But for us to take advantage of His goodness—we must prepare our hearts for that place.

"Have you considered what you must do? Christ will keep His word. The place will be prepared and waiting. It will be ready when you depart this world—if you also have made preparations.

"God has told us in His Word what we must do to prepare. 'Believe on the Lord Jesus Christ and thou shalt be saved.' Repent—turn from your wickedness and unto God. Ask God to forgive those wrongs—those sins of the past—and to give you a clean heart—clean thoughts, clean actions—so that you might be prepared for the place He has prepared. Accept the forgiveness of God through the death of His Son, and be baptized in faith."

As the sermon continued, Angela stole a look at the crowd of neighbors all around the graveside. How many of them might need to hear the words being spoken? Had she really been concerned about their eternal destinies—or had she been too busy caring for her family? *Mama would have found the time—I know she would have,* Angela thought. *I must be careful so I don't get too taken up with duties that I forget people.*

Angela glanced again at the three menfolk at the grave. Carter stood respectfully, yet locked away. Angela could not read his thoughts or feelings. Charlie mourned openly. Poor little Charlie. The long illness of his boss and friend had almost done him in. Gus looked uncomfortable, as if he wished the parson would hurry. His hand supported Charlie by holding his elbow. It was touching to see the two elderly, wizened little men sharing their grief in such a manner.

———

"What will you do now?" Angela asked Charlie and Gus.

She had bundled up a few loaves of fresh bread in a clean kitchen towel and taken them across the field. She sat in the big kitchen. Now that Gus had been freed to return to his regular duties, he had scrubbed and polished until everything shone again.

"I guess I jest go back to my cookin'," said Gus lightly.

"And you?" asked Angela turning to Charlie. "Will you be riding again?"

Charlie shook his head slowly. "I'm too old for ridin'. Got no yen to be back out in the sun and the snow. My bones ache and the old breaks give me a twinge now and then. I guess I'll just find me a little shack somewhere and sit and rock."

Angela smiled. If anyone deserved to sit and rock, she felt Charlie did.

"Why do you need a shack? There's plenty of room here."

"Thet's what I been tellin' 'im," cut in Gus. "No reason I can see fer 'im to be lookin' fer another place. No reason."

Charlie shook his head.

"I ain't no use to nobody here anymore," he insisted. "Ain't gonna sit around an' jest get in the way."

"Why don't you come live with us?" Angela asked so suddenly that she surprised even herself.

Charlie looked up quickly to see if he had heard her right.

"We can make room," Angela continued, her mind busily trying to work out her plan.

Charlie was shaking his head slowly.

"Sure we can," she said. "I'll speak to Thomas. We'd love to have you—all of us would."

"No-o-o," spoke Charlie, but Angela was sure the idea appealed to him.

"We have a nice wide veranda that Papa built—"

"Nothing wrong with your place," cut in Charlie. "It's me. I ain't good for nothin' anymore."

"Of course you are. Don't say that. You are still worn out from your long ordeal, but you'll get your strength back again. Just wait and see. And if—if you don't—then—then we'd still like to have you."

Charlie reached out a calloused hand and patted Angela's soft young one. "You are kind, girlie—jest like yer mama. But thet arrangement wouldn't work."

"Will you at least think about it?" insisted Angela.

Charlie chuckled. "Think about it! Shucks, I'll dream about it."

Angela left feeling that with Charlie dreaming and her praying, surely something would work out.

Chapter Fifteen

A Caller

Carter caught Angela unexpectedly with his first call, and she had to excuse herself and go to her room to change and repair her hair. While she was gone, Thomas and Carter exchanged views on the weather, the year's crops, and the coming winter.

Angela returned to the kitchen quickly, and Carter turned his full attention to her.

She wanted to ask him about Charlie—but she dared not. After all, it really was none of her affair. Still, it seemed that after all his years of service to Carter's father, Charlie was due some sort of consideration.

They spent the evening in light conversation. Angela was tempted to have Thomas lay a fire in the parlor so they wouldn't have to spend all their time in the kitchen, but she withheld the suggestion. She decided to assess the situation to see if Carter was really calling on her or just paying a neighborly visit.

He was so smooth, so proper, so elegant in his plaid jacket with velvet lapels and his diamond stick-pin that Angela could not believe he could actually be interested in a simple girl like her.

Yet his eyes, his shared laughter, his absolute attentiveness—all stated that indeed he was interested. It was a puzzle to Angela—a puzzle that sent her pulse racing.

"How soon may I come again?" he asked, his eyes teasing her as she saw him to the door. Not "may I come again" or "would you mind?" but "how soon?" Angela held her breath in a little gasp and looked up into the dark eyes.

"Well, I—I—" Then she smiled and tipped her head slightly, answering in a joking mood. "April?"

"I would never last until April," he said, his eyes looking seriously into hers.

"Then perhaps we could make it a bit sooner," she responded. "How does Friday night sound?"

"This Friday night? This is Tuesday—that is only—"

"Three long, long days," he finished for her.

Angela took a deep breath and nodded, a smile playing softly about her lips. "Friday night will be fine," she said in little more than a whisper.

He nodded and turned to go, replacing his dark Stetson as he stepped out into the chill of the night.

Angela closed the door and leaned against it. She wondered if Thomas had heard the conversation.

"I'm going up to bed," Thomas announced.

Angela realized that to Thomas, Carter's call was little more than a neighborly visit.

"Thomas, Carter is coming again on—on Friday night."

Thomas looked up, his eyes filled with surprise.

"I was wondering—could we—could we have a fire in the parlor? That way—should the rest of you like—like to read— or—or whatever—in the kitchen, we won't be in one another's way."

There! She had stated her case clearly enough. She was being courted. She needed a bit of privacy. She fixed her eyes on Thomas, her blood pounding through her veins.

Thomas stood quietly, just looking at her; then he reached a hand to the chair in front of him and pushed it back against the table. His eyes looked down at the kitchen floor as though he were studying something. Then he swallowed. Angela could see his Adam's apple work up and down. At last he spoke.

"Is this what you want?"

"Why, y-yes. I—I guess it is."

"You're sure that he shares your standards? Your faith?"

"He goes to our church—almost every Sunday."

"Angela—it is more than going to church on Sunday. You know that."

She nodded. It was her turn to swallow. She twisted her hands. There were so many things about Carter that seemed so—so perfect. But she wasn't sure—not quite sure—if he actually shared her faith.

She lifted her head resolutely. "If I find that he doesn't, I can stop seeing him," she said.

"I hear it isn't always that easy," replied Thomas.

"What do you mean?"

"Well, Hazel Conroy said that about her Fred. I hear that he's already forbidden her to attend services."

That piece of news was a shock to Angela. "But Carter goes to services," she reminded her brother.

"So did Fred," Thomas answered soberly.

Angela remembered that it had been so.

"And—and what about Thane?" asked Thomas pointedly.

"Thane?"

"Thane most always comes on Friday night. Have you forgotten?"

"He can still come," she answered. "You and he can play checkers or something and—and I'll fix lunch for all of us."

Thomas looked at Angela with unbelieving eyes, shook his head sadly, then turned to the stairs.

Angela knew something was wrong. Thomas never turned his back and walked away from her. She wished to call out to him, but she closed her lips firmly. He was acting foolishly. There was no reason for him to be so upset about Carter coming to call. After all, she was an adult. She could choose her own friends.

Angela stiffened her back and lifted her chin, but she could do little about the tears that insisted on slipping out from under her long lashes.

She recalled her feelings of fear and jealousy when Thomas had seemed to enjoy the attention showered on him by Trudie. Maybe he felt the same way now. But Angela would never leave the family. Thomas should know that. He had nothing to worry about.

———

Carter did call on Friday night. Thane did not. Angela missed seeing him, but quickly pushed all thoughts of him from her mind and gave her full attention to Carter.

Thomas started the fire in the parlor fireplace as Angela had requested and he also must have told the children that Angela was not to be disturbed, for no one came near the parlor door.

Angela prodded Carter gently with leading questions, hoping that he would disclose his beliefs about God. But either he did not understand her meaning or was skillful in evasion, for she never did get a satisfactory answer.

Perhaps another time, she told herself and allowed the conversation to turn to other things.

He told her about his mother. He told her of the home where he had grown up and described it so well that Angela could almost smell the sweet honeysuckle and hear the katydids.

"It must have been hard for you to leave all that," she sympathized.

"On the contrary," said Carter. "I was quite bored with it all. I wanted to come west when I was about fifteen, but Mother would not hear of it. I toyed with the idea for years before I finally found the resolve to actually do it. Mother was dead set against it, you see. At first I hoped I could change her mind. But that didn't work. Finally we had a big quarrel. I'm sorry it had to happen in that way—but I'm not one bit sorry I came."

He reached down to take the small hand that rested on the sofa between them, and Angela flushed slightly. Courting was all new to her, and she was not good at knowing what to say and how to say it. She was quite sure Trudie would have had a ready response—and would have invited another compliment. But Angela sat tongue-tied.

Carter studied the small hand he held in both of his own. "How do you keep them so soft—when you work so hard?" he asked.

Angela was flustered again. She wasn't sure if she was supposed to answer the question or if it was just a flattering remark. She let it go.

"You should have someone waiting on you—rather than you doing all of the caring for others," he continued.

"I—I like to care for others," she stammered.

"I know you do." His eyes held hers. She knew he was paying her tribute. "You are the most sincerely selfless little creature I have ever met. Any man would be honored to get such tender care."

Angela wasn't sure she understood the full meaning of his words, but she was sure he intended them as a verbal caress. She withdrew her hand slowly and took a deep breath. "Perhaps I should see to refreshments," she offered, rising before he could object.

She was surprised when she reached the kitchen to discover

the lateness of the hour. There was no one at the table or in the big chair beside the stove.

"Oh my!" she exclaimed. "They must all be in bed. I wonder if they had their milk and cookies?"

Angela took her time in preparing the serving tray and arranging the coffee cups. She needed to calm her nerves and to think soberly.

By the time she returned to the parlor, she was in control again. She took over the role of hostess easily and efficiently. She was even charming, without being forward.

After his third cup of coffee, Carter withdrew his pocket watch and looked shocked as he read the time.

"My word!" he exclaimed. "Where have the hours gone? You see the effect you have on me, Angela. I lose all track of time and place."

"It has gone quickly, but we had much to talk about," Angela said as she began to gather the lunch things and place them back on the tray.

"Yes," agreed Carter, his eyes serious as they studied her. "We have had. And so much more that we haven't yet discussed. I'm afraid I will have to insist that you allow me more of your time, sweet Angela." His eyes and voice were teasing again. Angela felt that she knew better how to respond when he was in a light mood.

"Well—maybe just a teeny, weeny bit of time," she said, indicating a small amount with her thumb and finger. She laughed softly and he smiled his slow, deliberate smile.

"And when might that teeny, weeny bit be available?" he asked her.

"Well—"

"And please don't tell me April," he said with a mock groan.

"What would you like me to say?" asked Angela coyly.

"How about tomorrow?"

She hoped he was teasing again.

"Saturday evening is always family time," she answered quickly.

"Could I take you to dinner on Sunday—somewhere? Where does one go for a fancy dinner around here?"

"One does not go for a fancy dinner around here," Angela laughed. "One could get a beef and potato meal at the hotel. But not on Sunday. And not me. I always prepare a special dinner for the family on Sunday."

She didn't tell him about their game and the Memory Book.

"See!" he pointed out. "It is like I said. You are always more concerned about others than you are about yourself."

"But I—"

He reached out to lay the tip of his finger on her lips, and she stopped protesting mid-sentence.

"When may I see you again?" he asked. "I really don't want to wait very long."

Angela raised a hand to remove his finger from her lips. His hand closed quickly over her own. She felt confused— crowded—unable to think straight. "Why don't we talk about it on Sunday—after church?" she suggested.

He seemed disappointed, but he accepted her arrangement.

"Until Sunday then," he confirmed and reached for the hat he had left lying on the sofa table.

Chapter Sixteen

The Will

Angela decided that Carter could call again on Tuesday. She felt it was a bit soon, but she could not turn down his pleading dark eyes.

They also had another caller on Monday. Charlie braved the weather to make his way across the field.

He sipped coffee, savored chocolate cake, and talked of neighborhood events until after the three younger children had been sent to bed. Then with just Thomas and Angela sharing the table, he brought up what he had really come to talk about.

"They read the will today."

For a moment Angela did not catch the meaning of his words.

"Mr. Stratton was wise to have drawn a will," commented Thomas, and Angela understood.

Charlie nodded.

They sat in silence for a minute. Thomas and Angela both sensed there was more on Charlie's mind.

"It held some surprises?" prompted Thomas.

"It did."

Charlie pulled a yellowed envelope from his pocket. On the front in scrawling handwriting was the name of Karl Peterson.

"Papa!" said Angela in surprise.

Charlie nodded.

"But Papa has been gone for—" began Angela.

"The boss must have written this letter before yer pa died— an' then forgot about it bein' in thet drawer with his will," responded Charlie.

Thomas took the envelope and turned it over and over in his hands.

"Why don't you open it?" advised Charlie.

Thomas carefully tore a corner off the envelope and slit the edge. He withdrew a short letter in the same scrawling script that appeared on the envelope.

"Dear Karl," Thomas read aloud. "I might not have been much of a neighbor over the years. I've been bitter about many things, but I see now that much of it was my own doing. If any-thing should unexpectedly happen to me, I just wanted you to know that I've been thinking on what you said. It does make a lot of sense. I don't know which way I will decide, but you have done your part. I admire a man with guts enough to speak his mind on what he believes."

It was signed simply, "Carter."

"Carter was named after his pa?" asked Angela in surprise.

Charlie nodded. "She did do the man that small favor," he admitted, speaking of the former Mrs. Stratton.

"Does Carter know this?" asked Angela.

"About the letter—or about the name?"

"Well—well, both. I mean, it must be—be special to him to share his father's name. And the—the letter. Why, what if—what if Mr. Stratton did think on the things Papa said? What if he did decide to ask forgiveness for all of those things from his past?"

Angela felt sudden excitement. Wouldn't it be wonderful if the man had made his peace with God?

But Charlie was not finished with his surprises.

"The boss named Gus an' me in the will," he said, and his voice broke.

Both Angela and Thomas looked up. The little man was fighting to control his emotions. He nodded and blinked hard, not wanting to allow tears.

"He left Gus three thousand dollars."

Angela caught her breath. It was impossible to imagine that much money.

"What does Gus plan to do?" she asked when she could speak again.

"He don't know. It caught him off guard. He says he ain't got no call fer the money. But I 'spect he'll find some way to spend it."

Charlie managed a smile.

"And you—?" prompted Thomas.

"He left me the parcel of land on the crick an' the little cabin thet sits on it."

"Oh, Charlie!" squealed Angela, and she threw her arms around his neck. "That's—wonderful. You'll have a place of your very own. You can just—just sit and rock—or fish or just do nothing."

Charlie was grinning. "I always had a feelin' fer thet little cabin," he admitted when Angela stopped squeezing and stepped back. "I guess the boss knew how I felt."

Then Charlie went on. "He left me a thousand dollars, too. Now I don't need to worry none about a grub-stake."

"Oh, that's wonderful! Just wonderful!" Angela exclaimed again.

Thomas reached over to pat the old man on the back.

"Well, I dunno," said Charlie hesitantly. "The new boss don't think it's so great."

"What do you mean?" asked Angela, a frown creasing her brow.

"Oh, he don't care none about the money. Got enough left anyway, I guess. His pa did leave him the rest of what he owned. But he don't cotton none to losing thet crick bottom. Says it's the best cattle piece he's got."

Angela's eyes shadowed with emotion. She felt bad for Carter. It didn't seem quite fair that a son should lose his property to an employee. But surely with all of the land he had now, he wouldn't need the bit that had been left to Charlie.

"Doesn't he have access to water on the rest of his land?" asked Thomas.

"Oh, shore. Shore," said Charlie. "Lotsa water. But I guess he took a fancy to thet piece, too."

Thomas shook his head slowly. "Well, it's too bad," he acknowledged, "but I guess a will is a will."

Charlie shook his head slowly. "Not really," he told them. "Shore it says in the will thet it's mine—but thet don't always hold, I guess."

"You mean—?"

"I mean the lawyer fella says thet even a proper will can be contested."

"Contested?"

"Yeah—taken to court to see if it is legally bindin'—or can be overturned."

"Who could do that?" asked Angela, shocked.

"The fella who thinks he has right to it," responded Charlie.

"Carter?" asked Thomas.

"Not Carter," objected Angela quickly.

But Charlie was nodding his head. "Told me straight out that he plans to go to court and get his property back," said Charlie. The mere mention of a court battle made him look tired and old.

"But you said—" began Angela.

"Shore. The will says it's mine. Carter says it's his." Charlie's eyes were coming to life. Angela saw the snap in them. The old man raised his head and his stubborn chin lifted slightly.

"So what do you plan to do?" asked Thomas.

"Fight it!" snapped Charlie. "I'm not gonna jest hand it on over to 'im. The boss gave it to me. I'm gonna fight it."

Angela felt a sickness begin to creep through her body. She had to sit down in the nearest chair.

Oh, dear God, she prayed silently. *And we—I—will be caught right in the middle.*

Angela longed to discuss the situation with Carter the next evening, but she didn't feel the freedom to bring up such a sensitive subject. They talked of other things. Little things. Funny things. Things from their different backgrounds. Carter did not even mention the will, and Angela was sure he was unaware they had any knowledge of its contents.

Thane would say just what he was thinking and feeling, Angela thought, and then checked herself. *What does Thane have to do with this? Why did I make that comparison?*

Angela quickly returned her thoughts to what Carter was saying. He was full of plans for the ranch, the house, and somehow Angela knew he expected her to be excited, to share his dreams.

"It sounds wonderful," she put in when Carter stopped for a breath.

"It will be," he said with confidence. "I am going back to Atlanta to do my shopping. I know the stores there and can get just what I want."

"How will you ever carry it all back out here?" asked Angela innocently.

"I'll ship it by rail. Shouldn't take too long. I figure by next spring—or summer at the latest—the house should have a whole new look."

"I think it's charming as it is," said Angela.

"Wait until you see what I'm going to do—you'll love it."

Angela had a strange thought—and the courage to voice it. "Does it really matter if I love it?"

Carter looked surprised. He opened his mouth to comment, but Angela quickly continued.

"I'm sure that your good taste will show throughout your lovely house," she smiled, "but what if I—what if I don't have the good sense to like the same things you do?"

For a moment he appeared surprised, but then he looked at her as if she must be teasing. He smiled, though his eyes did not lighten, and he spoke in bantering fashion, "Well, then—I guess we just throw it all out and start over," he said with a laugh, but Angela wasn't convinced.

When he left he promised that he would see her on Friday night, and Angela moved to the kitchen to wash the dishes.

She was still troubled as she prepared for bed and tucked herself in under the snug quilt made by her mother's hands.

"Oh, God," she prayed earnestly, "I wish I had my mama now. I need her so. I just know if she were here she'd be able to help me sort this all out."

Angela finally fell into a restless sleep.

Carter did not come on Friday night. He stopped by on Wednesday to inform Angela that he would be out of town for several days. He promised to come over the minute he returned, then surprised her by pulling her gently forward and kissing her on the forehead.

Angela felt sure the trip had something to do with his father's will. In the afternoon she bundled up against the cold wind and headed across the field to the big house. She didn't have baking to take along, but Gus was back in his own kitchen so he no longer needed her cooking.

She was welcomed by both Gus and Charlie. Angela was not surprised by this until Gus inadvertently mentioned that he missed Charlie since he no longer lived at the ranch house.

"You don't live here?" exclaimed Angela. "Where do you live?"

"I moved into my little shack," said Charlie with satisfaction.

"Is it warm enough?" Angela asked, thinking of the cold winter winds and the driving snow.

"Sure is," said Charlie proudly. "It's as snug as a nest in there—and lots of good wood piled up at the back, too."

Angela was relieved. "So how come you're here?" she asked.

"Oh, I still sneak over for a cup of coffee now and then when I know Gus will be alone."

"You knew?"

"We have us a little signal system worked out," he said with a grin, and Gus winked at Angela.

Angela did not ask them to reveal their secret.

"We sure do. We sure do," Gus chuckled.

"Then you know that Carter has gone to the city—and why?"

Charlie nodded. "He's settin' the wheels in motion for the trial over the will. Wants him the best lawyer he can find for the case."

Angela nodded slowly. She had feared that was the reason. "And you?" she asked Charlie.

"Figured I'd be my own defense," Charlie told her. "Me and thet there piece of paper thet says the land is mine."

"But—?" began Angela.

" 'Course I got me a piece of advice from ol' Ed Stern. He said thet possession is nine-tenths of the law, or somethin' like thet. Advised me to move right in without hesitation."

Angela nodded. The pieces were falling together.

"And, I was anxious to move anyway. Nothin' fer me to do here but hassle Gus."

The twinkle had returned to Charlie's eyes.

"How will you get supplies?" asked Angela.

"Neighbors been right good about it."

Angela knew that the Conroys and Blackwells lived in the direction of Charlie's shack. Before she could make further comment, Charlie went on.

"Ol' man Blackwell is a rather decent sort. An' him tied to thet woman fer all these years. Don't know how the man has stood it. Sneaks over every now and then fer a bit of chin-wag or a cup of strong coffee. He popped in on the way to town an' says he will do thet whenever he's goin' by."

Angela smiled. It was good that the two men had each other. "Do you have any idea when—when this trial might come up?" asked Angela. She felt far more free to talk to Gus and Charlie than she did to Carter, but she did not stop to analyze the reason.

"Carter would like it all done up before Christmas," said Charlie, "but Ed Stern says those things can sometimes take a good while."

Angela nodded. It really wasn't long until Christmas.

"Well, I'd better be getting home," she said, pushing back her cup and getting to her feet. "Thank you, Gus, for the coffee."

"You're welcome," said Gus. "Anytime. Anytime."

"Come over when you can," Angela invited, her words directed to both men but her eyes resting on Charlie.

"Well, now, I reckon I would need to know the time fer thet," said Charlie, who had always just dropped over in the past. "I hear me through the locals' report thet you sometimes have a caller."

Angela reddened. "But that doesn't mean—" she began.

" 'Course not," said Charlie. "Jest a bit uncomfortable, if you know what I mean."

"You can come any Saturday night or Sunday afternoon," Angela informed him and then promised herself she would be sure not to invite Carter on those days.

―――――

The hearing was set for January 15. Carter did not speak of it to Angela. She heard it from Charlie. She admitted to herself that she was a bit hurt that Carter had not discussed it with her. But perhaps he wanted to spare her feelings, knowing how she cared for Charlie.

Angela decided to push the whole matter aside and concentrate on preparations for Christmas.

Chapter Seventeen

Christmas

Angela went to town to do some shopping. She hadn't seen the Andrewses, except at church, for what seemed ages. She decided to leave a little visiting time in her schedule.

Mrs. Andrews greeted her warmly, as always, and ushered her into their living quarters behind the store.

"How are things going, dear?" the woman asked as she pushed the teakettle forward over the heat of the firebox.

"Fine—I guess," said Angela as she removed her heavy coat and placed it on the back of a chair.

"We hear you have been entertaining Mr. Stratton," Mrs. Andrews said openly.

"Yes," admitted Angela. "He calls." She felt she should be making her announcement with a gleam in her eyes and excitement in her voice. She was aware that there was neither.

"Ma Andrews," Angela began, calling the woman by the name she had used for many years, "have you heard about the trial?"

"I guess everyone around has heard of the trial," the woman answered.

"Well, do you think—do you suppose there is any danger of Charlie losing his land and cabin?"

"I really couldn't say, dear. I have no knowledge of legal things, but most folks are saying that Charlie has a fairly good case."

Angela wasn't sure that was good enough, but she held her tongue. It would be such a shame if Charlie were to lose his small cabin.

Mrs. Andrews asked, "What does Carter say—?"

"We haven't talked about it," Angela answered quickly.

"I see," said Mrs. Andrews as she poured the tea.

The conversation turned to Christmas. "I've been hoping you would get to town," Mrs. Andrews said. "I wanted to check to be sure you and the family are planning to have Christmas dinner with us."

"Oh yes," responded Angela before she even had time to think. The Peterson family had shared Christmas dinner with the Andrews family ever since their mother had passed away.

Then Angela thought of Carter. Was he expecting an invitation to the Petersons'? Well, she would just explain to him the long-standing tradition. She couldn't very well invite him to accompany them. Could she? She glanced up at the kind woman who was pouring the tea and was about to blurt out her request when she thought better of it. Carter hardly knew the Andrewses, whereas she had thought of them as family for a number of years. Certainly Carter would not feel comfortable in such circumstances.

They talked further of Christmas and of the church Christmas pageant and the costumes Angela needed to prepare for Louise and Sara. Derek had announced quite forthrightly that he was too big to take part in the Christmas drama now. Angela had not argued. She was pleased to have Derek showing a mind of his own.

"Will Louise be wearing her hair up this year?" Mrs. Andrews asked. "Agnes has talked of nothing else for the past several months. Especially since she saw Louise at Hazel's wedding."

Angela looked at the older woman. "What do you think Mama would do?" she asked. "I don't want to be fighting Louise all the time, but she is constantly pressing me to let her do this and let her do that. I really don't know the proper time for these—these various things of—of youth."

Mrs. Andrews smiled. "Do you remember when you went through it?" she asked.

Angela shook her head slowly.

"Well, I do. Your mama handled you so wisely. 'Yes,' she said, 'you may have your hair up just as soon as you take over the chore of baking bread. A lady should never make bread with her hair hanging loose about her face.'"

Angela did remember then. She had been only eleven when

she had begun to pester her mama about putting up her hair. She flushed slightly.

"I remember. I was even younger than Louise," she admitted.

"Yes, but you put it off for another two years after your mama's little talk."

"I was thirteen—and I had to take over baking the bread. Mama was much too ill."

Mrs. Andrews nodded solemnly, remembering the young child who had been forced into an adult role.

"Well, then, I guess, if it's all right with you, Louise and Agnes will wear their hair up this year," said Angela.

Mrs. Andrews agreed with a hearty laugh. "We will have two happy girls when we tell them."

Angela looked at the clock. "Oh, dear. I must hurry or I won't be home in time to make supper." She picked up her coat, hugged Mrs. Andrews, and hurried through the door into the store.

Thane was there waiting on a customer. Angela hung back until he had finished and then approached him. She had not seen him for several weeks, other than at church. She greeted him warmly.

"Hello. I guess your father is keeping you busier than ever. We've missed you."

Thane smiled, but Angela thought she saw sadness in his eyes. It reminded her of the look on his face at Hazel's wedding.

"Is something wrong?" she asked softly, drawing closer to the young man.

"I'm not sure," he responded. "Are you happy?"

Angela was taken by surprise at his question. "Well, yes—I guess."

"Then I'm happy," he said, and this time he gave her a full smile and a chuck under the chin. "How's Tom?"

Angela answered that Thomas was just fine—but missing their Friday night checker game.

"I hear you have other company on Friday night," Thane said frankly.

Angela flushed slightly but quickly recovered. "Well, that doesn't mean there isn't room for old friends."

"Well—room maybe—but it might be a little—uncomfortable. All those people crowded into one kitchen."

"Oh no!" exclaimed Angela. "Carter and I use the parlor."

The sad look returned to Thane's eyes. "You need some groceries?" he asked as he turned to the shelves behind him. Angela laid her list on the counter.

———————

Carter did not look happy when Angela explained their Christmas arrangements.

"I was counting on us being together," he said, his dark eyes shadowed.

"But we have always gone to the Andrewses'," Angela explained. "Ever since Mama died. The family would be heartbroken if I suggested something else."

"Why don't you let them go and you and I make our own plans?" he suggested.

"Be separated on Christmas?" Angela couldn't believe her ears.

"Well, you won't always be together. Perhaps now is a good time—"

"There is never a good time to break up a family," Angela said firmly, surprised at her fervor.

He nodded reluctantly. "Fine," he said but his voice held disappointment. "Then how do we get a bit of Christmas?"

"Could you come over Christmas Eve? We'd love to have you join us. We always exchange our gifts and read the Christmas story and discuss our memories of other Christmases. Then we have popcorn and pull taffy and—"

"Angela," cut in Carter, "I meant just the two of us."

Angela bit her lip. She had not even thought of it being just the two of them. "I'm sorry," she said, "but I don't think I can do that. It's important for us to all be together on Christmas."

Carter looked upset but he still pressed. "What about the evening of Christmas Day?"

"We always stay late at the Andrewses', and if the weather is nice we go for a sleigh ride."

"The evening before Christmas Eve?"

Angela thought about that. There was no reason Carter couldn't come calling on the twenty-third.

"That would be fine," she agreed and gave him one of her smiles.

———————

The days slipped by quickly and Angela scarcely had time to finish her baking and her gift-making before Christmas was upon them. She had seen Carter twice a week in the intervening time and he always made special mention of the evening of the twenty-third. Angela felt that he was gently reminding her that she had put her family before him, but she held firm and gave him a smile whenever he mentioned the coming evening.

He still had not discussed the trial, and Angela did not have the courage to bring up the subject.

When the twenty-third arrived Angela dressed carefully in her blue voile. She had not worn it since Hazel's wedding. She smoothed the skirt over her slender frame and studied herself in the mirror. The dress, in its very simplicity, did become her. She turned to the task of pinning up her hair, leaving little tendrils to gently curl against her cheeks. Then she fastened Thane's cameo about her neck and looked again at the total picture.

"Well," she said to her reflection, "that's about as good as it's going to get. I can't do much more." And so saying, Angela went downstairs to make sure the parlor fire had been lit and that the refreshments were ready for later.

Carter came promptly at eight. Angela ushered him inside, noting the cold gust of air that accompanied him.

"It's dreadful out there!" she gasped. "What a horrible night to be out."

Carter laughed and allowed her to take his heavy coat and his hat. Angela hung them up while he greeted the other family members.

Then she beckoned him to the parlor. "Come in and warm yourself by the fire," she invited, and he followed her into the room.

"It is cozy in here," he observed as he seated himself on the sofa. Angela moved to place another log on the cracking flames.

"Come," he invited. "Sit here beside me and we'll enjoy the fire together."

Angela accepted his invitation.

"Now," he said taking her hand in both of his, "tell me what you have been doing to get ready for Christmas."

Angela felt that it would be a rather boring account so she countered, "Most of my time has been in the kitchen. You tell me what you have been doing instead."

"Well—I made another trip to the city," he offered.

Angela noted the gleam in his eyes. "Business?" she asked.

"No. Pleasure," he answered, and he lifted her hand and placed a kiss on her fingers, studying her carefully as he did so.

Angela did not withdraw her hand—nor did she flush with embarrassment.

"I think that if I ever went to the city it would be for pleasure also."

"You have never been to the city?" he asked.

Angela shook her head.

"Then we must right that," he said, kissing her fingers again.

"So-o," said Angela. "Are you going to tell me all about your pleasurable trip?"

His dark eyes flashed. "I'd love to," he said, so softly that she barely caught his words. "I went to the city shopping—just in case a certain lovely lady I know accepts my offer of marriage."

Angela's eyes widened and her breath caught in her throat. She almost withdrew her hand.

"Well," he prompted. "Do you? Will you?"

"Are you—?" began Angela.

"I am asking you to be my wife."

"But I—I never dreamed—"

Angela stopped short. She had dreamed. Well, sort of. But she had not really prepared herself for anything like this. This seemed so soon. So sudden. So unreal.

He pulled her close and kissed her cheek, letting his lips brush her hair and linger near her ear.

"Will you, Angela?" he asked again. "I am still waiting for your answer."

Angela pulled back and looked into his eyes. She lifted a hand to touch his cheek.

"Are you sure?"

"I am sure," he whispered.

"But—but don't you think it's too soon? Have we known each other long enough? Do we know each other well enough?"

"Angela, I know all I need to know about you. You are the sweetest, most caring, most unselfish woman I have ever met. And on top of that, you are lovely to look at. What more could any man want? What could we possibly gain by waiting? Please, don't put me through that agony. I need you with me."

"Oh, Carter, I do so want to do the right thing. I do want to make you happy." She stared into his dark eyes. "Yes, yes, I will marry you. I will be happy to be your wife."

He pulled her close and kissed her. Angela had never been

kissed in such a way before. She felt the blood rushing through her body, pounding at her temples. For a moment she felt faint.

So this is how it is to be in love, she thought, and she lifted her lips so he might kiss her again.

I'm getting married. I'm getting married, her heart sang. *Oh, if only Mama were here now.*

Chapter Eighteen

News

It wasn't until morning came that Angela realized the seriousness of her commitment. She was about to announce her good news at the breakfast table, but when her eyes traveled from one face to another she bit her tongue. Thomas was impatient to get off to town before the weather had a chance to delay him. He had a hog to sell, and the price he got would determine the kind of Christmas the family would be celebrating. Derek, Louise and Sara were riding along into town to do their own Christmas shopping.

Louise fussed as she dished out the porridge. Her hair had not cooperated when she pinned it up. It looked precarious to Angela even now, in spite of the many combs attempting to hold it.

Derek was quiet again. Angela had told herself that he was gradually coming out of his shell, but on this particular morning he seemed withdrawn. Angela felt herself tensing up as she looked at him.

Sara bubbled as usual, completely oblivious to the moods of those about her. Her whole little body bounced as she went about her morning task of setting the breakfast table. And while she bounced, she talked—a steady stream that seemed to get on Louise's nerves even more than usual.

"Sara, why can't you ever be quiet?" Louise demanded at last, flipping her head impatiently.

It was the wrong thing for her to do. Rolls of hair came tumbling down about her ears, causing Thomas to snicker in spite of himself. With a wail, Louise headed for her bedroom, hair streaking out behind her as she fled.

Angela gave Thomas a look of reproach, then retracted it with the hint of a smile. Louise did look pretty funny.

Sara stopped her chatter long enough to look from Thomas to Angela and back again, her eyes asking what would happen next.

Angela finished serving the porridge and then quietly slipped from the room to see if she could get Louise, and her unruly hair, back under control.

Now is definitely not the time to share my good news, she decided as she headed for the bedroom and the sound of sobs.

"Louise." She spoke softly as she approached the distraught girl. "Louise?"

The only response was louder wailing.

"Louise." Angela tried again, sitting on the edge of the bed and brushing back the tangled hair. "Don't get your eyes all red and swollen. I can fix your hair, but I can't do much to help puffy eyes."

Louise seemed to be considering the comment, for her crying diminished some.

"Come. I'll try pinning it. Hair can be terribly obstinate—until it gets used to being up. Let me see if I can fix it for you."

"I'm not going to town," wailed Louise.

Angela sat in silence for a moment and then responded with a firmness that surprised even herself. "Oh yes you are. You still haven't done your shopping. And if you don't, it will spoil everyone's Christmas. A few locks of unruly hair are not going to keep you from it. Now, get yourself up. You'll be mussing your dress."

Angela took the girl's arm and gave it a gentle tug.

"But, Angela," protested Louise, "my eyes are already red and swollen."

Angela could not be so easily put off. "You have a long ride ahead—and it is sharp this morning—with a brisk wind. By the time you get there, your eyes will be back to normal—or else red and stinging like everyone else's."

Louise hoisted herself up on her elbows and gave Angela a disdainful look.

"Right now," Angela said sharply. "You are making the others late."

Louise arose and settled herself at her vanity but refused to pick up her mirror or give Angela directions as to how she wished her hair pinned.

Angela tried to ignore the pouting girl. She swept the thick hair back with the stout brush and gathered it neatly together in the palm of her hand. Then she began to twist and lift, pinning as she went. In a few moments the task had been completed and Louise couldn't resist just a tiny peek in the mirror.

She made no comment, but Angela caught the flash of satisfaction that crossed her sister's face before she could hide it.

"Now—mop up your face and come for your breakfast," Angela said. "The rest will have finished by the time we get there."

Louise was not the only one who avoided eye contact when the two returned to the kitchen. Angela was afraid that if she observed a twinkle in Thomas's eyes she might not be able to hide a titter of her own. Nor did Angela want the incident to trouble Derek further. And Sara would be watching for the tension to ease so she could resume her chatter, and Angela wasn't quite ready to listen to more prattle about incidental things.

So Angela crossed to the stove, brought back the bowls of porridge meant for her and her younger sister, and settled herself at the table without lifting her eyes.

The others had finished. Angela gave a slight nod to recognize the fact and then said, as softly as her tense throat would allow, "You may all be excused."

"But we haven't had our morning Bible story," objected Sara, and Angela's eyes did lift then. She looked quickly at Thomas who sat, Bible in hand.

"So we haven't," she admitted, a flush touching her cheeks. Then her look turned to one of beseeching. "We are late," she said simply. "Perhaps this once you could read while we eat."

Thomas nodded and began the morning reading. By the time he was ready for prayer, Angela and Louise had finished their porridge and were sitting with hands neatly folded in their laps. They prayed together.

After the door had closed on the four family members, Angela dropped back into a kitchen chair, coffee cup before her.

What will Carter think of all of this? was her first thought. *Well, he did ask me to marry him. I didn't just dream it,* she reminded herself, and then another thought quickly followed. *It's going to be so—so wonderful to have someone to share the responsibility of caring for the family. I know I have always had Thomas—but he can go now—go away to do the work he has always dreamed of. He will be so happy—*

Tears formed in Angela's eyes. She would miss Thomas. They had been so close. Had worked together for so many years as a team, raising their younger siblings.

She brushed impatiently at the unbidden tears. "Here I am, on the happiest day of my life, sobbing like a buffoon," she scolded herself. "Why, I should be singing my way through the morning chores—and here I sit crying in my coffee."

Angela decided not to drink the second cup of coffee, after all. She took the cup to the slop pail and poured out the contents, then turned her attention to the morning dishes.

"It is just that the morning did not start out well," she informed herself. "Things will soon be right again."

She cast a worried look toward the kitchen window. The sky had darkened and a stiff wind was blowing.

I do hope Thomas makes it to town and back before it storms. And I hope the children are bundled up warmly enough against the wind. I wonder if Louise wore her muffler. She is getting so full of silliness that she'd rather freeze than be thought out-of-style. Oh, dear! What will I ever do with the girl?

Angela's mind turned to prayer. "Lord, you know how hard it is to be growing up. And Louise seems to be having a particularly bad time with it. How can I help her, Lord? Mama would have known just what to do and say—but I stumble along and make so many blunders. Give me wisdom, Lord. Give me wisdom. With Louise. And with Sara. Give me patience with her constant chattering, too, Lord. And with Derek and his buried grief. Help me, Lord. And help me to pick the right time to share with them the news that I am to marry. May they be just as excited about a new home as—as I will be—as I am."

Angela did not say Amen. She knew her prayer might be taken up again many times throughout her day.

In the afternoon, Angela was surprised to see Thane. He had been out their way delivering groceries to the Widow Thorson and had decided to drop in, he said. Angela pushed the kettle forward and prepared a cup of hot lemonade to help take the chill from his bones.

They chatted and laughed as old friends. Then he said he must get home since the day before Christmas was always a busy one in the store. As he left, Angela called after him that she would be seeing them all on the day following, and he called back that he hoped it wouldn't storm and prevent them. Angela turned again to her preparations for the family evening.

The family arrived home in a flurry of excitement and much laughing and bantering as they headed for bedrooms to wrap gifts before the evening gift exchange. Angela called out orders as to chores to be done before supper. The girls responded good-naturedly, but Derek was still quiet and withdrawn. Angela was relieved that Louise had returned to good humor—probably something to do with the fact that she had been given a nice compliment on her hair by Claude Sommers. Sara shared the news and, though Louise shrieked and scolded, Angela was sure Louise was secretly pleased that Sara had told.

The stock was cared for, the woodbox stacked high, and extra water carried from the well before they gathered around the kitchen table, where the lamp cast a soft glow on wind-chilled faces and the kitchen stove sent out waves of warmth.

Angela looked at the little circle of family. Everyone was relieved to be in out of the cold and most anxious for the evening's festivities—simple as they were.

Angela had taken special care with the meal. The chicken was fried just the way Thomas liked it. The biscuits were high and fluffy. The peas had been creamed to suit Sara, and there was cranberry sauce to please Louise. The fruit cake was especially for Derek.

"Are we having company?" asked Derek, casting a furtive glance about.

Angela laughed. "Who would come out on a night like this?" she asked, and Derek just shrugged his slim shoulders and looked relieved.

"Thane used to," put in Sara.

A hush fell on the room and all eyes turned to Angela.

"Why doesn't he come anymore?" went on Sara, wistfulness in her voice.

"Why, he comes. He stopped by for a few minutes today."

Angela thought she saw a smile play about the corners of Thomas's mouth, but he made no comment.

Sara did not let it pass. "He did? And I didn't see him," she mourned. Then she went on. "But he doesn't come much. He used to come—lots and lots. Why doesn't he do that anymore?"

"I—I don't know. He's—he's been very busy helping his father expand the store, I guess," said Angela. "He says they are finally done with it. He'll have more time now."

"I miss him," continued Sara. "I haven't had any lemon drops for—for just years."

"Sara!" Angela scolded. "I hope that Thane means more to you than lemon drops."

Sara fidgeted in her seat, but Derek raised his eyes to Angela's.

She could feel a probing, a questioning, and she wondered what he was thinking. She felt like squirming under his gaze, yet didn't know why. To Angela's relief he dropped his eyes to his plate.

"Did you fight?" asked Louise bluntly.

"Who?" asked Angela, knowing full well whom she meant.

"You. You and Thane."

"Of course not! What do you mean? Why would Thane and I fight?"

"Well, he used to come see you all the time and he doesn't anymore," said Louise with a shrug.

"He—he didn't come to see me. He—he came to see us—all of us," Angela protested, her cheeks flushing.

"Oh no," denied the chattery Sara. "He used to come to see you. I know. I saw him looking at you."

"Don't talk foolish," Angela hushed Sara as she rose to replenish the chicken platter that was still piled high.

She had planned to share her proposal with the family over the supper table, but now did not seem like a good time to declare her news.

"Sara, that's enough chatter," Thomas said softly. "Stop your talking and clean up your plate or we'll all need to sit and wait for you."

Angela noticed that each family member still had a full plate. Sara was no slower than the rest of them, yet she felt thankful that Thomas had put a stop to the conversation.

———

"What is it?" Thomas asked when the two of them sat alone at the kitchen table sharing the warmth of the stove and the dim light of the lamp. The taffy-pulling and popcorn-making was over for another year and each gift had been exchanged and received with proper fuss and appreciation. The three younger children had been sent off to bed, with Angela and

Thomas left to clean up the kitchen and then catch their breath.

Angela raised her head.

"You've got something on your mind," Thomas continued.

Angela did not deny it. It would be wrong—and foolish—for her to do so.

"I—I had a proposal for marriage," she answered, trying hard to hold her voice steady.

A glimmer lightened her brother's face, and Angela breathed a little sigh of thanksgiving. Thomas looked pleased—not upset.

"And you have given an answer?" prompted Thomas.

Angela could not speak. She simply nodded her head, but there was a gleam in her own eyes now.

"I take it from the shine in your eyes that the answer was yes," said Thomas.

Angela nodded again, a smile blossoming on her full mouth, her cheeks flushing faintly.

"When?" asked Thomas simply.

"No date has been set," responded Angela. "We really have not had much chance to make plans at all."

"I know," nodded Thomas. "He's been terribly busy."

"And it wouldn't seem right to—to hurry into marriage with circumstances as they are, and all."

Thomas looked a bit puzzled. "Circumstances?"

"With his father just being buried and—"

Thomas jerked upright, his whole body tensing. His eyes looked startled and unbelieving in the dim light of the lamp.

"What are you talking about?" he demanded.

"Carter wouldn't want to marry quickly. His father—"

"I know about his father."

Angela understood then. Thomas had not been thinking of Carter Stratton when she had announced that she was to marry. Thomas had thought she was speaking of someone else. But who? Who other than Carter would Thomas have assumed to be the one? Who had already been given Thomas's blessing? And why were his eyes now filled with concern?

"I—I don't understand—" began Angela.

Thomas had dropped his head and was running a nervous hand through his thatch of blond hair. At last he looked up, his eyes dark with anxiety.

"It's not that—I mean—" He hesitated and took a deep breath. "Are you sure? I mean, do you really—?"

"Of course," said Angela with more confidence than she felt. After all, wasn't her marriage to Carter going to solve problems for all of them?

Thomas looked at her for a long moment.

"Then you have my blessing," he finally said, but to Angela, his voice sounded weary.

She reached out to squeeze his hand, flashing him a smile so that she might receive one of his in return.

He managed the smile. And he responded to the pressure of her hand. But Angela wondered if both were forced.

"I—I wonder," he finally managed, "if it would be wise to just—just keep your secret—for a—a while—until—until we get this matter of the land settlement behind us."

Angela nodded. She had forgotten about the will. Although she wasn't sure she understood exactly what Thomas was saying, she was content to abide by his wishes.

Chapter Nineteen

Carter

It was difficult for Angela to keep her secret from Mrs. Andrews on Christmas Day. But each time she was tempted to bring up her engagement, she remembered Thomas's request and fought back the urge. She didn't let herself think about the fact that Thane seemed to be avoiding any eye contact with her. She had enough on her mind already.

At the end of the day, the family bundled up with robes and blankets and started off for home. They were filled with turkey and trimmings and new memories of fun and laughter with their good friends.

But as Angela reflected on the day, she felt a stab of pain. This would likely be the last Christmas spent with the Andrews family. Surely Carter would expect to celebrate Christmas in their own home in the future.

Angela brushed away tears that started to spill. She loved the Andrewses. They were like family.

January turned bitterly cold. Angela hated to send the youngsters off to school. A few mornings she did keep them at home, putting them to work on their lessons at the kitchen table.

Carter had not been to call. Angela kept telling herself that it was much too cold for anyone to be out, but she did wonder about his absence.

The trial date was drawing closer. Angela could hardly bear the suspense. She was tempted to bundle up and head for the nearby farm. Surely Gus would be able to give her some news.

Perhaps she would even be lucky enough to visit at the same time Charlie was making one of his calls.

But what would she do if Carter should be there? So Angela did not head across the field. She knew Thomas would oppose her going out in such weather. She stayed put, trying to ignore her troubled thoughts, and waited.

Thane dropped in a couple of times in spite of the weather.

"I hear you've been missing me," he said to Sara with a wink. "Or is it just the lemon drops?"

Sara denied the charge with a shake of her blond pigtails, but she did smile brightly when Thane produced her favorite candy.

Thane and Thomas set up the checker board by the cozy kitchen fire and spent the next hour noisily challenging each other. Angela felt a strange comfort in the familiar banter that accompanied the game. She had to admit that she had been missing Thane's visits, too.

By the trial date, the weather had eased some. Angela dressed the children in extra layers and sent them off to school. She fought the urge to hitch the team and head for town. From the reports she had received, the trial was to be held in the town hall. But this word had not come to her from Carter. He had not mentioned the hearing, nor had he called since his pre-Christmas proposal of marriage. Angela began to wonder if she had dreamed it, after all.

Thomas must have noticed her agitation but he made no comment.

"I think I'll go on into town," Thomas announced at the dinner table one evening. "Do you care to come along?"

Angela paled. "I don't think so," she answered slowly.

So Angela watched him go, feeling that whatever word he brought back would somehow affect her.

If Carter only had brought it up, Angela kept saying to herself, *I might have been able to explain to him how important the little place is to Charlie.*

At other moments Angela tried to see Carter's point of view and found herself feeling put out with Charlie. *He could have taken his money and gotten a nice little place in town,* she protested during her inner debates. *He didn't have to take Carter's land.*

But no matter which way Angela argued, she could not find peace of mind.

When Thomas returned from town, he told her the matter still had not been settled. Angela felt more agitated than ever.

Thomas did, however, bring with him a note from Carter.

"My darling Angela," he wrote in bold, firm script. "The days have been unbearably long since I last saw you. I cannot wait until this ordeal is over and I will be free to call again and we can make our plans. It shouldn't be long now. Things went well today—in my favor, I might add, and I propose that soon I will be granted the land that is rightfully mine. This fool of a little man really doesn't have a logical argument on his side. So please bear with me. I will call the moment I am free to do so. With my deepest affection, Carter."

Angela was relieved to hear from him but troubled at his assessment of Charlie.

He's not a fool of a little man, she argued to herself. *He is a dear, good friend and he does have right to the land. It was left to him.*

But Angela would not have shared her thoughts or her words with anyone. Not even Thomas. To do so would have been to put some blame on Carter.

"It will all be over soon," she said out loud, pretending to find comfort in that fact.

Angela hoped that Carter would call, but two days passed and still he had not visited.

"That trial must be dragging on and on," she fumed in exasperation. Thomas nodded and went back to the farm account numbers on his sheet of paper.

It was Charlie who eventually brought the news.

When she heard the knock Angela jumped to her feet, brushing first at her hair and then at her skirt, sure that Carter was on the other side of the door. But when Thomas opened it, it was Charlie who stood there, a grin on his face.

"It's over?" asked Thomas.

Charlie grinned wider.

"Come in," welcomed Thomas.

Charlie moved into the kitchen, pulling his worn hat from his head as he did so. He beat the hat against his leg a couple of times to shake the loose snow from its brim, then tossed it toward the corner and moved to the warmth of the fire.

Angela held her breath. She couldn't have said a word if the kitchen had been on fire.

"How did it go?" asked Thomas, though Angela felt that he already knew.

"I licked 'im," boasted Charlie. "Licked 'im fair and square."

Angela had never heard Charlie gloat in such a fashion before. For a moment she felt sick to her stomach.

"So you got your land?"

"They said the will stood—the way it was written."

Thomas nodded, looking from Charlie to Angela. He wasn't sure how to respond.

"That's good," said Thomas.

Angela said nothing.

"Yeah," said Charlie, slapping his thigh with a heavy mitten. "Yeah."

Then Charlie turned the conversation abruptly. "You busy tomorra?"

"No," said Thomas.

"Wondered iffen you'd bring thet big team of yours and help me move my shack. I figured as how, iffen I could get about four big teams, I could skid it right on over here."

"You're going to move it?"

Charlie turned to Angela. "Remember how you once said to me thet I'd be welcome to live here?"

Angela nodded. She had said that—but things were so different then. What would Carter think about her harboring the enemy? Angela was sure Carter would consider Charlie the enemy now.

"Well, I thought as how I'd like to have thet shack right up there in the corner by the garden—iffen the offer still stands, thet is?"

Angela felt that it was hardly the time to tell Charlie they themselves might not be living on the farm for long. When she married, the children would go with her, and Thomas would go off to do his research work. She opened her mouth to speak, but Thomas shook his head. She closed her mouth quickly and turned to the stove.

"I don't understand," said Thomas slowly. "Of course you're welcome here. But you don't want your shack on your own land by the creek?"

Charlie began to chuckle as if he had just played a delightful joke on someone.

"Don't have any land by the crick," he informed them.

"But I thought you said you won."

"I did. I did," said Charlie with shining eyes. "They gave me the land—then I took the deed—and I looked young Mr. Stratton straight in the eye an' told 'im thet I'd move my shack and he could have his land fer all I cared—an' I handed thet deed right back to 'im."

"But—but if you didn't care about the land, why did you go to court?" asked Thomas incredulously.

Charlie's eyes began to snap. "I weren't gonna be pushed around by some young city-slicker," he sputtered. "The land was mine. Fair and square. It was given to me by the *owner*. The *inheritor* doesn't have no say so in the matter. He needn't think thet he can jest walk in and stomp all over folks."

"But court cases cost—"

"Didn't cost me," said Charlie, his eyes twinkling again. "Cost 'im. He had to pay the court costs." Charlie continued chuckling. "An' he got hisself laughed at, too. The whole court room was laughing. Here he spent all thet money, I won the case, and then I give it back to 'im. Iffen he'd asked face-to-face like a man in the first place, I'd a give it to 'im to begin with, but bein' ordered around by a bunch of papers don't sit well with me."

Poor Carter, Angela thought. *No wonder he hasn't come around.*

Then Angela felt anger toward both men begin to seep through her. Carter was wrong to try to muscle his way with Charlie. But Charlie was equally improper to let the whole mess get to court just to prove his silly point. In Angela's thinking they had both acted like spoiled children. She turned her back and headed for the stairway.

She stopped mid-stride, realizing she was being just as foolish herself. *Never return evil for evil,* she heard the words clearly in her memory. Her mama would have been ashamed of the way she was acting.

It took a moment of silent prayer for her to regain her composure, but at last she was able to turn and speak evenly.

"Cup of coffee, Charlie?" she asked and even managed a small smile.

———

It was almost the end of January before Carter finally got around to calling. Angela had begun to think she would never see him again. But when he came he was just as solicitous as ever, as though he had not been absent for an entire month. He seemed to take up right where he had left off, offering no explanation or apology for his long absence.

"I hear the trial is finally over," Angela eventually said.

"Yes," he nodded, seeming pleased with himself. "I have all my land back in one piece."

Angela wondered if he had noticed the small shack tucked away by the back garden. If so, he made no comment.

"I am leaving soon for Atlanta again," he informed her. "I have workmen coming to start on the house, but there are a few more things I need to finalize."

He beamed at Angela, and she knew he expected her to be happy at the news. She simply nodded her head in acknowledgment.

He took her hand. "What special thing might I bring you, my dear, as an engagement gift?" he asked.

Angela was taken by surprise. She had not thought of an engagement gift and had no idea what would be appropriate.

"I—I don't know," she stammered. "Perhaps you should do the choosing."

Her answer apparently satisfied him. He nodded as though it made the best of sense.

"How long will you be gone?" she asked.

"I have no way of knowing. I do hope it won't take too long. I can't bear to be away from you. Perhaps I can arrange for us to take a trip together later on. There are so many things I want to show you. There is so much shopping for you to do for your trousseau. There is so much for you to learn about the proper running of a house." He flushed slightly and then hurried on, "Of course, I know you have kept house for years. But now you will have help with the work—it will be the supervision you will need to learn."

Angela couldn't imagine herself supervising rather than doing the work herself.

"We have so many things we need to talk about," he went on.

"Yes," agreed Angela. "We do."

"Would you like me to look for an extra housekeeper while I am there?"

"An extra housekeeper?"

"For here. For the children."

"Oh, but the children won't be staying here," Angela quickly said, wondering why it was necessary to explain this to Carter.

"You have some place else for them?"

"Why, they'll be with me," replied Angela.

"But my dear," responded Carter with one of his measured smiles, "I plan to take you to live with me."

Angela nodded. "Of course."

Carter seemed to catch on at last. "You mean," he said slowly, "that you propose to bring all of them along with you to my house?"

Angela nodded, her stomach beginning to churn. By the look on his face she realized he really had meant to leave the youngsters here on their own.

He shook his head slowly and then his eyes began to twinkle. "How you tease," he laughed, giving her a playful shake.

"Carter," said Angela, her back straightening, "I am not one to tease about such serious matters."

She looked directly into his eyes and saw her own image reflected in them, a bit of a girl with honey blond hair. Her blue eyes held his steadily, and her small frame did not flinch. Carter shifted his weight to his other foot.

"You can't be serious!" he finally exclaimed.

"They go—or I stay," stated Angela simply. "I haven't been much of a mother—but I am the only mother they have. I will not leave them until they have been properly raised."

Carter shifted again. "I can't believe you," he said at last, his eyes narrowing. Then he smiled, but not his sweet, charming smile. "I'm afraid, my dear, that you are all set to be an old maid. No man will marry a woman who brings along three younger siblings—even if she is pleasing to the eye."

Angela swallowed hard and nodded. "Then so be it," she replied with all the courage she could muster. She moved to get his hat and coat and handed them to him without a word.

He looked at her, anger filling his eyes, and then he began to laugh, a coarse, bitter laugh that made Angela shiver. She felt as though she had been struck, but still she did not flinch.

"Good night, my dear," he said.

"Goodbye, Mr. Stratton," she replied and turned back to the fire until she heard him leave the room.

It wasn't until Angela was in the privacy of her own bedroom that she allowed the tears to flow. She didn't bother to remove her clothes before throwing herself onto her bed and letting the sobs shake her slender body.

"He's right," she cried into her pillow. "He's right. I will be an old maid. No one will ever, ever marry me with three others to care for. I know it. I know it."

Angela cried long and hard, but in the end she wiped her tears and resolutely got up to prepare for bed.

"I don't care," she told her image in the mirror. "I am quite ready to be an old maid. I made Mama a promise—and with God's help I will keep it. I will raise them. I will. I will. And I will never—never look at another man again. How could I have been so foolish? Why did I say yes so quickly? Mama taught me more sense than that. Thomas was right. I never really knew Carter. I did not realize the kind of person he really is. I am just so thankful—so thankful—that I found out in time to prevent—to prevent a—a tragic mistake."

She lifted her chin and straightened her back in resolve—but she couldn't keep another tear from trickling down her cheek.

Chapter Twenty

Changing Plans

Charlie came in for coffee the next morning.

Angela sensed something was bothering him, but he made no comment. Instead, he talked with Thomas about the latest storm, wondered how Gus was getting along with his new boss, and promised Angela that come spring, he would help her with her garden.

"Is your cabin warm enough?" Thomas asked.

Charlie nodded, pride in his eyes.

"I helped the boss build thet little place. We made sure thet it was sound and solid," he said, the gleam in his eyes again. "Got everything in there thet a man needs."

So why aren't you happy? Angela wanted to ask, but she held her tongue.

Thomas asked the question Angela was thinking, though in a roundabout way. He simply gave Charlie the opportunity to bring up what was bothering him. "What can we do for you, Charlie?"

Charlie sat and stirred the cream in his coffee. Round and round went his spoon, and Angela imagined his thoughts going round and round, too. It was a long time before he spoke.

"Been doin' some thinkin'," Charlie said at last. "It really weren't right the way I handled young Mr. Stratton. I mean— well, he is the boss's boy—an' I reckon iffen it had been me—I woulda wanted all of my pa's land myself. I coulda jest given him back his land—not made a public show of it like I did."

There was silence again. Charlie raised his head, his eyes troubled.

"Reckon yer pa would've done it different," he said with conviction.

Thomas nodded. "Reckon," he agreed.

"Well, I been thinkin' as to how I owe the young feller an apology," said Charlie.

Angela stiffened. At one point she would have agreed, but after the events of the previous evening she had little compassion for Carter Stratton.

"Well, I figure as how I best hike myself on over there and speak my little piece. Don't know if he'll accept my words or not—but I gotta be a sayin' 'em—iffen I want to live with myself, that is."

Thomas nodded.

They sat in silence again. Angela wished to speak—wished to stir—wished to flee—but she did none of those things. Her own thoughts went round and round in her head.

"I watched yer folks fer a good number of years," Charlie went on slowly. "I don't think they would have taken things on—jest fer spite, like I done. Now, mind you—I don't claim to be religious like yer folks were—but they was good folks. Funny—" Charlie hesitated and then chuckled softly, "I find myself thinkin' about yer pa and askin' myself, 'What would Karl have done?' An' yer ma. Well, she was kindness itself. Never done a thing in her life fer spite, yer ma. One time she says to me, 'Charlie, the Lord says we are to forgive seventy times seven,' she says. 'I figure as how I never get much past ten.' She says thet to me, and she smiles an' I think within myself thet I never get much past two. Fact is, I most often never even get started."

Angela felt her face warming. She was harboring a little resentment of her own. Charlie was right. Her mama would want her to forgive—if indeed she had any reason to be angry at all. Other suitors had changed their minds about the person they had asked to marry. Certainly Carter had a right to a wife without—without a whole family to tend.

Angela went for more coffee. She would spend some time with the Lord in prayer just as soon as Charlie left on his little errand.

―――――

"Thomas . . ." Angela spoke slowly, hesitantly. She wasn't sure just where or how to start. She could feel tears forming and willed herself not to cry like a silly child.

Thomas lifted his head and waited.

Angela turned her attention back to her dinner plate. She

had determined that Thomas would be told of the change of plans before the children arrived home from school.

Angela lifted her head, took a deep breath and said, "There won't be a wedding, after all." Her voice was matter-of-fact and straightforward.

Her brother's eyes clouded. Angela read anger in them, and Thomas seldom got angry.

"He backed out?" he said through clenched teeth.

"Let's just say we changed our minds," Angela hurried on. "There were some things we had not discussed—before. And when we got to them, we couldn't work out a compromise," she said simply.

The eyes before her remained dark. Angela hurried on.

"I—I'm sorry," she whispered. "I know that it means— means—" but she could not go on.

The darkness began to fade from her brother's eyes. Thomas gave a little sigh. Was it one of relief? Angela wondered. He reached for her hand and gave it a squeeze. "Are you terribly disappointed?" he asked.

Angela shook her head, tears coming now. "I—I honestly don't know," she managed to say. "In some ways—yes—I—I guess any girl is disappointed when—when things don't work out—as planned." Angela stopped to sniff and wipe at the tears with her handkerchief. "But I—I've done some praying and I think—I think that—well, I think it's best this way. I don't think Carter and I—that we were—well—right for each other. But I'm awfully sorry about you. I mean—"

"About me?" cut in Thomas. "What do you mean 'about me'?"

"Well, you could have left the farm. Gone to do your work with seed like you've always dreamed—"

Thomas stood. "You mean you thought—"

"I know how much it means to you," she rushed on, "and as long as you need to be here—for the children and me—I know you won't just leave us and go," said Angela with a little shrug.

Thomas sat down again and leaned toward his sister. "Angela," he said softly but firmly, "don't you ever marry anyone— *anyone,* you hear?—to try to make things better for the rest of the family."

"But it wasn't—wasn't just that," Angela fumbled. "I mean— I mean I—I liked Carter. He was—was—"

"Arrogant, conceited, and totally uncaring of another's feelings," Thomas said, his voice hard.

It was Angela's turn to stand to her feet. Her eyes were wide with shock and her lower lip trembled in spite of her attempts to still it with her teeth.

"You thought that?"

Thomas was already repentant. He lowered his head and ran his hand through his hair. "I'm sorry. I'm sorry," he muttered.

"Thomas," said Angela reaching out a hand to her brother. "Why? Why didn't you say so?"

For a moment Thomas could not respond, but at last he looked directly at Angela. "Because I thought you loved him."

Angela dropped to her chair again. "So did I," she whispered. "For a short time—so did I."

"And now?" asked Thomas.

"I spent a good part of the morning in prayer. Oh, Thomas. I don't think it would have been right at all. Mama would have— Mama would have known right from the start. I know she would have. I could have been saved the heartbreak if only Mama—"

"Don't," said Thomas. "Don't berate yourself. You got it worked out. That's all that matters now. We'll just—we'll just go on as though it never happened."

Angela shook her head. She knew she would always be aware of the fact that she had been engaged—then jilted. But she lifted her chin and looked at Thomas. Then her eyes began to twinkle and her lips formed a wobbly smile.

"I'll live," she said. "I've been wooed and—and forsaken—but the worst is already over. Life will go on." She blinked back an insistent tear.

Thomas stood and pulled her into his arms. For a moment Angela leaned against his broad chest, comforted by the strength of the arms that held her. She would have missed Thomas. But she was so sorry—so sorry that he couldn't pursue his dream.

"Good girl," Thomas said.

His voice sounded so much like their father's that Angela felt like a little girl again, held safe in her pa's strong arms.

"Good girl," Thomas said again; then he released her and went for his cap and heavy coat.

———

Life did go on for Angela. Nothing further was said about the broken engagement. Angela was thankful that Thomas wisely had asked her not to tell anyone of her wedding plans. There were no questions from friends and neighbors to answer. But in her heart, Angela still felt moments of pain.

Fortunately there were few occasions for her to see Carter. Word had it that he was much too busy on the ranch to make it to Sunday church. He did manage the Easter Sunday service, but he sat near the back and Angela did not have to greet him. Occasionally they met on the streets of the little town and Angela managed a stiff smile and a "good morning." Carter responded in a manner to indicate that Angela had never been anyone special in his life. Angela heard that he was calling at the home of Trudie Sommers, but she did not make any effort to verify or discredit those rumors.

Winter turned to spring and Charlie kept good his word about helping Angela plant her garden. She was surprised how much time it freed when Charlie manned the hoe.

Thomas planted a large plot of his special seed even before he did the regular planting. He could hardly wait for the new grain to appear so he could judge its success.

School ended and the children were home again. Angela always looked forward to that time of year. It wasn't hard to keep them busy as there were many jobs around the farmhouse. Derek spent his time helping Thomas in the fields. He was filling out, and even though Angela still thought of him as a young boy, she knew he was quickly becoming a young man.

His attitude about himself and about life seemed to improve—but very slowly. Angela knew the pain in his past would likely always haunt him. They still played the memory game, and Derek shared along with the rest. Some stories were poignant, some funny, others joyous. Angela hoped their game helped healing to occur.

Louise had far more interest in socializing than in fulfilling household chores. She begged and pestered until Angela was tempted to tell her to just be gone and leave the household in peace. But Angela knew her mother would not have handled it in that manner.

"You may have one outing a week," she told her young sister. "You must decide whether it is to be an evening, an afternoon, or a Sunday."

Louise sulked for a time but at last accepted the arrangement.

Sara had grown so much over the winter months that Angela

had to let down every inch of her sister's skirts. She would soon be passing on to Louise's hand-me-down dresses. Angela sensed that Sara would be the tall one—tall and slim like their father. But the growth of the young girl made Angela uneasy. Did it mean that she was about to lose the joyful, teasing, carefree little bundle of energy called Sara and gain another changing, pouting, testing adolescent? Angela wasn't sure she would be able to cope with two moody teenagers.

Thane was back. He spent every available minute in the fields with Thomas and Derek. He challenged Thomas to checker games and teased Louise about young men of the community. He brought Sara her lemon drops and licorice sticks and helped Derek fashion a bridle for his new saddle horse. He brought groceries from the store for Charlie and recommended medication for his arthritis. He lounged on the front veranda, talking and laughing, while the long hours of dusk wrapped a soft, dark cloak about the farm. He admired Angela's garden, asked for her company on summer evening walks, brought her books from his own bookshelves, and listened to her plans for sewing new curtains.

And it was true. He did watch her carefully—just like Sara had said. But Angela hardly noticed. She felt at ease with Thane. He was as close as one of the family. There was a security—a fellowship—a feeling of belonging. Angela sensed it, though she could not have defined it. But she, like the others, was very glad that Thane was back.

Chapter Twenty-one

The Picnic

The day was warm with just the hint of a breeze. Angela spent the morning in her kitchen preparing potato salad and deviled eggs. From the oven the chicken sent out the most inviting aroma. Angela had browned it in the big frying pan, then covered it with herbs and rich cream and put it into the oven to simmer. Louise cut thick slices of homemade bread, and Sara spread them generously with farm butter, making sure that even the corners and crusts were given a portion.

"Thomas hates dry edges," she observed as she worked.

Louise looked at the cake on the table. It was her first baking for the community picnic and she appeared proud of her work. With a toss of her pinned-up hair, she went back to slicing the bread.

"What time is dinner?" she asked.

Angela answered without looking up from her task. "One o'clock."

Louise glanced toward the mantel clock. "I hope the boys hurry or we'll be late."

Angela looked at the clock as well. "There's lots of time," she assured the younger girl.

"Does Trudie still like Thomas?" asked Sara without any preamble.

Angela shifted her gaze to Sara. Her dress, even though let down to the limit, was still a bit too short. She sighed. How would she ever keep up with the growing child?

"I—I hear that"—Angela almost said Carter, then changed it quickly to Mr. Stratton—"that Mr. Stratton has been calling on Trudie."

"Good!" said Sara with emphasis but made no explanation.

The back door slammed and Derek entered the kitchen, his eyes shining. "Ready?" he called in an excited tone.

Angela felt her pulse quicken. It was the first time she had seen the boy so enthusiastic.

"We just need to bundle things up," she told him. "Bring those boxes from the shed and we'll wrap the chicken so it won't cool."

Derek hastened to obey, and Angela began to gather the picnic foods for packing. With the help of the girls, she soon had things ready to go, and Thomas and Derek carried the boxes to the waiting wagon. Charlie was already standing by, looking pleased.

"Been ages since I found myself at a picnic," he observed. "And with a real live family too," he added, smiling around on them all.

Angela noticed that he looked pleased at the prospect.

They all climbed aboard and found places to sit; then Thomas clucked to the team and they were off.

Angela lifted her eyes to the cloudless sky. "Well, it looks like we won't be rained out," she observed. "Though it could get a mite hot before the day is over."

"Just right," said Derek, slapping a well-worn baseball into the mitt on his hand.

Angela knew why Derek was excited about the day. He loved sports, and he lost no opportunity to take part in a game.

"Well, if you want to play ball," Thomas counseled good-naturedly, "remember not to eat too much. Hard to play ball on a full stomach."

"Why don't we play ball first?" asked Derek.

"Because the food wouldn't stay hot—or cold—whatever it is supposed to be," explained Angela.

"Still think they have it backwards," mused Derek, showing little concern as to whether hot dishes became cool or cold dishes became warm.

"You'd get sick," said Louise with a familiar toss of her head. "Food spoils real fast in the summer heat."

The occupants of the wagon fell silent then, each sorting out personal thoughts. Angela wondered if she would need to face Carter and Trudie as a twosome. The thought didn't bother her as much as it would have a few months previously, but still it would be a less-than-pleasant experience. She marveled, though, that she had returned to emotional health so quickly.

A number of teams had already gathered by the time Thomas hitched his team to the rail fence. Sara had jumped out to join her friends before the wagon even rolled to a stop. Angela was about to call after her to walk like a lady, but she shook her head and turned back to the dinner items.

Long tables had been constructed for the food, and Angela directed Thomas and Derek to carry the pans and boxes. Charlie lent a hand and soon the task was complete and Derek was free to find other young men with whom to discuss the ball game. Thomas drifted to where young fellows his own age had gathered. Louise tossed her head slightly and displayed her cake, obviously wishing someone would ask her who had made it.

The meal was first on the agenda. Long lines of chattering, laughing neighbors queued up, and impatient children crowded to the front of the line to get "first pick." Angela found herself in line beside Thane.

"Sara tells me that Louise baked a cake," he whispered in her ear. "Which one is it so I can make an announcement?"

Angela laughed as she pointed out Louise's cake. Thane nodded, and Angela was sure then that Louise would receive all of the recognition she desired.

Sure enough, when they reached the spot, Thane declared in a loud voice, "Look at that cake! It looks delicious. I wonder who made it. Do you know?" he asked Mrs. Blackwell, who was on the other side of the table.

She shook her head.

"Do you know?" he asked Mrs. Sommers.

She gave the same response.

"It looks delicious," he repeated and went on helping himself to a generous portion. "Must be a good cook. Louise, do you know?" he called to her just ahead of them in the line.

Louise's face reddened, but she admitted ownership. "I did," she said with a self-conscious tilt of her blond head.

"By yourself?" asked Thane in astounded tones.

Louise nodded. Angela could see the pleased look in her sister's eyes as heads turned to look.

Thane, who had already dipped his fork into the piece on his plate as though he couldn't wait another second, was smacking his lips. "Yum. It tastes even better than it looks. Delicious!"

Angela chuckled. If Louise wanted recognition, word had certainly gotten to the right person. Angela was about to give Thane a nudge to caution him not to go too far. But Thane suddenly turned the compliment toward her, making Angela blush as red as Louise.

"Well, she should be good," he whispered into her ear; "she's had the community's best teacher."

Angela was eager to quiet Thane's embarrassing comments, so she led him to the shade of tall poplar trees that bordered the school property. The Andrews family joined them, and their talk turned to a more comfortable topic than cakes and cooks.

After dinner the games and races began. Thomas took part in everything for which he was eligible. Sometimes he won, sometimes he lost, but he accepted both outcomes with good humor. He took first place in the woodcutting competition with no difficulty, retaining his title for the third year.

Derek proved to be good at foot racing. But Derek entered only those events in which he felt he would make a fair show.

Derek does not do very well at losing, Angela observed, noticing the intensity of his face.

Louise scorned involvement in competition. She tossed her head, trying to look mature, but she wasn't always able to quite manage it. Sara, on the other hand, had no inhibitions and would have raced with the boys had it been allowed.

From one event to another the day progressed with everyone having a lot of fun. Then it was time for the ball game, and the Merrifield brothers were called on to choose up sides. Spectators moved their blankets to grassy spots near the diamond, and folks settled themselves for some cheering. Roger Merrifield chose Derek to be on his team, and his brother Peter chose Thomas.

"Brother against brother," Angela heard someone say, and the comment was followed by a laugh.

About the time of the first pitch Angela saw Carter's team of bays enter the schoolyard. By his side sat Trudie, proudly holding his arm with one hand and her hat with the other. The team came to a halt in a small cloud of dust, and Trudie descended like a queen. She leaned close to Carter as they walked toward the crowd and laughed noisily as he spread their blanket. Angela turned her eyes back to the game. It did bother her—a little.

The game held her attention, though. The score remained even inning by inning. Derek's team was ahead by a run—then Thomas's team would lead—back and forth, back and forth. Angela hardly knew how to cheer, so she cheered for both.

When they went into the ninth inning the score was tied. Thomas's team batted first. Peter struck out. Ernest hit the ball down the first base line, and Thane disposed of that batter. The third batter hit a long fly ball. Angela held her breath. It was heading straight toward Derek. No, it was going to his right. There was no one else who would be able to reach the ball. Derek raced toward it, and Angela squirmed and grimaced. She was sure he had no hope of getting to the fly ball and would be injured in the attempt. At the last possible second, Derek made a valiant dive, rolling head over heels in the grass. When he stopped tumbling he jumped to his feet to show that he had the ball in his gloved hand. The crowd cheered, and Angela started breathing again when she saw the grinning boy running in from left field.

The score was still tied. Angela felt this would be a good time to end the game. No winners or losers. Then she noticed the look on Derek's face. It was clear to Angela that his thinking did not match her own. Derek wanted to win. She watched as he swung the bat in preparation for his turn at the plate. On his face was a look of determination she had never seen before.

Thane was the first batter. He hit the ball well, but Peter managed to catch it. Angela did not know the young man who batted in second place. His family was new to the community. He popped up a foul that was caught by the catcher. There was just one more chance for a win, and Derek stepped to the plate. Angela felt her stomach tighten. She didn't want to watch, but she couldn't bear to turn away.

To make matters worse, the pitcher was Thomas. Everyone talked about what a good pitcher he was. Angela knew little about baseball, but she was willing to take the word of the neighborhood young men. If they said Thomas was good, she concluded he must be.

Brother faced brother. Thomas stood on the mound, his face relaxed, his eyes showing both humor at the situation and pride in his younger brother. Derek stared back, his jaw tight, his eyes intense, his whole frame flexed for action. He had faced Thomas many times before. They often filled vacant moments with a ball and bat in the farmyard. But Thomas had always thrown balls he wanted his brother to hit. This time, Derek knew, there would be no mercy.

Derek whipped the bat in little flicking motions that Angela likened to the tail of a hunting cat. Thomas's moves were slow, deliberate. He took his sign from the catcher, started his windup, then reared back and threw a sizzling fast ball. Derek swung—but too late.

"Strike one," called Mr. Andrews from behind his umpire's mask.

Derek shuffled, digging in his forward foot with determination.

Thomas looked at the catcher and ground the ball in his mitt.

Angela's stomach was twisting now. Men had risen from their blankets, their eyes squinting against the afternoon sun. An occasional yell rent the stillness, but most leaned forward in silence, ready to explode should the drama intensify.

Thomas threw two balls in succession. "Just nicked the plate," Angela heard the man to her left exclaim. "Andrews missed that call."

But the count stood—two and one.

Another pitch came spinning in. Angela wondered how Derek could even see it, but he swung, sending the ball reeling into the dirt at his feet.

Two and two.

The next pitch was in close. For one horrible moment Angela feared it would strike Derek, but it veered away and Derek jumped back, avoiding any contact.

Three and two. Full count. The crowd leaned into the play. Even Carter had deserted Trudie to stand with the others, his jaw working, his eyes intense.

Angela's eyes shifted quickly back to her two brothers. The one on the mound, rubbing the ball in his glove, and the other at the plate, sweat beading on his forehead, his bat flicking, his muscles taut.

Another pitch. Angela could not look. She closed her eyes just as the ball was about to reach the plate. Then she heard a sharp, loud crack.

She jerked her head up again and was on her feet before she realized what she was doing. "Run, run!" she screamed as Derek headed for first base. The ball was still in the air. It was sailing farther and farther. Angela saw Thomas, his back to home plate. He was shading his eyes and watching the flight of the ball.

When Angela's eyes returned to Derek she was surprised to see him rounding second—then on to third. The ball had gone over the heads of the outfielders and was being chased by the center fielder. The throw was coming in as Derek tagged third, but he kept running full speed toward home base.

"Slide! Slide!" Angela heard someone yell, and she thought the voice sounded like Thomas's.

Derek dove head first beneath the catcher. The ball smacked into the glove just as Derek's hand stretched forward to touch the plate. He had averted the tag. A cheer went up. The crowd surged forward as one. Derek's team had won the game.

Angela felt tears stinging her eyes. She knew how much the win would mean to her little brother. She had no fear that the loss would adversely affect Thomas.

She fought her way back to her blanket against the pushing crowd, her face flushed at her lack of composure.

A strange silence settled about her. She turned back to the diamond, bewildered. Something was wrong. Had Mr. Andrews called Derek out? But he was safe. He had slid.

And then, through the gathering crowd, Angela saw the reason for the stillness. Derek was still on the ground. He had not picked himself up from the dirt. He lay—just where he had fallen. Thomas was bending over him, speaking his name, brushing his cheek. Angela saw fear in his eyes. Derek lay still. Very still.

With a cry Angela grabbed up her skirts and ran toward them. She tried to pray but the only words to come from her lips were "Oh, God. Oh, God."

"Bring some water," someone was saying.

"He must have hit his head," said another.

Angela fell on her knees beside Thomas and reached out a hand to Derek.

"Don't move him," cautioned Thomas, brushing her hand aside.

Angela looked up at him, her eyes filled with terror.

"Is he—?"

"I don't know. I don't know," said Thomas. "But we can't move him until we're sure he hasn't hurt his neck or something."

Angela nodded, tears spilling down her face. *Oh, God, if anything happens to Derek*—She couldn't finish the thought.

He was so still. So pale. Angela reached a hand to his cheek and gently brushed off a smudge of dust.

"They've run for Doc," someone said, and someone else knelt beside her and wiped Derek's face with a water-soaked towel.

A moan escaped Derek's lips. It was the most beautiful sound Angela had ever heard. Then he stirred slightly.

"Don't move," cautioned Thomas, holding the boy steady. "It's all right, Derek. It's all right. Just lie still. Lie still."

Derek moaned again.

The doctor came from his shaded spot on the other side of the schoolyard, and the crowd receded while he knelt beside the young boy. Angela frantically watched his probing fingers as they felt Derek's neck, shoulders, chest.

"Just winded," he said at last. "He got the breath knocked right out of him."

Derek's eyes fluttered open and he looked up, bewildered, then embarrassed by all the attention.

"Just lie still a minute, son," the doctor said. "Just lie still. Here, Thomas—help me turn him onto his back."

An older man placed his hat on the ground for a pillow, while the Doc and Thomas turned Derek. Doc took over sponging the boy's face, and Angela saw the color gradually return. The crowd started to breathe again.

"That's better," said Doc. "That's better." Then with a twinkle in his eye he said to Derek, "Hear you won the game."

Derek grinned and the whole group erupted into a cheer. The tension broke. Derek was going to be fine.

Angela felt her knees buckle beneath her. She had never fainted before, but she knew she was going down now. But someone caught her and helped her to the blanket she had earlier deserted. She heard a voice ask for a cup of water. She felt her head cradled against a shoulder, and she left it there until her world stopped spinning. She accepted the water offered to her and soon her equilibrium began to return.

"I'm fine," she finally muttered, embarrassed at her near collapse.

"You're sure?"

She nodded her head emphatically and looked up into the face of Thane.

"I'm fine," she said again. "It just sort of—sort of gave me a scare."

Thane nodded. Then his eyes began to twinkle. "He won," he whispered. "He won. He beat Tom's best pitch. You should see Thomas. Now that he's over his fright—he's fairly bursting his buttons."

Chapter Twenty-two

Visitors

Angela had just finished the morning laundry and Louise was hanging the last of the socks on the clothesline when Mrs. Blackwell arrived, panting from the effort of her walk. Angela ushered the woman into the coolness of the kitchen, fearing that she might suffer from heat exhaustion if she didn't soon get in out of the summer sun.

Angela pushed forward a chair and urged the woman to be seated. Mrs. Blackwell dropped into the chair with a glance toward the icebox.

"Would you like some lemonade?" asked Angela.

The woman nodded, and Angela hastened to produce a large glassful.

After a lengthy drink, Mrs. Blackwell placed the glass on the table but did not release it.

"I hear there's to be a weddin'," she announced.

Angela raised her eyebrows.

"Thet there Stratton fella is hitchin' hisself to Trudie," continued Mrs. Blackwell.

"Really? I hadn't heard," responded Angela. She kept her voice even.

"My man heard the news in town this mornin'. Says it's to be soon—in the church. 'Course her folks wouldn't be none too happy iffen she didn't marry in the church."

Angela nodded.

"Well, I don't like the smell of it all," went on the woman. "Seems awful fast work to me. He ain't been here in the community fer thet long."

Angela wondered what the woman would say if she knew

Carter Stratton had already been betrothed to another since his arrival in their community.

Mrs. Blackwell took another long drink.

"Some folks is sayin' thet he's jest out to spite his ma. He and her had 'em a big fight before he left home." She spoke the last statement in a hushed, confidential tone.

When Angela didn't respond, Mrs. Blackwell continued. "His ma wants him to marry a city girl. Even had one all picked out fer him. He's pickin' his own jest to get back at her."

She finished the lemonade and pushed the empty glass toward Angela.

Angela refilled it and passed it back.

"His ma won't even come to the weddin'." She made a disapproving sound at this last bit of information.

Angela wondered how much truth there was to the report. If true, if Carter was marrying just for spite—she herself could have been the unfortunate bride. *But surely, surely he wouldn't do that,* she reasoned. Not to Trudie. Not to anyone. Angela forced the gossip from her mind and attempted to divert the conversation.

"How is your garden doing?"

"See thet man out hoein' yours 'most every time I go by," the woman stated instead of answering the question. "You really think yer ma would have been happy with an old man livin' with ya?"

"He doesn't live with us," corrected Angela. "He lives all alone—in his little cabin."

"Same thing," said the woman with a dark look. "He comes an' goes like he lives here. An' you with two innocent young girls an' all. Yer mama—"

"My mama was a charitable woman," Angela stated flatly. "And she did not look for dirt on a polished table. Charlie needed a place for his cabin—and Thomas appreciates an older, wiser head for farming advice. And as for me and the girls, Charlie is like a—like a grandfather—and we need all the family we can muster."

The woman's mouth dropped at Angela's frankness. Her eyes flashed, but she held her tongue and reached for another drink from the glass.

Angela spun away from her. The idea that anyone would even hint there was anything wrong with Charlie sharing their yard made her tremble with anger.

But she had only taken two steps before she turned again. She stood for a moment in silence and then dipped her head. "I'm sorry," she said softly, lifting her chin again. "My mama would not be proud of my sharp tongue. Charlie is a dear friend of the family and we are—are happy to have him living here. But Mama—Mama would never tolerate sass or disrespect of our elders. For that, I apologize."

The older woman did not decline or accept the apology, and Angela went for some sugar cookies to accompany the lemonade. When she returned, the incident seemed to have been forgotten.

The very next day Trudie came calling. Angela was in the kitchen kneading dough for a batch of bread. Louise worked over the ironing board, and Sara labored over stitching a torn pocket on one of her frocks.

Trudie bustled into the kitchen without waiting to be invited. Her eyes shone and her mass of red hair, carelessly piled on top of her bouncing head, danced in rhythm to her enthusiasm.

"Guess what?" she squealed, holding out her arms to Angela. Angela did not have to guess, but she remained silent.

"Oh, guess what?" Trudie repeated. "I'm going to be married!" She threw herself at Angela with an excited squeal, and Angela returned the embrace even though her heart was not in it. The young woman's face glowed and her eyes shone.

"Oh, look!" Angela exclaimed when they backed away from each other. "I've smeared flour all over your shoulder."

Trudie just laughed as though the flour was part of the exciting world she inhabited. Angela grabbed a towel and tried to brush Trudie's dress, but Trudie just laughed harder.

"Don't fret. Don't fret," she giggled. "Carter is taking me shopping in the city anyway. I'm to have all new clothes. Everything. He said so."

Angela tossed the towel down on the seat of a nearby chair. "In that case," she responded with a laugh, "another hug." Angela was surprised that she could enjoy this moment with her friend. She sincerely hoped Trudie would be happy with Carter.

Trudie accepted the second hug with the same enthusiasm she had given the first, and Angela did not try to keep her floured hands from the shoulders of the blue dress.

"Now sit—and tell me all about it," Angela invited.

"We are getting married in two weeks—on Sunday afternoon

in the church. We will have the dinner at the farm. We have a big yard there as you know, so just—just everyone will be able to come. Do pray that it will be a nice day. I'll just die if it rains—or is windy.

"Carter is arranging for flowers—they have flowers in the city for their weddings—and I am wearing a gown right from a city shop. Carter has it already, but he won't let me see it until the wedding morning."

"Well, that is a turn," mused Angela. *I thought the groom was the one who was not to see it.*

"Carter is paying for everything. He has told Mama exactly what he wants for the ceremony and the dinner and everything."

Angela said nothing.

"But he is letting me choose my own attendant," Trudie continued. Then she squealed again and held out her arms to Angela as before. "I picked *you.*"

Angela felt the blood draining from her face. "Oh, but I—"

"No, don't you try to say no. You are my best friend."

"But what will Carter—"

"I've already told Carter. He says he'd love to have you share our happy moment. He was so sweet about it. He will even shop for a dress for you. He insists—he says he'll pick one just made for you."

Angela had to sit down. She was glad to find a chair nearby. She couldn't guess what Carter would choose for her. An ugly dress that looked frumpish and demeaning—or a stylish gown to remind her of what she could have had. Either way, she was not looking forward to seeing the dress or taking part in this wedding.

Trudie was still babbling. "And he said he would look after everything. And, oh—you should see the house! Carter has had it completely redone. It's gorgeous! And I am to have help—in the kitchen and with the cleaning. Not Gus, of course. Gus has been dismissed. There's a new cook coming from the city. Carter says he is sick and tired of flapjacks and fried bacon." Trudie stopped to laugh as though the comment had been witty or cute.

Poor Gus, thought Angela. *I wonder if Charlie knows. Poor Charlie.*

Trudie went on and on about the wedding, about the house, about Carter. Angela tried to listen but her thoughts kept wandering. Louise had stopped ironing and was listening with wide eyes. Even the young Sara had let her garment fall into her lap and was sitting still, taking in the one-sided conversation.

Angela continued to knead the dough, giving it such a thorough rolling and pounding that she wasn't sure it would have the strength to rise.

At length Trudie slowed down. "Well, I must run," she bubbled. "I have so much to do."

"But I thought Carter was doing it all," responded Louise with youthful frankness.

"Oh, he is—at least all of the big things. He has saved me so much, the dear, but I still have a multitude of little things to attend to. Oh, I'm so glad that you are to be my bridesmaid, Angela. It's going to be such a wonderful day." And with those words Trudie left in a flurry, just as she had arrived.

"Did I say I would be her bridesmaid?" Angela asked her two sisters, shaking her head.

"I don't know," responded Louise, "but I sure would. Wow! It's going to be so exciting. And a new dress. Do you s'pose it'll be from the city?"

"I have no idea," spouted Angela as she dropped the last roll of dough into the big pan and smacked it hard with her floured hand.

"You are going to do it, aren't you?" asked Sara.

"Of course. For Trudie. As a friend." And then she added, to herself, *for I fear that in the days to come Trudie will need every friend she has.*

Angela watched Derek carefully in the days following his mishap and was finally convinced he had suffered no permanent injury. But what a scare he had given them! Gradually she ceased protesting each time Thomas suggested some heavy task for the boy. Derek didn't want to shun responsibility and looked at Angela with embarrassment when she tried to divert his tasks to herself or to one of the girls. Still, it was hard for Angela to go on as before and even harder to keep silent when she saw Derek grab his glove after a day in the field and climb onto his horse for a trip to some neighbors.

Don't slide. Don't slide, she wanted to call after him.

Seeing her anxiety, Thomas always tried to ease her concern. "The boy is fine. I've watched carefully and he's just fine."

Angela knew Thomas was as concerned for Derek as she was, and she tried to assure herself that Thomas would know whether or not there was any reason for further worry.

Eventually Derek returned to haying, manning the heavy forks, and sweating his way through the hot and dusty summer.

Angela found herself taking frequent trips to the hayfield with the excuse of bringing her brothers a cool drink or a light snack. Other years it had been Sara's job, but this year Angela wanted to keep an eye on her young brother.

On one such trip she stopped to feel the heads of Thomas's experimental grain. They were filling out, but Thomas admitted disappointment in his new seed.

"It's not quite right yet," he said. "I need to bring in another strain that has more resistance to the hot summer winds."

"You mean you have to start all over?" Angela queried.

"Oh, no. Not all over. It takes years to produce just what you are looking for—and I haven't given it much time."

Angela slid her hand over a shock of the new grain, wishing again that Thomas might be freed to work on his seed instead of being saddled to the cares of the farm. She moved on, her shoulders heavy with concern.

As she passed Charlie's shack, Charlie rose from his front porch and greeted her.

"How is he, girlie?" he asked. Angela flushed. She hadn't realized her missions had been that obvious.

"Fine," she responded. No sense denying her purpose in making trips to the hayfield.

Charlie walked along with her to the house and settled himself on the cool back porch.

"You want some cold buttermilk?" Angela offered, and Charlie was quick to accept.

Angela took the lunch dishes to the kitchen and returned with two glasses of buttermilk.

Charlie sipped slowly. His thoughts seemed to be far away.

"Been doin' a lot of thinkin' lately," he said at last. "Guess you heard thet Gus is out of a job."

Angela nodded.

"Feel sorry fer Gus. Been wonderin' iffen there's room in thet little shack fer two old duffers."

Angela pictured the two little rooms. It seemed a bit crowded to her way of thinking.

"Been thinkin' thet a fella could build on another bedroom," Charlie went on. "Right out thet there side toward the east."

Angela nodded again. It seemed workable.

"Maybe Gus would like to spend some of his money on it," Angela suggested.

"I'd forgot all about his money," mused Charlie. "Shucks—with all thet money—what'd he ever want to live with an old geezer like me fer?"

"Because you're his friend," replied Angela.

Charlie nodded then, turning the empty glass in his hands. "I've been doin' some more thinkin' too," he went on.

He was silent so Angela prompted. "About?"

"About yer ma and pa. Their religion. What they used to say. You know what?"

"What?" asked Angela.

"I even been tryin' to live like they did." He straightened his shoulders and looked directly into her eyes. Then he seemed to sag.

"Guess I don't know enough about it—'cause I keep gettin' all tripped up. Just when I think I got the hang of behavin' proper, I go an' do somethin' all wrong. Don't know how your folks kept all those rules straight."

"You think that their—their faith was a bunch of rules?" asked Angela softly.

"Wasn't it?"

"No. No—it wasn't rules—not as you think."

Charlie seemed confused, and Angela wasn't sure she could explain it properly.

"It doesn't start with rules," explained Angela hesitantly. "It starts with the heart."

Angela remembered kneeling at her mother's knee as a child of seven. She, too, had thought she could be good by keeping the rules, but her mother had explained that it wasn't her self-righteousness that would prepare her for heaven; it was her trust in the Savior who had paid the penalty for all her wrongdoing.

"It starts with the heart," Angela said again, placing her hand over her own heart. "We are all sinners. We can't be—be good enough to earn our way into heaven—none of us. God knew that. That's why He sent His Son Jesus to pay the penalty for sin. He said that the wages for sin was death. That part He didn't change. But instead of making each one of us die for our own misdeeds, He allowed Jesus to die for us—for all of us. But even though the—the penalty has been paid, it's of no effect unless we accept it. It's like getting a—a present that you don't accept. Like you—and the will. It said that you could have the land—but you wouldn't take it. You can do the same thing with God's pardon. You have to accept it like a freely offered gift—with thankfulness."

Charlie was silent while he pondered the words.

"That's all?" he asked at last.

"Well, not quite. I mean, when we admit we're sinners, then we ask for His forgiveness and accept His gift—like I said. Then He does the rest. He cleanses us. The Bible says He gives us a new heart—a clean heart—so that we can keep His rules."

Angela groped for an explanation that Charlie might understand. Through the window she spotted a pot on her kitchen stove.

"See that pot," she said, pointing her finger. "If I pushed it over the heat and it boiled over—what would spill out on my stove?"

Charlie hesitated, chewing on a corner of his mustache. "What's in it?" he asked slowly.

"That's it," replied Angela excitedly. "Whatever is in it spills out. That's the way it is with us. That's why we can't be consistently good if our heart is evil. As soon as things get a—a little too hot for us to stand—the evil spills out. We need to be cleansed. King David prayed, 'Create in me a clean heart, O God.' We all need that first. Then what you call 'the rules' sort of come in."

Charlie waited for her to explain.

"Even after we've been cleansed we need His help," went on Angela. "We can't do it on our own—none of us. We ask for His help—daily. Why, I remember my pa praying every morning that God would give him wisdom and power and patience for the day."

"He did that?"

"And so did Mama. In fact, I think she did it many times throughout the day. I heard a prayer on her lips so often."

Angela fell silent as her thoughts turned back to her mama's whispered prayers.

"Is thet all?" Charlie asked at last, his voice low and solemn.

"Well, the Bible says we are to be baptized—as our testimony to the Lord. And believers read the Word and pray often to get to know God better."

Silence again.

"Go to church?" asked Charlie.

Angela nodded. "The Bible says not to forsake the gathering of ourselves together for praise and fellowship," she confirmed.

"I figured as how they'd get thet in there somehow," mused Charlie.

"You don't like church?"

"Know'd too many hypocrites," responded Charlie.

"You are not responsible for the hypocrites," Angela assured him. "They must answer to God for their own deeds. You are responsible only for you."

Charlie seemed to be chewing on the matter as he continued to gnaw at his mustache.

"An' thet's what yer folks taught ya?" he asked.

Angela nodded.

"No wonder I couldn't git it to work on my own." He laid a gnarled hand over his own heart. "I ain't been changed none in here—and boy, I sure do need me some changin' on the inside iffen I'm ever gonna do any changin' on the outside."

"We all do," admitted Angela softly.

"Ya got an extry Bible?" Charlie surprised Angela by asking.

"We all have Bibles. Mama saw to it that we each got one for our eighth birthday. As we grew up we could hardly wait till it was our turn."

Then Angela thought of her mother's Bible with its marked passages. It would be better for Charlie. Her mother had written little comments and explained certain scriptures. She went to get it and handed it to Charlie. He accepted it hesitantly.

"I'll take special care of it," he promised. "I know it's a heap special to ya."

Angela nodded. "If you have questions," she said, "speak with Thomas. He's much better at explaining these things than I am."

"You done jest fine," Charlie told her. "Now I guess it's up to me."

Chapter Twenty-three

Trudie's Day

Trudie's wedding was set to take place right after the morning church service. The girls were going to dress for the ceremony at the Merrifields'. Angela had come to terms with taking part as Trudie's bridesmaid, but she was not pleased at the prospect of wearing a gown purchased by Carter Stratton. She would have offered to pay for it, but her common sense told her that this might squander the family's income for the entire year. Instead, she suffered the humiliation in private, making no comment even to Thomas.

The sun was shining and the breeze gentle as Trudie and Angela hurried to the parsonage following the last amen. Trudie, so excited she was giddy, told Angela breathlessly that she still had not seen her wedding dress.

What if it doesn't fit? Angela asked herself. In that event, there was little time to do any alterations.

"Carter made me send all my measurements in a sealed envelope to the seamstress," Trudie babbled. "Oh, I'm so nervous, I can scarcely think."

So what did he do about me? Angela wondered. She had been asked for no measurements.

When the girls arrived at the house, Mrs. Sommers had Trudie's dress spread out on the parson's bed. It was truly a magnificent creation. Angela had never seen anything so beautiful. The satin shimmered in the sunlight that spilled through the bedroom window.

"Oh!" cried Trudie, "look at it! It is—it is beautiful—just like Carter said."

If Trudie had not already been so excited, she may have

wept. As it was she giggled like a child, and Mrs. Sommers had to prompt her to hurry and change into the wedding gown. Angela was full of misgivings about what the dress she was to wear would be like, but when she saw it, she was stunned. It was absolutely perfect.

The soft blue satin had folds and folds of skirt. The bodice was fitted and the sleeves puffed and then fitted from the elbow down. A row of delicate pearl buttons in the back went from hip to neckline. Angela wondered distractedly how she would ever get them all fastened in time for the ceremony. She asked someone to go get Louise to help. In the bedroom she slipped out of her summer voile and into the soft depths of the satin.

The dress fit to perfection, accenting her slim waistline, her creamy skin, and her deep blue eyes. She could not believe her reflection in the mirror.

"It—it's beautiful," she whispered, and for one awful moment she felt that she would never forgive Carter Stratton. Then Louise burst through the door, panting from her run across the churchyard. Her eyes opened wide and she gasped at the sight of Angela.

"You look like a blue angel!" she cried.

"Don't talk silly," Angela said curtly. "I need you to button me. There are more buttons back there than I can count."

Louise set right to work on the buttons. Even so, Trudie was already waiting, fully gowned and coifed, by the time Louise had Angela buttoned up.

"Oh, Angela. You look beautiful!" Trudie cried. "The dress fits as if it was made for you—oh, how silly of me—of course it was!"

"Thank you," returned Angela. "What a beautiful gown. And your red hair looks stunning."

Trudie flushed. "Then I guess my wedding will be the most charming event in the county," she responded. "Both of us look magnificent."

They made their way the short distance across the grassy lawn to the little church. Angela could hear the organ playing.

Nervousness brought a flush to Angela's cheeks. She had never been in a wedding party before. She stepped to the back of the church and waited for the cue from Mrs. Merrifield; then she began the slow procession toward the altar. On her arm were white camellias and blue forget-me-nots. A spray of baby's breath was tucked in her loosely coiled hair.

As she neared the front of the church her eyes met those of Carter Stratton. He nodded ever so slightly and gave her one of his measured smiles. Angela dropped her gaze. She wasn't sure of the message in his eyes and she did not want to understand it.

All heads turned when Trudie appeared at the rear of the church. Eyes glowing, she came down the aisle on her father's arm, her full-skirted gown swishing against the sides of the pews. Her head bobbed under the satin and lace of her veil.

Oh, God, breathed Angela silently. *May she always be this happy.*

Trudie reached the front amid murmurs of awe, and Pastor Merrifield stepped forward to begin the ceremony.

Angela stood as if in a trance. She watched and listened in a daze, but soon someone nudged her and she realized that Trudie was now Mrs. Stratton. An arm was extended to her and she took it. She hadn't paid any attention to the man standing next to Carter Stratton and to her surprise she saw that he was a total stranger.

"I'm Carter's cousin on his mother's side," the young man whispered to her as they walked back down the aisle together. "And you are Miss Peterson?"

Angela nodded her head.

"Carter said that I'd be pleased to escort you," he continued, "but that was an understatement."

Angela tilted her head and studied him, wondering if he had the same controlled charm as his cousin. But instead Angela saw warm, humorous eyes, held in check by proper manners.

"And your name is?" she prompted.

"Bradley Whitteker," he responded. "You may call me Brad."

"I think I shall call you Mr. Whitteker," Angela returned, but there was teasing in her voice.

They went directly from the church to the Sommers farm. Ladies that Angela did not even know scurried about loading long tables with sumptuous-looking dishes.

The wedding couple and their attendants were ushered to the head table. There were bouquets of flowers everywhere. Angela eased her skirts gently around them. She did not want to chance any kind of soil on the expensive gown that belonged to Carter Stratton. Carter gave a short speech of welcome to the guests, then seated his bride and took his place beside her.

Angela had to admit that it was an impressive event. Everything was done in the most elaborate fashion possible. Her escort behaved himself as a true gentleman and provided her with interesting conversation, seasoned well with a dash of wit. To her surprise, she found herself enjoying the meal rather than enduring it.

At length the feast was over and the crowd started to mill about while the new couple opened their wedding gifts. Angela wanted to escape the crowd and noise for a bit and enjoy some fresh air. She moved away and took refuge under the shade of a large elm. She felt as if her hair were pinned to her scalp. She wanted to pull out the combs and just let the tresses spill about her shoulders, but she told herself that for Trudie she could endure the discomfort a few moments longer.

The day had turned warm. Too warm. Angela longed for a bit of the wind that Trudie had prayed away. The tight bodice fitted her like a corset. She would be relieved when she could slip out of the gown and replace it with her own comfortable voile.

She was tempted to sit down on the cool grass, but she could not risk getting stains on the beautiful satin. She didn't even dare lean against the trunk of the elm tree. She stood erect, wishing the minutes by so she might be released from her satiny blue prison.

"There you are," said someone at her elbow. She turned to see Thane studying her.

"Tired?" he asked, concern in his voice.

She nodded her head. "Tired and warm," she admitted, "and so anxious to—to get out of all this—these layers."

"You look beautiful," he whispered, and his eyes told her he meant the words.

Angela felt flustered. Thane had never given her such an intimate compliment before.

"Why, thank you," she managed, and let her eyelids fall to hide the confusion she felt. "The dress is—is most fashionable."

"It's not the dress," he continued. "Though you do make it look awfully good."

Her eyelashes fluttered up again. Was this really Thane speaking?

"I noticed you are wearing the cameo," he commented softly.

Angela nodded. "I like it," she admitted, lifting the cameo so she could see it too.

He opened his mouth to respond, but before he could get the words out someone called for Angela.

"I must go," she apologized, begging him with her eyes to understand.

He nodded, but as she stepped away he reached out and took her hand, halting her.

"Angela," he said, in a voice little more than a whisper. "May I come calling?"

For a moment she did not understand his question. He always came calling. Had always been welcome. Why would he ask—? And then his meaning reached through to her. Thane was asking permission to call—on her. Her heart fluttered within her chest and her breath caught in her throat.

"May I?" he asked again.

She forced herself to look into his eyes. They were pleading. Angela had never seen such a look in his eyes before.

"Please," he said again, and the pressure on her hand increased.

"I would be honored," she managed to whisper and lingered just long enough to read the relief on his face before she withdrew her hand and slipped away.

———

Angela didn't stop to analyze her happiness as she hummed her way through her morning chores. She just knew she felt like singing. Even Louise's bad temper at the breakfast table did nothing to daunt her good spirits. Angela coaxed the girl into better humor and sent her off to school with at least the scowl removed from her face.

After the kitchen was in order, Angela went to her room and spread the blue gown out on the bed. She carefully surveyed each inch of material. She did not want to return it in soiled condition.

She wasn't sure what Carter Stratton would do with the dress. Trudie could never wear it. She was much more "full-figured," her mother called it, than Angela.

When Angela was convinced that the dress was in mint condition, she wrapped it carefully in tissue paper and bundled it into a large box. Tucking the box under her arm, she started across the field to the Strattons'. She wasn't sure who would greet her. Gus was no longer there. He and Charlie were busy making plans for adding a room to the small cabin.

In answer to her knock the door was opened by a stiff-looking woman in a starched apron. Angela wondered if the

woman and the garment had been dipped in the starch together.

"I have a box for Mr. Stratton," Angela explained with a
smile.

"Mr. Stratton is presently on his honeymoon and isn't expected home for some time."

The woman even spoke stiffly.

"Yes," admitted Angela. "I know. There's no hurry about the
box. It can await his return. I would be appreciative if you'd see
that he gets it—after he gets home."

The woman nodded in a short, clipped manner, accepted the
box and moved as though to close the door. Apparently the interview was over. Angela smiled her thanks and stepped back.
She just had time for a quick glance at the new hallway. Carter
had certainly changed things. The walls were papered in a
leafy green pattern and trimmed with cream woodwork. The
floor was covered with thick sea green pile rugs. Rich tapestries
hung at the tall windows, and brilliantly colored pictures almost covered one wall.

"I think I liked it better before," Angela muttered to herself
as she made her way down the brick steps.

She remembered Carter's words on his wedding day. "You
must come and see Trudie often. She regards you as a dear
friend."

Angela thought of the many years she had puzzled over
whether she was a friend or foe of Trudie Sommers, but she
pushed the thought aside. Perhaps she could be a friend to
Trudie in the future, but she did hope that the visits would take
place at her own farmhouse, not at the mansion-like house behind her.

As Angela started back across the fields her song returned.
She was happy to be going home. Happy that her family was
well. Happy that both Charlie and Gus were going to share her
yard. But especially happy that Thane was to call.

Chapter Twenty-four

Commitment

Thane had sent word with Thomas that he would come calling on Friday night if it was convenient for Angela. She would not have dreamed of turning him down. After all her years of close friendship with Thane, Angela felt strangely nervous and excited.

"Stop it," she scolded herself, lifting a trembling hand to brush her hair back into a neat knot. But she could not control her feelings. She had never been this agitated when Carter was calling.

Carter! With his name came the painful memory of his curling lips and final cutting warning: "You are all set to be an old maid. No man will marry a woman who brings along three younger siblings."

The words brought Angela's hands to a halt. She clutched at the combs she was about to place in her hair.

Carter was right. No man—not even Thane—should be expected to take on a ready-made family.

Angela leaned against the bureau and shut her eyes tightly, but the tears squeezed out from under the lids.

"It wouldn't be fair. It wouldn't be fair," her heart cried. "Oh, God, if only Mama—" But Angela checked her thoughts. For the first time in her life she had been about to blame her mama for not staying with them.

Forgive me was her next cry. *I didn't mean it. I didn't. I know Mama did not will to die. I know she—she wanted to be here for her family. I know that—that she—she trusts me to take her place.*

And with those thoughts, Angela straightened her shoulders, brushed the tears from her eyes, and finished pinning her hair.

She took one more look in the mirror to be sure no traces of tears lingered, then smoothed the skirt of her blue gingham. She preferred her voile, but Thane had always been partial to the gingham.

Thane and I have always been dear friends, she told herself. *There is no reason for that to change. We can remain friends—I will tell him so.*

When Thane arrived, Sara hurled herself at him, assuming he was there just to see her. He pulled her braids and tweaked her nose and then handed her a small package of sweets. Louise stood by, grinning and blushing, and Thane paid her a nice compliment, gave Derek a playful punch on the shoulder, and turned his attention to Angela.

He did not say actual words, but Angela felt she had been paid a high compliment as well. It was in his eyes as he noted her appearance and smiled his greeting.

To Angela's consternation, Thomas moved to set up the checkerboard. But Derek, not Thane, took the seat opposite him. Angela breathed a sigh of relief and indicated that the parlor was available. Thane did not need a second invitation.

"I'll see you later—if you haven't been sent off to bed," he promised Sara, as her lip began to protrude.

"None of that," he said, pretending to tweak her nose again.

Sara grinned impishly.

"See that she gets her homework done," he told Louise in mock seriousness.

Louise nodded and then began to grin.

It was a warm evening so Angela had not asked Thomas to lay a fire in the hearth. She waved a hand to indicate that Thane could be seated on the brocade settee and she moved toward the rocking chair.

"Sit here," said Thane, patting the seat beside him. "I have something to show you."

Angela obeyed, curious.

Thane reached into a jacket pocket and drew forth a small packet.

"Pa got in a new shipment, and I thought of you," he explained. He lifted a tissue-wrapped object from the brown paper and held it out to Angela.

She took the gift and carefully folded back the tissue. Inside were two of the most delicate, dainty lace hankies she had ever seen.

"Oh, Thane!" she exclaimed. "They are beautiful."

"You're welcome," he said, and they both laughed.

"I was going to get around to a thank you," Angela chuckled. "Really I was."

Her nervousness left her. She settled easily onto the seat beside him and they talked as they had done over the years. As the evening wore on, Angela forgot all about her little we-can-be-friends speech. It seemed so right for the two of them to be there—to be sharing thoughts and dreams. She almost forgot to offer refreshments. When she went to get the tea and tarts she was surprised to discover that the rest of the family had retired.

"Why don't I just join you in the kitchen?" Thane asked. "Then you won't have to bring everything in here."

Because it was Thane, Angela did not argue. Instead, she chuckled and nodded her head for him to follow. They pulled chairs up to the kitchen table and shared the food and continued to talk.

When Angela told how frightened she had been when Derek winded himself playing baseball, Thane reached out and took her hand. It never occurred to her to withdraw it. Thane listened attentively, nodding his head in understanding, increasing his pressure on her fingers.

"He seems fine now," he said comfortingly.

"Yes, thank God," breathed Angela, and without thinking she reached over with her other hand to clasp Thane's fingers.

Thane's hold on the slim hand tightened. Then he glanced at the clock. "Oh—oh!" he exclaimed. "I'd better get out of here before your big brother throws me out."

Angela followed his gaze to the clock and was shocked that it was almost one. She laughed and tried to pull her hands away. Thane reluctantly released them.

"I'll get your hat," she told him and walked the few steps to the wall pegs where the hat hung.

"So you are throwing me out," he teased, but he accepted the hat and then stood up.

"Angela," he said, taking her by the shoulders and turning her slightly so the glowing lamp filled her face with light, "I have enjoyed the evening—tremendously."

"So have I," she whispered honestly.

He drew her gently toward him and brushed a kiss on her forehead.

"May I come again?" he asked softly.

She could not speak. She pulled back so he could see her; then she nodded her agreement.

"Thank you." He lifted a hand to brush her cheek gently and then he turned and was gone.

Angela floated up the stairs and down the hall to her bedroom. She had never felt so—so light—so treasured—so filled with joy.

"Oh, God," she breathed as she placed her hand on the doorknob, leaning lightly against the door, "I think Mama would be happy for me."

But you didn't explain that you are just to remain friends, said an accusing inner voice that shattered Angela's peace.

"Next time," she promised herself. "We'll talk about it next time."

But the weeks passed and the visits continued and Angela could never quite remember at the right time that she had something important to discuss with Thane.

———

"I miss Thane," pouted Sara, and Angela's eyes opened wide in surprise.

"Why, he is here two or three times a week," she responded.

"But I don't get to see him. Just when he first comes. Then you hurry him off and—and hog him all to yourself," Sara continued, her lip trembling and her eyes accusing.

"Why I—I," sputtered Angela, and then admitted meekly, "I guess I do."

"Well, I think we should all get to see him. He belongs to all of us," Sara declared.

Louise nodded, for once in total agreement with her younger sister.

"All right," said Angela. "We'll have him over and we'll all share him. What would you like to do?"

"For supper," clapped Sara, her eyes now sparkling.

"For supper," agreed Angela.

"When?"

"Is he coming tonight?" asked Sara.

"Yes—but it's too late to get word to him about supper."

"But we can ask him tonight. Let's ask him for Friday. We'll have our supper and wash the dishes and play our memory game and then we'll all make popcorn and play games together."

Sara seemed to have it all worked out.

Angela nodded. "All right," she said. "You may extend the invitation."

As soon as Thane stepped through the door, Sara hurled herself at him, her plan pouring out in an excited torrent of words.

Thane looked over the young girl's head and received a slight nod from Angela. "It sounds like a wonderful plan," he said, giving Sara a brotherly squeeze. "I accept."

Sara squealed her glee, reached for the ribbons that Thane held out to her, and promised to do her homework.

"How's harvest coming?" Thane asked Thomas.

"All done for another year," Thomas responded.

"New seed produce?"

"Yeah, but it needs some more work yet. Have to add another strain. But I did get a nice bunch of seed to work with."

Thane looked over at Derek. "Hear you're still tearing up bases," he teased, and Derek glanced up and grinned. It was now acknowledged that he was the best baseball player at his school.

"How do you spell sedimentary?" asked Louise from her spot at the kitchen table.

"What are you ever going to do with a big word like that?" asked Thane, stopping beside her and looking down at her book.

She lifted her head and screwed up her face. "I have to do a report for school."

Thane spelled the word for her and then followed Angela to the parlor.

———

On Friday Thane spent the evening with the whole family, and even Sara seemed satisfied with the outcome.

"See," she told Angela, "it works just fine. Why don't we do that all the time?"

"Because—well—because Thane and I like to talk."

"I like to talk too," protested Sara.

"That you do," Angela agreed, but she could find no words to explain the situation to the young girl.

Louise cut in with a toss of her head. "They're sweethearts. They don't want company."

Angela opened her mouth to protest and then closed it again. What could she say? She still hadn't had her talk with Thane— and each call was bringing them closer together.

Sara had a birthday. To please her and the rest of the family, Angela again invited Thane for supper. She did not promise her family the entire evening, however. Thane had hinted that he wanted some time alone with her.

The celebration went well. Louise had baked the birthday cake and Thane praised it liberally while Louise flushed in pleasure and embarrassment.

Thane presented Sara with her first pair of soft kid gloves. Sara and Louise both had to try them on—just to see how they felt.

Thane helped with the dishes, but Angela sensed that he was in a hurry to get the task over and escape the kitchen.

"How about a walk?" he asked Angela when they finished their work.

Angela agreed. She loved to walk. It was late fall now and the evenings were cool, so she went to get a heavy shawl.

When they stepped out onto the back porch a full moon was shining. Angela stood for a moment and looked up into the heavens to get her thoughts under control.

Somewhere up there her mama was dwelling. She had been reunited with Papa. Angela felt sure they were happy. Still, she often wondered if they could see their family struggling to make their way without the example and counsel of wise parents.

Thane took her arm, and Angela allowed herself to be led around the house and toward the long country lane.

"Look at all the stars!" she exclaimed.

Thane released her arm and let his hand reach down to enfold hers. She wrapped her fingers around his large sturdy ones and walked closely enough that her shoulder brushed against him.

"Sara's growing up," Thane observed.

Angela nodded. "She's growing fast. I sometimes fear that she'll soon catch me," she laughed.

"Well, you're nineteen—almost ancient," teased Thane. "She has a long way to go yet."

Angela laughed.

They walked in silence for a few moments; then Thane picked up the conversation.

"My mama always said that a girl is old enough to know her own mind at nineteen." His voice still held a teasing note.

"You have a very wise mama," responded Angela in the same tone.

Thane stopped and turned to the lane fence. He lifted an arm to lean on the top rail, drawing Angela close beside him, still holding her hand.

"Then if you know your mind," he began, his voice serious now, "do you—are you ready to promise to be my wife?"

Angela was aware that his hands tightened on hers, but then her world began to spin. She caught her breath and found herself straining in the semidarkness to study his face. He was not teasing now.

"Do you mean—?" she began but could not finish. She should have known this would happen. She should have been prepared. She should have explained to Thane that she could not leave the children until her task was completed. She could not.

"I—I can't!" she cried, a sob catching in her throat. She saw in the moonlight the surprised and hurt look that crossed Thane's face. But he did not release her hand. He drew her even closer.

"What do you mean, you can't?"

"I just can't. I promised Mama that I'd—that I'd care for the family—"

"You can still care for the family," he interrupted. "That won't change."

"But I—I have to live with them—" began Angela.

"We'll both live with them."

"But—but you won't want to—to take on a whole family when you wed," she sobbed and leaned against him to cry.

Thane took her by the shoulders and looked into her eyes. "Angela, when I asked you to marry me, I already knew that you'd never leave them. I have always known that it would mean caring for the family. I love you, Angela. I love Thomas and Derek and Louise and—and Sara. I feel they are my family, too. But it is you that I want to marry. You that I want to share my life. You that I love."

Angela was silent while his words found their way to her mind and to her heart.

"I—I didn't know that you—cared—like that," she managed at last.

"I have always cared—like that," he assured her, gazing deeply into her eyes.

I should have known. I should have seen it, thought Angela. *It has always been there, boldly declaring itself in his caring, his eyes, his touch.* As soon as Angela accepted that fact, she knew with a certainty that Thane meant every word. She looked up into his earnest eyes.

"You gave me the scare of my life when—when you were seeing Carter," Thane went on solemnly. He drew her back into his arms. She could hear the beating of his heart as she lay her ear against his chest.

"It would have been all wrong," she whispered.

"I know," he answered. "All wrong. I'm so thankful to God that you realized it before it was too late. I have never—never prayed so hard in all my life."

Angela closed her eyes tightly and breathed a prayer of her own.

"I'm still waiting for my answer," he prompted, whispering into her hair.

"Oh, Thane," she responded, looking up at him. "I—I don't think it's a bit fair to you. It won't be an easy task. You have no idea just how hard—"

Thane's arms tightened around her. "Angela, just answer me."

"Yes—yes, I'd be happy to be your wife."

Thane kissed her then while a million twinkling stars clapped their hands above them. The moon dipped thoughtfully behind a cloud, allowing them a few moments of total privacy. When the silver glow of moonlight restored light to the world around them, Thane spoke. "Would you like to go in? We have a lot of plans to make."

Angela agreed. Her heart was singing. Her blood was racing. Her world was spinning in a flood of glorious light and color.

She lifted her face to the open sky. "Oh, God," she breathed. "I'm so happy. Tell Mama, will you, Father? I want so much to share this moment with her."

Chapter Twenty-five

One More Memory

In a way, Sara got her wish. She shared Thane. In fact, the whole family shared in the planning for their future. They held long discussions around the kitchen table. The coming marriage affected them all in more than a usual way.

"I'd like to farm," Thane said candidly. "I always have wanted to. I've talked to Pa about it. He'll help to get me started on my own place."

"No need for that," put in Thomas. "The farm is here. You may as well farm it."

"And you?" asked Thane.

Thomas grinned slowly. "I'd still like to get a chance at seed experimentation."

"Do you know where you could go?" asked Angela.

"I've written a few letters," Thomas admitted. "One university is quite interested in my projects."

Angela was surprised to hear that Thomas had already approached a school about his work.

"Then I'd be happy to farm your land—until such time as Derek might want to take it over," agreed Thane.

"I don't want to farm," Derek said quickly.

"So what do you want to do? Play baseball?" teased Thomas, reaching out to ruffle Derek's hair.

Derek blushed, then grinned. "I want—I want to teach," he said. "Maybe coach some—and sure, I'd like to play baseball. But I don't want the farm."

"Then we don't have to move!" cried Sara, clapping her hands.

"That's right. We won't have to move," agreed Angela.

"We can keep right on going to the same school." Sara seemed very pleased that her life would not change drastically.

Louise tilted her head and looked at Thane. "Will you be our new pa?" she asked.

"Is Angela your mother?" he asked in return.

"No-o-o. But she's our boss."

"Then I will be your—your big brother, and I will help with the bossing a bit, too. In place of Thomas."

Louise shrugged. She certainly didn't need any more bosses, but she didn't seem too upset by the arrangement. Perhaps she thought it wouldn't be too bad to trade one boss for another.

"You can boss me—if you want to," conceded Sara amiably.

Thane reached out an arm and drew the young girl onto his lap. "I can't imagine you needing a boss," he told her and pulled a pigtail.

The wedding was set for the month of May. Angela marked off the days on the calendar. There was so much to do and she had such limited knowledge of how to plan a wedding. Over and over she visited the Andrews household, getting much-needed help from Thane's mother.

But her usual duties still had to be cared for. The housework was just as demanding. Sara had outgrown everything she owned, and Angela spent hours at her sewing machine.

Louise still had her emotional swings from high to low. Some days Angela felt as if she was at the end of her patience. Thomas would only shrug and say, "You're a woman; you understand her better than I do."

But Angela could not recall going through such a tough time in her own growing-up years.

Mama would have known, she told herself over and over. *She would have known when to make an issue and when to let it pass.*

Then she would find herself praying, "Oh, dear God, please help Sara pass through the years of change with more ease and less turmoil."

So Angela's days were filled to overflowing with scarcely time to think. Between caring for a growing family and preparing for a coming wedding, she felt as if her world were spinning out of control. Thane often came in the evenings, and Angela sometimes darned socks or hemmed skirts while they chatted. He did not seem offended that he did not have her full and undivided attention.

"I wish there was more I could do to help," he fretted. "Perhaps we should just elope."

"Mama wouldn't have been in favor of that," responded Angela, not seeing the teasing glint in his eye. "She always felt there was something special and sacred about vows taken before the Lord and the congregation."

Thane did not joke about eloping again.

Angela had seen little of Charlie or Gus over the winter months. The small addition had been made to the cabin, and Gus had moved in his few belongings and his bed roll and now shared the three-room home. Angela wondered if he did the cooking duties, but she had never gotten around to asking.

With the receding of the winter storms and the warming of their world, Charlie and Gus came out of hibernation.

"Sure good to be out in the open," Charlie said to Angela one day when she went out to feed the hens. "Man can get cabin fever all shut up like that."

"You could have come over," Angela informed him. "We would have been glad to have you."

Charlie chuckled. "Well, girlie. Seems to me thet you had about all yer evenings taken."

Angela flushed slightly but accepted the teasing with a smile.

"There were mornings—and afternoons," she teased back.

Gus approached slowly. Angela noticed that he was limping.

"Lumbago," explained Charlie to her unasked question.

"I'm sorry," sympathized Angela.

"Oh, it'll get better with some sunshine. Always does," said Gus cheerfully. "Always does."

"So why don't you come in for some coffee?" asked Angela, ashamed of herself for neglecting her two old friends.

They accepted immediately. As they waited for the coffee to boil, Charlie began to question Angela about her plans for the spring garden. Angela admitted that she had not begun to think of gardening.

"Why don't ya just give us the seed and let us go at it?" asked Charlie.

"Oh, that would be unfair—" began Angela.

"What's unfair? We plan to eat from it. We'll plant lots fer everyone. An' we still can swing a hoe. The time outta the cabin an' in the sun will do us good."

Gus nodded in agreement, and Angela finally agreed, telling them what a relief it would be to let them take over.

"Been readin' yer ma's Bible." Charlie announced a complete change of topic.

Angela raised her eyes to look at the old man.

"Understand a lot of things I didn't understand before," he went on.

Angela moved her gaze to Gus to catch his reaction.

"Gus an' me figure as how it's about time we got ourselves straightened out and attendin' church."

"As soon as it warms up we figure we'll have the preacher baptize us in the crick," put in Gus. "Right in the crick."

"Oh—but first," began Angela, "first you must make your—your commitment—to the faith."

"Did thet," said Charlie simply.

Gus nodded. "Yep. Yep. Did thet."

"You did?" said Angela, her eyes opening wider.

"Did thet," said Gus. "Both did thet."

"But how did you know—I mean, what did you—"

"Jest followed the Book," said Charlie. "Yer mama had all the places marked—jest like ya said. We jest followed the Book."

"Jest followed the Book," parroted Gus.

"It works," continued Charlie, tears trickling down his weathered cheeks. "I got thet there new heart—right in here." He placed a calloused hand over his shirt front. "Feel changed. New. Just like the Book says."

"Yup," put in Gus, tears forming in the corners of his own eyes. "Changed—jest like the Book says," and he reached up a twisted hand to cover his own heart.

Angela had tears of her own now. To think that years after the seed had been sown by her parents, it had now born fruit. "I—I just—don't know what to—to say," she stammered. "I'm so—so happy. Papa and Mama would both be so—so pleased."

"Yup," said Gus nodding his head. "Yup."

When May arrived, Thane had joined Thomas in the fields to get all the planting done before the wedding. Feeding hungry men and sending children off to school kept Angela's already busy days even fuller. Derek took on a man's share of farm chores. Daily Angela breathed a sigh of thanks that she didn't have the responsibility of the big garden. Charlie and Gus had kept their promise, and plants were peeking their heads above the ground, already promising an abundant yield.

Thane and Angela had little time to themselves, but they promised to make up for it in the years ahead.

The morning of the wedding Angela turned to her bedroom window and was disappointed by the sight of drizzling rain. "I had so hoped for a sunny day," she mourned, and then remembered her mama telling how her own wedding day had been greeted with a shower as well.

"But by wedding time," her mama had said, "the clouds had rolled on and the sun was shining."

Angela prayed that it might be so for her and Thane as well. "But if it isn't," she determined, "this will still be the happiest day of my life." Angela rose from her bed with a song and hurried down to prepare the family breakfast.

"Aren't you the cheery one this morning," greeted Thomas as he lifted the milk pail from its hook in preparation for his trip to the barn.

Angela beamed at him.

"Have you noticed the weather?" asked Derek as he struggled into a light jacket.

"I noticed," said Angela. "To be honest, it's not what I would have ordered—had the choice been mine—but we'll make do."

Thomas nodded. "I think it will clear by midmorning," he predicted cheerily.

They hurried through the morning chores and breakfast to get an early start on their trip to town. The girls were to change for the wedding at the Andrews' house after the morning service. Mrs. Andrews had helped Angela sew her wedding gown. It was not nearly as elaborate as the gown Trudie had worn, but Angela was content. It suited her.

Louise was to wear a dress of pale blue and Sara one of soft pink. Angela was allowing Sara the privilege of pinning up her long blond hair.

"It is rushing things a bit," she explained, "so tomorrow it is back to braids again."

Sara nodded, but her eyes danced with the excitement of being considered grown-up—even for a day.

"We must hurry," coaxed Angela as they finished their breakfast. "We don't want to keep everyone waiting. Thomas, are you ready with the Scriptures?"

Thomas lifted the family Bible and was about to begin the morning reading when Louise interrupted.

"Couldn't we play the game? Just once more? Please. It won't take us long. Please."

"But we can still play the game. Just as often as we like," said Angela. "Thane is always happy to play it with us."

"But Thomas will be gone," said Louise, fighting hard to keep back the tears. "It just won't be the same anymore."

No. It would not be the same. Thomas would be gone—leaving for his dream of schooling and research just as soon as she and Thane returned from their short wedding trip. And then Derek would be leaving them to make his way in the world. And before they all turned around, Louise would be grown—then little Sara.

Before Angela could start crying, a new thought came to her. She would always have Thane. There would be no day when he would grow up and leave her. That was the marvel of God's great plan. Through good times and bad, through sickness and health, in weakness and in strength, Thane would be with her as long as God granted them years on earth. It was a comforting thought to Angela. She rose from her chair and lifted her head, her eyes shining in appreciation for the wisdom and love of her Father.

"All right," she agreed. "One more time with Thomas."

Louise, satisfied, settled back in her chair. Angela hurried to the buffet drawer and came back with the fifth scribbler they had been filling with their memories.

Thomas started the memories. "I remember," he said, "the morning I was baptized. It was a very special morning for me—I was telling all my friends that I intended to put aside selfish plans and try to live my life in the manner Christ taught His disciples. Mama took me in her arms and told me she was proud of me for making the right decision—then she looked me in the eyes and said, 'Thomas—always be true to the step you are taking. Don't ever—ever think of turning back.' "

As Angela hurriedly wrote to keep up with Thomas's words, she noted to herself that *somewhere along the way we have changed from just sharing memories to also thinking of the lessons Mama so subtly taught with each little incident of our childhood.*

After a moment of silence Derek cleared his throat and said, "I remember one morning when I went out to feed the chickens and the mother cat was running across the yard with a little dead bird. I chased her and got it back. I cried—and I brought it in to Mama. She just hugged me for a long time and let me cry and then she said, 'Son, don't fight death. Death, too, is a part of life. One thing dies that another might live. God is a wise God. He has a purpose for all things—even death. And for us—His special creation—death is the only gate to eternal life. When the time comes for me to join Him, though we might wish to linger a bit, it will be a triumphant time. Remember that.' "

Derek stopped and swallowed hard. "I had forgotten that," he went on, "until just now."

Angela blinked away tears. To some it might have seemed morbid to be talking of death on her wedding morning, but it wasn't morbid to Angela. She felt that Derek had just made an important step in dealing with his grief.

"I remember," said Sara, "the little pink quilt Mama made for my dolly. I got the dolly for Christmas and she didn't have any blankets and it was cold. I remember. We shivered even in the kitchen that winter."

Angela remembered that cold spell of which Sara spoke. It hadn't lasted long but it had been bitter.

"Well, I wanted my dolly to be warm. I tried to hide her under my sweater, but then Mama said she would make her a quilt—and she did. And when she gave it to me she said, 'Sara, always show as much—much passion—' "

"Compassion," corrected Angela softly.

" 'Com-passion,' " Sara continued, " 'toward others as you are showing for your dolly now. Share your warmth, Sara. Share your love.' "

Louise wriggled on her chair as if she had changed her mind about wanting to play the game. By the time Angela had finished writing Sara's memory, however, Louise was ready to begin.

"I remember," she said in a whispery voice, "one morning

when Mama came to call me for school. I didn't want to get up so I thought I would just pretend I was sick."

Louise stopped and fidgeted some more.

"Well, Mama laid a hand on my forehead and she said there was no fever—then she had me open wide my mouth and she looked at my throat. She said it was fine. She pressed on my tummy here and there and asked if it hurt and I said 'No.' Then she asked me if I had—had broken my leg and I said 'No' again, so she said I must really be quite fine then. Nothing seemed to be wrong—so she told me to get up. After breakfast when I was kissing Mama goodbye, she held me close and said, 'Louise, don't ever try to pretend you are something that you are not. Folks always see right through the sham. Be true to others—and to yourself.' "

Louise paused for a moment and then admitted softly, "Sometimes it is still hard for me not to pretend—a little. But I—I am trying to learn."

You poor darling, thought Angela as her pen stopped writing for a minute while she considered the words. *Perhaps you are growing up.*

Angela was the only one left. She looked around the table at her family members and cleared her throat.

"I remember," she began with trembling voice, "when I was about ten years old. Mama was sick in bed and I was sent to the field to take lunch to Papa. On the way home I found some early roses. They were the first ones I had seen that spring—just beginning to open—bright and pink and sweet-smelling. I knew how much Mama loved the spring roses so I stopped to pick some. Just a little handful. That's all there were. I remember how I got some thorns in my fingers. I even got a drop of blood on my pinafore where I wiped my hand.

"Then I started on home, thinking how happy Mama would be when I arrived with the flowers. I had to cross the creek and it was higher than usual. Papa had thrown a log across it, but I wasn't very good at walking the log. I was about halfway across when I started to lose my balance. I grabbed frantically for an overhanging limb and managed to keep myself from falling in. But in clutching at the tree branch—I dropped the roses. I stood there crying as I watched the stream carry them off. When I got home I was still crying.

"I went into Mama's bedroom and threw myself against her bed and told her what had just happened.

"She put her arms around me and pulled me close. 'Angela,' she told me, 'you are my flowers. My roses. You and your brothers and sisters. You make up my bouquet. And a more lovely bouquet never graced the home of any woman. I will always—always—see you as such—my beautiful, beautiful roses. I don't need any others.'"

Angela stopped to wipe her eyes. They would be red and swollen for her wedding if she wasn't careful. At least Thane would understand.

She lifted her head and looked around the table. "And that is how I see you, too," she told them softly. "As Mama's roses. She would be so—so proud of you—if she could see you now. Just as Thomas and I are."

They leaned forward for an impromptu family embrace and then wiped away tears, smiled at each one, and rose from the table.

"I don't want to keep Thane waiting," spoke Angela softly as she replaced the Memory Book in the bureau drawer. She turned to her brother. "I'm afraid you'll need to push the team a bit, Thomas."

"Thane will wait," Thomas said with confidence, "but we'll see that you're there on time."

He stopped long enough to pull her into his arms and give her a brotherly embrace.

"You're going to make him a beautiful bride—and a wonderful wife—Mama's rose," he said softly. Then he released her slowly, turned, and was gone to fetch the team.